M

Consent

She wanted to be more than just his mistress…

Three passionate novels!

In November 2007 Mills & Boon bring
back two of their classic collections,
each featuring three favourite
romances by our bestselling authors…

MISTRESS BY CONSENT

Mistress by Agreement by Helen Brooks
The Unexpected Mistress by Sara Wood
Innocent Mistress by Margaret Way

PREGNANT PROPOSALS

His Pregnancy Ultimatum
by Helen Bianchin
Finn's Pregnant Bride
by Sharon Kendrick
Pregnancy of Convenience
by Sandra Field

Mistress by Consent

MISTRESS BY AGREEMENT
by
Helen Brooks

THE UNEXPECTED MISTRESS
by
Sara Wood

INNOCENT MISTRESS
by
Margaret Way

MILLS & BOON®
Pure reading pleasure

All the characters in this book have no existence outside the
imagination of the author, and have no relation whatsoever to anyone
bearing the same name or names. They are not even distantly inspired
by any individual known or unknown to the author, and all the
incidents are pure invention.

All rights reserved including the right of reproduction in whole or
in part in any form. This edition is published by arrangement with
Harlequin Enterprises II B.V./S.à.r.l. The text of this publication or
any part thereof may not be reproduced or transmitted in any form
or by any means, electronic or mechanical, including photocopying,
recording, storage in an information retrieval system, or otherwise,
without the written permission of the publisher.

This book is sold subject to the condition that it shall not, by way of
trade or otherwise, be lent, resold, hired out or otherwise circulated
without the prior consent of the publisher in any form of binding or
cover other than that in which it is published and without a similar
condition including this condition being imposed on the subsequent
purchaser.

Haringey Libraries

CC		
Askews		29-Oct-2007
AF ROMANCE		
		HA 926

Harlequin Mills & Boon Limited,
Eton House, 18-24 Paradise Road, Richmond, Surrey TW9 1SR

MISTRESS BY CONSENT
© by Harlequin Enterprises II B.V./S.à.r.l 2007

Mistress by Agreement, The Unexpected Mistress and
Innocent Mistress were first published in Great Britain by
Harlequin Mills & Boon Limited in separate, single volumes.

Mistress by Agreement © Helen Brooks 2003
The Unexpected Mistress © Sara Wood 2001
Innocent Mistress © Margaret Way, Pty., Ltd. 2004

ISBN: 978 0 263 85528 9

05-1107
Printed and bound in Spain
by Litografia Rosés S.A., Barcelona

MISTRESS BY AGREEMENT

by

Helen Brooks

Helen Brooks lives in Northamptonshire and is married with three children. As she is a committed Christian, busy housewife and mother, her spare time is at a premium, but her hobbies include reading, swimming, gardening and walking her old, faithful dog. Her long-cherished aspiration to write became a reality when she put pen to paper on reaching the age of forty, and sent the result off to Mills & Boon.

CHAPTER ONE

'MISS MILBURN? Mr Ward is here for his ten o'clock appointment.' Rosalie's secretary's disembodied voice from the intercom was not as calm and businesslike as usual, and Rosalie knew why, having met the said Mr Ward at a dinner party a few weeks earlier.

She glanced at her neat gold wrist-watch. Eight minutes to ten; he was early. She forced herself to breathe deeply before saying, 'Ask Mr Ward to wait a few moments, please, Jenny.'

'Yes, Miss Milburn.'

The intercom clicked goodbye and Rosalie sank back in the big leather chair, her heart racing. This was stupid; this was so, so stupid. What on earth was the matter with her? She had been like a cat on a hot tin roof since Kingsley Ward had made the appointment a week ago—or rather his secretary had liaised with her secretary, to be exact.

Of course she could have *insisted* he see one of the other three partners in the firm of chartered quantity surveyors she was part of, after her polite message—again via the two secretaries—that she was terribly busy but had arranged for Mr Ward to see a colleague had been turned down flat.

Mr Ward was quite happy to wait until she was available, his secretary had told Jenny, and there was no question of seeing someone else. Miss Milburn had been personally recommended, and Mr Ward *always* went on personal recommendation.

And now he was here. Rosalie glanced nervously round the big, light-filled office that tended to be her home from home with the long hours she worked. She even slept on the couch that occupied one corner when the occasion warranted it. Kingsley Ward was here and it was only at this precise moment that she acknowledged the meeting had been weighing on her spirit like a ton of bricks. It wasn't even as if they had got on that evening at Jamie's house—just the opposite, in fact.

Rosalie stood, walking across to the massive plate-glass window that overlooked half of Kensington. She stared into the street below without really seeing any of the little ant-type figures scurrying about, a frown wrinkling the pure line of her brow.

She could remember the exact moment she had walked into Jamie's large and very plush drawing room in Richmond and glanced across the assembled couples, only to find her gaze held and transfixed by a pair of piercingly blue eyes, which had narrowed to twin points of light on her face. She had been aware of David at the side of her saying something, but for the life of her she had been unable to move or speak. And then the cerulean gaze, its deep blue as clear as a summer's sky, had released her, the man in question turning his head in answer to something the woman on his arm had said. She had taken a deep and very necessary gasp of air, deep enough for David to say anxiously, 'Are you all right, Lee? What's the matter?'

'The matter? Nothing,' She forced a smile, before adding, 'How are you feeling? That's more to the point.' David was an old and very dear university friend who had just been through a painful and acrimonious divorce, which had caused him to totter on the edge of a nervous breakdown for months. The evening was his first venture into the social scene since his wife had left him, taking their two children to live with her new lover, and he had been visibly shaking in the taxi earlier. Only the fact that they were as comfortable together as a pair of old shoes had persuaded him to leave his recently acquired bachelor flat when she had called for him.

'I'm okay.' His smile was more of a grimace and Rosalie felt for him. 'It's just that I've never been much good at this sort of thing, dinner parties and such. Ann was always the one who was the life and soul of the party.'

Ann had been a cold-hearted, predatory exhibitionist who had systematically alienated every other female she had ever come into contact with, along with making a play for every man. However, Rosalie thought it wasn't the right time to point that out.

'Nonsense,' she said briskly. 'You're great company, you always have been, it's just that your confidence has taken a bit of a mauling lately.' Which was putting it mildly. 'Now, we're just going to circulate and smile and make polite conversation whilst we sip one of Jamie's magnificent cocktails and contemplate the superb dinner ahead. Did you know he's buttonholed one of the chefs from Hatfields tonight? Apparently he's a friend of a friend and Jamie's offered him a small fortune to come and put on this dinner on his evening off.'

'Really?' David was an accountant and now the pound sign showed in his eyes. 'How much is a small fortune?'

'Ask Gabby, she'll be sure to know.' Rosalie guided him over to one of their more inquisitive friends who had a reputation for winkling anything out of anyone, and stood listening with some amusement to their conversation.

That died abruptly when a smooth voice at her elbow

said, 'Rosalie. Unusual name. French origin, I think?' and she turned to see the possessor of the faint American burr.

Kingsley Ward was tall, very tall, with a muscled strength that made the beautifully tailored dinner jacket sit on him like a designer's dream, Rosalie remembered now, her cheeks flushing at the memory. He was hard and ruggedly handsome, his face one of sharply defined planes and angles, which said he took no prisoners, and she gazed up at him with a sensation akin to numbness freezing her response. Ebony hair cut very short along with ridiculously thick eyelashes emphasised the brilliant blue of his eyes even more close to, but it was the overall sense of maleness that was so intimidating. Uncomfortably, unsettlingly intimidating. Enough to make her want to turn tail and run.

Instead she lifted her chin ever so slightly, calling on all the resources of her thirty-one years as she said coolly, 'My mother was French.'

'That explains the chic and classical elegance.'

Yuk, what a smoothie! And if there was anything she disliked it was handsome smooth-talkers who thought they were God's gift to the female race.

She was unaware that her thoughts were mirrored in her eyes until the warm social smile and interested expression on the hard face vanished. His gaze took on the quality of blue ice, and he said coolly, 'I have obviously interrupted a riveting conversation you are anxious to get back to. Excuse me,' at which point he turned and walked away, leaving her feeling more than a little ashamed of herself. And she *hated* feeling like that.

The way the evening had gone thus far she supposed it was inevitable she was seated between David and Kingsley Ward for dinner. He was coldly polite to her, and charming and amusing to everyone else, and as she

sat and liste...
was forced t...

But of cou...
cellent compan...
from the window...
for one thing, and...
devastating good...
kill for, they had a...
edness that was an a...

Was *that* why she h...
ing? And then she answ...
from her conscience w...
always made sure she wa...
...for the office,
and with a prospective ne... was extra important.
That was all. That *definitely* was all.

The wrist-watch reminded her it was a minute to ten and bite-the-bullet time. She sat down again at her desk, smoothed her hair and took a deep breath. She resisted the impulse to check her make-up in the mirror in her cosmetics bag and felt quite proud of herself for doing so.

'Right.' She pressed the intercom. 'I can see Mr Ward now, Jenny,' she said brightly.

A moment or two later the door opened and Jenny all but curtsied Kingsley Ward into the room, Rosalie noticed with a dart of annoyance as her back stiffened for the onslaught of the piercingly blue gaze. But she was prepared for it this time. Her heart was thudding but outwardly she was the epitome of the successful businesswoman, cool, collected and *very* in control. 'Good morning, Mr Ward.' She had been determined to get the first word in and set the tone. 'Won't you sit down?'

She hadn't offered to shake his hand, which was something that would have been automatic usually, but—and

pid—she didn't want to

no such inhibitions. He strode
hand outstretched, as he responded,
, Rosalie. I may call you Rosalie? And you
e Kingsley, or King if you prefer.'

last was said in just the same brisk voice as the
of his opening gambit, but Rosalie had looked into
his face and she was sure she saw something mocking
there.

As her small hand was enfolded in a giant one that was
warm and hard, she steeled herself to show no reaction at
all. Nevertheless, her breathing wasn't quite even when
she said, withdrawing her hand the very second it wasn't
rude to do so, 'How may Carr and Partners help you?' as
she gestured again for him to be seated.

She was a cool one all right, and just as sleek and
sophisticated as he remembered from that damn awful
dinner party. Kingsley folded himself into the seat opposite the desk, his long legs crossed one over the other and
his arms going out along the arms of the upholstered chair
in a pose that was naturally masculine. True, the elegant
cocktail dress had been replaced by a beautifully tailored
business suit, but the silver-blue shade brought out the
copper tints in that wonderful chestnut hair and turned the
grey eyes mother-of-pearl. He hadn't seen such a naturally
lovely woman in years, so how come his careful enquiries
had revealed there was no man in her life at present, nor
had there been for some time as far as anyone knew? Of
course she could just be an obsessive career woman married to her job, but... The soft mouth was too full and the
small chin too vulnerable for that.

He smiled, slowly. 'We started off on the wrong foot

at Jamie's dinner party, didn't we?' he drawled easily. 'How about we try again?'

How about we don't? Rosalie lifted fine eyebrows in polite enquiry. 'I'm sorry, I don't quite understand?' she said frostily.

He stared at her for a moment, just long enough for her cheeks to begin to turn a definite pink, and then he shrugged, straightening in the chair and picking up the briefcase he had placed at the side of him when he had sat down. 'Ward Enterprises acquired just over a hundred acres of land situated between Oxford and London a few weeks ago,' he said curtly as he opened the briefcase and extracted some paperwork. 'I want to build a hotel and country club, with an eighteen-hole golf course, landscaped gardens, helicopter landing pad and so on, similar to the ones I own in the States. Here is the architect's plan and the full brief. Interested?' He pushed the papers over the desk before settling back in his chair again.

Interested? Suddenly becoming aware that her mouth had fallen open in a small gape, Rosalie shut it with a little snap, her cheeks brilliant now. She had been so rude to him—*so rude*—and all the time there had been the possibility of this fabulous project for Carr and Partners. Why hadn't anyone at Jamie's told her that he was an entrepreneur—and a pretty wealthy one if this was anything to go by? But she had been looking after David for most of the evening, she reminded herself feverishly; that was when she hadn't been ignoring Kingsley Ward, of course.

'May I examine these for a moment?' Her voice sounded remarkably normal considering she felt about an inch tall.

'Sure, take all the time you want.'

Concentrate, Lee, concentrate. As she spread out the

plan and attempted to look at it it danced before her eyes for a second or two before she took a deep breath and willed her racing heart to behave. It didn't help that Kingsley Ward was straight in front of her with his gaze fixed on her face—she might not be looking at him now but she could feel those twin lasers on her skin.

After a little while professionalism took over and she became engrossed in the plan and brief, excitement growing like an expanding ball in her stomach. This was a terrific job and a fantastic opportunity, but she had to admit one of the other partners—*any* of the other partners—was more qualified for such a massive undertaking than she.

Mike, Peter and Ron were all well over forty. Mike was approaching fifty-five, with a wealth of experience to draw on, and she was very much the junior partner. She would have to make it clear to Kingsley Ward that if Carr and Partners were given the job, one of the other partners would almost certainly insist he took over.

She raised her head. He was sitting in the same pose as before, leaning back against the seat, breathtakingly relaxed and sure of himself, but this time the almost tangible authority brought no irritation, all her senses tied up with how best to put what she was going to say. 'Mr Ward—'

'Kingsley,' he interrupted, very softly.

She nodded, her cheeks—which had just cooled—firing up again. She had always loathed the way she blushed so easily but it went hand in hand with the red lights in her chestnut hair and there was nothing she could do about it. 'Kingsley,' she began again, 'this is a wonderful job and I know Carr and Partners would be thrilled to take it on if you saw fit to put it our way—'

'But?'

She had always taken exception to being interrupted, she considered it the height of rudeness, and now she breathed out just once before she continued, 'But I'm afraid you are talking to the wrong person. My partners are all older and more experienced, and they would be able to tackle this project far better than me, much as I would love to do it.'

He shifted slightly in the chair, lean male thighs outlined for a moment or two under the Armani suit, and Rosalie's nerves jerked. 'You would love to do it?' he said quietly.

'Yes, of course, but you would need someone who—'

'Then do it.' It was as though he hadn't heard her. She stared at him, and he said softly, 'Let me put it another way. I am not a fool, Rosalie, and I would not offer you the job if I did not think you were capable of doing it. I have been assured from various quarters that to date you have handled your work competently, ethically and thoroughly, and more than one person has told me that you are particularly skilful in detecting problems with builders before they occur. Am I right?'

She was pinned by the blue eyes and could do no more than nod her head.

'Good.' He spoke as if the matter was settled and Rosalie had a moment of panic.

She cleared her throat. 'The thing is, the decision is not up to me,' she said carefully.

'No, it is up to me,' he agreed shortly, standing. Rosalie rose quickly, her head spinning. Was he leaving already? It appeared so. 'Discuss the job with your partners, by all means, but make it clear I am engaging *you*, please. If they need to speak to me you have my number in England and in the States on the information I have given you.'

He was already walking to the door as he spoke and

then he paused, turning to look at her. 'Do you feel you could do the work, given the chance?' he asked quietly. 'You said you would love to do it but that isn't necessarily the same thing. The time angle is not so much of a problem, I can be flexible to a degree.'

She was still reeling with the suddenness of it all but there was no hesitation in her voice when she said, 'Yes, I can do it. I've not tackled anything on this scale before, I have to admit, but, yes. The job I'm working on at the moment will be finished within a week or so, and after that there is nothing planned which I can't pass on to one of the others.'

'Good.' It was silky soft. 'My secretary will liaise with you as necessary, but I am a hands-on kind of guy, Rosalie, so we'll be seeing quite a bit of each other over the next months.'

Rosalie blinked. The words sounded innocent enough but there had been a smoky flavour to them that had set her antennae waving. And then she told herself not to be so silly. This was work, business, that was all. Kingsley Ward was obviously an enormously successful and wealthy mogul, and with his looks, not to mention his money and male charisma, he must have the women lining up in droves. It had been one of the things that had set her teeth on edge at Jamie's wretched dinner party—the way every woman present had been all but dribbling with lust. And of course he'd lapped up the attention; what man wouldn't?

He was waiting for a response. She pulled herself together as the realisation hit, stitching a polite smile on her face with some effort. 'We've still got a way to go before you give Carr and Partners the work, surely?' she said evenly. 'You haven't asked the fee for my services.'

She realised too late she could have put that better when

the blue eyes flickered, just once, and he said, very dryly, 'What exactly do you charge, Rosalie?'

With anyone else she could have turned it into a joke or frozen the individual out with one of the icy looks she had perfected years ago, but Kingsley Ward wasn't anyone else. And she was burning up with enough heat to spontaneously combust.

Rosalie took the coward's way out and acted dumb. 'For a job of this kind we tend to estimate a cost,' she said tightly. 'It isn't always possible to be specific when one is dealing with contractors and subcontractors, and things don't always go according to plan. Materials might not be available when they ought to be, for example, or there may be a technical hitch which makes the job more difficult and therefore more time-consuming. Of course, this is not usually the case,' she added quickly.

'Quite,' he said soothingly, making her aware she was gabbling.

'The first thing I would need to do is to draw up a bill of quantities, which is a list of all the materials needed to complete the project right down to the smallest detail. This would extend to several hundred pages for a job of this nature.'

He held up a restraining hand, his voice even dryer when he said, 'You are telling me you don't come cheap, is that it?'

She had never met anyone she would like to punch on the nose more, or anyone who could make the most normal conversation sizzle with sexual undertones like this man. Or was it her? The thought kicked like a mule. Was she imagining all this? She didn't like being confused and it sounded in her voice when she said, 'It's always worth paying for the best in the long run.'

'My sentiments exactly,' he drawled silkily, his

American accent suddenly strong. 'And that being the case I am sure I will hear from you shortly with a tidy breakdown, and some sort of ceiling cost, okay?'

'Yes, of course.' He had opened the door before she realised she hadn't thanked him for what was the most fantastic opportunity of her career to date, but even as the words hovered on her tongue he had gone without a backward glance or a goodbye.

CHAPTER TWO

ROSALIE worked harder than she had ever done over the next few weeks. Once she'd finished with the job she'd been engaged on when Kingsley Ward had made his amazing proposition, she began working on the bill of quantities for the Ward project, which was an enormous undertaking. It didn't help that she was aware her three senior partners were a little anxious about it all.

When she had told Mike Carr and the other two about the meeting with Kingsley Ward, Mike had called Kingsley the same day, after which he had come and perched on her desk in the late evening just as Rosalie had been thinking of going home.

'There's no doubt he wants you for the job.' Mike looked at the slim, beautiful woman in front of him, whom he both respected and admired, and in whom he had taken a fatherly interest almost from the first day Rosalie had begun at Carr and Partners fresh from university ten years before. 'Know much about him, do you?'

Rosalie stared at him in surprise. Mike was more than a working colleague; shortly after she had been engaged by the firm she had discovered she had been at university with his daughter, Wendy, and after a reunion with the other girl it had become common for her to spend the odd weekend at the Carrs' lovely old house in Harrow. The family's friendship had come at a painful time in her private life and had meant the world. It still did, even though—with Wendy now married and living abroad, and Rosalie having been taken on as junior partner, which had

17

doubled her workload and made for less socialising—she
saw less of the family as a whole.

'Not a thing, really,' she admitted after a moment or
two. 'Why? Isn't he creditworthy?'

Mike smiled. 'You really don't know anything about
him, do you? Oh, yes, he's creditworthy, all right, Lee.
Ward Enterprises was begun by his father over thirty years
ago, but until Kingsley was old enough to come on board
it was just a moderately successful little hotel chain com-
prising of some three or four fairly middle-of-the-road es-
tablishments. Kingsley changed all that. He had the vision
to buy up land and make the Ward name synonymous
with luxury hotels complete with a couple of golf courses,
hundreds of acres of parkland and so on, the sort of places
the rich and famous would go to to enjoy peace and se-
clusion where their every need is catered for. To put it
crudely, my dear, Kingsley Ward is loaded.'

Rosalie smiled, before raising her eyebrows as she said,
'So why that note in your voice when you asked me if I
knew anything about him?'

'What note?' And then Mike smiled himself at the expression on his junior partner's face. 'Oh, all right,' he
said a little shamefacedly. 'It's just that, along with the
wealth and jet-set lifestyle the man now has, has come a
certain reputation.'

Rosalie's eyebrows rose higher.

'He's partial to a well-turned ankle.'

Dear Mike. Only he could use such a quaint old-
fashioned phrase to describe a womaniser, Rosalie thought
fondly, before she said teasingly in a mock American accent, 'You mean he likes the broads?'

Mike wasn't smiling now. 'He likes them, all right,' he
said quietly. 'Lots of them.'

'What's that got to do—?' Rosalie stopped abruptly.

'Oh, come on, Mike,' she said disbelievingly, 'you don't seriously think a man like the one you've just described would waste time trying to seduce a little provincial mouse like me, do you? He's used to the celebs and model types who have been everywhere and done everything for sure.'

'Rosalie, you're a very beautiful woman, and no one in his right mind would describe you as a mouse,' Mike said matter-of-factly. It was always amazing to him that she seemed so completely unaware of her effect on the opposite sex. What did she see when she looked in the mirror, for crying out loud? It was a question he'd asked himself many times, and now he answered it as he usually did; she saw something different from everyone else for certain. And she had Miles Stuart to thank for that. 'Anyway, all I'm saying is watch him, okay? I'd say the same to Wendy in a similar situation, you know that.'

'Yes, I know, Mike.' She put out a hand and touched his jacket sleeve. 'And I appreciate it, but, really, there's no need.'

Nevertheless, that conversation of a few weeks ago was now on Rosalie's mind as she finished the last item in the bill of quantities and settled back in her seat in front of the word processor. Kingsley had asked her to contact him once she had this ready and before she sent copies to various contractors to put a cost on each part of the work. She had got the impression he was the type of man who liked to keep his finger on even the tiniest pulse. She would try the English number he had given her first and ask his secretary where he was in the world. Since the conversation with Mike she had made it her business to find out everything she could about Kingsley Ward, and she had discovered he had hotels in the Caribbean as well as the States and was constantly on the move. She had also found out that Mike had not exaggerated about Kingsley's love life.

She dialled the number herself; she had come into the office very early to finish off the list of materials and, as it was now still only eight o'clock in the morning, Jenny hadn't arrived. Undoubtedly her call would be intercepted by an answer machine in Kingsley's new English office in Oxford, but that was all right. It was another thing off the multitude of jobs she'd got lined up for the day, and his secretary could call Jenny later.

'Kingsley Ward.'

Rosalie almost dropped the telephone at the sound of the deep cold male voice, her heart giving a resounding thump. It was a moment or two before she could say, 'K...Kingsley?' Oh, don't stutter, girl, for goodness' sake, she told herself in the next instant, hearing her breathless voice with utter contempt. Her voice was stronger as she continued, 'It's Rosalie Milburn here from Carr and Partners.'

There was a pause, and then, 'Yes, Rosalie?'

She gulped. She preferred the first abrupt cold voice to the warmer, faintly sexy burr with which he'd spoken her name. And then she told herself not to be so darn ridiculous and to get on with it. 'I'm sorry to bother you so early,' she said politely. 'I was expecting to just leave a message on your secretary's answer machine to say that the bill of quantities is ready that you wanted to look over, and to ask where to send it. I wasn't sure if you were in England or America.'

'That was quick,' he said appreciatively. 'I'm in London today, I'll call in for it. There were a couple of things I wanted to discuss with you anyway. Are you free for lunch?'

'L...Lunch?' She was doing it again! Her brain scrambled. She wasn't doing anything for lunch but the last thing she wanted was to spend a couple of hours in close proximity to Kingsley Ward with no hope of escape. And then logic and reason took over. This was a massive job, she was going to have to liaise with Kingsley considering he was the type of man who insisted on overseeing everything. She forced her voice into neutral. 'Lunch would be fine.'

'Great.' If he'd sensed her hesitation he gave no sign of it when he said, 'I'll pick you up round noon, okay?'

'Yes. Thank you.'

The phone went click. No goodbye, no social pleasantries. A man of few words, obviously. Rosalie sat staring at the receiver for some seconds, aware that she was feeling rail-roaded but that it wasn't really fair on Kingsley. She could have said no to lunch, but if he needed to talk to her there was no point, added to which she had to make herself get on enough with him for them to establish a working relationship.

She looked down at what she was wearing. She had dressed for an unremarkable day in the office—pencil-slim grey trousers and a wrapover white buttoned shirt, with a pearl-grey bouclé wool jacket for later in case the May evening turned chilly on the walk home. Her flat was only half a mile from the office and she always travelled on foot, enjoying the wake-up in the morning and the wind-down at night. The only time she drove was when she needed to call on site or visit an architect or contractor or something similar.

She wrinkled her nose at her clothes. Kingsley Ward would be used to women who dressed to kill, for sure. And then she caught the errant thought, horrified at herself. What did it matter what he was used to? This was a business lunch with a client, that was all. As long as she was presentable that was all that mattered, and Kingsley probably wouldn't notice what she was wearing anyway.

Kingsley did. He arrived to collect her just before noon, his gaze going over her steadily as Jenny ushered him into Rosalie's office. Rosalie made a huge effort to act as she would with a man who wasn't drop-dead gorgeous, smiling brightly and forcing herself to extend her hand this time as she said, 'Kingsley, how nice to see you again.'

His smile was lazy, with a mocking quality that suggested he knew she was lying. 'Likewise.'

'I've got everything ready if you'd like to glance through before we leave?' she asked briskly, once her flesh had left contact with his. The tingling in her hand she could do nothing about.

'Later. I'm hungry.' His gaze hadn't left her face, his eyes like blue crystal.

'Fine.' She busied herself in collecting the wool jacket and her handbag, hoping her bustle hid her agitation. She had forgotten what a startlingly deep blue his eyes were; if it were anyone else but Kingsley Ward she would have suspected they were wearing cosmetic contact lenses.

'I hope you had nothing pressing this afternoon? I would like to visit the site after lunch. The architect will be there and it would be good for you to meet him.'

'Of course.' Rosalie thought of her work schedule and prayed for calm. 'I'm all yours.'

The carved lips twitched. 'How generous.'

It was, actually. She had already visited the site twice and didn't really need to meet the architect today, Rosalie thought aggressively. There would be time enough for that once the tenders were returned, a builder selected and the work began. It would be her job to see the chosen builder kept to his prices, and she would be visiting the site frequently to value the work done for interim payments.

'Shall we?' He had taken her arm and whisked her out of the office before she had time to reflect further, and it was with dark amusement that Rosalie noticed Jenny's expression of envy. If her secretary had but known it she would have swopped places with her for the lunchtime like a shot!

Carr and Partners was situated in a row of terraced houses, and once out on the pavement Kingsley led the way to a nifty little silver sports car that would have done credit to James Bond. Rosalie was eternally grateful to her guardian angel that she'd decided to wear trousers that day; the car's low interior was not conducive to entering and exiting in anything else. As it was she slid into the leather interior with more than a measure of aplomb. This faded somewhat when Kingsley climbed into the driver's seat. He was close, very close, and he smelt nothing short of delicious.

Rosalie hit her traitorous libido a sharp crack on the knuckles and swallowed deeply a few times. Her voice higher pitched than usual, she said, 'Is it far? Where we're eating?'

Damn it, but she was like a cat on a hot tin roof. Was it him or was she like this with the whole male race? 'No, not far,' he said easily as he pulled out into the traffic, the car's engine growling softly. 'A friend of mine owns a little place near Finsbury Park where I often eat when I'm in London. Unless there's somewhere else you'd prefer?' He glanced at her.

She shook her head, making the silky swirl of hair move and shimmer. Kingsley felt his loins tighten in response and turned his head, concentrating on the traffic.

After a few tense moments during which Rosalie registered every single movement he made and the car's interior seemed to shrink still more, she said carefully, 'I'm really excited about this job, and I never did thank you for looking me up after the dinner party. Who mentioned I was a quantity surveyor, anyway?'

He executed a manoeuvre that was totally illegal, receiving a few kindly gestures from passing motorists in the process, before he said, 'What? Oh, I don't remember. Is it important?'

He turned to look behind him as he changed lanes and Rosalie glanced at the back of his head where his hair had been tapered into his neck. It was so sexy it wasn't true. As the big body turned again her head shot to the front. She felt like a voyeur, for goodness' sake, she admitted to herself crossly, willing each taut muscle to slowly relax. But she hadn't expected to be cocooned in an inch-square box with him, that was the thing.

Kingsley was clearly a man who didn't go in for chatter when he was driving, and the short journey was accomplished in almost total silence. By the time they drew up outside a small neat restaurant Rosalie felt she'd got her act together, in spite of not quite being able to identify what it was about Kingsley Ward that threw her into such a spin.

True, he was silver-screen handsome with the added authority that came with wealth and influence, but he was also hard, ruthless and possessed of a giant ego, from all the background she'd gathered on him. Women galore had been enjoyed and discarded if half the stories about him were true, and Rosalie didn't doubt that they were, looking at the man. And she loathed men like him, individuals who took and never gave, plundered and demanded what they wanted as though it were their God-given right. In fact they disgusted her.

'Don't you like it?'

'What?' She spun round in her seat as the quiet voice registered on her, becoming aware in that moment that her face must have reflected her thoughts as she gazed out unseeing at the building in front of them. 'Oh, I'm sorry, I was thinking of something else,' Rosalie said quickly. 'This looks very nice.'

'Don't let the nondescript appearance fool you,' he said evenly as he cut the engine. 'Glen isn't into glitz and glamour, but he has the punters fighting a path to his door now word has got out about the food here.'

He exited the car in a smooth, controlled uncurling motion that Rosalie could but envy; she knew she was going to have far more trouble levering herself out of the low seat. As it was he had opened her door and extended a hand before she had to try, and once she was standing on the pavement she tried to ignore his towering height and the fact that she was all flustered again.

Kingsley opened the door of the restaurant for her and then waved her through in front of him, thinking as he did so, Nice bottom. In fact nice everything. She was one hell of a woman and yet there was something so fiercely defensive about her it screamed disastrous love affair. Who had let her down and had it been recently? Certainly Jamie and one or two other of her friends who had been at the dinner party claimed they knew nothing. He wasn't sure if he believed them. Whatever, she intrigued him. She'd intrigued him that night, enough for him to follow through and arrange for her to get the quantity surveyor's job, after he had checked her credentials, of course. Much as he liked the idea of being the hunter for a change, he wasn't about to endanger what was a very tasty business opportunity because he wanted a woman who had made it clear she didn't want him.

'King! My friend, my friend.'

Rosalie hadn't expected the said Glen to be foreign, somehow—Glen sounded too English for that—but the slim, wiry man who came rushing up as they entered was Italian or she'd eat her hat. He kissed Kingsley on both cheeks—something Kingsley had obviously been expecting and which didn't phase him at all—before turning his attention to her, saying, 'You have brought the most beautiful lady in London to grace my restaurant. How can I thank you, my friend?'

'Cut the spiel, Glen,' Kingsley said dryly, 'it won't work on this lady. And she's a business colleague, before you get too carried away.'

'So there is hope for me? Even better!'

The black eyes were wicked but full of laughter, and Rosalie found herself laughing back as she said, 'If the food is as good as the welcome, no wonder you are so popular.'

'Rosalie; Glen Lorena, the biggest sweet-talker this side of the ocean. Glen; Rosalie Milburn, my new quantity surveyor for the English job.'

'This is true?' The Latin face expressed surprise. 'But you are too lovely to do such work. I cannot believe this.'

'Believe it, buddy.' Kingsley had noticed the dimming of Rosalie's smile and took swift action, ushering her further into the restaurant as he said over his shoulder, 'Usual table free?'

'Of course, my friend, of course. The moment I received your reservation the table became yours.'

Glen joined them a moment later, taking their order for drinks as he presented them with two dog-eared menus before disappearing again. Rosalie glanced round. The room was not large and it was packed with diners, in spite of the furniture being on the basic side without a taste of luxury anywhere. They were sitting in what was clearly a prime position in a small alcove, a table that gave an element of privacy without obstructing the view.

As her eyes returned to Kingsley he leant forward slightly. 'Glen didn't mean anything by that last remark,' he said softly. 'It's just his way. His wife used to work as a barrister before they got this place so he's got no problem with women and careers.'

Rosalie nodded stiffly. It was true she hadn't appreciated the Italian's comment about her job; she'd suffered the same sort of surprise too often in the past, normally accompanied by a distinctly patronising interest afterwards. After a degree course followed by three years of practical training and then the Assessment of Professional Competence, she felt she'd served a good apprenticeship before she began working as a fully qualified surveyor in what was still very much a male-dominated environment.

She had found she had to be just that bit better than her male colleagues at first to be taken seriously, but being a female in such a position was definitely a situation of swings and roundabouts. Most of the builders were tickled pink to see her arrive on site, and, once they realised she knew her onions and wasn't going to be fooled or cajoled into accepting late dates or poor quality work, they were pussy-cats in her hands.

She'd often heard Mike and the others bemoaning the fact that they got all the stick from both the builder's own surveyors and also the client when things went wrong, but usually, with just a smidgen of charm, her jobs ran on nicely oiled wheels.

'Whilst we're on the subject of careers,' Kingsley continued smoothly, 'what *did* make you take up quantity surveying?'

Rosalie stared at him. She hadn't been aware they were

on the subject of anything. She shrugged after a moment or two, her lashes sweeping down and hiding her gaze from the piercing one opposite as she said carefully, 'I liked the mix of office work and getting my hands dirty on site, I suppose.'

'Commerce is a hard world,' Kingsley said quietly, 'especially for a woman dealing with men who might not like being told what to do or not to do by a female, and a young and attractive one at that.'

Rosalie shrugged again. 'I'm tougher than I look,' she said without smiling.

He gazed at her, one dark eyebrow quirked and a disturbing gleam in the back of the brilliant eyes. 'Are you now?' he murmured softly. 'A lady of mystery?'

'There's no mystery.' She had spoken too quickly and she knew it as well as he did. She buried her face in the menu.

So, he'd hit a nerve? Kingsley's eyes narrowed a fraction as he sat back in his seat just as one of the waiters arrived with the bottle of wine and another of sparkling mineral water. Life had taught him a few lessons in his thirty-five years on the earth, he reflected as he watched the waiter filling their glasses. One, expensive wine was worth every dollar compared to the other stuff. Two, gambling was a mug's game. Three, never trust a woman, especially a beautiful one with hair like bronzed silk and eyes the colour of a stormy sky, eyes that carried secrets in their cloudy depths. For sure the secrets would be nothing more important than what hair dye she used to colour her hair, and within a few weeks he would be itching to move on. Although Rosalie's hair looked natural...

He picked up the menu, suddenly annoyed with his thoughts and the world in general although he couldn't have explained why. 'The roasted shallot and lemon thyme salad is very good to start with,' he suggested mildly. 'One of Glen's specialities. Or the mediterranean fish soup? And I can recommend the roast lamb or braised tangerine beef with herb dumplings.'

Rosalie smiled politely. She chose watercress soufflé followed by poached fillet of sea bass with asparagus tips, and after she had given her order to Glen, who had reappeared like the proverbial genie out of a bottle, she sat back in her seat and had a couple of hefty swallows of the very good wine whilst she watched Kingsley discussing the merits of the lamb against the beef with his friend. If ever she had needed a drink it was now, she thought with wry self-mockery. Why ever she had agreed to come out to lunch with this disturbing individual she didn't know, let alone commit to spending what virtually amounted to a whole afternoon in his presence.

When the food came it was utterly delicious, although Rosalie had to admit that Kingsley's Mediterranean fish soup and roast lamb looked and smelt wonderful, added to which she had never particularly cared for sea bass. But her food was excellent, all of it, along with the wine and the chocolate macadamia steamed pudding drenched with whipped cream she chose for dessert. She didn't think she had ever tasted food so good, and she told Kingsley so as they drank their coffee.

He smiled. He'd smiled quite often during the meal as they had made light conversation, and she had to concede he'd got the art of conversation, along with the smile, down to a T. But the smile had never reached the cool blue of his eyes and the conversation was such that she knew nothing more about him than when they had first sat down at the table. Which was enough, more than enough, she told herself dryly.

'Glen's easily the best chef I've ever come across.'

Kingsley drained his coffee-cup and gestured to the hovering waiter for the bill. 'As the waiting list for a table bears out.'

'Surely he could earn a fortune if he chose to work somewhere like the Savoy or the Ritz?' Rosalie asked, her eyes wandering round the interior of the restaurant again.

'He's done the big-time thing and ended up nearly ruining his marriage *and* his health,' Kingsley said shortly. 'He got out of the rat race, bought this place and set up with Lucia, his wife, who does all the behind-the-scenes work. He's had offers galore to go back as a head chef or expand here to bigger and better, but the bottom line is he doesn't need it. He's happy here, Lucia's happy, that's all that matters to Glen in the long run. He's found his Shangri-La.'

Rosalie stared at him. 'You sound as if you envy him,' she said at last.

He smiled but this time it didn't even crinkle the skin around his eyes. 'Why would I do that?' he said easily. 'I'm exactly where I want to be in life. How about you?'

'Me?'

'Yes, you. Are you where you want to be in life?' he asked with a silkiness Rosalie immediately suspected. 'Doing what you want, being who you want, with whom you want?'

She didn't like this conversation. 'Certainly,' she said briskly.

'Then we are both very fortunate.'

Rosalie's jaw set. She couldn't quite put a label on the quality of his voice but it suggested disbelief, and who the hell was Kingsley Ward to question her, anyway? 'Yes, we are.' She rose from her seat. 'I won't be a moment,' she said coolly before making her way to the door marked 'Signorinas' at the back of the restaurant.

Once in the small but immaculately clean little cloak-room Rosalie walked across to the two tiny washbasins situated under the plain, unframed mirror. She stared at the flushed reflection and two angry eyes stared back at her. She had done what she'd promised herself she wouldn't do weeks ago when she'd taken the job, and let Kingsley Ward get under her skin. Her soft lips tightened but her irritation was at herself and not Kingsley.

Self-control. It was all about self-control, everything was, she knew that. If *anyone* knew that, she did. She shut her eyes, shaking her head as it drooped forward, but today the memories she usually kept firmly under lock and key surfaced in a flood. Suddenly she was a little girl again, sitting shivering on the landing with her eyes straining down into the shadowed hall as she listened to the familiar sound of her father shouting at her mother in the sitting room below. Other sounds followed, they always did, but what made this occasion more memorable than all the ones that had gone before was that in the midst of the sound of slaps there came a silence, and then her father's voice, the tone agitated, saying, 'Chantal? Chantal, get up. Come on, get up.'

The memory blurred at this point but she could recall the bright lights of the ambulance and then the police car when they had arrived at the house. It had been a police-woman who had come and found her, still sitting in numb silence on the stairs. They had taken her to her maternal grandparents—her father had been brought up in a chil-dren's home and had no family—and it had been a day or two later when her grandmother had told her, very gently but with tears streaming down her face, that Mummy had gone to see the angels in heaven. Her beau-tiful, tender mother, who wouldn't have hurt a fly, had never recovered consciousness from the aneurysm that had begun to bleed in her head, caused by one of her husband's blows.

On the day of the court appearance her father had taken his own life, and at the age of five she had become an orphan. Her grandparents had looked after her from that point, and with her mother having had younger siblings who had gone on to have children her childhood had not been an unhappy one. But there had been a void, a massive gap because she had been a mummy's girl from the moment she had been born. As she had grown she had begun to understand why her mother had absorbed herself so completely in her child. Her grandparents had told her that her father had been an unhappy individual as a result of a traumatic childhood, insanely jealous of any attention his wife had paid to another adult, be they man or woman, and consequently her mother had led a life isolated from the rest of the world in an effort to keep the peace. Her headstone was a memorial that this hadn't worked.

Rosalie raised her head, her eyes large and dark with the painful memories. When she'd been eighteen and entering university her grandparents had decided to return to their native France to live their autumn years with the relatives there; her grandfather's health had been poor and he'd wanted to be close to his brothers.

She had agonised for some time whether to give up her university place in London and go with them, but she had been born in England and she didn't want to study in France, besides which there were all the friends she would leave behind. In the end she had stayed, and then she had met Miles Stuart...

'Enough.' She spoke the word out loud, her mouth setting in a grim line as she ruthlessly put a check on her mind. Why was she thinking of all this today? But she knew why. Miles and Kingsley Ward were miles apart in many ways, but they both had one attribute that was unmistakable: male magnetism.

It was indefinable, something elusive and subtle, but when a man had it, it cut through all the layers of civilisation and refinement and brought a woman right back to grass-roots level, forcing her to acknowledge a sexual response whether she wanted to or not. A powerful weapon. Her eyes darkened still more. And unfortunately mother nature seemed to excel in bestowing it on two-legged rats who didn't give a damn.

She breathed deeply before washing her hands, taking a moment or two to run her comb through her hair and apply fresh lipstick before she left the cloakroom and walked to where Kingsley was waiting near the front door of the restaurant. Glen was standing talking to him, and Rosalie kept her eyes on the Italian man as she said pleasantly, 'That was the best meal I've had in a long time, Glen.'

'It is a pleasure to cook for such a beautiful woman.' He grinned at her as he spoke, and Rosalie had to laugh. He was outrageous but somehow you knew he was as harmless as a kitten.

She turned her gaze to the long, lean figure beside the restaurateur, and eyes of blue ice looked back at her. 'All ready?' Kingsley asked easily, smiling the arctic smile.

Once out on the pavement in the fresh May sunshine, Rosalie remembered her manners. 'That was a lovely lunch,' she said politely. 'Thank you.'

'The pleasure was all mine.' An ordinary phrase, but he managed to make it sound like a criticism, as though she'd been churlish. She glanced at him and the azure eyes gazed back innocently.

This was going to be one great afternoon!

CHAPTER THREE

ROSALIE asked herself a hundred times afterwards how it had happened. Over the last ten years she had been to umpteen sites, clambering about measuring foundations and walls and areas of land, and not one accident. So why, *why* had it been this particular day at this particular site and more especially with this particular man that she'd had to go and make the most almighty fool of herself? One minute she had been talking to the architect and hopefully impressing Kingsley with her handle on the job, the next she'd been flat on her face with her ankle feeling as though it was broken.

The architect, a nice middle-aged man, was all concern, but it was Kingsley who picked her up in his arms after she had tried to rise and nearly passed out with the pain.

'I…I'm all right. Please, I can walk.' Through the excruciating throbbing the fact that she was being held close to a hard male chest with her head on an eyeline with his throat took precedence.

'Keep still.' She had tried to wriggle free and his voice was curt.

'Really, it feels better already,' she lied through gritted teeth.

'And I'm Mickey Mouse.'

The architect, who was now trotting alongside them as Kingsley carried her over to the parked cars, said soothingly, 'It might just be a sprain, Miss Milburn, but you really should get it checked at a hospital.'

'I'm not going to a hospital,' she responded quickly. 'Not for a sprain.'

'That's exactly where you're going,' the deep voice just above her head said flatly.

She would have argued better if she weren't so horribly conscious of being in his arms, but, with the feel of his body as he moved and the overall heady scent of faint whiffs of the most delicious aftershave, she wasn't feeling herself. 'If you'll just take me back to the office I will be fine,' she said as firmly as her twanging nerves would allow.

They had just reached the car and he didn't reply. As the architect opened the passenger door Kingsley placed her into the seat as carefully as one would a piece of Dresden china, but even so the action caused an involuntary gasp before she bit her lip hard, her face white.

'And you're talking about going straight back to the office?' he said disgustedly. 'Your ankle's already twice its size and swelling as we speak, or hadn't you noticed?'

Yes, she had darn well noticed; she was the one feeling the pain, not him!

He shut the passenger door, said a brief word to the architect who was now standing peering worriedly into the car, and then proceeded to make a call on his mobile phone. Rosalie was sure it was about her although she couldn't hear what was being said. He slid into the car, saying shortly, 'I'm taking you to a doctor.'

The man was like a cruise missile, but suddenly, what with the pain and the nausea it was causing, she couldn't argue anymore. Her face must have spoken for itself because he swore softly before reaching into the glove compartment and pulling out a small silver hip-flask, unscrewing the top and handing it to her. 'Drink some, it's brandy.'

'Brandy? I don't want—'

'*Drink some.*'

She drank, just a sip or two but she had to admit the neat alcohol burnt up the nausea causing her to feel more herself. And then she froze as Kingsley took off his jacket, bundling it into a roll and leaning over her as he said, 'I'm going to put this under your foot to cushion it as best we can, but I'm afraid the journey's not going to be pleasant.'

And then his head was practically in her lap as he positioned the clump of material that had been a very nice Armani jacket under the injured foot, easing off her court shoe as he did so.

She looked down at the short, spiky jet-black hair and muscled shoulders, and almost asked for another swig of brandy.

'Thank you.' She hoped he would put her breathlessness down to pain and ignore the flush of embarrassment that had flooded her cheeks with colour. He had only taken off his jacket, for goodness' sake, so why did it suddenly feel as if he were almost naked?

He eased himself back into the driving seat, loosening his tie and letting it hang slackly as he undid the first couple of buttons on his shirt.

He had a magnificent body. Her eyes just couldn't tear themselves away from the broad chest under the silk of his shirt. Powerful and lean, without an ounce of fat anywhere. She gave up trying to be cool and reached for the hip-flask again, taking another sip gratefully.

'Okay?' The blue eyes met hers, his voice low with sympathy now, and she gave a brave smile, nodding because she didn't trust her voice. Suddenly the hospital didn't seem such a bad idea—anything to get out of the claustrophobic confines of this car.

Having experienced Kingsley's driving technique earlier in the day, Rosalie appreciated he was driving extremely cautiously once they were underway, but nevertheless every slight jolt or bump of the car had her biting on her lip to stifle the gasps of pain.

She was conscious of him glancing at her a few times before they reached their destination, which looked to be a hospital nearer Oxford than London. As they drove into tree-filled grounds and she saw the long, modern attractive building in front of them she said, 'This isn't a private hospital, is it?'

'What's wrong with that?'

She hadn't got private health insurance, for a start.

Whether he guessed what she was thinking he didn't say, but what he did say was, 'This is where a friend of mine works and, as luck would have it, he's around today. He said he'd take a look at the ankle as a favour, and we'll go from there. Okay?'

This whole thing was running away from her and she didn't like that, besides which Kingsley seemed to have a friend for every occasion, Rosalie thought resentfully. It might be nasty of her in the circumstances when he was being so helpful, but she couldn't help the way she felt—he brought out the worst in her. She sat stiffly in her seat, her cheeks flaming. 'I would have preferred to go to a National Health hospital,' she said primly.

'Tough.' Her eyes shot to meet his at the tone, widening as he went on, 'I haven't got time to waste sitting in an emergency department even if you have. I have another appointment later.'

She glared at him. 'Well, excuse me!'

'Certainly.' The carved lips twitched at her fury. 'Now sit still until I can help you.'

Much as she hated to obey him she had no option, and

unfortunately she knew she was not going to be able to walk on the ankle either. Even trying to flex her toes brought acute agony. But the thought of him carrying her again… Could she hop, perhaps? Darn it, she'd never felt so helpless in all her life.

When he opened the passenger door the decision was taken out of her hands. He scooped her up before she could so much as utter a squeak. The warm masculine feel of his body was worse this time with just the silk of his shirt covering his chest.

'Put your arm round my neck,' he said quietly as he hotched her more securely against him. 'Don't worry, I don't bite.'

She was startled into looking up into his face; there had been a smoky quality to his voice that was pure dynamite. There had been wry amusement in his face at first, but then as their eyes locked she watched the amusement replaced by something else and found she was holding her breath, not daring to move a muscle.

Another car entering the car park broke the spell. Rosalie lowered her head, grateful for the wings of hair that covered her hot face, but by the time they walked into the reception of the hospital the burning colour had subsided due mainly to the ache in her foot.

The next half an hour was a painful one, and at the end of it Rosalie could have cried with frustration when X-rays confirmed Kingsley's friend's prognosis that a small bone was broken, necessitating a plaster cast on her ankle for a few weeks.

Another hour or so and they were back in the car again, the ankle feeling better now it was supported but Rosalie's head spinning as her brain scrambled all the appointments and deadlines of the next days. Fortunately a great deal of the work could be done from the office, she decided thankfully after a few minutes of thinking hard, and site visits would have to be undertaken by one of the others until she could drive again, unless she called on taxis. She would manage somehow, anyway. There was no way she was going to hand this job over, lock, stock and barrel, to someone else.

'How does it feel?'

'I'm sorry?' As Kingsley's voice penetrated her whirling thoughts Rosalie turned to him. She had to admit, albeit reluctantly, that he had been very good over this whole affair—refusing to let her pay for anything although she knew he had written a cheque at the hospital, and displaying a patience she hadn't suspected he possessed.

'The ankle. How is it?' he repeated, the patience she had noticed not so much in evidence now.

'Fine.' His irritation reminded her he'd had an appointment. 'I hope I haven't delayed you too long,' she added politely. 'You mentioned an appointment?'

'A dinner engagement.'

With a woman, she dared bet, and obviously one he was anxious to see if he was prepared to pay the expenses of a private hospital to keep his date. A dart of something Rosalie didn't care to put a name to made itself felt, causing her to silently upbraid herself. A man like Kingsley Ward would have any number of women, for goodness' sake, and gorgeous ones at that, but his private life was absolutely nothing to do with her.

She slanted a sideways glance at him from under her eyelashes. She had got used to the muscled contours of his body now—she'd had a couple of hours to do that at the hospital as he had insisted on staying with her—but still something warm curled in her stomach as she took in the hard profile and clean-cut lines. He was intensely sexy, she thought drowsily, the combination of the trauma of the accident and the pain-killers Kingsley's doctor friend had prescribed making her sleepy in the car's warm womb. She yawned before she could stop herself.

'Put your seat back and have a snooze,' Kingsley suggested a moment later, even though she hadn't been aware he had noticed.

For some reason the thought of being asleep and in a position where Kingsley could look at her and she wouldn't know was quite untenable. It woke her up better than a bucketful of cold water. 'No, it's okay,' she said quickly, adding, perfectly truthfully, 'I wouldn't sleep tonight if I had a nap now. I don't sleep well as it is.'

'No?' One rapier-sharp glance raked her face before returning to the road ahead. 'Why is that? Have you always been that way?'

Since Miles she had. Rosalie kept her voice even as she said, 'In latter years. It's not exactly unusual, after all.'

'First sign of stress.'

Rosalie stiffened at the hint of criticism. 'I don't think so. I enjoy my work,' she said very stiffly, eyes to the front.

'It doesn't have to be work that's the problem,' he countered smoothly. 'Work's not the be-all and end-all of life, surely.'

'The rest of my life is also perfectly stress-free, thank you,' she said tartly. As if it were anything to do with him, anyway.

'Rosalie, in this day and age *no one's* life is perfectly stress-free. Do you keep a healthy balance between work and play?' he persisted, knowing he was being unfair in pursuing this when she had just been through one hell of an afternoon, but sensing her defences were low. He wanted to know more about this woman who kept herself so very much to herself, he admitted silently, capitulating to the truth he had been ignoring all day. She had aroused his curiosity as well as his body, damn it, and, yes—it *was* pique he was feeling at her total disinterest in him. Which made him a lesser man than he had thought he was.

'That's my business, surely?' It was frosty, and exactly what he had expected.

'I'm sorry,' he said with lazy innocence. 'I've obviously touched a nerve.'

She glared at him. 'Of course you haven't,' she said sharply. 'That's absolutely ridiculous.'

The black eyebrows rose but he said nothing, which was ten times more aggravating than an argument, Rosalie thought irritably. It was hard to argue with silence.

'I mean it,' she said again. 'You haven't touched a nerve.'

'Methinks the lady protests too much.'

Methinks the gentleman is an arrogant pig.

'So, do you have a current partner, a boyfriend?' he asked softly, knowing the answer full well.

She was longing to tell him to mind his own business but in view of their conversation to date didn't think it appropriate. 'No.' It was so wintry ice tinkled.

It would have discouraged a lesser man, but Kingsley wasn't a lesser man. 'How long since you've been on a date, then?'

She was fairly quivering with the rage she was trying to hide. How dared he cross-examine her like this? 'In spite of this being the twenty-first century and therefore licence for most people to behave like rabbits, I prefer quality rather than quantity,' she responded icily, hoping that would be enough to satisfy him. She had never met such rudeness in her life.

Of course it wasn't. 'That taken as read, how long?'

Suddenly, horrifyingly, the rage had gone and the urge to burst into tears was paramount. Twelve years long. Twelve years since I was hurt and abused and brought to the brink of losing my mind. The words were so fierce in her head that for an awful moment she thought she'd spoken them out loud, but when the chiselled features didn't change she knew she was safe. She had never spoken about her relationship with Miles to anyone, not even her grandparents before they had died, and she never would. All old friends and family knew was that she'd been married and then it had finished. New friends didn't even know that much.

She took a deep pull of air, praying her voice wouldn't reveal her inward trembling. 'Some time, I can't remember. I'm not the sort of person who puts notches on the bedpost, unlike some.' She turned to look at him as she spoke.

It was pointed, and she saw his mouth tighten with a dart of gratification. You can dish it out but taking it is a little harder, isn't it? she thought bitterly.

'Meaning I am?' he asked grimly.

'I didn't say that.' She paused purposely. 'But if the cap fits…'

'It doesn't, not in this instance.'

'Right.' She put a wealth of meaning into the one word.

'I have my faults, Rosalie, but promiscuity is not one of them,' he said, very coldly.

'Methinks the gentleman protests too much.'

For a second she wondered if she had gone too far as she cast a sidelong glance at his angry face, and then the wind was completely taken out of her sails when he laughed ruefully, turning to look at her for an instant with eyes that were smiling for the first time since she had known him. *'Touché, mademoiselle,'* he said dryly. 'I guess I asked for that one.'

Oh, no, don't do this. Her mind was gabbling. Don't step out of the mould like this. You aren't the type who can laugh at himself. You're arrogant and self-opinionated and a control freak. It's written all over you in great big black letters.

'So…' It was a lazy drawl. 'You've got me down as a philanderer, is that it?' He glanced at her again.

She hesitated a mite too long.

'Charming.' It was dry but not too bothered.

'Look, Kingsley, I didn't exactly say that,' she said quickly as she reminded herself he *was* the best client Carr and Partners had had in ages. 'I don't know you, do I?'

'True.' They had just paused at some traffic lights and he turned to watch her with narrowed eyes. 'So how do we remedy that so you can give an informed opinion?'

'My opinion doesn't matter one way or the other, surely?'

His eyes travelled to her mouth, the fullness of the lower lip naturally pink and tender, and his voice was deep when he said, 'Perhaps I object to being misunderstood?' as he smiled again, sexily.

He was flirting with her. Rosalie stared at him for a moment and then the traffic lights changed to green and they were away. Whenever anyone had tried that in the past she had firmly repelled them, dealing with them gently or harshly depending first on their martial status, and then the nature of their persistence. Some of the married ones had been the worst, necessitating arctic freezing of the most severe magnitude, but there had been the odd young buck who had fancied his chances—along with his own sexual attraction—who had needed an icy put-down.

She hadn't found it difficult to deal with them, whatever

their age or experience, mainly—she realised right at this moment for the first time—because she hadn't been tempted by their overtures.

Kingsley was different. She gazed blindly ahead as the car growled and leapt forward. Which made him dangerous and to be avoided at all costs. She had done the falling-madly-in-love thing and it was a con; a repeat performance would make her the biggest fool on earth. Unfortunately, however, she had learnt over the last ten years that she wasn't the type to go in for sex without love; it just wasn't in her make-up. Therefore she'd decided a first-class career, and all the benefits that would accrue from it, was her goal in life.

Good friends, a nice home, enough money to travel to foreign parts when the fancy took her—that would suit her just fine. But the main thing, the most important thing, which transcended anything else and negated all other considerations and benefits, was that she remained autonomous. In control, with a capital C.

'I need an address.'

'What?' She came out of the maelstrom of her thoughts as his voice penetrated the turmoil.

'A finite end to the journey?' Kingsley could see her face even when he was concentrating on the road ahead, and he'd noticed the tight set to her mouth. He had known from the first moment he'd laid eyes on her at that damn dinner party that she spelt trouble, he told himself moodily. It was in the touch-me-not restraint of the slim, elegant body, the wary coolness in those magnificent eyes.

'If you could drop me at the office, I'll be fine.'

And who in hell had grey eyes anyway? He acknowledged her voice with irritation. Why not brown or blue or green? Those colours were good enough for most of the population, so why not Rosalie Milburn? 'I'll take you home.' It was a statement that did not invite argument.

'There's things I need to do.'

'Perhaps, but they'll keep till tomorrow. Those pain-killers are not to be messed with,' he said evenly. Why had she hovered on his consciousness from that first evening? He wasn't short of female company—the thought carried no pleasure, merely irritation—so what made this woman different? But then she wasn't, not really. She just played the game differently, that was all. Nevertheless, she stirred his blood until he couldn't think straight.

He ran his hand through his hair, more than a little annoyed with himself. He was too realistic and too cynical to pretend he believed in anything other than animal attraction between the sexes, he reassured himself in the next moment, but this woman had the plus factor in a way he hadn't come across in a long, long time. Which made it more strange she wasn't with anyone.

On the perimeter of his vision he saw Rosalie shift her injured foot, wincing as she did so, and the action emphasised to him how stubborn she was in asking to be taken to the office. She needed a hot meal and some more pain-killers and sleep, in that order, he thought flatly. Crazy woman.

'So, do I get an address or do we just drive round London all night?' His thoughts had made his voice abrupt, for which he offered no apology. She rattled him, he admitted it.

Rosalie glanced at him, her nostrils flaring at the tone. 'I live quite close to the office in Kensington,' she said shortly. 'I'll direct you when we get nearer.'

'Thank you.' It was sarcastic.

'You're welcome.' Why did he have to make everything into a confrontation?

The rest of the journey was conducted in silence until they reached Kensington, whereupon Rosalie duly directed him to the crowded terraced street where she lived. Number twenty was identical to its neighbours, and as Kingsley drew up outside the house he glanced at the five steps leading from the pavement to the front door. His expression said it all.

'I know; not ideal in the present circumstances,' Rosalie acknowledged tightly. But then she hadn't rented the flat with the possibility of becoming injured in mind. 'I'll get Jenny to bring some crutches round tomorrow,' she added, to let him know she wasn't totally oblivious to what was needed. 'That way I can be mobile again.'

'Mobile in the very loosest sense, I take it,' Kingsley qualified coolly, opening his door as he spoke.

As the tall lean figure exited the car Rosalie did something she hadn't done since childhood, and stuck out her tongue at the departing back. Okay, childish maybe, she thought guiltily, but he made her so mad she could spit.

When he opened the passenger door he didn't swoop on her immediately, letting his eyes wander over her face for a moment before he said, 'Do you often regress to kindergarten?'

The man must have eyes in the back of his head. Rosalie refused to blush this time. 'You deserved it,' she said stiffly. 'I'm trying to make the best of what is going to be a difficult and awkward situation for me, and your comment wasn't exactly helpful.' She glared at him, her mouth set tightly.

He considered, head slightly on one side. 'You're right. I apologise.' It was said with what sounded like genuine remorse.

She blinked. 'Yes, well, I should think so,' she said lamely. She didn't know what else to say.

'I'm glad you've accepted my apology so graciously.'
He had gathered her up as he spoke and Rosalie was immensely pleased she'd had the foresight to get her key
ready. He held her as she opened the door and then
stepped with her into the wide hall. The house was three
storeys high with a flat on each floor and a basement that
housed the landlady of the property, and as Kingsley
glanced about him and then looked towards the stairs, his
voice was resigned when he said, 'Don't tell me, you live
on the top floor?'

'This one actually,' she said smugly. 'That's my front
door just there.' It felt enormously good to put him right.

He glanced down at her, his lips twitching at the satisfaction in her voice. 'Clever you,' he said softly, his eyes
so blue they seemed luminous. His gaze intensified as it
had done once before, but this time they were not in a car
park and there were no interruptions.

Slowly his head bent and Rosalie made no move to
avoid his mouth, watching with fascinated eyes as it came
nearer. His lips were warm and firm as they touched hers
in a fleeting kiss that held no threat, lingering just for an
infinitesimal moment before he straightened, saying,
'Let's get you inside, you've had one hell of a day.'

He took the two or three steps to the white-painted front
door before she had time to collect her scattered wits, and
then she realised she was still holding the main front door
key rather than the one to the flat. Her cheeks flushed, she
found the appropriate key on her bulky keyring, which
housed numerous office keys as well as personal ones,
aware her hands were shaking and praying all the time he
wouldn't notice.

She had allowed him to kiss her. Was she mad? She
had to be! What on earth was he thinking now? Did he

imagine it was an invitation for more of the same? Over her dead body!

She pushed the key into the lock, turned it, and then they were in her small square hall. 'I'll be fine now.' She tried to straighten but he took no notice of her efforts to be free, even when she said, 'Could you put me down, please?'

'Sitting room?' It was cool and unconcerned.

'What?' And then she collected herself, pointing to the first door off the hall as she said quickly, 'In there, but really you don't have to stay now. I know you have an appointment and it was good of you to bring me home.'

'This is great.' Once they were in the sitting room he glanced about him appreciatively, but Rosalie was in no mood to admire the décor, even if she had spent months decorating and furnishing her flat so it was exactly how she had imagined it on the morning she had first viewed it some years before.

The sitting room was the largest room with big windows that ensured there was lots of natural light, and she had made the most of this with a colour scheme of soft yellows and buttery cream, and pine furniture. She pointed now to the huge pine sofa that took up most of the far wall, and which was brimming with scattered cushions in varying shades. 'If you put me down there, I'll be fine,' she said again, making sure she kept her head bent so he couldn't possibly think she was propositioning him.

'I'm not going to leap on you, Rosalie.'

He put her down as requested as he spoke, gently and with care, and for a ridiculous moment she felt a sense of loss as the close contact finished before his words shocked her into raising her head. 'I know you aren't,' she lied vehemently. 'But you have a dinner engagement.'

'Did have,' he drawled, watching her with narrowed

eyes as he stepped back, crossing his arms. 'When Kirk was sure something was broken I cancelled it.'

'You shouldn't have done that,' she protested shakily.

He shrugged. 'Perhaps postponed is a better word. Does that make you feel better?' He didn't try to hide the mockery.

'But I'm—'

'Don't say fine.' He raised a hand, palm facing her. 'I couldn't stand it. Look, what sort of a guy do you think I am? You're in pain and the least I can do is to make sure you have something to eat before you turn in. Okay? Where's the kitchen?'

This was crazy. Her lips were still tingling from the brief contact with his and she wanted to ask him why he had kissed her, but the fact that he had seemed to dismiss it as totally unimportant made it difficult. In fact, if it weren't for the tingling she'd have wondered if she'd imagined it. But he *had* kissed her, and that wasn't in the contract. No way, no how. But how did you throw a six-foot-plus-a-few-inches, hard, lean, muscled man out of your flat when you couldn't even walk properly?

Her heart was beating so hard it hurt, but she managed to keep her voice very matter-of-fact when she said, 'I am more than capable of making myself a sandwich and after that lovely lunch I couldn't eat anything more.' That was a lie. She was amazed to find she was starving. Perhaps breaking a bone in your ankle was an appetite enhancer? Or perhaps it was all the nervous energy she expended around this man?

'A sandwich?' He eyed her reprovingly. 'It's—' he consulted the magnificent gold watch on his wrist '—now nearly eight, and we ate at one. You need something more than a sandwich and so do I.' It was a definite statement of fact, which brooked no reply.

It seemed churlish to tell him he was perfectly welcome to leave and go for a meal somewhere—considering he'd just told her he'd cancelled his dinner engagement for her—but that was exactly what she felt like doing. Rosalie bit back the words, saying instead, 'I'm afraid I don't have anything in. I was going to shop tonight on my way home.'

'Freezer food?' he suggested easily.

'Don't have one.' She tried to keep the triumph out of her voice. 'Cooking for one doesn't necessitate a freezer, besides which I prefer fresh produce.' So goodbye, Mr Know It All.

He smiled. 'That's okay, I was going to order some food in. Chinese, Indian, Italian, Thai?'

Rosalie gave up. Her ankle was too sore and she was too tired to argue any more. 'Chinese.'

He beamed. 'My favourite. Anything in particular you fancy?'

'Surprise me,' she said testily.

'Nothing I'd like better.' One dark eyebrow arched. 'Got a menu handy anywhere?'

'No, sorry.' She wasn't trying to be difficult, she genuinely *hadn't* got a menu. 'But there's an excellent Chinese take-away on the corner of the next street.'

He nodded, before walking across the room and switching on the TV, handing her the remote as he said, 'Keys? I shall need to get back in.'

She passed them over without a word, and when the front door clicked shut a few moments later exhaled a long breath of air. The day had taken on a life of its own; she had never felt so railroaded in all her born days. And she must look a mess.

The last thought prompted her to pull herself upwards, and she found by hitching and hotching along the walls and furniture the short journey to the bathroom wasn't too bad. She gazed at her reflection in the bathroom mirror. Her face was shiny and almost devoid of make-up, most of her mascara smudged under her eyes creating a faintly panda-style image. She groaned. Why on earth he wanted to stay and have dinner with her looking like this she didn't know!

She set to work feverishly, washing her face and then creaming it, before using just a touch of mascara on her lashes and careful foundation to take away her paleness. She brushed her hair until it curved in sleek wings against her cheeks, applied a few drops of her special French perfume, which cost an arm and a leg, and surveyed the results. Better, much better, but with her ankle throbbing like mad and her other leg protesting at the flamingo pose she'd had to adopt she really needed to sit down rather than get the plates ready.

Nevertheless, she struggled into her small but wonderfully compact little kitchen, flopping on one of the two pine stools and sitting limply for a moment or two. Her trousers were absolutely ruined; the nurse had slit the right leg to above her knee, and they were covered in dried mud from her fall. She didn't feel up to changing though, she decided as she fetched out plates, cutlery and wineglasses.

Ten minutes later she was ensconced at the small pine table in a corner of the sitting room, a gargantuan feast spread out before her and her wineglass full of orange juice—he was driving and she was on pain-killers that didn't mix with alcohol, Kingsley had informed her on his return with the food.

'Kingsley, this would feed a small army.' Rosalie gazed at the mixed hors d'oeuvres, beef with black peppers, pork in Kung po, chicken with ginger and pineapple, fried rice, prawn crackers and several other dishes crammed onto the table.

'I'm hungry.' He grinned at her, and her nerves jerked.

'Good, because I can't eat a quarter of this, let alone half,' she said evenly, refusing to relax her guard.

She wouldn't have believed how much food he could pack away if she hadn't seen it with her own eyes, and when the table was practically clear he fetched her pain-killers without her asking him to, along with a glass of water. 'Thanks.' It was reluctant. She didn't need looking after, especially not by Kingsley Ward. She was well able to look after herself. And she refused to consider how nice it had felt.

He recognised the tone, but as she had the pallor of a ghost and was clearly bushed he let it go. 'Want me to help you get ready for bed?' he asked helpfully.

Grey eyes met blue, and when she saw the gleam in his she was forced to smile, albeit grudgingly. 'I can manage.'

'Do you want a coffee before I go?'

She shook her head.

'Tea? I know you English like your tea.'

'No, thanks.' Just *go*, for goodness' sake.

'Cocoa? Bovril? Ovaltine?' he offered.

'Nothing.' Not unless he wanted it thrown at him, that was.

'Correct me if I'm wrong, but I suspect I've outstayed my welcome,' he said with lazy self-mockery. And then he bent down, taking her hand and turning it over in his before he put his lips to her pink palm in a caress that was as fleeting as the previous kiss. 'Goodnight, Rosalie.' He straightened, still holding her hand. 'Sleep tight.'

'Goodnight.' Tingles were radiating from the point of contact with his mouth, but she was immensely proud of herself that she hadn't jerked away or shown any signs of the frantic thumping of her heart. 'Thank you for everything you've done today,' she added carefully, remembering her manners.

'It's a speciality of mine, damsels in distress.'

Her hand was her own again, and the return of it enabled her to smile fairly naturally before he turned and left the room. She heard the front door open, and then close with a click. She listened, her ears straining and her eyes narrowed.

He had gone.

CHAPTER FOUR

ROSALIE didn't know what she had expected after the fiasco of her day with Kingsley Ward, but it wasn't the ginormous basket of flowers that was delivered the next day with a card that simply said, 'Heal fast, K', followed by three weeks of no contact whatsoever.

For a week or so after the accident she had been as jumpy as a cricket, and, with the flowers scenting out her flat and acting as a constant reminder of Kingsley, she'd actually preferred being at the office. But at home or in the office, every telephone call had her heart beating fit to burst and her nerves jangling.

By the second week she had begun to wonder if she'd got all the signals wrong, and he wasn't interested in her at all except in her professional capacity.

By the third week she'd accepted her imagination had run away with itself, and he had just been acting out of kindness and concern. Kingsley was the type of man who would flirt mildly with any woman he was with, she told herself firmly on the Saturday morning as she dumped the wilting flowers in the bin. And the flowers had been a polite gesture of commiseration, nothing more. And as that was exactly what she wanted, it was all to the good, wasn't it? Of course it was.

Monday morning saw Mike calling for her in his top-of-the-range Jaguar as he'd done each morning since her accident. The crutches Jenny had obtained were fine for pottering about at work and home, but negotiating her way on crowded London pavements was a definite no-no. But it shouldn't be long till she had the plaster off now, Rosalie comforted herself as she plumped down in the passenger seat. Kingsley's doctor friend had sent her notes to her GP, and he in turn had arranged for any further treatment to be carried out at her local hospital. After a check-up the Friday before, they'd confirmed another two weeks and the plaster would be off. And it couldn't be a day too soon, Rosalie thought grumpily as the itching under the plaster, which had made itself felt for days now, made her wriggle in her seat.

'Something you might be interested in in this magazine.' As Mike slid into the car after helping her into her seat he reached over to the back seat and then threw a glossy magazine into Rosalie's lap. 'Hannah noticed it.'

'Oh, yes?' Hannah, Mike's wife, devoured periodicals ranging from gardening magazines right through to high fashion and everything in between. Mike had coined the word 'magaholic' with his wife in mind.

'Page with the corner turned down,' he said shortly before pulling out into the traffic.

Ridiculous, really, *really* ridiculous, but she felt as though someone had just punched her in the stomach as she gazed down at Kingsley in morning dress with a voluptuous brunette draped all over him. Painfully aware of Mike's studied nonchalance, she kept her face blank with tremendous effort, reading the short caption under each of the five photographs of the high society wedding in New York without commenting. It would appear he had been best man to a very old friend, a very rich old friend, and the brunette—who featured in each of the three photographs Kingsley was in—was the groom's baby sister and chief bridesmaid.

Rosalie got a measure of savage comfort from the fact that both the style and the colour of the bridesmaid's dress—citric yellow—did nothing for the girl in question. But then she was lovely enough for it not to matter too much, and the last picture—coyly captioned 'The best man taking his duties very seriously'—showed them wrapped in each other's arms so closely Rosalie was surprised the girl hadn't got in Kingsley's suit with him.

'Lovely dresses.' She slung the magazine over her shoulder back onto the seat. 'And Kingsley looked the part, didn't he?'

Mike darted her a quick glance before he said, 'There's talk that's the girl who's going to snare the ultimate bachelor.'

'Really.' It was cool. 'Lucky old bridesmaid.'

'Rosalie—' Mike stopped abruptly. 'Hell, I thought you should know,' he said irritably.

'Know?' She turned to him, stitching a smile on her face. 'Why on earth should I know, Mike? I shouldn't think the wedding, if there is one, would interfere with the job we're doing for him. Beyond that…' She shrugged.

'Yeah.' Mike was clearly out of his depth and she would have felt sorry for him in any other circumstances. As it was, she wanted to hit him. But why shoot the messenger? she asked herself in the next instant. And what was she getting all hot under the collar about anyway? Kingsley Ward was nothing to her, absolutely nothing.

She took a deep breath, turned to Mike and began to engage him in conversation about a couple of minor problems with Kingsley's job, as though this were just another ride to work.

The week went steadily down hill from that point, but finally it was Friday and the last few days of petty irritations, delays, broken promises—something builders excelled in—and general aggravation were over. She was spending the weekend with one of her aunts—her mother had had two sisters and, although Rosalie didn't see a great deal of them and their families, they were always there if she needed them—who lived in Kingston upon Thames, and as her aunt was collecting her at the office she had taken a weekend bag to work with her that morning.

She was deep into checking a list of figures and calculations at five o'clock when there was a knock at her door, and, Jenny having gone home early with a migraine, she called out, 'Come in, Beth. I won't be a sec.' Her aunt was only ten years older than Rosalie, and their relationship had always been one of friends on an equal level rather than a traditional aunt/niece affair. One of best friends even though their lives were different.

'I've been called a lot of things in my time, but never Beth.'

Her head shot up at the deep, amused voice from across the other side of the room. Her mouth dry, Rosalie said, 'Hello, Kingsley.' She was so glad she was sitting down.

'Hello, Rosalie,' he returned softly.

He was leaning against the open door, looking more attractive than any man had the right to. The Armani suit was not in evidence today, but the more casual light charcoal trousers and open-necked cornflower-blue shirt were killers. Or rather the body inside them was.

'I thought you were my aunt,' she said stupidly.

'But as you can see I am not.'

'No.' She sucked in a hidden breath, forcing a smile as she said, 'What can I do for you at this late hour?'

He strolled further into the room, his flagrant masculinity suddenly dwarfing the place, and to her horror he perched on the side of her desk as though he had the perfect right to sit wherever he liked. The ebony hair was even shorter than she remembered, the severity of the style emphasising his beautiful eyes with their almost feminine lashes. But of course he would have had it cut for the wedding, she thought testily. In order to look his best for…

'Do you mind?' She gestured at the papers covering the top of her desk. 'You might disturb them.'

He glanced at the papers and then raised his eyes to her face, keeping them there as her colour rose. 'What's the matter?' he asked quietly.

'Nothing is the matter,' she said coolly. 'I just don't want things muddled up, that's all.'

He folded his arms over his chest. 'I muddle you?'

'That's not what I meant.' And he knew it, darn him.

'How's the foot?' he asked softly.

'Much better.' She belatedly remembered her manners and added, 'Thank you for the flowers.'

'Your aunt? Are you seeing her tonight? I was hoping we could do dinner.' And he actually had the nerve to smile at her.

She didn't believe she was hearing this! He hadn't even bothered to contact her for weeks and then he breezed in expecting her to be available? To just drop everything?

'Sorry.' Her eyes narrowed coldly. 'I'm busy.'

'That's a shame.' Considering he had flown straight back across the Atlantic the moment the business deal he'd been setting up over the last weeks was in the bag. That, and Alexander's circus of a wedding. 'Are you free tomorrow?'

'I'm away for the weekend.' Funny, but it wasn't as satisfying to turn him down as she had imagined during the last few days when she had let her mind dwell on such a remote possibility occurring. In fact it wasn't satisfying at all.

'The aunt,' he said flatly. 'Right?'

She nodded. And then she did what she had promised herself she'd rather cut out her tongue than do, and said, 'How did the wedding go?' her voice as causal as she could make it.

'The wedding?' He showed his surprise but as far as she could determine there was no guilt in his eyes. The rat. 'Did I mention it before I went?'

He knew full well he hadn't; neither had he seen fit to call attention to Little Miss Canary. Rosalie shook her head. 'Mike's wife takes a magazine which covered the event,' she said pleasantly. 'You're famous, it seems.'

He grimaced. 'Alex is, you mean. He owns half of New York State, or rather the family do. He's a great guy but life in a goldfish bowl can get a little tedious.'

'I'm sure it can,' she said with no sympathy whatsoever.

'Okay, Rosalie.' He leant towards her, ignoring a couple of pages that drifted onto the floor. 'Why the big freeze?'

'I don't know what you mean,' she said stiffly.

'Sure you do.' His mouth had thinned but his voice was softer than ever. 'I ask you out to dinner and it's like I've committed the ultimate insult. No, thank you is simple enough surely?'

'You happen to be in London and at a loose end, and you expect me to fall on your neck with gratitude because you deign to offer to pass a couple of hours slumming?' she said tightly, regretting the words the second they had passed her lips. She had determined to be so cool and in control the next time she met him, and here she was practically demanding to know why she hadn't heard from him before this. Worst possible line to take, Rosalie, she thought miserably, but she just couldn't seem to think straight around this man.

'Is that what you think?' He had slid off the desk, moving round to her chair and pulling her to her feet regardless of her injured ankle. 'That you're a number in a little black book?'

He had his hands on her forearms and she couldn't move, but she raised her head defiantly, looking him full in the face. 'Actually, yes.' And she made sure he knew she meant it.

She waited for his temper to rise but he considered her dryly, his head to one side. 'Some girls wouldn't mind that,' he said softly. 'Being wined and dined with no strings attached is what plenty of career women call for these days. No messy complications or irritating ties.'

She didn't know quite how to answer that. 'You have an answer for everything, don't you?' she muttered crossly. Her voice wasn't as acidic as she would have liked, mainly because, with the palms of her hands pressed against his chest so hard she could feel the beat of his heart, and the smell and feel of him all around her, her head was beginning to spin.

'Do I?' There was a strange note in his voice, and when he lifted a hand to her face, his fingertips caressing the silk of her cheek, she was quite unable to move.

'Oh, I'm sorry!'

A flustered voice from the doorway brought Rosalie's head jerking round, but Kingsley continued to hold her for another moment or two before he turned, managing to put an arm round her waist and pulling her firmly into him as he did so.

'Beth.' Rosalie had never felt so rattled. 'I didn't hear you come in. I mean—'

'You must be Rosalie's aunt.' Kingsley was all charm

as he deposited Rosalie gently back into her chair before striding across the room with his hand outstretched towards the pretty, plump woman in the doorway. 'I'm Kingsley Ward. How do you do? I was hoping to surprise Rosalie and take her out to dinner, but it appears I'm too late.'

He was all white teeth and winsome smiles, Rosalie thought furiously, watching Beth go down before him like a ninepin.

'Oh, what a shame.' Beth darted one quick glance towards Rosalie, who groaned inwardly at the delighted gleam in her aunt's eye. Beth had been on at her for years to find herself a nice man and enjoy life—the two were synonymous in her aunt's mind—and Kingsley was clearly the answer to all her hopes. 'Have you come far?' she asked worriedly.

'New York.' He grinned winningly. 'Not too far.'

Beth wasn't going to be taken in by this drivel, was she? It appeared she was.

'Really? But that's too bad. Look, Rosalie's coming to us for the weekend; why don't you come too? We've a couple of spare bedrooms now the children are all doing their own thing. We've two at university and one's up in Scotland doing goodness knows what on an archaeological dig.'

'A dig, how interesting, but I couldn't impose…'

'It wouldn't be imposing, we'd absolutely love to have you. Wouldn't we, Rosalie?' Beth was really going for it now.

Two pairs of eyes looked her way; one pair earnest brown, and the other alive with wicked blue delight. Rosalie warned herself her aunt had had a sheltered life and might faint on the spot if she said what she was thinking. 'I'm sure Kingsley has things to do over the weekend,

Beth,' she said tightly. 'He's a very busy man.' She glared at him pointedly as she spoke.

'But all work and no play…' Beth beamed at the tall, dark and wonderfully handsome man in front of her. If she had gone out and sifted through all the men in London, she couldn't have found better for Rosalie, she thought happily. He was a hunk.

Oh, he plays all right. Boy, does he know how to play! Rosalie opened her mouth to set her aunt straight, but Kingsley was there before her. Wouldn't you just know it?

'If you are sure it's okay I would love to come,' he said with outrageous humility. 'I called here to see Rosalie straight from the airport so I've all my things in the car, as luck would have it. It'd be great to have a relaxing weekend.'

This was too much. Rosalie was almost choking with rage. And how could Beth invite him like this without checking with her first? But she knew how. Her aunt had been looking into those blue eyes and had lost all reason.

'Lovely.' Beth was almost wriggling like an ecstatic puppy. 'That's settled, then. And it will give you a chance to meet my husband, George—that's if we can manage to drag him out of his study. He's in the middle of preparing a paper on the origins of anthropomorphism, whatever that is.'

'The attribution of a human form or personality to a god or animal or thing, I think,' Kingsley supplied helpfully.

'Yes, that's right!' Beth gazed at him admiringly. 'Goodness, aren't you clever? You'll get on like a house on fire with George. He's a lecturer at City University and I think he despairs of intelligent conversation now the children have all flown the nest. They all take after him, you see, rather than me.'

'Then I'm sure that's their loss.'

She'd be sick if she listened to much more of this. Rosalie coughed meaningfully, and, having got their attention, said crisply, 'I'm sorry but I'll be another ten minutes finishing in here. Why don't you give Kingsley the address, Beth, and he can make his way later?' Which would enable her to fill her aunt in on the background to this crazy situation, and make it very clear any matchmaking possibilities were out of the window.

'Or why don't I disappear and do a bit of shopping I need to get, and see you both back at the house?' Beth put in cheerfully. 'You can show Kingsley—that's an unusual name, isn't it?'

She interrupted herself mid-flow, not an unknown occurrence for Beth. Kingsley smiled. 'My friends call me King, and I'm sure we're going to be friends?'

Beth giggled. 'King, it is, then. Gosh, how grand.'

Rosalie shut her eyes for an infinitesimal moment.

'Anyway, as I was saying, Lee can give you directions, then, if that's all right?' Beth continued. 'And I'll see you later.'

'That would be great. Thanks, Beth.' Kingsley turned to Rosalie, his eyes taking in her burning cheeks and hot eyes. 'I'll wait outside in your secretary's office until you've finished,' he said gently, ushering Beth out with him and shutting the door behind them both.

Rosalie stared at the door for a full ten seconds. Then she sagged back in her chair, the breath leaving her body in a long whoosh. She didn't know whether to laugh or cry, she thought helplessly. Who else but Kingsley would have managed that so perfectly for his own ends? He was amazing, and she didn't mean that in a laudatory sense either!

She lowered her gaze to the papers on her desk, but she had completely lost the thread of what she'd been doing, along with the will to continue. A weekend with Kingsley. This whole thing was surreal. And what about Tweety Pie? Where did she fit into the scheme of things? Was she one of those career women he had talked about who liked being wined and dined with no strings attached? Or were the rumours Mike had spoken about true and she was due to be the future Mrs Ward? Not that it made any difference to her, of course, Rosalie reassured herself in the next instant, but if the latter *was* the case he shouldn't be here right now.

She put her hands to her hot cheeks, her heart thumping a tattoo. She didn't want this, any of it. Panic rose, the taste acidic in her throat. She had made a life for herself, a good life, and she didn't want anyone or anything to spoil it. And Kingsley had the potential to do that.

She smoothed her hair away from her flushed face, aware her hands were shaking but unable to do anything about it.

Control. It was all about control, just as it had been with Miles. Miles had bulldozed his way into her life too, captivating and holding her with his charm and good looks and dominating her to the point where she had begun to believe black was white. She had been eighteen when she had met him and nearly twenty-one when they'd split up, and apart from the first few months of their relationship she'd existed rather than lived. Terrified of upsetting him, of losing his love; accepting always that she was the one to blame whatever the circumstances. *Her mother's daughter.*

She straightened, shame and humiliation making her

back rigid. Non-involvement spelt safety where a man like Kingsley was concerned, and she needed to remember that this weekend. This was just an amusing diversion for him, that was all.

It was another fifteen minutes before she left her office and by then Rosalie was in command of herself again. Kingsley glanced up from where he was sitting perched on the edge of Jenny's desk, leafing through a car magazine. He rose, slinging the magazine on a pile on the occasional table next to a comfy chair reserved for visitors, his voice expressionless as he said, 'Don't frown like that, you'll get lines before your time.'

Don't react, that's exactly what he wants. Rosalie's smile was brittle, her eyes cool, but she kept her voice pleasant. 'I'll take my chance.'

'You won't say that at fifty when you resemble a wrinkled prune instead of a peach.' He grinned at her, one of the grins she'd seen only once or twice, which touched the clear cold blue of his eyes with warm sunshine. It was hard to remain annoyed and try to freeze him in the face of such a metamorphosis, but she persevered.

And then strong arms caught her and he wasn't smiling any more. 'What was his name?' he asked softly.

'What?' She was so taken aback she made no move to free herself, her senses registering the shirt was made of silk as her hands rested against the wall of his chest.

'The guy who put the ''Keep off'' sign in place.'

Her eyes flickered. 'I haven't the faintest idea what you're talking about.' She looked at him defiantly.

'Liar.' His gaze moved over her face, burning where it touched. 'Someone's hurt you, and badly. What was his name?'

'Kingsley, let me go—'

'We can stand here all night like this if you like, but I

want to know his name.' And now the softness covered pure steel. 'The more I get to know you, the less I know you, and I don't like that.' The blue eyes were clear and steady and unrelenting.

She raised her head a fraction. 'I would have thought you are too busy to worry about me,' she said tightly.

He looked at her, his expression unreadable. 'Now something tells me you aren't referring to my work schedule,' he said quietly. 'Right?'

Darn right. She shrugged, attempting to move away, but the grip on her arms tightened. Now he was bullying her. Charming.

'And this is a follow-on from the little-black-book dig. Right again?' His voice was even and faintly quizzical.

'It was you who brought up the little black book,' she protested. 'I merely said—'

'I know what you said, Rosalie.'

He lowered his head and kissed her. His mouth was urgent, hungry, and this kiss was as different from anything that had gone before as ice from fire. She made a brief movement of withdrawal but then as it continued, his mouth slowly and deeply taking what it wanted, she felt desire rise hotly in the core of her being. She felt weightless, the feel of him and the warmth of his body causing her to melt into him even as a tiny part of her mind that was still capable of rational thought warned her that this was madness.

His hands were stroking the silky skin of her back under the thin blouse she was wearing, his fingers delicately exploring even as they urged her closer into him. She could feel what the kiss was doing to him, and it was sweet, potent, to know she could arouse him so easily.

It was the ringing of the telephone on Jenny's desk that penetrated the world of touch and taste that had taken her over, and Rosalie had no idea how long they had been standing wrapped in each other's arms. As the answer machine took a message from someone concerning an account problem, Kingsley said softly, 'I wouldn't kiss you like that if I was involved with someone else, Rosalie. Oh, I might take you out to dinner or for a drink, a date where everything remained on the level, but there would be no lovemaking.'

'Just platonic friendship?' She tried to make her voice lightly disbelieving, but she was trembling too much.

'Just so.'

Did she believe him? She stared into the piercingly blue eyes and admitted she didn't know. She had believed Miles and look where that had got her. The thought of Miles caused her heart to give an unsteady slam, and something of the impact must have registered in her eyes because Kingsley said, 'Sooner or later you have to put a toe in the water again; you know that, don't you?'

It didn't dawn on her what she had admitted when she said, 'Why do I?' until much later.

'Because you are far too beautiful and desirable not to, that's why. Whoever he was, Rosalie, and whatever he did, the future is yours and what you make of it. Do you believe that?'

She remained silent, the euphoria of how it had felt to be in his arms, to be kissed by him, gone. And then she said very quietly, 'His name was Miles Stuart.'

There was a second of stillness. It seemed to go on for ever.

'And?' he said gently. Very gently.

'And we met when I was eighteen, married when I was nineteen and were getting divorced when I was twenty-one.' Her voice was louder now, her face painfully defiant. Story done.

'When you were at university?' he persisted softly.

She nodded. This was as far as she was going to go.

Kingsley Ward had had fifteen ruthlessly hard years of experience in the market place of big business to know all about keeping poker-faced, and this came to his aid now, enabling him to maintain an impassive countenance as he said, 'And he hurt you?' knowing he really had no right to ask.

'I don't want to talk about it.' It was unmistakably final.

He took a deep breath, finding his guts had twisted like a corkscrew. 'Fine,' he said calmly, 'but what I said earlier still stands. He is the past, you have to look to the present.'

He didn't have a clue what he was talking about. Rosalie looked at him steadily. Decisions and consequences was a rotten game to lose at eighteen years old.

'Have you had therapy?' he asked after a moment or two.

'This is England, not America.' It was too sharp and she moderated her voice when she said, 'Like I said, I don't want to talk about it.'

'But you have talked it through with someone? At the time, when it all happened, or later?' he said quietly.

Rosalie could hear the beat of her own heart. She didn't want to think about Miles, not even for a second. It made her feel sick. She swallowed audibly. 'I'm not like that,' she said carefully. 'It wouldn't have helped.' In fact it would have killed her; it still would, even ten years later. There were some things so degrading that to share them with another human being was unthinkable. 'I married him and it was a mistake, that is all anyone needs to know.'

The hell it was. Kingsley nodded. 'Sure,' he said easily, 'whatever. But coming back to us—'

'Us?' Where did us come from?

There was real panic in her voice and now his tone was velvety smooth when he said, 'There's an us, Rosie, whether you like it or not. There was from the moment we laid eyes on each other. Call it the X-factor or whatever you like, but your body knew what it wanted long before you could bring your mind to accept it.' His eyebrows rose, daring her to disagree.

'You're talking sex,' she said flatly. 'That's all.'

Blue eyes glinted. 'Sex is spelt with three letters; it's not a four-letter word, Rosie.'

'Don't call me Rosie. Everyone shortens Rosalie to Lee.' A small point but somehow vitally important.

And then Kingsley hit the nail on the head and summed up what she was feeling when he said softly, 'But I'm not everyone, am I?'

Her skin shivered. No, he wasn't.

'Besides which, Lee is cold, abstract, almost boyish. Rosie is warm and soft and as sexy as hell.' He bent and picked up her crutches from where they'd fallen seconds after he had taken her mouth. 'But enough of this getting to know each other,' he said dryly. 'Beth will be waiting at home for us.'

'I can't believe you virtually invited yourself along this weekend,' she muttered, disturbingly aware that she seemed to have lost on every twist and turn of this conversation.

'Believe it.' He eyed her unrepentantly. 'And you ain't seen nothing yet, Rosie. Trust me on that if nothing else.'

CHAPTER FIVE

THE June evening was warm with all the delicious smells of summer when Kingsley's car drew into Beth and George's pebbled drive, and Rosalie got an inordinate amount of pleasure from the fact that Kingsley was speechless for once. She hadn't warned him what to expect, and it was clear the quaint old thatched cottage engulfed in roses, honeysuckle and jasmine, and set in a perfectly Victorian garden, had stunned him.

'What a place.' He turned to her after a moment or two, his voice richly appreciative.

'Gorgeous, isn't it?' They hadn't said much on the way and it was a relief for some of the crackling tension to diffuse. 'The back garden is just as beautiful. It's full of hollyhocks and wallflowers and all the old-fashioned types of flowers. I've always thought of this place as a piece of heaven on earth. A very English heaven, of course,' she added with a smile.

'Wooden benches and a rose garden and arbours?' he said smilingly. 'I bet it has all those?'

She nodded. 'And rambling roses scaling old stone walls and apple and plum trees. It's just perfect—to me, that is.'

'It must be worth a small fortune,' he said softly, glancing at the mullioned windows. 'I didn't realise lecturers were paid so well over here.'

'They're not. George's father was something big in the city, a real wheeler and dealer, which is pretty amazing to think about when you meet George. He's a dear but

70

hardly of this world, such a genius in his own field he doesn't know what day it is most of the time. Beth's perfect for him; she's more mother than wife. Anyway, as the only child he got everything when his parents died in a car accident just after he and Beth married, and so they decided to plough the lot into their own little piece of English heaven which is near enough the university for it not to be a huge problem. Of course that was over two decades ago now, and the price of property has gone crazy since then. As an investment it was pretty cute. I think George's father would have been proud of him for once!'

'Undoubtedly.' He turned fully to face her in the tight confines of the car as he reached out a hand and touched the shining silk of her hair, letting one finger trail down the smooth skin of her cheek. 'Real peaches and cream,' he murmured almost to himself, 'and very English. And yet the French side is apparent too.' Rosalie had told him during the wait at the hospital some weeks before that both her parents had died when she was young, but that was all, and now he asked, 'Your parents? Was it an accident like George's parents or something similar?'

She answered the way the family had decided to handle it at the time of her father's suicide. 'My mother died of a brain haemorrhage, and my father felt he couldn't go on without her…'

'He took his own life?' he said very quietly.

She nodded, flushing slightly. She had never found it hard before to leave out the more pertinent facts that clothed the bare truth in quite a different garment, but now she felt uncomfortable. Therefore it was with a real sense of relief that she saw Beth at the front door beckoning them into the house. 'Beth's calling us.'

She turned to open her door but he caught her hand for

a second, saying quietly, 'You've had a tough start in life one way or the other.'

'People have worse.' He was making her feel twice as guilty. 'My grandparents were wonderful to me, and my mother's two sisters spoilt me rotten. You might meet Jeanne—she normally calls round if she knows I'm here, like Beth does if I visit Jeanne. She lives quite close.'

Why had she said that? It was too cosy. As if he were her boyfriend or something. She didn't want him to meet her relatives, or know all about her. She pulled away from him now, cross with herself and everyone else. She had always been so careful to keep the opposite sex at a distance since Miles, even the harmless ones, and now she was in the most farcical situation and through no fault of her own. Beth might be one of the warmest and most hospitable creatures under the sun, but right at this moment she wasn't in the mood to appreciate her aunt's generosity.

She hoped George and Kingsley would take an instant dislike to each other, and Kingsley would be bored stiff here. She always spent time with Beth when she visited, knowing how lonely her aunt got with the children gone and George ensconced in his study most of the time he wasn't at the university, and she saw no reason to change things because Kingsley had engineered an invite. Perhaps he'd give up and leave early if things were too dull? He was used to the jet-set lifestyle, after all.

'You're frowning again.' Kingsley had come round to the passenger door, opening it and helping her out, and now his voice was soft when he added, 'Smile sweetly for Beth. We don't want to upset your lovely aunt, do we?'

She murmured a word that was rude enough to make him blink, and, encouraged at that small victory, stitched a smile on her face as she hobbled off towards the front door, cursing the plaster and the fact she couldn't sweep elegantly in front of him.

George and Kingsley did not take an instant dislike to each other at all. Kingsley displayed such an interest in the other man's work that George was in danger of becoming positively effusive over pre-dinner cocktails, and Rosalie groaned inwardly as she contemplated her aunt's gratified expression, for all the world like a satisfied mother whose brilliant child was being appreciated.

'I'm just going to show Kingsley the garden.' When she couldn't stand it a minute more, Rosalie put down her cocktail and all but frogmarched him out through the open French doors and into the last of the spangled evening sunshine.

'You don't have to humour him quite so enthusiastically, you know,' she said snappily once they were far enough away from the house not to be overheard.

'I'm interested,' he protested mildly, pulling her down onto a sun-warmed bench near an old tree providing a giant sculpture for sweet-smelling roses to ramble over. 'Sit awhile and relax, you're too tense,' he added reprovingly. 'You need to learn to chill out.'

Chill out? *Chill out?* She might have got some very nice chilling-out time this weekend, but with Kingsley around relaxing was not an option. She'd never felt so edgy in all her life.

A couple of blue tits were busy stocking up for the night from a nut feeder Beth had hanging from the tree, and Rosalie kept her gaze on the small birds, willing herself to calm down. She had a whole weekend to get through; she couldn't afford to let him get to her like this.

Nevertheless, she was painfully aware of him sitting

next to her, one arm stretching along the back of the old wooden bench so that his body was inclined towards her. She had noticed the faint dark shadow of body hair under the blue shirt earlier, and now the delicious scent of him she had smelt once or twice before teased her nostrils, forcing her to acknowledge her heightened senses.

Kingsley stretched out his long legs, his voice easy as he said, 'This is great, isn't it? You could believe the rest of the world didn't exist here, it's so peaceful.'

'I wouldn't have thought you were the sort of man who wanted peace.' It slipped out and she regretted it immediately.

'No?' He bent closer, turning her face to him. 'Why is that?'

Rosalie flushed. 'Just your reputation,' she said after a moment. But she knew he would persist with this now.

'Which is?' He didn't seem inclined to let go of her chin.

'Work hard and play hard.'

'Ah, I see.' She wasn't quite sure what he saw, but then he said, 'Amazingly I'm not a robot, Rosie. I get tired, I get sick on occasion, scratch me and I bleed, just like any other man.'

She lowered her eyes; the intensity of his gaze was unnerving 'I know that,' she said awkwardly. 'Of course I know that.'

'I don't think you do.' He let go of her, and they continued to sit without speaking in the warm, scented air. Fat honey-bees buzzed busily among the profusion of flowers, paying special attention to the roses, and the evening was alive with bird song. Why had she never brought Miles here? Her hands were clasped too tightly together and she forced herself to relax her fingers one by one. Had it been because university life had been so frantic, so busy, their circle of friends so absorbing? Or because she had been frightened the cracks in their relationship, which had begun to appear shortly after the quick register office wedding, would have been apparent to Beth? That her aunt would have recognised the same spirit of tyranny and oppression in Miles that had been in her sister's husband?

She shifted slightly on the seat, brushing a wisp of hair from her face. But at least her father had had some excuse for acting as he had, or not an excuse, exactly, she corrected herself, but a reason behind his actions that explained his obsessive peremptoriness with her mother. And he had loved her too, tortured and twisted as that love had become. Miles had been the original spoilt little rich kid, the adored and indulged only son whose every whim had been granted since birth.

'You haven't left him behind yet, have you?' The voice at her side was very quiet, and as Rosalie's eyes shot up to meet his Kingsley covered her hand with one of his own, refusing to let go of it when she tried to pull away. 'He's right here now, isn't he?' he said softly. 'The silent spectre at our shoulders.'

Rosalie's stomach clenched. She looked away, her mouth unconsciously tightening. How come he could read her mind?

'Do you still love him?' Kingsley said evenly.

'Love him?'' It carried such distaste Kingsley couldn't doubt her antipathy.

So, he'd been barking up the wrong tree there. He knew a second of quick relief, before the question of what *was* wrong kicked in. 'So you don't still care for him. Why is he such a big deal in your life, then?'

'I told you before, I don't want to talk about Miles,'

she said shakily, her voice refusing to obey the command to be firm and cool. 'I'm cold, let's go in.'

'No, you're not,' he challenged softly, squeezing her hand as he spoke. 'And I'm just trying to understand where you're coming from, that's all. I don't want to drag up painful memories for the sake of it, but right from the first moment I met you there's always been a silent third party present. I didn't know what the problem was at first, but it's him, the ex, isn't it?'

He felt the withdrawal even though she hadn't moved a muscle and he knew he was right. He also knew he was getting in way over his head. This wasn't the way he did things. He cursed himself for being a fool. He had done the love and commitment thing once and had been left with enough egg on his face to keep him in omelettes for the rest of his life.

'You've no right to question me like this.'

She was damn right, he hadn't. 'Yes, I have,' he said grimly. 'You're here right now with me, not him, and I don't like threesomes.'

The control thing again. He couldn't have said anything worse as far as she was concerned. They were all the same under the skin, the whole male race, apart from the occasional being from another planet like George. 'I didn't invite you to be here, remember?' she bit back harshly.

'Do you want me to leave?' he asked grimly.

Did she? It was a drenching shock to find out it was the last thing in all the world she wanted, and it caused her to say, her voice quivering despite all her efforts to control it, 'Yes, that's exactly what I want.'

The world was motionless, and then with a low growl of irritation he took her into his arms. He kissed her over and over until her weak, fluttering protests faded, each kiss deeper and hungrier than the one before, and somehow she found herself lying on his lap with her hands clinging to his shoulders. And still he kissed her. His mouth was warm and wonderfully experienced and his arms were strong, the heat between them explosive.

It was Beth's voice calling from the house that eventually brought them apart, Rosalie blinking and staring at him with huge drugged eyes as he raised his head. 'You don't want me to leave,' he whispered gently, his eyes so blue it hurt her to look into them. 'Say it.' He kissed the tip of her nose, a tender, curiously intimate caress. 'Say it, Rosie.'

She looked at him. 'I don't want you to leave.'

'Good.' As Beth's voice called again he stood up with her, lowering her gently to her feet before reaching down and handing her the crutches. 'That's good, because I had no intention of going away.' He grinned at her, purposely breaking the spell that their lovemaking had woven round them because they had to go into the house and pretend the world hadn't suddenly tilted and changed direction. 'And for the rest of the weekend we're just going to enjoy being in each other's company and have fun,' he added softly. 'Okay? No more questions, no more big debates.'

She blinked again. He was like a human chameleon, changing his persona so swiftly and completely she couldn't keep up with him, she thought helplessly.

And as though he had read her mind, his smile faded. 'There's nothing to be afraid of,' he said quietly. 'We're two adult people getting to know each other a little better and neither of us is hurting anyone else. What is wrong with that?'

Put like that, nothing. But one of the adults was Kingsley Ward, which took this into a vastly different ball game.

'Come on.' As though he had suddenly tired of the

situation Kingsley's voice was brisk. 'I'm starving. I hope Beth's a good cook.'

'She's a brilliant cook.' This was safer ground. 'Three super-intelligent children and a near genius husband inspired her to excel in the thing she's always had a gift for, and her meals are second to none. Even your friend, Glen, would have a hard job to compete. And she's something of a wine boff too.'

Kingsley smiled again, a very cat-with-the-cream smile. 'I think I'm going to enjoy this weekend in more ways than one,' he said softly. 'Wine, woman and song.'

'Shouldn't that be wine, *women* and song?' Rosalie said breathlessly, taking a second to stop and brush back the hair from her face as they walked to the house, her crutches proving a mixed blessing, as always.

He let his eyes roam over the high, rounded breasts, slender waist and long, long legs, before lifting his gaze to the beautiful face with its curtain of shining chestnut hair. 'Not from where I'm standing,' he said gruffly.

The meal was as delicious as Rosalie had promised, and, with the wine flowing as freely as the conversation, and even George cracking a couple of jokes and proving quite witty in Kingsley's company, Rosalie found she was enjoying herself.

Kingsley had a way with people, she thought towards the dessert stage of the dinner, watching Beth positively bask in his appreciative comments about the food, which had actually prompted George to take a break from Planet Antiquity long enough to give his wife a rare compliment. But then Miles had always been able to charm the birds out of the trees too.

The thought was like a punch in the chest and she was angry with herself for letting Miles intrude into her thoughts once again. She hadn't thought about him in a long time, and now it seemed he was at the back of her mind all the time, or, as Kingsley had said, a spectre at her shoulder. *Was* Kingsley like her ex?

She surveyed him from across the table as he held Beth and George captivated with another of the many funny stories he'd related during the evening, the sting in the tail often being directed against himself.

Certainly Miles hadn't been able to laugh at himself, but then Kingsley was probably quite aware that it was a definite plus in winning people over, she thought, with no apology for the cynicism.

Miles had been tall, dark and handsome—like Kingsley. Rich—like Kingsley. Possessed of the certain something that, along with wealth and power, proved to be an almost irresistible draw to the average female—like Kingsley.

Miles had also been cruel and unreasonable, a harsh despot who hid his true nature under blindingly good looks and a winsome boyish manner. He had been the perfect man until they had got married, the catch of the university, and she'd known all her friends had been green with envy. Who would have believed that behind locked doors he could turn into a vicious, brutal sadist when crossed, a savage, and for something as trivial as his toast being burnt? The flat they had rented had become a place of terror, and it had got so she had only felt safe when she'd been at her lectures or out in a group with their friends.

Why had she stuck it as long as she had? Probably because she'd believed marriage was for life back then, and she had been desperate to make it work after what had happened to her parents. Every time he had hurt her she'd told herself she had to try that bit harder to be a better wife. It had to be her that was at fault, surely? Miles was perfect; everyone said so. And then had come the night of their graduation...

'...don't you think, Lee?'

She came out of the horror to see Beth's dining table and three pairs of eyes looking at her. 'I'm sorry.' She forced a smile. 'Thinking about a problem at work.'

'Not my job, I hope?' Kingsley's voice was easy, lazy, but the piercing blue of his eyes told her she hadn't done quite such a good cover-up job as she'd have liked.

'Yours is fine.' She turned her gaze to Beth, who had been the one who had spoken her name. 'Sorry,' she said again. 'What were you saying?'

The conversation progressed naturally from that point, but Rosalie was aware that, although he laughed and joked as before, Kingsley's gaze was thoughtful when it rested on her.

They didn't reach the coffee and liqueur stage until just before midnight, and by then the conflicting emotions Rosalie had suffered since Kingsley had walked into her office had her aching for sleep. Fortunately Beth and George were normally in bed by ten, and once everyone had finished their coffee and brandy Beth made no bones about retiring.

The four of them walked up the exquisite curved stair-case the cottage sported together, and once on the landing Beth and George disappeared into the master suite after the customary goodnights, leaving Kingsley and Rosalie alone on the landing.

'Goodnight, Rosie.' He had bent his dark head and captured her mouth before she could react. Warmth spread through her, and then a rising passion, the blood rushing through her body like hot mulled wine. He had pulled her hard into him, kissing her with almost violent intensity before he suddenly let her go.

Her legs were trembling as he held her away from him so she could stabilise herself, and he looked at her with hungry eyes. 'There was a woman once, when I was twenty, and I got my fingers burnt badly,' he said roughly. 'Since then I've always been up-front about how I feel; no promises of for ever, no commitment beyond that whilst the affair lasts I'll be faithful and I expect the lady to be. Honesty and loyalty, and no regrets, no recriminations. Not a bad philosophy, is it?'

She stared at him. What was he saying, that he wanted an affair with her? A no-strings-attached kind of affair? For a moment her brain wouldn't work, and then she sidestepped the issue by saying, 'And the women are happy with that?'

'Of course.' He sounded surprised she had asked. 'When you get down to basics most women acknowledge that love might sound a pleasant concept but it just doesn't work in the real world. Sooner or later mistrust and doubt rear their ugly heads, and if you find out your partner has been cheating on you…' He shrugged. 'It happens. All the time. The divorce rate is evidence of that. Sexual compatibility is something else. That's real and honest and not reliant on trusting someone or being trusted.'

Rosalie took a deep breath. 'Are you propositioning me, Kingsley?' she asked expressionlessly.

'You want me, Rosie. And I want you—from the first second I laid eyes on you I've been burning up with the need. You're single, I'm single. It's the most natural thing on earth.'

She wasn't sure how she felt exactly, but she knew she wanted to hit him, and that didn't seem quite fair when he was being so honest. She tried for lightness. 'Sorry, but I don't do affairs,' she said pleasantly.

'I know that.' He pulled her closer again, his palms cupping her sides and his fingertips splaying over her lower ribs. 'And I respect how you feel.'

She could feel his strength and warm virility flowing into her, and the lure of it made her voice husky when she said, 'But? And don't tell me there isn't a but. "But" this is different. "But" we'd be so good for each other. "But" it's not often people have the empathy we have. Am I right?'

For an answer he moved, pressing her back against the wall of the landing, holding her there with his body as he took her mouth again. His thighs were hard against hers and she could feel every inch of him as he drained her will to protest, his mouth and tongue fuelling the burning desire that had exploded the moment his lips had touched hers. She could feel his heart pounding like a sledgehammer, mirroring her pulse, and for a second the urge to give in, to open the door of her bedroom and pull him in with her was paramount.

It was enough to shock her back to reality. Her arms had been round his waist but now she brought them up to his chest and pushed, her voice shaking as she said, 'Don't. I don't want this, Kingsley. Let me go.'

Kingsley had known many women over the years and thought he understood the female species pretty well, but the fear in Rosalie's voice stunned him. He stopped instantly, taking a backwards step that removed his body from hers, but kept his arms outstretched either side of her body, holding her within the circle of his maleness. 'What the hell did he do to you?' he asked softly, his voice very deep. And then, at the look on her white face, he straightened. 'Okay, okay, I know. You don't want to talk about it.'

'I can't.' It was a whisper. 'I can't talk about it.'

'You don't trust me enough.' His expression was unreadable.

'I don't know you,' she said truthfully. And yet part of her felt as though she had known him all her life, which was even more scary. Petrifying, in fact.

His brow furrowed, and she could almost see the formidably astute and intelligent brain considering the implications of what she had said. Then he nodded, his face giving nothing away as to what he was thinking. 'I can accept that,' he said after a moment or two. 'So we remedy the situation.'

She stared at him. 'What do you mean?' she asked warily.

He smiled, his astonishing eyes as warm as cornflowers in a sun-drenched meadow. 'We date for a while,' he said matter-of-factly. 'Nothing heavy, we can take it as slow as you want, but I'll be there for you and you'll be there for me.' His American accent was very strong suddenly.

'I don't think—'

'This is not a suggestion, Rosie.' Now the blue gaze resembled cool water. 'It's either that or I kiss you until we end up in bed together right now. And I could do it with very little resistance from you if I put my mind to it.'

Arrogant swine. She was furious at the picture he'd painted but at the same time her innate honesty forced her to accept he had a point. Certainly she wasn't confident enough in her powers to resist him to put it to the test, anyway. She contented herself with a glare, before she said, 'This dating? A kiss goodnight at the end of the evening is all you'll get, so if you're thinking—'

'I said we would take it as slow as you want.' He was standing with his legs slightly apart and his powerful arms folded over his chest, and he looked big. Big and rugged and so incredibly sexy it made her mouth dry. 'Contrary to what you so obviously believe, I can actually wine and dine a woman without expecting a pay-off at the end of the date,' he added dryly.

No doubt because his dates in the past had been panting to get him in the hay! She cleared her throat. It was only fair to put him in the picture. 'Look, since…since Miles I haven't dated,' she said flatly, dropping her eyes from his and staring at the carpet because it made it easier to say what she needed to say. 'And I don't want to get into another relationship again, not ever. I have my work and my home and—'

'And you are perfectly happy to coast the rest of your life; no highs, no lows, just flat, calm water endlessly in view?' he drawled softly. 'I don't think so, Rosie.'

'How would you know?' she shot back indignantly, her eyes shooting up to meet the slightly taunting gaze. 'You don't know me.'

'We seem to have completed a full circle.' He studied her face, the confusion she was trying to hide apparent in the dusky darkness of her eyes. 'And I suspect every avenue of argument would come back to the same thing. So…we date. No discussion, no debate about it, we do it. All right?'

And with that he turned, reaching out for the handle of his door and opening it without another word before he stepped into the room and closed the door quietly behind him.

She didn't believe this! Rosalie stood for a few moments more, glancing almost pleadingly about the cool, gracious landing as though it were going to provide an answer to her bemusement. Kingsley Ward was as male as you could get—aggressive, strong, ruthless and possessed of a sexual magnetism that was as powerful as it was formidable. He was the last man on earth she should date. So how come she found herself in a position where she was doing just that?

She shook her head at herself, going back in her mind over their conversation to see where she had slipped up. 'Oh, to heck with it.' She glared one last time at his closed door, hoping it would penetrate the wood and pin him where he stood, and shrugged her shoulders. She could refuse the dates when they occurred—or at least a number of them—once this crazy weekend was over. Give him the cold shoulder. Freeze him out.

It was scant comfort. Possibly because she didn't believe it. To date, trying to freeze Kingsley out had been about as successful as a snowball surviving in hell.

Whatever, she'd cope. She squared her shoulders, entering her own room and determining to ignore the fact that Kingsley was right next door, possibly getting undressed, or perhaps even naked in the shower? Enough. She banished the erotic images before they had a chance to take hold.

Yes, she would cope. She had survived Miles Stuart, hadn't she? Not only survived him, but gone on to make something of herself and carve out her own life on her own terms. So she could hold her own with Kingsley. She wasn't a trusting, nervous little eighteen-year-old now, bowled over by the fact that the most gorgeous boy she had ever seen said he wanted to love her and take care of her.

Take care of her... She flopped down onto the bed, dropping the crutches on the floor. Miles had taken care of her all right, taken care that she came close to a nervous breakdown, damn it.

But Kingsley was right about one thing—Miles *was* the past. She nodded to herself, the churning in her stomach the stark memories always caused making itself known. But if Kingsley thought he had taken out a contract for an affair when he'd signed her up to work for him, he was wrong. Her eyes narrowed and she looked resolutely ahead, her gaze inward-looking. Boy, was he ever wrong…

CHAPTER SIX

THE next day Rosalie was awoken at seven in the morning by a distraught Beth. The dean at their youngest son's university had rung. He had been careful what he'd said, but it had transpired one of the students in Jeff's block had been diagnosed with meningitis and was now in isolation at the local hospital. All the other students had been put on antibiotics as a precautionary measure, but three of them—of whom Jeff was one—were unwell. There was no need to panic, the dean had assured Beth, but to be on the safe side they had also been taken to the hospital and some tests were being run.

'We're going straight to Cambridge now.' Beth was all but pulling her hair out. 'Will you and Kingsley be all right? There's plenty of food in the fridge and freezer, but could you possibly feed the cats at six tonight? Tuna in sunflower oil, it's in the right-hand kitchen cupboard over the sink. And they like full cream milk and will only eat and drink off their china saucers. They'll be turning up wanting milk soon, no doubt.'

'They'll be fine, we'll look after them.' Rosalie thought it was just like Beth to worry about the cats rather than her guests at a time like this. Beth was primarily concerned with the needy and vulnerable, which was one of the reasons Rosalie loved her so much, but she had always thought that her aunt's anxiety over the cats—two enormously fat, amber-eyed females with filthy tempers—was misplaced. If ever anything could look after itself, those two could.

'We'll probably stay in a hotel somewhere overnight and see how things are tomorrow, but I'll ring you.' Beth gazed at her with tragic eyes. 'Oh, Lee, I'm so worried.'

'Jeff will be fine, I'm sure of it. Now you go and Kingsley and I will look after things here.'

Rosalie tried to be encouraging as she saw Beth off, and she had just made her way into the kitchen to make a cup of tea when she became aware of a presence behind her. She turned sharply, almost losing her balance as her plaster foot slid on the terracotta tiles, and Kingsley smiled at her from his vantage point in the doorway. 'Hi.'

'Hello.' She instantly became aware of the fact that she hadn't even brushed her hair in the mad scramble to get her aunt out of the house before Beth completely went to pieces, and the nightie and thin robe she was wearing were not her prettiest ones.

Kingsley, on the other hand, had obviously recently showered as his damp hair bore witness to, but he hadn't shaved. His stubble was dynamite. As were the midnight-blue silk robe and matching pyjama bottoms, which emphasised every line and contour of the hard, powerful body in a way that should be illegal. The robe was pulled loosely together, the casually tied belt allowing a tantalising glimpse of his thickly muscled torso and the silky black hair on his chest, and his whole demeanour was one of contented ease. He was a man very much at ease with his own body, that much was for sure, but the overwhelming maleness was such that Rosalie found her throat was dry and her hands were damp.

'Tea?' It was a squeak and she heard it with annoyance.

'Coffee, if that's okay.'

Of course, she should have known.

'The instant variety will do,' he offered helpfully as she made a move towards Beth's coffee percolator. 'As long as it's hot and strong first thing in the morning I'm not fussy.' He strolled fully into the kitchen as he spoke, and her senses went into hyperdrive. Beth's kitchen wasn't small, in fact it was the sort of oak-beamed old country kitchen that would accommodate a whole London flat in its cavernous depths, but suddenly it had shrunk alarmingly.

She hastily explained about Beth and George's sudden departure, opening one of the big windows as she talked and letting in the cats, who had been prowling up and down the windowsill for a few moments. They trod delicately over the draining-board and jumped neatly onto the floor—obviously an old and practised route into the house—and then both of them began to wind themselves round Kingsley's legs, purring loudly.

The air was clean and fresh as it poured into the room, the sun already warm, and the cheerful twittering of the birds in the surrounding trees and bushes almost drowned out the sound of the boiling kettle.

'They like you.' She gestured to the cats, who had continued their elegant homage even though Kingsley was now perched on the edge of the massive old kitchen table, his long legs ensuring his feet still touched the floor. 'They aren't normally so friendly'.

'Perhaps you should take a leaf out of their book,' he suggested in a lightly mocking tone. And then as her foot slipped again he said firmly, 'Sit down, I'll do it.'

She sat down, mainly because the pure male sensuality was a little unnerving at just after seven in the morning when she hadn't quite got her armour in place.

'Toast? Cereal?' He placed a cup of tea in front of her as he spoke, his tall, lean frame lending itself surprisingly easily to the domestic scene. 'Or eggs done the Ward way?'

She eyed him suspiciously. 'Which is?'

'Nothing more alarming than scrambled with butter and onion, and served on toasted bread with a slice of bacon or ham. Delicious, even if I do say so myself.'

'You cook?' She almost added 'too?' and stopped herself just in time. His ego was already jumbo size; she didn't need to add to it. No doubt plenty of women did that already.

'Of course.' He grinned at her. 'As long as you want eggs the Ward way, that is.'

'For breakfast, dinner and tea?' she guessed dryly.

'You've got it.' Blue eyes laughed and she had to join in.

Oh, help, why did he have to be so drop-dead gorgeous? It was first thing in the morning and he looked good enough to eat, whereas she probably resembled something that had been pulled through a hedge backwards. Perhaps he'd go off the idea of them dating now he'd seen her in all her morning glory? Funny, but the thought wasn't comforting.

However, Kingsley didn't seem put off by the gargoyle at the table as he lifted a strand of hair from her face, letting it run through his fingers as he said almost absently, 'Raw silk, and such beautiful colours when the sun catches it. Who do you get your colouring from?'

'My father. He had grey eyes too.'

There was a tightness to her voice that hadn't been there moments before but he didn't comment on it, merely letting his fingertips rest against the smooth skin before he turned abruptly. 'Four eggs for me. How many for you?'

'Two would be heaps.'

She watched him as he found and prepared the onions first, cutting them expertly under a little water before drying them and adding them to the fat sizzling in the frying-pan. 'Now whilst they're browning it's time for the toast.'

He turned as he spoke, smiling at her, and she was aware her breathing became quick and shallow. This was too nice, too delicious. Forget the food, she could feast for ever just looking at his body as he moved with an animal grace that was pure magic.

'As you're in charge of the food, the cats want breakfast,' she said dryly, hiding her trembling under a veneer of nonchalance.

'Of course. Are they boys or girls?' he said lazily.

'With names like Meg and Polly, girls, I hope. Either that or they're very confused felines.'

'Then I know just the thing.' He dived into the back of Beth's enormous fridge and came out with a carton of cream. He poured a little into an earthenware dish before she could tell him about the china saucers, but wouldn't you just know it, she thought helplessly, the darn cats lapped it up nevertheless.

'Don't know a woman in the world who can resist cream,' he said, turning to the onions and moving them around the pan with a wooden spoon.

'And of course you know most of them,' she said sweetly.

'Miaow.' He glanced at her for just a second, the blue eyes glittering. 'Meg and Polly are ashamed of you, you're giving cats a bad name.'

She stuck out her tongue at him and he grinned again, adding the beaten eggs to the onion and putting the lid on the frying pan whilst he buttered the toast, and cut several slices of ham from a joint he had found in the fridge. 'This is delicious.' Some of the ham had found its way into his mouth. 'Beth's rolled it in brown sugar, by the look of it, and perhaps a touch of mustard. I could get used to living here, given half a chance.'

She took a big gulp of her tea. As a hard businessman and entrepreneur he had been pretty devastating, and the side of him she'd seen the evening before had knocked her for six, but this morning the domestic Kingsley, clothed in the silk robe and pyjama bottoms, was every maiden's prayer. How could anyone make cooking so sexy? she asked herself breathlessly. He could knock all those TV chefs off the face of the planet.

By the time he placed a heaped plate in front of her, along with a glass of ice-cold orange juice, she had expended enough nervous energy to be absolutely starving. 'This is wonderful.' There was a note of surprise in her voice.

'Thanks.' It was very dry.

'No, I mean—' She stopped abruptly.

'Don't try to explain,' he said, his voice so flat she knew it was hiding amusement. 'It will either make you sound like one of those women who are convinced only the female race can do things like cooking and cleaning and—'

She threw a napkin at him, hitting him square in the face.

He placed it carefully at the side of him, continuing with barely a pause, 'Or plain jealous at my expertise.' He eyed her thoughtfully. 'I rather suspect the latter.'

'You wish.'

'Oh, I do, Rosie, I do. I wish for all sorts of things, things that would make your hair curl.'

The heat in his eyes left her in no doubt as to what form these wishes took and she grabbed for her orange juice, swallowing it hastily. When she nerved herself to look at him again he was calmly eating his food, a twist to the firm mouth telling her he had loved every moment of the little skirmish.

Breakfast set the tone for the day. For the first time in years Rosalie found herself being looked after. They had a lazy morning in the garden with the Saturday papers, and it was Kingsley who saw to elevenses, bringing out the most delicious whipped-cream coffee and shortbread fingers to her where she sat reclining in one of Beth's deckchairs. For lunch he took her off to a nearby riverside pub, where they sat in the shade of a huge red and blue striped umbrella, drinking velvety smooth, cold draught Guinness and eating chicken in the basket, whilst watching a pair of swans teaching their new signets the tricks of the trade and marshalling them into order every now and again.

Rosalie had phoned Beth's mobile three times during the morning, and just before they had left for lunch her aunt had got back to her informing her that Jeff had a bad attack of flu but that was all. 'I feel I want to stay the night up here, though, if that's okay with you?' Beth had said anxiously. 'I just want to be with him for a while, after the shock and everything. Will you and Kingsley cope all right? There's steaks in the fridge I'd got in for tonight, and salad and baby new potatoes, and a whole stack of frozen desserts in the freezer. Don't go hungry, will you?'

There was no chance of that. After a drive in the afternoon Kingsley stopped at a cottage advertising cream teas, and the mouth-watering homemade scones brim full with jam and cream and cream cakes melted in the mouth. Kingsley won the heart of the elderly owner by asking for a second round, and by the time they left they had had the older woman's life story, including the account of the giddy affair she'd had in the war with a visiting GI. 'Spoke just like you, he did,' the rosy-cheeked, bright-eyed lady—who wasn't an inch over four feet ten inches—said confidingly to Kingsley. 'And with the accent and his charm, the local lads didn't stand a chance. Course, everyone told me it'd come to nothing, but I loved him and he loved me. No doubt about that. But he got killed, see. Just a week before the war ended. I've had three husbands since then. Divorced one and buried two but there was still no one like my Hank.'

Rosalie hadn't known whether she'd wanted to laugh or cry. The little woman was a born comic and she had known it too, regaling them with one story after another about her life, which had been a fruitful one to say the least, but there had been something in her eyes when she'd spoken about her Hank that had gripped Rosalie's heart and made it ache. It hadn't helped that as they'd been leaving the lady had grabbed Rosalie's arm, forcing her to bend her head closer to the lavender-scented little body, whereupon the woman had whispered, 'Don't you let him get away, dear; you'll regret it the rest of your life if you do. And I know. Oh, yes, I know all right.'

'What did she say to you?'

Kingsley had gone ahead and was waiting on the threshold, holding open the door for her, and as Rosalie edged through the narrow aperture with her crutches she said quietly, 'Nothing really. Just that she still misses Hank.'

He shook his head as they walked towards the car. 'That's a real shame after all these years.'

'Yes. Yes, it is.' She glanced at him as he walked beside her, so attractive he made her head spin. He smelled nice. A clean, sharp aftershave with a faint scent of lemons, she thought distractedly, suddenly aware she would remember this moment—the bright sunshine, the man at her side, the smells and colours—for the rest of her life. It produced a feeling so poignant it was physically painful.

She was getting in too deep here. Panic had her heart beating a tattoo. This seductive feeling of being enclosed in his aura, of being safe from the buffeting of the storms of life, was an illusion. At the moment he wanted her in his bed and so everything was hunky-dory. All that could change with the wind.

He opened the car door for her, taking the crutches as she lowered herself into the seat and slinging them in the back before he walked round to the driver's side. She watched him, the little old lady's words ringing in her ears. But the woman hadn't known that they were just ships passing in the night, that Kingsley wouldn't want it any other way and neither would she. *She wouldn't*, she reiterated fiercely when her heart lurched. He wanted a brief affair; she didn't even want that.

Home again, Kingsley saw to the two cats who met them on the drive as though they hadn't been fed in years and were starving. Stiff tall tails expressed feline disapproval at the lateness of the hour—eight o'clock just wasn't an acceptable dinner time in their opinion.

'Steak, salad and new potatoes okay for you?' Rosalie asked when she joined him in the kitchen after checking the answer machine for messages. 'Beth's left us well provided for.'

'Sounds great.' On the way to the cottage the evening before he had insisted on stopping at an off-licence and buying several bottles of—what was to Rosalie—frighteningly expensive wine, and now he said, 'Which wine would you prefer: red, white or *rosé*?'

'*Rosé*, please.' They'd had a bottle of Kingsley's wine the night before as well as one Beth had provided, and she had to admit—wine connoisseur that her aunt was—Kingsley's had had the edge. Of course he wasn't supporting three children all doing their own thing at university or whatever, she qualified hastily, as though the thought had been disloyal to her aunt in some way. 'And while I get underway with the food, you could set the dining table if you like,' she added. The dining room was much more formal than the way they'd eaten breakfast, close together at the kitchen table, with his shoulder seeming to brush against her every so often, and she needed the distance between them—mentally as well as geographically. It might be weak and pathetic but that was the way she felt.

'It's a beautiful evening, why not alfresco?' Kingsley suggested lazily. 'I believe in making the most of summer.'

'If you like.' Beth's round wooden patio table was an enormous one with eight chairs—bought in mind for when the children and their partners descended—and again was less cosy than the kitchen.

After opening the wine Kingsley left a glass at her elbow before wandering off. Rosalie was determined to make the fairly plain meal as good as she could, and after seasoning the steaks she put them under the grill on a very low heat, and with the potatoes bubbling away she set to work preparing the salad. The beauty of Beth being such an accomplished cook was that she usually had every ingredient you could imagine somewhere in the kitchen, along with plenty of fresh vegetables and fruit.

Tomatoes, avocado, baby spinach, celeriac, apple, walnuts—that should be enough. Rosalie cut and grated, and was just mixing a creamy dressing—one of her aunt's recipes—consisting of double cream, dry mustard, lemon thyme, black pepper and nutmeg, the juice of an orange and lemon, and a teaspoon of Barbados sugar, when Kingsley reappeared, dipping his finger in the mixture and licking it. 'Mmm, gorgeous.' He eyed her wickedly. 'And the dressing tastes great too.'

She couldn't help but smile, even as she said warningly, 'No tasting until I say so.'

'Promises, promises…'

He refilled their glasses before coming to stand near as she mixed a pinch of coriander and parsley with garlic butter for the potatoes once they were cooked. He gently brushed a wisp of hair from her forehead, his touch feather-light, and Rosalie felt the contact shudder through her body.

'Could you check how the steaks are doing?' Her voice was breathless and she heard it with a dart of despair. She had to get a handle on all this. The trouble was she was a bunch of contradictions where Kingsley was concerned, she admitted silently. Part of her wished she had never met him, and the other part was beginning to wonder how she had managed for so long without him in her life. And that was dangerous.

She pounded the butter to within an inch of its life before she became aware that Kingsley was looking at her thoughtfully. 'Is that better?' he asked softly.

'Is what better?' she prevaricated carefully, the tell-tale burning in her cheeks causing a feeling of acute irritation with both Kingsley and herself. Why did she have to blush so easily? It was such a give-away.

'Now you've worked off some of that excess frustration, do you feel more relaxed?' he asked with aggravating composure.

She glared at him. 'How are the steaks?'

'Well and happy and demanding to be eaten.' He

walked over to her. 'So why don't you hobble off like a good girl and sit down and I'll bring everything through?'

The glare intensified. 'I've got to drain the potatoes and—'

'I am more than capable of doing that. You've done all the hard work, now it's my turn.' He handed her her glass of wine. 'Concentrate on getting to the patio with that without spilling it, okay?' He picked up the salad bowl and then the smaller one holding the dressing. 'Vamoose, woman!'

She really couldn't do anything else. By the time she had limped through to the sitting room, which led to the patio area, Kingsley was already on his way back to the kitchen, smiling at her with an unsettling blend of amusement and softness as he passed.

She was glad he wasn't with her when she walked onto the patio because she groaned out loud. He had set a corner of the table intimately for two, two candles burning in small star-shaped crystal holders and a vase of richly perfumed white roses between them. A small scalloped tablecloth covered the area of the table they were sitting at, and he'd used Beth's best plates—white china edged with platinum—and silver cutlery.

The sky had provided its own magnificent backdrop to the scene, its dusky blue streaked with tumescent crimson and violet and enriched with bands of gold, and the scent of jasmine and honeysuckle vied with the heavy perfume of the roses to create a riot on the senses.

She stood staring for a moment or two, the soft indigo dusk beyond the table warm and fragrant, and then slowly made her way to her seat. So much for distance.

Kingsley reappeared in the next moment with the potatoes and wine, looking at her with shadowed eyes. He refilled her wineglass, which had been almost empty, before he went back to the kitchen with the plates for the steaks, but he didn't speak and neither did Rosalie. Not until he was back and sitting beside her. Then she said, 'This is the way summer evenings should always be,' raising her wineglass as she added, 'To the new hotel and the continuing success of Ward Enterprises.'

He gave a phantom of a smile as he lifted his own glass. 'To the most beautiful quantity surveyor I've ever seen and getting to know each other.'

He noticed the withdrawal in her eyes his words brought forth but he didn't comment on it, gentling his voice still further as he said, 'Let me serve you.' And then he released her gaze, reaching out and picking up the bowl holding the succulently coated potatoes.

They talked of inconsequential things as the meal progressed and within minutes Rosalie was wrapped in his easy mood. He set out to make her laugh and he succeeded, creating a lazy, relaxed atmosphere enhanced by the sleeping garden and the whispering stillness of the velvet night. The moon rose, the sky becoming a dark canopy pierced with tiny flickering lights, and the rest of the world outside the garden melted away.

It was Kingsley who cleared away the dishes, returning after a while with a board containing a selection of cheeses and crackers, and another holding green and red grapes, after they'd agreed they were too full for one of Beth's rich desserts.

He handed her a cup of coffee with thick whipped cream floating on top, similar to the one he'd made earlier in the day, but this time there was the taste of orange liqueur along with the fragrant spices.

'This is delicious,' Rosalie murmured as he sat down beside her again, one arm draped casually on the back of her chair. 'Where did you learn to make coffee like this?'

He shrugged 'I don't remember.'

She stared at him. There had been something, just the faintest something that told her he was lying. He remembered all too well. Rosalie straightened in her chair. 'It was her, wasn't it?' she said flatly. 'The woman you mentioned last night, the one where you got your fingers burnt?'

He didn't prevaricate further. 'Yes, it was.'

'Why didn't you say so?' she asked quietly.

'Because I didn't think mentioning another woman would add to the evening,' he said bluntly.

'Do you mind talking about her?'

He removed his arm from the back of her chair, settling back in his seat and folding his arms as he looked at her quizzically. 'Which means you think I do,' he observed softly. Then he shrugged. 'The answer is no, not now. Not for a long time.'

She knew it wasn't fair to ask because she wasn't prepared to reciprocate regarding Miles, but she couldn't help herself. 'What happened?' she asked quietly.

'Maria was Italian and worked at one of my father's hotels. We were in love, or so I thought. What I didn't know was that I was one of many. She liked nice things, you see, and where she had come from—in a particularly poor area of Naples—a beautiful girl could make a lot of money very quickly in the age-old way. Shocked?' he asked softly.

'No,' she lied quickly. 'Of course I'm not shocked.'

'I was.'

'So…so you finished with her?' she said carefully.

'Not exactly.' He drained the cup of coffee. 'The way I found out about all the others was when she ran off with some rich oil baron she'd forgotten to mention when we got engaged. She obviously considered him a better bet than a hotel owner's son. I'm not complaining. It was the spur I needed to take hold of the business by the throat and shake it into shape. It also taught me a salutary lesson that I've never forgotten. Women lie best when they're in the horizontal position.'

She blinked. 'Some women don't lie at all.'

He smiled, coldly. 'I told you mentioning another woman wouldn't add anything to the evening.'

'It's not mentioning *her*, it's that last statement,' she returned heatedly. 'Lumping all women under the same banner.'

'Something you would never do with regard to the male sex,' he agreed smoothly. 'Right?'

She stared at him, her face reflecting her shock, and such was the expression in the dove-grey eyes that Kingsley felt like the biggest heel in the world.

She didn't try to deny the sudden self-awareness or make excuses, thus heaping—unwittingly—coals of fire on his head. What she did say was, and in a shaking voice, 'You're right, I suppose I am guilty of the same crime, but I do have my reasons.'

This was not the finish to the day he had envisaged. Damn it. And certainly not the way to penetrate that inch-thick steel armour of hers. He didn't want to make her feel bad.

He nodded. There was nothing else he could do. 'I'm sure you have,' he said flatly.

Why was it important to make him see? Rosalie sat motionless, her head whirling. And then to her absolute amazement she found herself saying, 'My mother didn't altogether die of natural causes.' She looked at him to see his reaction.

Her mother? What the hell did her mother have to do

with any of this? They were talking about this Miles guy, weren't they? 'I don't understand,' he said evenly.

'My father…he…' She didn't know how to say it because she had never spoken it out in the whole of her life. And then she found herself telling him, clearly and almost matter-of-factly, about the night when her life had been changed for ever. How she had sat on the stairs in the dark, not daring to move, but knowing something was terribly wrong. The overwhelming sickness she'd experienced, born of fright and panic, and the vomiting. But still she hadn't moved.

When she finished speaking she looked into Kingsley's face and saw the horror there. *She shouldn't have told him*, she thought desperately. He was disgusted, repulsed…

'Hell.' It was deep in his throat. And then he reached out for her, pulling her into his arms and holding her tight as he said, 'I don't know what to say, Rosie,' and such was the tone of his voice that she relaxed against him. He wasn't disgusted, she thought tremblingly. And that was enough for now.

He held her close for some time, his hands warm and strong, and then, with one hand, he tilted back her head and made her look at him. 'I'm so sorry,' he said, sincerely and softly. 'No child should have to go through something like that.'

She swallowed hard. This was too much; it was happening too fast. She was giving too much of herself.

Something of her panic must have shown in her face because he kissed her lightly on the mouth, a non-demanding, easy kind of kiss, before lowering her into her seat as he said quietly, 'Your coffee's cold and I could do with another cup before I turn in. Won't be a minute.'

She stared after him as he left, and in spite of the heat

redolent in the air and stone slabs of the patio after the hot June day, she shivered. Kingsley was the most exciting man she had ever met, the most attractive, the funniest—oh, she could go on for ever, but he was also the most lethal. He wanted a light-hearted little affair. He'd spelled it out for her just in case there had been any doubt. He wanted to make love to her, he'd told her. And what about her? Did she want to make love with him?

She swept back the hair from her face helplessly. Yes, she did, but that only showed how crazy she was and what foolishness it had been to get involved with him thus far. She had told him something she'd never told another living soul, not even Miles. Her family—her grandparents, and her mother's sisters—had never discussed the true facts about her mother's death and her father's suicide after the one time they had spelled out for her what she had to say as a child. It had been a dark and shameful secret, something to be hidden at all costs, that was what they'd all intimated. Perhaps it hadn't been intentional, but that was what she'd grown up with. And it had added to the feeling that what had happened was in some way her fault. If she hadn't been around, if she hadn't been born, her father would have had her mother all to himself and she might still be alive.

She bit down hard on her lip, shutting her eyes tightly for a moment. Reason and logic told her to think in such a way was rubbish, that there would always have been someone for her father to be jealous of, but reason and logic didn't always hold sway when the heart was involved. But now she had finally admitted the truth about the night her mother had died and why her father had taken his own life to someone, she felt the need to talk about it with Beth. To ask more about her parents' relationship, more about them as people. It had always been such an emotive issue with her grandparents. She knew they had loved her but right until the day her grandmother had died, some seven years ago, followed by her grandfather five years later, she'd known the subject was a closed book.

She supposed in a way she had been a sitting duck for someone like Miles who liked to dominate and control. She'd been so full of self-doubt and guilt, so easily crushed…

'One coffee.' Kingsley's voice in her ear brought her out of the dark thoughts.

'Thank you.' She smiled up at him as he placed the cup in front of her and then tensed as he bent down, his lips caressing her neck before moving up to her mouth. Warmth spread through her and she no longer felt the chill of the past. Her eyelids were closed, and in the safe velvety darkness she let herself be carried along on the wave of desire, responding to the voluptuous exploring of her mouth and the slow, insistent building of sensation. He took his time, pleasuring himself as well as her, and by the time his lips left hers she was aching in her inner core and ready for more.

'Drink your coffee.' His voice was husky.

She opened her eyes as he straightened and took his seat, flushing hotly at the knowledge that he knew how completely he had aroused her. Why had he stopped? She lowered her head as thoughts tumbled about in her mind. To prove that he was the one in control, was that it? And then she chastised herself in the next instant, sipping the coffee almost without tasting it. It had been her who had insisted they progress slowly; he was only keeping to the bargain.

The kiss had left her tense and frustrated, and the former easy atmosphere had disappeared. Kingsley sat quietly, not trying to diffuse the electricity vibrating between them, and Rosalie found herself gulping down the coffee in silence, screamingly aware of the big male body just a foot or so away.

Had he kissed her like that in preparation for a big seduction line in a few minutes? she asked herself as she drained her cup. Was that it? Certainly his kisses and touch swept her away from caution, but she wasn't seriously considering sleeping with a man who didn't love her and wanted an affair without any serious commitment. *Was she?* Alarm overwhelmed her that she had had to question herself, and now she emphasised strongly, No, she wasn't. She was not.

'Why don't you go on up and I'll clear away down here?' His voice was level, cool even, and she raised startled eyes to his face, the flickering candles turning him into a monochrome of black and white in the shadows of the night.

'No, I'll help,' she said quickly.

'What's to help? There's just a few things to carry through and the dishwasher will take care of everything.'

So...no seduction scene, then? She didn't allow herself to recognise the thread of disappointment, shrugging lightly as she said, 'If you're sure?'

'Sure I'm sure.' He smiled but his eyes were searching. 'But once the plaster's off it'll be a different story. I'll expect to be waited on hand and foot then.'

'Expect all you like.' She smiled too but it was forced. He spoke as if they were going to go on seeing each other, as though this was just the beginning, and it frightened her. And thrilled her—which was even more scary.

She stood up carefully. She hadn't bothered with the crutches tonight—they were more trouble than they were worth in the house. He rose with her, reaching out for her but holding her away from him slightly as he studied her face, a half-smile curving his lips. 'You're a very complex woman,' he said softly. 'Do you know that? But I'm not complaining. I've a feeling boredom is not an option around you.'

'Is that a compliment?' She could feel the colour that had crept into her cheeks whereas he was annoyingly cool, calm and collected. But then Kingsley never gave anything away.

'What do you think?' he drawled slowly.

His hands were warm on her back, his eyes piercingly blue as they held hers, and he just looked at her, saying nothing as she searched for an adequate reply and found her brain had stalled. Which happened fairly often around him.

Surprisingly, he didn't kiss her. Instead he raised a hand to the smooth silky skin at the side of her face, stroking down one cheek as he said quietly, 'Goodnight, Rosie.'

'Goodnight.' It was a whisper, and his arms held her for one more second before she was free.

Beth and George were home in time for Beth to insist on cooking a huge Sunday lunch the next day. According to George, in a low aside to Rosalie when his wife was out of the room, Jeff was now back home in his flat and had made it clear he preferred the current girlfriend feeding him grapes and ministering to his every need, rather than his mother. 'Understandable at his age,' George had added quietly, 'but I think Beth was a bit upset. Let her spoil you today, eh?'

She had smiled back, whispering, 'A nod's as good as a wink. I'll explain things to Kingsley.'

*   *   *

After that, the first time Rosalie and Kingsley were alone again was in the car on the way back to Rosalie's flat.

'Thanks for being so nice to Beth today,' Rosalie ventured as she settled back in her seat after waving goodbye to her aunt and uncle. Kingsley had dutifully eaten everything put before him and had second and even third helpings when Beth had prompted him, played cards for part of the afternoon with the older couple although Rosalie could tell it wasn't his kind of thing, and discussed the different merits of French, Italian and Australian wine with Beth for ages—although wine definitely *was* his thing. Nevertheless, she realised he had put himself out for her aunt after she'd explained the reason for the older couple's sudden arrival back at the house; being deliberately amusing and teasing Beth until the hurt look at the back of her eyes had faded and she'd become her old self.

'It's not difficult, she's a very warm and giving lady,' he said quietly. 'She reminds me of my mother in a way.'

'Your mother?' He hadn't spoken of his parents at all. She glanced at him, the chiselled profile doing funny things to her heartbeat. Ridiculous, but she couldn't imagine him ever being child size.

He nodded. 'She died when I was twelve. She'd had a hard time having me and had been told any more babies might be fatal, but eventually she persuaded my father to try for another...' He shrugged. 'The unborn child died with her. My father married again three years later. My stepmother and I did not get on.'

'I'm sorry.' She stared at him, not knowing what to say.

He shrugged. 'It's history now. My father died when I was thirty and my stepmother has since remarried.' He glanced at her, a wry twist to his mouth. 'I was not invited to the wedding. It was a relief not to have to refuse the invitation.'

'Things were still as bad as that?'

'I can see now, looking back, that I wasn't the easiest kid in the world for her to handle. As far as I was concerned my father's interest in another woman besmirched my mother's memory and they both had to pay for the desecration, added to which she was a hard, blonde, painted bimbo with pound signs for eyes.' He shrugged. 'Believe me, I don't exaggerate.'

'Right.' She took another glance and wondered if she dared risk a quip to lighten what had suddenly become a heavy conversation. 'Don't mince words, Kingsley,' she said softly. 'Tell it as it is.'

He grinned at her, totally unabashed. 'I always do, honey,' he assured her evenly. 'I always do.'

Once they drew up outside the flat Rosalie felt she could do nothing else but invite him in for coffee, an invitation Kingsley accepted with alacrity.

Late evening sunshine was streaming in through the sitting-room windows when she opened the door, enhancing the soft buttery colour scheme and mellowing the pine furniture. 'Sit down, I won't be a moment.' She gestured to the sofa and then hobbled off to the kitchen. She had bought a small wheeled trolley since the accident and found it indispensable.

Kingsley was sitting on the thick carpet looking through her music collection when she wheeled the trolley in. 'No jazz?'

'Sorry, not my scene.'

'I can see I'm going to have to educate you in all manner of things,' he said softly.

She ignored that; it seemed appropriate when he looked so broodingly sexy. He finally decided on some classical music she'd had for some time, and she was just beginning to relax after he had moved to sit beside her when he said, out of the blue, 'Did I mention I'm looking for a house in London?'

For a moment she was speechless. 'You are?' she managed at last. 'Why on earth are you doing that?'

He glanced down at her, putting his coffee-cup on the little table at the side of the sofa and slipping an arm comfortably round her shoulders as he said, 'It seems more sensible than all the inconvenience of hotels.'

'But you'll have your own—hotel, I mean. Surely you can have a suite reserved in that for your own use when you're in England? And your main business is in the States, isn't it?'

'At the moment,' he agreed smoothly. 'But I want to develop the English project to include at least three more hotel complexes over here.'

'You do?' She just didn't know how to handle that.

She hadn't realised the tone of her voice until he said, his drawl silky but with an edge to it, 'I'd have thought you'd be pleased. No doubt Carr and Partners will get the business again, if the job is done right this time, of course.'

Her throat had locked and she had to swallow twice before she could say, 'Of course it will be done right,' knowing she was skirting the main issue.

'In spite of the business I'm in, I've never liked staying for any length of time in a hotel,' he continued, the hardness of his thigh against hers setting up a chain reaction Rosalie could have done without. 'On the one hand they are impersonal, not like a home, and on the other—with me owning the damn thing—my employees are a sight too nosy about my comings and goings. It's like living in a goldfish bowl at times.'

And no doubt his love life made interesting observation, she thought testily. She schooled her voice to show no expression. 'I can understand that.'

'Me not liking hotels or my staff's intrusiveness?'

She took a sip of her coffee. 'Both,' she said coolly.

She felt the blue gaze searching her face but she kept her eyes focused on the cup in her hands, and after a moment he said, 'So, any suggestions?' as he settled back, one knee over the other.

'Suggestions?' She raised fine eyebrows in bland enquiry.

'On property,' he said patiently.

'I wouldn't have a clue on the sort of thing that might interest you,' she pointed out carefully. 'Would you want a flat or a house or what?'

'Not a what.' He was smiling above her head; she could feel it. 'Probably a flat. I've got the house in New York and a villa in Jamaica, so maybe a flat would be appropriate here.'

A house and a villa? Lucky old him. Rosalie didn't know why the thought of Kingsley buying a base in London was so unsettling, but it was. Which was crazy when you thought about it. London was more than big enough to take the pair of them and make sure they never bumped into each other for the rest of their lives! She took a deep breath. 'You'd be better going to an expert,' she said pleasantly.

'Do you know, I might just do that.'

Her heart gave an unsteady thud. She should never have agreed to work for him in the first place, that way none of this would be happening. But Mike would have thrown a blue fit if he had learnt she was turning business away, especially the sort of business Kingsley represented.

Her hands tightened on the coffee-cup. No, she'd had

no choice, she reassured herself firmly. Since Jamie's dinner party events had unfurled almost of their own accord—aided and abetted by Kingsley, of course.

She glanced up at him and the blue eyes were waiting for her. 'I'd better be going. I fly back to the States first thing in the morning,' he said, the tone lazy.

'You do?' She was surprised. 'But…'

'Yes?'

'You only arrived on Friday, didn't you?'

He nodded, his eyes tight on her puzzled face.

'But surely the business you came to England about, the hotel…' She tried to get her thoughts in order. 'Don't you need to deal with it?' she asked.

His thumbs traced patterns along her cheekbones before he kissed her, very thoroughly. 'Who said I came over on business?' he murmured huskily, rising to his feet. 'Sleep tight, Rosie.'

And he left.

CHAPTER SEVEN

'So WHEN are you seeing him again?'

It was the following night, and, lo and behold, Beth had turned up on Rosalie's doorstep as soon as she'd got in from work. Her aunt had apparently come into town to do a spot of shopping—believe that, believe anything, Rosalie thought irritably. As soon as she'd answered the door to Beth the one and only topic of conversation had been a tall, dark American, and it was clear Beth had been completely bowled over.

'I told you, I don't know.' The two women were sitting having a relaxing glass of wine whilst they waited for the pizza Rosalie had ordered to be delivered, or at least it would have been relaxing but for Beth's one-track mind.

'But you *are* going out together, officially, I mean? It's not one of these horrible modern arrangements where each party is free to do this, that or the other?' Beth asked anxiously.

'Beth—'

'Oh, it's not! Tell me it's not, Lee.'

'I can't get a word in edgeways to tell you anything.' Rosalie softened the words with a smile, but inwardly she was wondering how on earth to explain her relationship with Kingsley to Beth, when she didn't know if she was on foot or horseback herself. 'I told you how we met and that I'm doing the quantity surveying for Ward Enterprises,' she said carefully, 'and we've agreed to date a little when he's in England and see how it goes from there.' And it would go absolutely nowhere.

'So he's not going out with anyone in the States in the meantime?' Beth leant forward, her eyes on Rosalie's face.

Good question. 'I assume not,' Rosalie said even more carefully. But who knew with a man like Kingsley Ward?

Beth wriggled a little, the way she did when she wasn't totally satisfied about something. 'Lee, he's absolutely gorgeous, the most divine man since…since—' words evidently couldn't adequately express Kingsley's divinity '—since *ever*, and you haven't even set up ground rules?' Beth wailed.

'It's not like that.'

'It never *will* be like that with a man as sexy as him if you don't insist on it being so,' Beth said anxiously.

'I'm not sure I want a relationship with Kingsley.' There, she'd said it, and now she waited for the storm to burst over her head as she stared straight at her aunt.

Surprisingly Beth just slumped back in her seat before reaching across and pouring herself another glass of wine, drinking half of it before she sighed, long and loudly. 'It's him, swine face, isn't it?' Swine face had been Beth's nickname for Miles since the divorce. 'You aren't still thinking about him, are you? In any fond way, I mean?'

Funny how she had been asked that twice in as many days. 'Memories softened by time and made sentimental?' Rosalie asked evenly. 'Beth, that just doesn't apply where he was concerned.'

Beth leant forward. 'It's probably the wine talking on an empty stomach,' she said earnestly, 'but has whatever went on between you and Miles put you off trying with someone else, Lee? Because if it has, don't let it. Not now, not with Kingsley. Men like him come along once in a blue moon.'

Rosalie hesitated, and then she said, very quietly, 'Marriage to Miles was a living nightmare, Beth. You don't know the half.' She took a big gulp of the wine.

'Oh, Lee.' Beth gazed at her, her plump, pretty face tragic.

Rosalie took a deep breath. 'I know the family don't like to talk about my mother and father, but compared to Miles my father was positively normal.'

Beth stared at her. 'It's not that we, me and George, don't want to talk about your parents, but we thought *you* didn't want to. You never have.'

'Because it was always an absolute taboo. I thought you were all too ashamed of what had happened.'

'No, no.' Beth was clearly horrified. 'But Mum and Dad, all of us, weren't sure of how much you actually saw and what you remembered, you were only a little dot after all, and Mum thought if we didn't harp on you'd get over everything quicker.'

'Oh, Beth.' Rosalie shook her head slowly, and then as she began to talk it all came out. All the doubts and fears and shame and guilt that had been shut away in her head for so many years, and the more she talked, the more Beth responded until the pair of them were crying on each other. But the tears were healthy and cleansing.

'Your father adored you, Lee,' Beth said at one point. 'Never think otherwise. We all used to say how strange it was that he was never jealous of you in spite of the way your mother loved you, whereas the rest of us... We had a job to get over the threshold. But he looked on you as an extension of himself and your mother, I think. That was the thing.'

Rosalie felt like a great weight had been lifted off her shoulders. 'What made you mention your mum and dad like that tonight anyway?' Beth asked suddenly.

Now it was Rosalie's turn to wriggle a little. 'I was

talking to Kingsley about them at the weekend,' she admitted.

'Ah, yes, Kingsley. Where had we got to on that subject?' Beth said immediately, homing in with the single-mindedness that often caused her offspring to turn tail and run.

'Leave it, Beth.' Rosalie eyed her aunt warningly.

'Oh, yes. You aren't sure if you want a relationship with the most gorgeous thing on two legs ever likely to hit these shores. Right?' Beth went on as though she hadn't heard.

Rosalie's gaze held more than a little exasperation. 'It's not like that,' she said firmly. 'We're—' what were they? '—friends.' It sounded incredibly weak, even to her.

Beth opened her mouth but whatever protest she was going to make was cut off by the buzzer to Rosalie's flat. Beth jumped to her feet. 'The pizza guy.' Beth jumped to her feet. 'I'll get it.'

Rosalie had pulled herself to her feet and was on her way to the kitchen when she was stopped in her tracks in the doorway to the sitting room by the sight of Beth almost buried under a mountain of flowers. The bouquet of tiger lilies and creamy pale orchids wasn't the average red-roses type of declaration of a man to a woman, but then Kingsley wasn't the average man.

Beth was clearly thinking the same thing because there was a significant little silence as the older woman gave the younger a long, meaningful look before she said, 'Friends…right.'

Rosalie counted silently to ten. 'That's all, Beth,' she said brightly, 'and who's to say these flowers are from Kingsley anyway?' As if there could be the faintest chance they weren't!

'You mean you've more than one gorgeous man after

you? No one could be that lucky.' Beth mirrored Rosalie's thoughts.

They were from Kingsley. The card simply said, 'Thinking of you, K'. Which was utterly Kingsley.

When the pizza finally arrived Beth bustled about sharing it out onto the plates Rosalie had got ready, carrying two trays through to the sitting room where they'd planned to eat watching their favourite soap on TV. In the meantime Rosalie arranged the flowers in two big heavy vases and then left them standing on the work surface in the kitchen. She'd bring them through to the sitting room when her aunt had gone, she thought flatly, otherwise they'd act as a spur to keep Beth twittering on about Kingsley all evening.

Her eyes returned to the card just before she left the kitchen. 'Thinking about you.' No kisses, no cloying message that dripped sentiment. Simply 'thinking about you'. Was he? His life was as far removed from hers as the man in the moon. Had he given her more than a passing thought since he'd left? Flowers were easy. Miles had bought her a bunch every day for weeks when they had first got together, sending the girls in her block at the university green with envy, but after she had left him she'd discovered that even then he had been messing about with other women.

She clicked her tongue irritably, annoyed with herself for both dredging up the past and allowing such cynicism to spoil what should have been rather a nice moment. They were unquestionably fabulous, the flowers…

Beth's taxi came just after nine and Rosalie decided to have a long hot soak in the tub with some wildly expensive bath oil she'd had for Christmas, and pamper herself a little. She took the remainder of her glass of wine through with her, lighting a couple of perfumed candles and turning off the main light so she could relax in the flickering candlelight.

She had long since stopped feeling slightly ridiculous due to having to wedge the plastered foot on the chrome bath rack that fitted across the bath, and now as she lay carefully back in the silky water she shut her eyes, sighing softly and contentedly. The sensuous warmth and evocative perfume emptied her mind of everything but the moment, and she felt the tension flowing out of her in a relaxing wave.

And then the telephone rang. And rang. And rang. When she couldn't ignore it a moment longer she hoisted herself out of the water, grumbling profusely, and warning of dire consequences should it stop the second before she reached it. Grabbing a bath towel, she shuffled out into the vibrating hall.

'*Hello?*' She had barked into the receiver, which wasn't her normal telephone manner at all.

There was a moment of startled silence, and then, 'Rosie? Is that you?' a deep, unmistakable voice said with some surprise.

'Kingsley?' Her voice was high and she fought to moderate it when she said a little breathlessly, 'I thought you were in the States?'

'I am.' She could tell he was smiling. 'Did you get the flowers?' The smoky tone to his voice curled her toes.

'The flowers? Oh, yes, yes, they're wonderful. Thank you.' *Pull yourself together, for crying out loud.* She was babbling like an idiot. 'What…what time is it there?'

'The time doesn't matter.' His voice was deep, husky, as clear as if he were in the next room, and Rosalie shivered, though not from cold. 'Had a good day?' he asked softly.

'Fine.' Her heart was thumping so hard she put her

hand on her chest before she could manage to say, 'And you?'

'So-so.' A slight pause. 'I've been dreaming of you, whether I'm awake or asleep. What do you think that means?'

She swallowed hard. Keep it light, Rosalie. 'You've eaten too much cheese?' she suggested levelly.

He chuckled and her heart turned right over. 'I wanted to hear your voice,' he admitted quietly. 'Right now, this minute. Crazy, eh? What have you done to me?'

She swallowed again, feeling the drips of water trickling down her skin where the towel wasn't touching.

'It was a good weekend,' he murmured. 'The best I've had in a long, long time. Thank Beth and George again for me when you speak to them. They're real nice people.'

'Beth's just left.' Her stomach was curling at the tone of his voice, its seductive quality mesmerising, and to combat the feeling she added, 'Utterly blown away by the flowers, incidentally. You'd have thought she'd received them herself.'

'I've sent her some, as it happens, a basket of freesias.'

'You have? That's kind of you,' she said carefully.

There was the briefest of pauses, and then his voice held a velvet touch when he said, 'And you're quite right in thinking it's a ploy to inveigle my way further into her good books. I've a feeling I'm going to need every weapon at my disposal where you're concerned.' It was totally unapologetic.

Rosalie blinked, a curious rush of exhilaration causing her to shut her eyes tightly for a second. 'What Beth thinks or doesn't think is neither here or there,' she said as severely as she could considering a big grin was trying to make itself felt. 'I'm my own woman.' Or had been before she'd met him.

'You wouldn't be so mean as to hold onto every little bit, surely? There's enough to go round for a starving man.'

'Are you saying I'm fat?' she said lightly, a part of her mind hearing herself flirting with amazement.

'You're perfect. For me, that is,' he said huskily.

Help. She was too rusty at this game to survive for more than a moment. Her thought process hiccuped and died.

'Rosie? Are you still there?'

'Yes.' Pull yourself together, act nonchalant and cool as though this isn't blowing you away.

'Look, I've got to go, there's a problem at one of the hotel sites here—some flooding. I was hoping to be back in England at the weekend but it's beginning to look as though it might be longer before I can get away.'

She took a deep breath. 'That's all right,' she said briskly. 'If there's any complications or difficulties with the job here, I've got numbers I can call, and your architect is very helpful.'

'Damn my architect,' he said levelly. 'I want to hold you, to kiss you, to—' Another pause and then he said, his voice dry, 'Goodnight, Rosie. Sweet dreams…as long as they're of me.'

'Goodnight.' She replaced the receiver in something of a daze.

Once Rosalie was back in the bath she found all thoughts of peaceful contemplation had been blown out of the water by Kingsley's voice. Just hearing the smoky tones had evoked all sorts of emotions, and not one of them sensible or sane.

She spent the rest of her time in the bathroom giving herself a severe talking-to. She was a modern career woman who had her sights set on advancement, and she'd already come a long way in the last ten years. Relationships—*any* relationships—meant give and take, and it was the law of dynamics that one partner would take more than the other. Control and manipulation weren't far behind then. And Kingsley was the type of man whose whole life had been built on the will to control, ever since his broken engagement anyway. He'd said himself that he'd carved his empire from a desire to reach out and take life by the throat and choke it into submission.

But all that aside, forgetting all she knew about the motivation that drove him and his cold-blooded attitude to affairs of the heart, it was her own feelings where Kingsley was concerned that told her it would be emotional suicide to get involved with him, even slightly. For some reason he had got under her skin, and, much as she would like to lie to herself and say it was just a physical attraction and easily dealt with, the weekend had shown her differently. She enjoyed being with him too much; she liked him too much.

Miles had swept her off her feet and into his arms, and she had married him in a fever of love and physical desire without knowing the real person beneath the façade. He had fooled her and she'd paid the price.

Kingsley wasn't like that. He had shown himself in his true colours from day one. Offended as she'd been, he had stated he would never fall in love with her and wanted an affair he could walk away from with no complications or messy feelings to complicate the nice clean finish.

She levered herself out of the bath, staring at her reflection in the misted mirror for a moment or two. She couldn't turn her feelings off and on at will, much as she would like to right at this minute. Neither did she want to put herself in a position where a man had the power to bring her to her knees again, and she had the feeling that, much as Miles had hurt her, Kingsley could hurt her a thousand times more. She'd survived devastation once and at least she hadn't brought it on herself knowingly. If she got involved with Kingsley she wouldn't have that comfort when it all went wrong.

She went to bed that night determined she was not going to agonise any further over Kingsley. It was simple, quite simple when you considered all the facts logically, that she would be crazy to let their association grow stronger. He had said they would take it as slowly as she liked. Fine. Then it *would* be slow, so slow a virile, red-blooded man like Kingsley would soon lose interest and move on to pastures new.

She would keep busy at work, go out with some of her girlfriends on a more regular basis and start letting her hair down a bit, book a sumptuous holiday somewhere for next year and generally revamp her life. Perhaps meeting Kingsley had done her a favour after all, motivating her to take stock and decide what she really wanted out of life? She nodded firmly, turning over and almost immediately falling asleep.

But the subconscious wasn't so easily conquered. In her sleep Rosalie was vulnerable to the ghosts she kept under lock and key most of the time during the day, and, probably because of the weekend and then Kingsley's phone call, she found herself in a deep, dark valley of shifting shadows and half-recognisable images, past and present interweaving.

She awoke some time in the middle of the night when it was still dark, tears running down her face and her whole body tense with the nightmare. Kingsley had been there, but a different Kingsley, one who had brown eyes and not blue, and who had been crimson with anger, shouting, hitting, punching...

She sat up in bed, aware her nightie was clinging to her damp body, and ran a shaking hand over her face, brushing back the hair sticking to her wet cheeks.

Why hadn't she left Miles long before their graduation night? It was a question she had asked herself many times. But she had been so much younger then, so confused and frightened. She had got used to him hitting her when he was in one of his moods, even punching her on occasion, but he had always been so sorry later she had forgiven him. He was Miles Stuart—the man everyone said she was so lucky to have married—so their rows *had* to be her fault.

And then that night, after they had partied with their friends and most people had drunk too much, she'd inadvertently walked into one of the bedrooms at the big house the party was being held in, thinking it was the bathroom. Miles and one of their friends had been in bed together.

She had shouted and stormed out of the house, intending to walk home to the flat they'd rented, and Miles had come after her in his sports car. She had actually thought he'd come to plead with her when she'd heard the car engine, but he had got out and hit her so hard she'd been dazed and barely conscious. He'd bundled her into the front seat and driven home, and there he had attacked her again. But that night the worm had turned.

Rosalie closed her eyes, hugging her knees to her chest as the past rose up on the screen in her mind. It had been a night that had finally killed the last remnant of love for him.

When Miles had begun punching her this time something had snapped and she'd fought back, kicking and scratching and biting for all she was worth. Quite when she had realised he'd intended to rape her she didn't know, but it had only been one of their neighbours kicking the front door in that had saved her, and that at the last moment.

The divorce had been quick and silent, Miles's parents had made sure of that once they had seen the evidence stacked against their son. They had been petrified she'd drag the family name through the mud along with Miles, and she would have. Oh, yes, she would have if he hadn't met all her requirements, even though it would have crucified her to reveal the facts of their marriage to anyone other than her kindly solicitor.

She could still remember how she had felt the moment she had finally and legally been free of him. She'd been physically and mentally exhausted the weeks leading up to the divorce, but on that day it had been as though an invisible weight, which had kept her mind and limbs leaden and dull, had been lifted off her body and she had felt as light as a bird. It hadn't lasted, of course—grim reality had had to be faced and she'd found the memories of the abuse and torment she'd suffered at Miles's hands reared up at the oddest moments, but always there was the recollection of that moment when her soul had soared.

Rosalie took a deep breath, slipping out of bed and padding across to the chest of drawers where she found a clean hanky and blew her nose unelegantly.

People went through far worse than her, she told herself firmly. She hadn't been disfigured or disabled in an accident or lost a child; she wasn't friendless or starving or living on the streets. She had a lovely home and a fulfilling job, and normally she was perfectly happy. Everything had only begun to go pear-shaped since Kingsley had appeared on the scene. Once he left she'd be fine.

She ignored the lurch her stomach gave at the idea of

a life in which Kingsley didn't feature, and snuggled under the covers again.

Mind over matter, she thought with determination, that was what all this was about. Hearing his voice so unexpectedly tonight had caused a little blip in the process, but she could cope with that. She had to distance herself from Kingsley Ward in her head and her body would follow suit. Simple, really…

CHAPTER EIGHT

SUMMER was in full bloom, and London was in the grip of a heatwave that sent hordes of office workers flocking to the capital's parks in their lunch hours, where they ate their sandwiches under leafy trees and grumbled about having to return to work in such beautiful weather.

All Rosalie was concerned about was the fact that the plaster was off, her ankle had mended well and the itching that had sent her crazy the last few days was gone.

It had been two weeks since the weekend with Kingsley at Beth's, and he had not been back in the country since then although he had phoned Rosalie several times. Each time he did she promised herself that the next time she wouldn't be breathless and shivery and excited. But then broken promises to yourself didn't count.

On the fifteenth day she had yet another call, this time at work. He was arriving at Heathrow around sixish, Kingsley drawled easily, his voice deep and smoky. He'd like to do dinner if she was available? He'd pick her up at eight and they could go to a club he knew, somewhere where the food was good and they could dance a little to celebrate the plaster coming off. How did that sound?

This was the perfect opportunity to slow things right down, Rosalie told herself silently. They hadn't seen each other in a while, and putting a date off would send a message even Kingsley's ego couldn't ignore. She could be pleasant but cool.

'Dinner?' She took a steadying breath. 'I'd love to.'

'Great.' His voice was warm and it caused her skin to tingle.

No, not great. Stupid, stupid, stupid!

There was a pause, and then he said very softly, 'Have you been good whilst I've been gone?'

Okay, you've already let the side down once, don't compound it by going all weak and fluttery just because his voice is reaching the parts no one else's could. 'Good? Well, I've shared my favours equally between all my many lovers, so would you say that's being good?' she said lightly, eternally thankful he couldn't see her flushed face and trembling hands. 'How about you?' she added, careful to keep her voice matter-of-fact.

'All work and no play isn't what it's cut out to be,' he said wryly. 'Not by a long chalk.'

Rosalie swallowed; the sensual quivers stirring her blood were drying her mouth too. She forced herself to say just as lightly as before, 'That's because you haven't had any practice in the art of denial, perhaps?' allowing a little sting in her tone.

'Perhaps. So, do I get a reward for being good?'

'Being good is its own reward,' she said primly.

'Like hell it is. I'll see you at eight. Bye, Rosie.'

She stared at the phone for a few moments before replacing the receiver, shaking her head as she did so. Mad, that was what she was. Stark staring mad.

Ten to eight that evening found Rosalie outwardly poised and perfectly groomed, but inwardly shaking. It was when she caught herself agitatedly pacing the sitting room that she warned herself to calm down. She wandered through to the bedroom again, checking her appearance in the long thin mirror to one side of the bed as though she hadn't already stood there for a long time already.

She had put her hair up for the first time in ages and now her slender neck was revealed by the upswept hairstyle, her eyes with their touch of eyeshadow and mascara seeming extra big and the scarlet gloss lipstick giving a touch of sophistication her confidence desperately needed.

The one-shouldered muslin and satin cocktail dress that ended just below her knees shouldn't have been her colour in deep scarlet, but it actually brought out the richness in her hair without clashing with the chestnut tones, and she had teamed it with simple strappy charcoal-grey sandals and clutch bag.

It had been thanks to Beth that she had tried the dress on some months earlier in one of the fashionable boutiques. Normally she wouldn't have touched the colour, but once on the dress had looked a million dollars—as it should have for the price! However, at the last moment she had chickened out of wearing it for the evening with the other partners and their wives and the rest of the staff at Carr and Partners' Christmas party, deciding it clung just a little too provocatively in places. But tonight... tonight the dress's unquestionable elegance and the way it transformed her figure into an hourglass was just what she needed.

When the buzzer sounded she counted to ten and then spoke into the little box on her hall wall. 'Yes?'

'It's Kingsley.'

Her heart thudded. She pressed the release for the house's front door and then opened the door of the flat, meeting him in the hall.

'Wow.' He smiled, and before she could say a word he was kissing her. It was a warm, confident kiss, a kiss that stated he had a perfect right to hold her and that he knew she would accept his embrace, but he didn't prolong the caress, raising his head as he released her and stepped back a pace. 'You look like all my dreams rolled into one,' he said lazily, with the touch of mockery she remembered.

'All of them?' she said smilingly, hoping he couldn't sense what the kiss had done to her equilibrium. 'Blonde, red and brunette ones?'

He didn't say anything for a second, but then one of his hands touched her hair. 'I only dream warm brown with tones of red these days.' His eyes moved over her face. 'And grey eyes, small nose, full, kissable lips. Mmm, very kissable lips…'

She stopped him with an upraised hand as he went to take her into his arms again, laughing as she said, 'I hate to tell you, but these kissable lips have left lipstick on yours. Unless you want to be thought of as a very modern man I suggest you wipe it off before we go out.'

He took her arm, gently moving her into her hall and closing the flat door before he said, 'One thing at a time…'

This time the kiss lasted longer and was more intimate, his arms moulding her body into his and his lips firm and warm as they took what they wanted. Rosalie was aware she was kissing him back and that it would be giving him all the wrong signals, but she couldn't help it, she told herself feverishly. He only had to touch her and she seemed to melt and lose all reason.

Not that that was any excuse, she admitted honestly in the next second when she was free again, but it was the truth none the less.

'I'll need to do my lipstick again.' She took a backward step as she spoke as though she thought he was going to reach for her again, her cheeks pink.

'Sure,' he said softly, his eyes laughing at her as he took out a crisp white handkerchief and began to wipe the scarlet from his mouth. 'Go ahead. I'm not going any-where.'

Once in the taxi—which had been clocking up the kissing time—he took her hand, asking her about her day and telling her about his, and what had been happening the last couple of weeks. They continued with the same kind of easy inconsequential conversation once they got to the nightclub, a lush affair with a very good jazz band and a dance floor that demanded closeness.

Their table was in a nice spot—not so near the band that they were deafened, but close to the dance floor—and after Kingsley had ordered a bottle of champagne he leant back in his seat, the bright blueness of his eyes holding hers. 'I'm glad the ankle mended so well,' he said quietly. 'We can do this more often now.' His eyes challenged her to disagree.

She stared at him, aware that the hint of intimacy that had been hanging in the air between them since the kiss in the hall was stronger than ever. 'As often as your busy life and mine allows,' she said at last, aiming to make it casual but knowing she hadn't responded quickly enough for that. 'Which won't be all that much, I suppose.'

He gave her a long, silent look. 'Then we'll have to make sure it is, won't we?' He shifted in his chair and every nerve in her body registered the movement. 'Friends should see each other often,' he drawled with lazy mockery.

Friends? She didn't know how to take that.

He was watching her with a kind of amused speculation, his lips curving just the slightest. He knew just how he affected her. She shrugged carefully just as the waiter appeared with the champagne, and once he had gone and she was sipping her glass of frothy bubbles Kingsley leant forward, all amusement gone. 'I like you very much,

Rosie,' he said huskily. 'It's important you know that. I didn't like the way you were on my mind at first, but then…then I welcomed it. I don't want to rush you, I still hold to that, but the way I feel about you…' One finger touched her mouth, slowly outlining her lips.

What was he saying? She took a big gulp of champagne. She didn't know where she was with this man from one moment to the next. One minute intense, the next mocking. Chameleon man.

He had sat back in his seat again as she had reached for her glass, and now he said quietly, 'Does that bother you?' He was watching her very closely.

Her smile was brittle. 'Of course not. Everyone likes to be liked, don't they?' A strange feeling was taking hold of her, uncertainty telling her she would be faintly relieved if he was still talking about just an affair and nothing more. But only faintly. Which was more crazy than anything that had gone before. A man like Kingsley wasn't for her. She knew that.

'I don't know,' he said levelly. 'You tell me.'

'There's no harm in liking.' She shrugged offhandedly.

'And if liking grows to something more?' he pressed softly.

She blinked, tearing her eyes away from his. She tried to think of something to say to bring the conversation back to normality and failed utterly.

'I see.' His voice was very soft, very deep.

Her heart quickened, her uneasiness transparent. 'What do you see?' she asked boldly, because she really wanted to know.

He didn't answer that. What he did say was, and still very softly, 'We've a long way to go, haven't we?' It was a statement, not a question. He observed her in silence, waiting.

A different waiter appeared with two menus, and Rosalie was so pleased to see him she could have kissed him. She took hers with such effusive thanks the poor man backed away with something like alarm on his face.

When he had gone with a promise to return in a few minutes, Kingsley took the menu out of her hands, his touch very gentle. He lifted her chin, forcing her eyes to meet piercing blue, and then he said, 'You told me about your mother and father, Rosie, can't you tell me about him?'

'No.' One word, but blatant in what it conveyed.

He gave her a long, searching look. 'Okay.' He released her, picking up her menu and placing it in her nerveless fingers. 'I'd recommend something but as it would mean you eating something else I won't try that one again,' he said pleasantly.

She glanced at him, relieved when he smiled at her. 'That was stupid,' she admitted weakly, feeling he deserved some sort of apology. 'But at the time you seemed so arrogant.'

'And now?' he asked with silky intent.

Oh, but he was good, he was very, very good, Rosalie thought helplessly. Didn't miss an opportunity, did he? But then that was undoubtedly one of the attributes that had made him such a formidable adversary in the business world. 'Now you still seem arrogant,' she said with a faint smile, 'but perhaps I'm getting used to it.' She raised mocking eyebrows, pleased with herself.

He grinned wickedly. 'There is so much more you could get used to, believe me.'

Rosalie floundered. You couldn't argue with some things.

Whether it was the champagne, or the fact that she was all dressed up and with the most gorgeous, fascinating man in the whole place, or simply that she'd had enough soul-searching for one night, Rosalie didn't know, but she found she enjoyed the rest of the evening. Kingsley had performed another chameleon manoeuvre, and turned into a perfectly charming, relaxed social animal with nothing more pressing on his mind than making the evening a good one for both of them.

The fact that this heightened the impact of his sex appeal considerably did cause her the odd problem, especially when they were dancing. He made sure she became acquainted with every inch of his undeniably powerful body, and more than once as she tottered back to her seat she wondered if other men could turn an ordinary dance into an experience of such epicurean intimacy.

He didn't realise the effect he was having on her, she was sure, but, held closely in his arms with the delicious male scent of him teasing her nostrils, she lost the rhythm more than once, excusing herself by blaming her faltering steps on her weak ankle rather than the weakness within.

It was very late when he took her home, sitting with her tucked into his side in the taxi, his arm round her and her head resting on his shoulder.

As they neared the flat the intoxicating effects of the dancing and champagne faded rapidly. She wanted to ask him in, she admitted silently, and not just for a nightcap. Could she handle what would inevitably follow? The sane, logical part of her brain told her she wouldn't be able to give him her body without giving her heart also; the other part, the part that cried out for tenderness and comfort and love, said why carry on being alone when she could be in his arms?

When the taxi drew up outside the flat Kingsley opened the door and helped her out, before leaning down and speaking to the driver through the passenger window, asking him to wait.

He wasn't coming in. Her heart thumped wildly and she honestly couldn't say if she was relieved or disappointed. Perhaps it was a mixture of both.

He took her arm and walked her to the door, standing with her on the top step as she opened it. As she went to say goodnight he pushed her inside, taking her in his arms and kissing her fiercely, without any restraint in the shadowed darkness. The taste, the smell of him spun in her head and she clung to him, running her hands over his hard body under his suit jacket, the soft silk of his shirt at odds with the hard muscles beneath.

His hands were exploring her curves, the delicate fabric of her dress doing nothing to hide the arousal evident in the peaked tips of her breasts, but although his mouth was urgent and hungry she sensed he was fully in control of himself and curiously she wished he weren't. If he got swept away by desire, taking the decision and the will to resist out of her hands, it would be *fait accompli*. She wouldn't have to think about things any more, she could just go with the flow.

And then she felt him very gently remove her from him, his hand stroking a wisp of hair from her face as though to soften the withdrawal. 'I have to go.'

She could tell him she wanted him to stay and make love to her, tell him to pay the taxi off and come back to her. 'Yes, I know.' She clenched her hands to avoid reaching out for him.

'I'll call you,' he murmured huskily. 'Okay?'

'All right.' She stared at him, her eyes huge.

He kissed her once more, and she had to restrain herself from pressing into him again, the feeling that she couldn't get close enough overpowering. Something was happening, something she had no control over and it was scary.

He touched her cheek in farewell and then opened the door fully, walking towards the taxi as she stood at the top of the steps watching him, her face as pale as alabaster. The night was almost silent except for the sound of the odd car beyond the end of the street, and just past the house a street lamp cast a circle of muted gold on the pavement. She didn't think she had ever felt so alone in all her life.

He turned and raised his hand before stepping into the taxi and she raised hers briefly in reply, letting it fall limply to her side as the taxi drew away. She watched it until it turned the corner and was lost to sight, but even then she didn't shut the door, but continued to stare out into the empty street. She wanted to cry and she didn't understand why.

Two small pinpoints of amber light shone further down the pavement as a cat sauntered out from the side of a house, a big apricot tom following a moment later.

Rosalie watched the first cat, a small dainty tabby, sashaying along in front of her beau, hips swinging and tail provocatively swaying. She fancied she could almost see the cat's eyelashes fluttering as it moved its head slightly at one point to make sure her admirer was still following.

'It's easy for you,' she murmured softly. 'No worries, no wondering if he'll still want you in the morning, no promises of for ever…'

She stepped inside and shut the door. She was beginning to talk to cats now, and ones that were out of earshot at that. The next stage was the men in white coats. Something told her it was time for bed!

That evening set the tone for plenty more in the following weeks whilst Kingsley was in England, along with long weekends when they walked in Hyde Park or took a boat on the Thames, went for champagne and strawberry picnics, visited Beth and George for enormous Sunday lunches, and generally enjoyed each other's company.

The hot spell held, and soon the newspapers were talking of hosepipe bans and water shortages, but the parks were full of happy, rosy children and tanned young mothers in short summer dresses, and everyone seemed to be smiling all the time. Including Rosalie. She kept warning herself it couldn't last, of course—the seductively so-far-and-no-further affair with Kingsley as well as the weather—but it was almost as though she was in a state of suspended animation about it all now.

She knew Kingsley wanted more from her, and she was beginning to suspect it wasn't just sexually but in all sorts of ways, but every time she asked herself what she would do if that proved the case she felt so confused she put the subject on ice.

She had known Miles for five months before she had married him, and on her wedding day she would have sworn her new husband would hold no surprises for her, except in the nicest possible way. She'd known Kingsley for less, but several times recently she had caught herself making judgements—and all of them good—about him, which just showed the old adage of once bitten, twice shy didn't always follow.

She did wonder if Kingsley might be biding his time about what he saw as the next stage of their relationship until she finished working on his hotel project. Sleeping with the quantity surveyor might not be his style, she thought wryly. He was the sort of man who would rarely mix business with pleasure, preferring to keep the different compartments of his life separate and straightforward.

Nevertheless, she had to admit to a feeling of surprise that he hadn't put pressure on her. Sometimes he kissed her with such fierce passion it stunned her, other times he was warm and tender, leaving her feeling cherished and desirable, and always wanting more. Always. Which might be a very clever strategy on his part? If he softened her up into accepting his terms he couldn't very well lose.

But in spite of debating the matter daily in her mind, and touching on all the reasons and rationalisations why she had to finish the relationship sooner rather than later, she always told herself one more date wouldn't hurt. And so it continued.

On a hot Saturday morning towards the end of July Beth arrived on her doorstep, and Rosalie knew the moment she opened the door something was afoot. She had some wonderful news, Beth announced in a flat voice. George had been offered a marvellous position in a top university in New Zealand, and with the children off their hands he felt it was the right job at the right time. It would mean moving there lock, stock and barrel, of course.

At which point Beth broke down in floods of tears. On the one hand she wanted to go, she sobbed; she certainly didn't want to hold George back and spoil things for him, and of anywhere in the world New Zealand was the one place she'd always had a hankering for, but on the other hand it would mean leaving everyone she knew and being faced with a new life in her middle age. Should they go? What did Rosalie think?

Rosalie hugged her and sat her down with a large slice of chocolate cake and a mug of coffee, and by the time Beth left an hour or so later she was brighter and seeing the positive side to the move more. Which was a good sign.

They *would* go to New Zealand, Rosalie thought, waving her aunt goodbye from the doorstep as Beth smiled at her from the taxi. And with Beth's ability to collect friends round her like moths to a flame, she'd soon find her feet. But Rosalie would miss her aunt terribly. Beth meant more to her than she'd realised.

She closed the door, wandering back inside and staring at the pile of work she'd brought home from the office the night before. Kingsley, in consultation with his architect, had accepted one of the tenders, and a builder had been engaged and had started work. Because it was such a big job various subcontractors were involved and she was visiting the site on a regular basis now, but she had other work that needed progressing for other clients, and there didn't seem enough hours in the day the last few weeks. Possibly because she was spending a large part of her free time with Kingsley, time that had been taken up with work previously.

She frowned as she collected up the empty plates and mugs, taking them through to the kitchen where she made herself another cup of coffee before starting work again.

Twenty minutes later there was another ring at the doorbell. 'Yes?' She spoke resignedly into the intercom. It was going to be one of those days where the world and his wife called, she could feel it. She was going to see a show in the West End with Kingsley tonight and they were having dinner first, so she had wanted to put in some good solid hours of work whilst she could. She needed to keep on top of things for her peace of mind.

'It's Kingsley, Rosie. I need to talk to you.'

When she opened the front door she was surprised to see him holding a suitcase. 'Is something wrong?' she asked quickly.

He nodded before kissing her, a perfunctory kiss that

nevertheless sent needles of sensation to her nerves. 'I need to fly to Jamaica urgently,' he said quietly, 'so I'm afraid tonight's off.'

She forced down her disappointment. 'Problem with a hotel?'

He shook his head. 'The friend I was best man to recently, Alex, has been involved in an accident,' he said briefly. 'Broken his neck jet-skiing. They aren't sure how bad it is and he's stuck in this hospital in Jamaica where they were honeymooning. I've known his wife as long as I've known Alex and she's got no family, poor kid. She phoned last night, hysterical, so I said I'd fly out today.'

'How awful.' She stared at him aghast.

'It was their last day there too, would you believe? He made the mistake of drinking at a party some friends they'd made threw to see them off, and then having a last ride round the bay before they changed to get ready to leave.' He shook his head. 'Damn fool,' he muttered hoarsely.

'I'm so sorry, Kingsley.' She could see he was struggling and she didn't know what else to say.

'Alex and his family were always there for me when Dad remarried; they helped me through a bad time.'

She had drawn him into the sitting room now, sitting beside him on the sofa and taking his hand as he talked.

'He's a nice guy, Rosie, you'd like him, and he lives for sport. Any kind, any place, it's a long-standing joke. It would be better for him to go straight away than be left paralysed. He wouldn't be able to handle it.'

'It might not come to that.' She squeezed his hand gently. 'Lots of people get better from such things. It just depends where the break is and what damage has been done.'

'I guess.' He sank back on the sofa, rubbing a hand

wearily over his face. 'Joanna phoned at one in the morning and I couldn't get off to sleep again. Hell, I can't believe he could be so damn stupid; he knows better than that.'

'What time do you leave?' she asked softly.

'In a couple of hours.' He stretched tiredly.

'Have you eaten?' And when he shook his head, 'Then first thing is a cup of coffee and then I'll cook us some brunch, okay?'

'Thanks,' he murmured, stopping her when she would have risen and putting a hand to her cheek, his touch so light it was like the brush of a leaf. 'I don't want to leave you,' he said huskily. 'Not like this.'

Suddenly it wasn't a time for pretending. 'I don't want you to go,' she whispered back.

He ran his fingers over her lips, outlining her mouth, and then down to her throat where he caressed the smooth silky skin delicately before pulling her into him. And then his mouth was coaxing hers open, sensation shooting to every part of her body as his lips and tongue explored hers, the hard pressure of his body as he slid her down beneath him intoxicating.

He kissed her until she was almost mindless with pleasure, his hands stroking and teasing her body as his lips plundered hers, and she knew she was trembling uncontrollably at the need he was drawing forth so effortlessly. He had kissed and caressed her many times over the last months, but never like this. Never like this.

She knew now, and in fact she had known it for weeks, that she'd been waiting for this time from the first moment she had laid eyes on him. It had been there between them, unspoken but alive and electric, the knowledge of how good they would be together.

Her breathing was coming in short pants and her breasts

felt tight and sensitive, her whole body sensitised. The will to think or hold back was gone, burnt up in the restless urgency that had surfaced under his lovemaking. She clung to him, responsive to his every demand, overwhelmed by a primitive yearning.

'You're beautiful, Rosie, so beautiful.' His lips were warm on her throat as he traced burning kisses over her skin. 'Inside and out. And you don't seem to realise it. I find that amazing.' He raised himself slightly, looking into her flushed face as he said again, 'So beautiful.'

She opened her eyes, staring into glittering blue made almost black with desire.

'I don't want an affair with you,' he murmured, his body as hard as a rock. 'I want more than that. I've fallen in love with you, Rosie. I've been fighting it since the first time I kissed you and I knew it deep inside, but I was hoping you would prove me wrong. That you would say or do something that showed me the image I had of you wasn't real. But it is.'

She had frozen in his arms, her eyes wide. This wasn't how it should be. Kingsley was a 'no complications, love 'em and leave 'em' type of guy, he'd *said* so.

'Don't you believe me?' he said softly, becoming aware of her reaction. 'Don't you, Rosie?'

Her voice was a long time in coming, and then it was a whisper when she said, 'I don't know.'

For a long moment he studied her face, his blue eyes searching hers with their penetrating light, and then he straightened up and away from her, pulling her into a sitting position at the side of him. 'You don't feel the same,' he said flatly. 'Is that it?'

She swallowed but she couldn't look at him. 'I don't know how I feel,' she said on a deep shuddering breath. 'This...this has all happened so suddenly.'

'Not from where I'm sitting.' There was a touch of wryness in his voice now. 'In the past I've wined and dined and bedded them a hundred times over by now.'

'Then…then how do you know you feel differently about me to all the others?' she managed. 'That this isn't a passing whim?'

'Do you really want to know?' He was staring at her.

She looked at him then; the note in his voice demanded it. 'Yes.' But she wasn't sure if that was true.

'Because I didn't want to wake up beside the others for the rest of my life,' he said simply. There was a ringing silence but for the life of her she couldn't speak. 'What makes you so afraid of me, Rosie?' he asked very quietly.

Her heart was pounding. This shouldn't be happening now, not when his friend was so ill and he had to fly thousands of miles away. It wasn't fair to him. 'I…I didn't say I was frightened of you.'

'You don't have to.' He gave a short, mirthless laugh. 'But for the life of me I don't understand why. At first I thought it was something physical, especially because you haven't dated in so long, but we're fine that way, aren't we?''

It was a question and she answered it. 'I think so.'

'So I waited on that score, trying to show you in every way I could apart from the ultimate act that it would be fine, that I wouldn't hurt you, that you just had to relax and let yourself know me a little. But today—' He stopped abruptly, raking back his hair. 'You were with me every inch of the way.'

Her body was rigid, her head whirling.

'So what is it, Rosie?' he asked softly after a moment or two. 'Why don't you know how you feel? Why aren't you *letting* yourself know how you feel? It's all to do with your ex-husband. What the hell did he do to you?'

She bit her lip hard. She couldn't think clearly any more. She wished she could make some sense of how she felt but she couldn't pin down any logic. Her emotions had taken over her reason and paralysed her judgement. How could she make Kingsley understand where she was coming from when she didn't understand herself? But she had to try; after all he'd said she owed him that at least. She sucked in a gasp of air. 'Miles…Miles wasn't normal,' she said shakily.

There was silence. Then very gently he said, 'In what way wasn't he normal?'

'I…he…' Her voice faltered. 'I…need to explain from the beginning. I met him the first year at university and I thought he was wonderful. He was handsome, funny, everything a girl could wish for. I suppose he swept me off my feet. His family were well off and he was the only boy at university with a sports car, that sort of thing. This makes me sound so shallow,' she added shakily.

'No, just a normal eighteen-year-old away from everything she knows and in love for the first time,' he said softly.

She looked at him, stunned by his understanding.

'And?' He pressured her very gently to continue.

'And he wanted me. I…I hadn't slept with anyone before and I think he found that a challenge.'

Kingsley looked at the beautiful face with its silky veil of chestnut hair and his stomach contracted. Whatever this guy had done, hanging was too good for him.

'Anyway, we…we got married because I…' she forced herself to sit up straighter, aware she had been slumping '…because I didn't think it was right to go to bed otherwise. Up until then he'd been fun and charming but…he changed. Almost overnight. He—' she shut her eyes tightly, unable to look at him '—became violent. Over the slightest thing. But only when we were alone. Everyone else thought he was the perfect husband, and I was young and I thought it was all my fault so I tried to humour him. Looking back, I think that made him even more of a bully.'

'He hit you?' he said grimly, his guts writhing.

She nodded. 'Where it didn't show, mostly. He was clever like that. After the divorce an aunt of his contacted me—she was the only one of his family to do so—and she told me he had always been violent and cruel from a small boy, but that his parents had made excuses for him. He was unbalanced, she said, and took after his father's father who had ended his days in a psychiatric hospital.'

She was shaking, she couldn't help it, the shock of hearing herself talking to someone about Miles making her nauseous.

'What made you leave him in the end? I presume it *was* you who walked out?' he said carefully, aware from her white face and trembling body she was near the limit of her endurance.

'I found him in bed with someone else and when he hit me I hit back,' she whispered. 'It sent him crazy.' She could almost feel the clothes being torn off her back. 'He tried to—' She couldn't say it but he understood anyway. 'Our neighbour broke the door down and pulled him off me.' She shook her head blindly.

His arms came around her and he drew her against him but she couldn't relax against him, the shame and humiliation of that moment making her stiff and unyielding. If Robert hadn't helped her Miles would have raped her that night for sure, because she had been all but naked and helpless by then.

But Robert had proved himself to be a true friend. He hadn't spoken of what had occurred to anyone except her solicitor when she'd asked him to give a statement, and when Miles's parents had whisked him home and the rumours had started no one had known anything for sure. It had been the only thing that had enabled her to go on. To be able to hold her head up.

'Where is he now?' The words were full of a dark, vibrating energy. No one could have doubted why he was asking.

'He crashed his sports car, killing himself and the girl he was with some time ago,' she said shakily. 'The aunt wrote and told me.'

'Pity,' he growled. 'He got off lightly.'

'Maybe,' she said thickly, wondering why she didn't feel better for telling him. Wasn't that what all the books said, that you felt better when everything was out in the open?

'So he was the reason you decided to step out of the human race and become autonomous,' Kingsley said gently. 'I can understand that, truly, but don't let him still beat you down. This is different, *we're* different. You do see that, don't you?'

She moved out of his arms, away from him. Miles had used those very same words on the day he has asked her to be his wife. 'We're different to the rest of them, Lee,' he'd said, his handsome face smiling and his brown eyes dark and compelling. 'We're two halves of one whole and life is going to be perfect from now on. I promise you.'

Her hands were clenched together now, tension radiating from her. 'He talked like that,' she said almost to herself.

'Like what?'

She shook her head. 'It doesn't matter.'

'It does to me,' he said quietly, struggling for calmness. 'I don't like being compared to him, Rosie.'

'I didn't mean...' Her voice trailed away. Perhaps she did mean it. There were so many similarities between Miles and Kingsley, not just the good looks and wealth but their iron wills. She had never imagined in her worst nightmares that Miles was so twisted and cruel under his outward veneer; how could she be sure about Kingsley?

'I'm me, Rosie, not that creep you married.' He stated the obvious. 'And I love you.'

'When you told me about Maria you said love was just a pleasant concept, that it doesn't work in the real world,' she said flatly. 'Sooner or later doubt and mistrust happen, that's what you said.'

One half of him wanted to shake her for being this way, the other wanted to make all the hurt go away. His frustration and resentment at the way she was putting him in the same category as her former husband showed in his voice when he said, 'I was talking out of the back of my head, and men are allowed to change their minds occasionally—it isn't just a woman's prerogative. I want to be with you, Rosie. Always.'

'And if you change your mind again, what then?' she said tensely, her chin rising as she stared him straight in the face. Miles had said that she had trapped him, ruined his life. That she was nothing, a parasite, unloving and unlovable. She had fought back against allowing his mental abuse to penetrate her perception of herself for the last ten years; she wouldn't survive a second time. 'What if you're not cut out for togetherness? Would you think I'd trapped you; blame me for being around? Would you say you were tripping over me all the time, that you couldn't breathe—?'

'Did he do that?' Kingsley interrupted softly. 'Did he say all those things?'

She jerked her head back, self-protection written all

over her. 'It doesn't matter; what matters is that I don't want any of this. I'm sorry, but I don't. I was honest with you from the very beginning.'

'Yes, you were,' he agreed slowly. 'So, where do we go from here?'

She stared at him. She had never felt so wretched in all her life. 'There…there's nowhere *to* go.'

'I don't accept that,' he said impassively.

Her eyes widened. She had expected him to storm out and call it a day. 'Kingsley, I meant all I've said.'

'You think you mean it.' He was careful not to touch her; it would only complicate things further if he gave in to his desire to take her in his arms and kiss her until she agreed black was white. This was deeper than that. 'But I don't believe you do.'

He closed his eyes and settled back on the sofa again, stretching his long legs as he made himself comfortable.

There were minuscule particles of dust dancing in a patch of bright sunlight just above his head, and Rosalie's eyes were drawn to them as she rose to her feet. She stood uncertainly, an ache in her throat and a churning in her stomach, and found she didn't know what to say. She'd learnt enough about him over the past months, both from her own observations and from business colleagues—who talked avidly of his ruthless reputation—to know Kingsley was not renowned for an excess of patience. This wasn't like him. At least not as far as she knew. Which brought her right back to the point in question—how sure could she be about anything to do with him?

'Did someone mention coffee and brunch?' His tone was deep, the laconic request bringing her back to herself and she turned, walking into the kitchen on shaky legs.

She couldn't believe she had just told Kingsley, *Kingsley* of all people, about Miles and her marriage.

What was he thinking? She stood at the kitchen sink, gripping the porcelain so hard her knuckles shone white through her skin. Did he think she was pathetic and stupid? Was he disgusted, with her as well as Miles? Why, oh, why had she told him? She squeezed her eyes tight, trying to stop the hot tears from falling.

'It's all right.' She hadn't been aware of him following her, but now he enfolded her into his arms and she had no more strength left to resist. 'I know it took a lot of courage to tell me about him, but he's gone, Rosie,' he said over her head as he held her against the solid wall of his chest. 'You get men like him in every generation, emotional cripples who prey on the gentle and the good. They're inadequate and deep down they recognise it so they compensate with cruelness. I'm glad he's dead because it saves me hunting him out and dealing with him as he deserves. Telling me has brought it all back right now and exposed the wound, but wounds can heal, believe me, and it's better when they're cleaned out, however painful.'

It wasn't as simple as that. There was so much more to this than just her marriage, but she hadn't fully realised it till now. The violent death of her mother, her father's suicide, the years of wondering if she had contributed to her mother's death simply by being born, and then—when she'd thought Miles was the answer to all her hopes and dreams, when she'd found someone who would love her, *really* love her—the nightmare of her marriage and its cataclysmic end.

She was a mess. This wasn't about Kingsley, it was about *her*. She drew away, pushing back her hair from her face as she said quietly, 'I'll see to the food and I'll bring your coffee through when it's ready.'

He made no move to hold onto her and he didn't say

a word before he turned and left the kitchen, his eyes just raking her white face for a moment.

They ate at the little pine table in a corner of her sitting room and it brought back memories of the first time he had been to the house, the evening he had brought her home from the hospital. She should have made sure any relationship between them had ended then. The thought caused her throat to close up and she had to force herself to eat, each mouthful threatening to choke her.

He glanced at his watch as they finished, his voice expressionless as he said, 'Are you coming to the airport with me?'

She stared at him. 'Do you want me to?' she asked in a small voice. 'After all that's been said?'

His voice held a touch of irritation as he said, 'Of course I want you to. What sort of damn fool question is that?'

She would have smiled if she had been able. His reply was so very much Kingsley, and another strand of the tensile net he'd thrown round her heart. A net she had to break. She couldn't let herself love him or anyone else, not again. She needed to be in control in every area of her life and love took that away, giving a terrible power to someone else.

She would go to the airport with him and she wouldn't say anything more to rock the boat before he left, not in view of the situation he had to deal with in Jamaica with his friend. But this was the finish. It had to be. He just didn't know it yet.

CHAPTER NINE

KINGSLEY took her hand in the taxi on the way to the airport and she let it lie there. They didn't talk but there was so much unsaid hanging between them that Rosalie felt the air were crackling. She was vitally aware of him at her side, his hard thigh touching hers and his big body seemingly relaxed. But he wasn't. She knew him well enough by now to know that he was playing a part, just as she was.

The airport was seething with people, and after Kingsley had checked in his luggage he took her arm and they made their way to one of the fast-food places. He ordered two coffees, which neither of them wanted, and once they were sitting on uncomfortable chairs at a table for two he took her hands in his. 'You're cold.' It was said with surprise.

She shrugged. She'd been chilled from the inside out since she'd decided what she had to do. 'My self air-conditioning has never been too good,' she said lightly.

Kingsley's eyes narrowed and he gave her a long look. 'I'm planning to come back at the end of the week,' he said quietly. 'Dinner on Friday night?'

'You might not be back,' she hedged quickly. 'Let's decide later.'

'No, let's decide now.'

Suddenly she felt they were discussing more than the dinner. She stared at him. He looked tough and strong, a man who would deal with any problem life presented and sort it out on his own terms. A man who wouldn't compromise, who would always want his own way because he would feel it was the best way. And yet he had been gentle and understanding with her, she had to admit that. And again this all came back to it being *her* who was the mixed-up kid, but she was a woman on her own—she had been for ten years—and she had managed just fine, hadn't she? She'd accepted she had to fight her own battles and stand on her own two feet and she had done it. Her life and what she did with it was down to her, and no one could rob her of that unless she gave over her independence, her self-respect, her autonomy.

True, the feelings of inadequacy that plagued her in the dark of the night were hard to deal with at times, especially since she had got to know Kingsley. She'd resolutely held back from giving way to the desire of imagining what it would be like to be in his arms, to have him holding her, loving her, banishing the demons with the strength of his presence. Dreams of that sort were all very well, but if they turned into nightmares…

'I wouldn't let you down, Rosie.' It was as though he had read her mind and she blinked at him. 'If I say Friday, I'll be here on Friday.' Again they both knew there was more to the conversation than the surface indicated. 'You are going to have to trust me sooner or later because I'm not going to go anywhere.'

'You're going to Jamaica,' she said, thinking, What a stupid thing to say at such a time.

'If you asked me to stay I would,' he said simply.

'What about your friend?'

'You come first.'

Her heart began to beat erratically. 'I wouldn't ask you to stay. You must go and see him; he needs you.'

'And you don't?'

She was silent. There was nothing she could say. Nothing at all.

He sighed irritably. 'I feel like I'm treading a minefield with you most of the time, do you know that? I never know when something I might say might be used against me, likened to the swine you married. You do that, don't you? Look for the same failings in me as you found in him?'

She was horrified and it showed, but she didn't deny it. How could she? It was true. And what man was going to put up with that in the months and years to come? Certainly not one like Kingsley who only had to click his fingers and have a hundred beauties lined up panting.

'If you think that…' Her voice trailed away.

'Why do I bother?' He finished the sentence for her. 'Why do you think I bother, Rosie? Why do you think I've been treading on eggshells the last few months? You've finally opened up about this sicko you married, but now the steel is inches thicker, isn't it?'

'What steel?'

'The stuff that coats the door to your heart,' he said, poetically for Kingsley.

There was a slight pause. 'I can't help how I feel,' she whispered, letting her hair fall in two wings at the side of her cheeks to hide her face from him and the tears she was struggling to keep behind her eyelids.

'Yes, you can,' he said, and his voice sounded oddly husky. 'Don't you think I went through hell when I realised I was falling in love with you? It's not just you who has the right to feel scared to death. After Maria I vowed I'd never let this happen again. Who needs it? A woman is a woman is a woman, and there were plenty out there who were only too willing to play the game the way I wanted it. Everything to gain and nothing to lose. Total safety. And then you came along.'

She didn't speak, she was crying, soundlessly, the tears slowly dripping down her cheeks, his honesty forcing her to admit what she had been trying to keep buried for weeks. She loved him. She had loved him for days, weeks, months, for ever. That was why the thought of giving herself to him terrified her so desperately. She loved him more than she had ever loved Miles, more than she would have thought herself capable of. Which meant his power over her was absolute. He mustn't know. He mustn't ever know.

He had stopped talking. He was breathing hard and she could feel he was looking at her although she didn't raise her head. After a moment a crisp white handkerchief was pushed into her hands. 'Don't cry.' His voice was gruff, painful. 'Damn it, the last thing I want to do is to make you cry. Drink your coffee.'

She wiped her face and drank the coffee, which was lukewarm and tasted foul, and then she raised her eyes, knowing his would be waiting for her. 'It would never work, Kingsley, you and I,' she said shakily. 'I'd spoil anything you're feeling for me right now because I can't be what you want me to be. When Miles did what he did—' she stopped, wondering how to explain the unexplainable '—something died,' she finished slowly. 'Something I can't get back.'

'I don't believe that,' he said with quiet emphasis. 'I love you, damn it, and I want to marry you and have children and grow old with you. I'm not Miles, I'm not anyone but myself and I've allowed you to see what that is, who I am. That has to count for something on this scorecard you keep in your head.'

She tore her gaze from his, wondering why she had

been so foolish as to come here with him. But she knew the answer to that. She'd wanted to be with him, this one last time. Every minute, every second was precious, and they were spending it arguing. She spoke the thought out loud. 'I don't want to fight, there's not much time.'

'I've never ducked an issue in my life and I'm blowed if I'll start with the most important one that's ever come my way,' he said grimly. 'I'll take a later plane if necessary.'

She shrank inwardly. She couldn't cope with much more of this. It was tearing her apart. 'Don't be silly,' she whispered brokenly. 'Your friend is waiting for you.'

'You don't get it, do you?' His voice was suddenly very quiet. 'You really don't get it. You don't have the faintest idea what you mean to me.'

'*I don't want to.*' It was wrenched out of her. 'This is hard enough as it is. Can't you accept I mean what I say and leave me alone? This is for the best and you'll see it one day.'

'The hell I will.' His mouth came down on hers and he kissed her hard, oblivious to anyone else.

'No.' She jerked her head away, panic-stricken. She couldn't weaken now and she always did when he touched her. This had to be the end, now, right here. He was away for a few days and it would give him time to reflect, to see she was right. They had no future. She loved him too much for there to be a possibility of a future but she couldn't say that, he wouldn't understand. But she mustn't weaken. He was too formidable an opponent, too intelligent and intuitive for her to show a chink in the steel he'd spoken of. 'I don't want this. I don't want you.'

He looked her straight in the eyes, his gaze so piercingly blue it was painful to hold. 'You don't mean that.'

'I do.' She nodded, her head wagging as though it were

on strings. 'I do mean it. And you've got to go. You'll miss your plane.'

He said something very rude about the plane, which made a passing customer gasp in shock and hurry to the other end of the seating area.

'I can't cope with you in my life, Kingsley. Is that plain enough?' she said desperately. 'I want it to be like it used to be before I met you. Mike or one of the others can take over the job from now on.'

'I don't want Mike or one of the others. The contract says you.'

'Then I'll resign and you can sue me if you want.' She glared at him, fear and defiance in her face.

He was silent for what seemed like a long, long time, his face full of a bewildered anger that cut her in two. 'You needn't resign your job,' he said at last. 'Not because of me. Put Mike on my project if you like, or one of the others. I really don't care.'

He stood up slowly, his face grey under his tan. 'Goodbye, Rosie.'

'Goodbye.'

She was conscious of a screaming toddler to the left of her who had just flung orange juice all over its mother, and two teenagers in the corner who were giggling at a magazine they had propped between them.

Something as momentous as their breaking up shouldn't happen in such mundane surroundings surely? she thought dazedly.

He looked at her one last time but he didn't speak again, merely giving her a curt nod and turning away, walking with calm, measured steps out of the restaurant and out of her life. And she let him go.

*　　*　　*

'You've done *what*?'

Rosalie winced at the pitch of Beth's voice. 'I've split with Kingsley,' she repeated flatly. 'It's over.'

It was Sunday afternoon and she was sitting in Beth's garden engulfed in the perfume of roses, honeysuckle and a hundred and one other scents from the profuse blooms adorning every nook and cranny, not to mention the flowerbeds. It was hot, it was very hot and a storm was imminent, but in spite of the weather Beth had cooked a big Sunday roast with all the trimmings, which Rosalie had ploughed through as best she could, considering every mouthful felt as though it would choke her. She hadn't slept a wink all night and had been prowling the flat at four in the morning crying her eyes out.

'But he adored you, anyone could see that,' Beth said agitatedly. 'Don't tell me another woman hooked him? I don't believe it.'

'You don't have to, it didn't happen like that,' Rosalie said carefully. 'We just felt it wasn't right, that's all.'

'We?' Beth looked at Rosalie's puffy eyes. 'The rotten, two-timing rat.'

'Beth, I promise you, Kingsley didn't do anything wrong,' Rosalie protested. 'There's no other woman, believe me.' Not yet anyway. 'It was just getting a bit...serious, that's all.'

'Oh, Lee.' Beth's voice dropped in horror. 'You didn't.'

'Didn't what?' Rosalie said uncomfortably.

'Freeze him out? Not Kingsley. Not the most gorgeous man you're ever likely to meet.' There was a slight pause, and then Beth said, 'You did, didn't you? And you're regretting it already.'

For the first time Rosalie could understand why Beth's children had been eager to escape the nest as soon as they could. There was something terribly annoying about someone who was always right.

'I'm not regretting it, not really,' she said flatly. 'It's for the best in the long run. He wanted more than I could give.'

'Sex without any commitment? Typical man. Is that it?'

'Not exactly.'

'You to move in with him? Bad mistake. You lose your independence and he keeps his. I can see—'

'*Beth.*' She was trying very hard to be patient. 'He wanted to—' She stopped. She didn't know how to put this. 'He was talking marriage,' she said at last.

'No…' It was a long drawn-out gasp. 'And you said no? Lee, are you mad?'

Perhaps it hadn't been such a good idea to come here today, but she couldn't have faced any of her friends feeling the way she did, and staying brooding in the flat just hadn't been an option.

'Probably.' She didn't smile. 'Very probably. He thinks I am, anyway. It wasn't an…amicable parting.' Her voice had quivered on the last words.

'Oh, baby.' Beth did what she did best and turned mother earth, springing up and kneeling down beside Rosalie's chair and hugging her tight.

It started an avalanche of tears that shocked them both and caused George, who had just wandered out from his study for a few moments, to beat a hasty retreat back indoors.

Over several glasses of Beth's iced lemonade liberally laced with lime and crushed raspberries, Rosalie told Beth the whole story throughout the sticky afternoon, discussing her fears and doubts for the second time in as many days but this time with someone who had no axe to grind. They were no nearer a solution when the heat of the day had gone and evening shadows spangled the slanting sunlight, and Rosalie couldn't honestly say she felt better for discussing the whole sorry mess, but, nevertheless, she was glad she had come to see her aunt. It had been hard to talk about Miles and exactly what had happened in their marriage, but strangely not as hard as she'd expected, perhaps because telling Kingsley had broken some mental barrier that had been in place before.

'I always loathed him, but then you know that,' Beth said of Miles. 'In all the time you were with him we hardly saw anything of you. It was all *his* friends, *his* interests, wasn't it?'

'I guess so.' Rosalie nodded. In that way Miles had been like her father, although her father's motive had sprung from a misguided, warped jealousy born of love, and Miles's had been pure selfishness. 'I didn't notice it at first as all our friends were mutual.'

'Kingsley isn't like him, Lee. You do know that, don't you?' Beth said earnestly as they made their goodbyes in the cool of the evening. 'He wouldn't use force or be violent. I know it.'

She nodded. 'I know it too, it's not that. But...' She shook her head slowly. 'I think I'm too scared by marriage to ever want to take a chance again, and then other times over the last twenty-four hours I'm almost picking up the phone to try and contact him and tell him I need him. How's that for inconsistency?'

'Perhaps if you said you'd live with him, without the marriage bit?' suggested Beth, the most staunch advocate of marriage in the whole of London, who drove her children mad by insisting anything else was living in sin.

Rosalie gave her aunt a hug. 'Beth, I'm really going to miss you,' she said, meaning it. 'But it's not even the marriage thing, although that is a sign of huge commitment. It's more...letting him know how much I love him, you know? Miles would always belittle me to puff himself

up and I know Kingsley wouldn't do that, but when someone is sure of your love they can change...' Her voice
trailed away as she gazed at her aunt. 'Oh, I don't know
how to put it,' she said flatly. 'I just know it scares me
to death.'

Beth looked at her for a long moment. 'And how much
does *not* being with him scare you?' she said softly. 'And
don't answer now,' she added as Rosalie opened her
mouth. 'Think about it. All right?'

Rosalie did think about it. She thought about it all through
the next few nights when she tossed and turned until dawn
in the sticky heat, the anticipated storm and change in the
weather yet to make an appearance.

She woke very early on the Friday morning when
Kingsley was due back, even though she hadn't managed
to fall to sleep until way after two.

She had made the worst mistake of her life. Even mar-
rying Miles paled into insignificance beside sending
Kingsley away. Suddenly her mind was crystal clear for
the first time since she had met him and she knew exactly
what she wanted.

Miles was gone—in every sense of the word. Gone
from her mind, her heart, her life and this world, so what
was she doing letting him ruin her life for the second
time? Beth was right, the possibility of *not* being with
Kingsley scared her a hundred times more than accepting
him fully into her life.

Kingsley was nothing like Miles, not in character and
he had shown her that. His honesty, his straightness, his
ability to face issues head-on—Miles had had none of
those qualities. Miles had been a pile of dead men's bones
beneath the outward façade of handsomeness and debo-
nair conviviality, nothing about the person he had pre-

tended to be before they'd married had been real. And she had allowed a man like that to convince her that love meant constriction and fear.

She sat up in bed, turning on the bedside lamp and staring into the dimly lit room. What a fool she'd been, what a blind, stupid fool. Kingsley had bared his heart to her, given everything he knew how to give and she hadn't even listened to him, not really. What had she done?

Her stomach twisted and she climbed out of bed, padding along to the kitchen and making herself a strong cup of coffee.

Why hadn't she found the courage to tell him she loved him? she asked herself helplessly. He hadn't phoned or contacted her since he'd gone and she didn't blame him. He'd clearly washed his hands of her. But how could she live in a world in which Kingsley was living, and not be with him? To know he was free to meet someone else, to marry someone else, to have babies with someone else.

She groaned, laying her head on the cool surface of the breakfast bar for a moment. She wanted to be with him more than anything in the world but she'd been too hung up by the terrors of the past to recognise it. When he'd left she'd thought a few days' separation would make him see that she was right and that they had no future together. What if that was exactly what he *did* think? How ironic when she'd done a full hundred-and-eighty-degree turn, if he'd done the same.

She drank the coffee scalding hot, and it was as she finished the last mouthful that she thought, What am I doing? What *am* I doing? If he loved her, if he *really* loved her it would be with warts, pimples and all. That was the sort of guy he was. So…did she believe he really loved her? She felt a surge of joy such as she hadn't felt since she'd been very young rise up. Yes, she did. She did. So it was logical to believe he hadn't changed his mind. Her fears and emotions might lead her down one path but she had to stand on logic and trust. She couldn't keep doubting him or herself, not if this relationship was going to have any future. And she wanted a future with Kingsley, oh, so much.

She found herself pacing the small kitchen and stopped abruptly, realising she was so tense her hands were clenched tight.

A bath. And then a call to the airport to see what time his flight arrived. She'd meet him. Whatever time he landed she'd be there waiting for him. She glanced at the kitchen clock. In fact she'd call the airport first, just in case it was an early arrival.

They were very sorry, the anonymous voice at the airport said politely, but there were no flights arriving from Jamaica today. Hadn't she heard about the cyclone?

No, she hadn't, Rosalie said tightly.

Cyclone Kimberley was heading straight for the coast and unfortunately holding course despite all predictions it would swing away; consequently all flights were cancelled for the foreseeable future. If she would like to ring tomorrow they might have news then.

She put the telephone down very carefully, her hands shaking. And then picked it up immediately to phone Kingsley's secretary in England for details of where he was staying, before she remembered it wasn't yet five o'clock.

The next four hours were the longest of her life.

She had a bath and washed her hair, cleaned the kitchen from top to bottom, including washing the inside of the cupboards and rearranging everything, after which she re-arranged it all back again. Her mind was plaguing her with vivid pictures. Kingsley buried under a pile of debris.

Kingsley trapped and injured or worse. And all the time thinking she didn't love him, that she didn't want him. She couldn't bear it. She just couldn't bear it.

She phoned Jenny at home at eight o'clock, explaining she had a few things she needed to sort out and that she wouldn't be in the office until much later, if at all. Apart from a little juggling with a couple of afternoon appointments there was nothing too vital to sort out.

At nine she spoke to Kingsley's secretary in the office at Oxford. 'Oh, hello, Miss Milburn,' the girl said politely. 'Mr Ward's number in Jamaica? Sure, I have it here. Just a minute.' There was the sound of rustling paper, and then the disembodied voice said quietly, 'Awful about his friend, isn't it? And not been long married too. And now there's all this panic about the cyclone.'

Rosalie's heart was lurching. 'His friend hasn't...?'

'Oh, no, he hasn't died, but it looks like he's paralysed, although they can't move him yet to a hospital in the States.'

'Right.' She took down the number, gave her thanks and put the receiver down, aware her hands were shaking so badly the numbers were barely recognisable.

It was around three in the morning in Jamaica—should she wait a while or phone now? Selfishly, she admitted, she was going to phone now. She needed to talk to him, to tell him how she felt, and she might not be able to get through anyway if the cyclone had hit. Her stomach went over at the thought.

The hotel receptionist sounded weary—no doubt she had been taking calls from anxious relatives and friends for most of the night—but she put Rosalie through to Kingsley's room without any argument, after indicating Mr Ward might have already joined a number of other guests who were preparing to shelter in the basement.

The phone was picked up immediately. 'Hello?'

'Kingsley, is that you?' Stupid opening line considering it was hardly likely to be anyone else. 'It's Rosalie.'

'Rosie?'

She was fighting back the tears that had sprung up with relief at hearing his voice and couldn't continue for a minute, and as the line cracked and popped his voice came again, louder, saying. 'Rosie? Are you there?'

'I'm so sorry.' Her bottom lip was trembling so much it was hard to speak. 'Can you ever forgive me?'

'Rosie, I can't hear you—the storm—you'll have to shout.'

'Can you ever forgive me?' she bellowed down the line, the urgency of it all providing the shot of adrenalin she needed to pull herself together. 'I've been so stupid.'

'You're not stupid—' The line faded and then crackled, and his voice came back again, saying, '…very brave, don't you know that?'

'I can't hear you!'

'I said you are the gutsiest woman I know and very brave. Look, it's getting worse—' there were a few more frustrating moments when the line shuddered and died, and then '—get back.'

'What? Oh, Kingsley, I can't hear you and I want to say I'm sorry and that I love you and that you must be careful.' But he was saying something too and she was almost sure he couldn't hear her.

'Kingsley, if you need to go and shelter, do it. I love you. Let me know you're all right when you can.' But the line had gone dead. She put down the receiver and burst into tears. He was in danger, and she wasn't sure if he knew she loved him or had heard anything she'd said.

She spent the rest of the day glued to the TV and radio reports, getting more and more worked up as they confirmed that Cyclone Kimberley was a biggie and was taking no prisoners. Rosalie drank numerous cups of coffee but couldn't eat a thing, and when Beth called in the evening, having heard the news on the TV, which had mentioned all power lines were down along with pretty severe destruction in places, she was all but climbing the walls.

'I'm coming over,' Beth said, at the sound of Rosalie's agitated voice.

'No, it's all right, really.'

'I'm coming. George is away at some conference or other and won't get back till tomorrow, and at least it won't seem so bad if there's two of us worrying together. Have you eaten?' she added in true mother-hen fashion.

'I don't want anything.'

'See you in a little while.'

Before she knew it Beth was on the doorstep, her arms full of tubs and boxes from an Indian take-away, along with a couple of bottles of wine.

'I'm…not hungry.' Rosalie was determined she wasn't going to cry again. She hadn't cried in years before she'd met Kingsley, but since he'd come into her life it seemed as if she'd done little else.

Beth ignored her, bustling about the kitchen heating food in the microwave and opening a bottle of very good red wine, saying as she did so, 'Listen to me, Lee. There have been worse cyclones than this one, much worse, and Jamaica and other such places are geared up for them. They're a yearly hazard, for goodness' sake, like…like snowstorms here.'

Rosalie's expression indicated what she thought of such a pathetic comparison.

'Kingsley's going to be absolutely fine, I know it, and you won't do him or yourself any good if you make yourself ill, now then. You are going to eat and drink, and wait for him to call you. Power lines always go down with these sorts of things, along with roofs being blown away and the odd boat or two being sunk, but that doesn't mean anyone gets hurt. I told you, they know what to do.'

Beth handed Rosalie a large glass of red wine. 'Drink some, *now*,' she commanded in the same voice she used to her offspring when it was a case of 'she who must be obeyed'.

Rosalie drank. The rich and full-bodied wine with the aroma of raspberries, damsons and spices left a warm glow and steadied the trembling in her stomach.

'Now go and set the table for two,' Beth said briskly, handing her the bottle and another glass. 'We're eating first and then you can tell me all about it.'

Amazingly Rosalie found she managed a good assault on her heaped plate before finally admitting defeat when it was half empty, another glass of wine helping enormously in forcing the food down.

After she had filled Beth in on her decision and the position to date, the two women sat sipping wine and talking until far into the night. Eventually, at gone two, Beth persuaded her to go to bed, insisting she would sit and doze in a chair by the phone.

'You look awful,' Beth said with her usual honesty. 'Get some sleep or you'll be meeting him with bags under your eyes big enough to shop with.'

Rosalie climbed into bed complaining that this was a wasted exercise and she wouldn't sleep a wink, and it was much more sensible for Beth to have her bed. However, she was asleep as soon as her head touched the pillow, the lack of rest over the last few days and the relaxing effect of the wine causing a deep, dreamless slumber.

She only slept for four hours, her subconscious then

kicking in and reminding her she ought to be awake and worrying, but she felt better for it as she tottered into the sitting room where Beth was snoring softly in her chair by the phone.

Beth went home after lunch, Rosalie having promised her aunt she would phone her as soon as she heard anything, and it seemed as though no sooner had the other woman left than the telephone rang.

'Rosie?'

It was Kingsley. She felt her heart give an almighty jump and then start thumping away like a sledgehammer. 'Kingsley.' She knew her voice sounded choked but she couldn't help it. 'Kingsley, I love you,' she said desperately, terrified they would lose the connection again. 'I was wrong about everything and I want us to be together. Can you hear me?'

'I can hear you, sweetheart.'

Sweetheart. He'd called her sweetheart. The tears were dripping down her face again but she didn't care. She'd cry every day all day if it meant he called her sweetheart.

'Listen, I've found a guy with a satellite mobile, there's still a virtual shut-down here, but he needs to make some urgent business calls so I need to talk fast.'

'Are you all right? You're not injured?'

'Filthy dirty, hungry, thirsty, but no, not injured. There's massive structural damage, especially in the shanty towns, and a number of us are helping out.'

'Oh, be careful. Don't take any chances.' She immediately had visions of buildings falling down the moment he went near them.

'I'm glad you phoned last night.' His voice was soft now, deep, and she shivered.

'So am I.'

'I love you.'

'I love you too.' She suddenly remembered she hadn't asked about his friend. 'How's Alex?' she said quickly.

'Not good.' Suddenly she could hear the exhaustion in his voice. 'I really needed that phone call from you. Fortunately the cyclone missed the hospital he's in so that's something.'

'Kingsley, you do forgive me?'

'Always, sweetheart.'

She gulped, giving an involuntary sniff. 'When do you think you'll be able to leave the island?'

'We're waiting to hear. Look, I have to go. See you soon.'

No, no, not yet. She wanted to protest, feeling something would go wrong, something would happen before she saw him again and really made everything all right. Instead she said, 'Take care.'

'I will. Goodbye, Rosie.'

'Goodbye.'

There was so much she'd wanted to say. As soon as she put the receiver down she went over their conversation in her mind. She needed to make him understand what had held her back from making a commitment, why she loved him so much, how special he was, just everything.

She sat for a few minutes collecting her thoughts and reliving the moment he'd called her sweetheart, and then telephoned Beth, who was ecstatic for her. Dear, dear Beth.

She walked into the bedroom and, fully dressed as she was, climbed into bed after kicking off her shoes and slept for several hours.

She awoke to the telephone ringing again and virtually fell out of bed, hearing Beth's voice with a disappointment that made her bite her lip.

'Sorry, Lee, did you think it was him?' Beth said cheerfully. 'It's just that I wondered if you've got the TV on? They're doing a bit on the news about the cyclone in a minute or two and I thought you might be interested.'

Not unless they could arrange a one-to-one with Kingsley for her. 'Thanks.' She put as much enthusiasm in her voice as she could. 'I'll switch it on now.'

Ten minutes later she sat as though turned to stone, the bottom having dropped out of her world.

CHAPTER TEN

'LEE, I'm sure there's some sort of reasonable explanation. Don't make up your mind about anything until you've heard what he has to say.'

Rosalie listened to Beth who had phoned moments after the news item had ended, politely agreeing and saying she was perfectly all right about it all, before putting down the phone.

She sat in the quiet of her sitting room for a long time, trying to make sense of it all. In the end, she knew she couldn't.

The news crew had veered towards the humanitarian aspect of the natural disaster, emphasising it was the poorest who had been affected most by the cyclone but that on such desperate occasions man's humanity to man could spring into action. Holiday-makers and visitors from abroad in the area had all pulled together with the rescue services to help those injured or trapped under the debris of their houses in the shanty towns, it had proclaimed, showing pictures of the good Samaritans in action. 'Courage and hope mingling with helplessness and despair' type of reporting.

Her heart had nearly leapt out of her chest when she had seen Kingsley. Her breath caught at the memory. Her body felt strange, all tight and hurting, as though she had been pummelled and kicked about by something.

He had been in the background actually involved in digging an elderly man out from under the tin shack that had been his home until a tree had demolished it. A miraculous escape, the man they'd been interviewing had said. Part of the roof had fallen in such a way that the man had been cushioned in a small chamber and was virtually unhurt.

Her eyes had been fixed on the tall dark figure in the background and she had barely noticed anyone else—until Kingsley had been joined by a certain familiar and voluptuous brunette, that was. And Little Miss Canary hadn't been at all shy about kissing him full on the lips as she'd flung herself into his arms.

The broadcast had shifted at this point to the story of a little girl, who had managed to save the family's goat by untying the animal from where it had been tethered in the nick of time and bringing it into their house, which had survived the tropical storm, but the images of Kingsley with the woman who was his friend's sister were burnt onto the screen of Rosalie's mind.

She exhaled sharply. Even Beth had been forced to admit that the kiss hadn't been a sisterly one, and as Kingsley's arms had gone round the girl she had pressed herself into him with all the finesse of a bitch on heat.

She could understand Alex's sister coming to see her brother after the accident, of course she could, and Kingsley had known her for years, but that kiss...

What was she going to do? Reality hit, and with it a gut-wrenching pain. Her body ached as it did when she had the flu but this wasn't a virus, unless you could call love a virus? Maybe you could at that, she reflected silently. She swallowed hard.

What had she said to herself only twenty-four hours ago when she had decided that she was going to plunge head first into this relationship? Her fears and emotions might lead her down a certain path, but she had to stand on logic and trust. Logic and trust were all very well but when millions of people had seen the man she loved embrace another woman...

Logic—Miss Canary had embraced him. Trust—maybe he could give her an explanation as to why Alex's sister thought she had the right to give him a body massage but without using her hands? And maybe pigs could fly. Helplessness at her ability to contact Kingsley right at this second and ask him what the hell he thought he was playing at gripped her.

Could she envisage a future with a man she couldn't trust? Would Kingsley want a future with a woman he felt didn't trust him?

Rosalie stood up, walking out of the sitting room and into the bathroom, where she washed her tear-stained face before straightening and looking at herself in the small round mirror set over the basin. Tragic, tear-swept eyes stared back at her from a face even her nearest and dearest would have to admit was blotchy.

She'd had enough of crying. The thought sent something hot and deliberate coursing through her blood, and she took a deep breath, speaking it loud. 'I am sick and tired of crying.' The eyes applauded her stand. She wasn't going to do it any more. Kingsley would contact her soon. Her throat tightened. And she wasn't going to play any games or pretend she was feeling anything else than what she was feeling. She would ask him about the Canary calmly and composedly, but only when she saw him face to face. That way she would know if he was lying.

Her whole instinct was to run at the moment. Run from any commitment, run from confrontation, run from Kingsley, from love. But she was a grown woman now, not a scared, confused little child who had just lost the two people she cared about most in the world, or a broken young teenager whose love had been trampled into the ground in the cruellest way imaginable.

She had to face this head-on. Not hysterically, admittedly, but neither was she going to brush what she'd seen aside and pretend it wasn't real. She'd done that with Miles, she realised suddenly. Ignored the tell-tale signs of his affairs because she hadn't been able to bear to think he would do that to her. But he had. And because *he* was weak and flawed, not because she hadn't been enough for him. As Kingsley had said, Miles had been an emotional cripple, inadequate and cruel. *Kingsley.* Oh, Kingsley, Kingsley. Please come through for me. Please give me an answer that I can believe because it's true.

He phoned her the next day. 'I'm coming home, Rosie.' She liked the way he said home, and then warned herself not to get too starry-eyed so she couldn't see clearly when she asked him about Tweety Pie. 'I land at Heathrow at seven on Monday evening.'

'I'll meet you,' she offered carefully.

'I was hoping you'd say that.'

He was smiling, she knew he was smiling, and for a moment she felt anger that he was all hunky-dory and smiling, and she felt wretched. She took a deep breath. 'How are the cleaning-up operations going out there?'

'Not too bad. It's tough when you see the poverty and some of the locals have lost everything, but it's incredible how they pull together. Family is strong out here, that's the thing.'

'And Alex?' she asked even more carefully.

'The doctor his father brought out with him from the States says he can safely be moved at the end of next week, but he's already seeing signs he feels are hopeful.

How hopeful will depend on the tests they run in the hospital back home. Rosie—'

'His father?' She interrupted his voice, which had gone into silky soft mode when he'd said her name. She couldn't handle how it made her feel right now and she needed to be strong. 'It's not just his wife who's out there with you, then?' she asked, thinking, *As if I didn't know.*

'No, they're all here.'

Aren't they just? 'Right.' Full marks for the cheerfulness, Rosalie.

'What's wrong?' he asked softly.

Or perhaps not full marks, then. 'Wrong?' Everything. 'Nothing,' she lied firmly.

'I don't believe you but I have to go. Take care, sweetheart. I'll see you tomorrow. I love you.'

'I love you.' At least she could say that and mean it. But the people who were supposed to love you the best always ended up hurting you. She closed her eyes for some time after she'd replaced the receiver. Was Kingsley going to hurt her? She had already hurt him when she had sent him away.

It was a different variation on what she'd been thinking since she had decided she wanted to be with him, and her brow wrinkled. He had conquered his demons for her but she had unwittingly given him a few more when she had refused him before he'd left for Jamaica. And now she might hurt him again when she asked him about Alex's sister. But he was a man, not a child. She had pussyfooted about with Miles, scared of hurting him or making him angry. If Kingsley was the one for her he would meet her halfway. He might not like what she asked but he could handle it. That was the sort of man he was. The ache inside her deepened.

She wanted to believe in a love that would last for ever.

She couldn't believe how much she wanted to. But that wasn't wrong or weak, was it? She had only stopped wishing for it when the hurt of being disappointed had been too much to bear, but since Kingsley she had dared to hope again.

Would she have the courage to ask him about Alex's sister when he was standing in front of her, and she could see what she might lose? She hoped so. She didn't want to be disappointed in herself just when she was beginning to like what she saw in the mirror for the first time since she had been five years old.

She got to the airport early, not because she had planned to but because she couldn't help herself.

She had agonised over what to wear since she'd left work at the unheard-of time of four o'clock in the afternoon, and the entire contents of her wardrobe were now strewn over her bed at the flat. Ridiculous. She wrinkled her nose at herself and then moved her head to catch her reflection in the shiny surface of a snack dispensing machine.

She had gone from sophisticated to smart casual to casual and then back to sophisticated again about ten times in the last three hours, but eventually she'd let the weather decide for her. Lightning was flashing in weird jagged streaks across the rooftops and thunder was rolling ominously, but as yet there was no rain, just a stifling heat that was oppressive. She had chosen a light, spaghetti-strap silk crêpe dress in white, which fell to just above her ankles and which was wonderfully cool, dressing it down with slip-on cork sandals. Simple, chic and with just the right touch of 'I haven't dressed like this especially for you, I always look this good'.

The plane was on time and her thudding heart belied

the outward picture of cucumber-cool, composed femininity that had more than one pair of interested male eyes turning Rosalie's way. But she didn't notice any of them. All her senses were tied up with the watching for Kingsley.

And then she saw him. Tall, confident and incredibly handsome. She thought, I've bared my soul to this man, told him things I'd never planned to tell anyone. How had it all happened? And then he saw her, raising his hand as his face broke into the smile that never ceased to make her heart jump.

'Hi.' He reached her, dropping his case and taking her in his arms. He bent down, pressing his mouth against hers and his lips were warm and firm, the familiar delicious smell of him teasing her nostrils and the hard body sending tingles down her spine. The kiss only lasted moments but she was trembling when he let her go, brushing a wisp of hair from her forehead with the tip of one finger as he said, 'You look beautiful, incredible.'

'Incredible's overdoing it a bit,' she managed fairly lightly, 'but I'll take beautiful.'

''My pleasure.' He grinned at her and her senses went into hyperdrive as his hands cupped her face as though he couldn't bear not to touch her. 'I've dreamt of you every night,' he said softly, 'but there's nothing like the real thing.'

Kingsley, oh, Kingsley. I didn't want to fall in love with you, that hadn't been the plan, but how do you stop an unstoppable force?

She glanced at the sea of people, her voice small as she said, 'Let's go, shall we?'

He looked at her, a searching look, but said nothing, simply reaching for his case and then tucking her arm in his as though it should be there. And she wanted it to be. So much.

Once outside she became aware that the first fat raindrops were falling from a sky that looked like something from a science fiction film. 'The storm's breaking at last,' she said quietly. How strange. It had hung on for days and it had to be the minute they'd met again that the elements unleashed their fury.

Kingsley had just hailed a taxi when the heavens let loose with a sheet of water that had her soaked before she could scramble in. Once in the taxi she realised that the dress that had been so chic and elegant moments before was now completely see-through, hugging her body in a way that would win first prize in any wet T-shirt competition.

'Hell!' Kingsley raked back his dripping hair, the thin black shirt and trousers he was wearing soaked through but still decent. 'What is it about me that brings storm and tempest?'

It was said jokingly but something in her face caught his attention, and as the taxi driver began to move gingerly away, windscreen wipers at Olympic speed, he reached for her again, drawing her into him as he said, 'Okay, what is it? And don't say nothing,' and now there was no amusement in the deep voice. 'This was supposed to be the grand reunion, not a tragedy.'

She shivered, and not just because she was wet through. He had given her flat as their destination, and she had been hoping to wait until they were inside before saying anything. She felt the warmth of his body begin to warm her and she sucked in a breath. She might ruin everything here. She wanted to touch him and hold him, talk with him, love him. But she had to know. She didn't know how to start. 'Did you really dream of me?' she asked a little breathlessly.

'Sure.' He moved his head, looking down at her with eyes as blue and clear as sapphires. 'But if I'd seen you in this dress before it would definitely have featured.'

'I didn't realise it went see-through in the rain.'

'I'm not complaining. It's all the welcome homes I've ever had rolled into one.' He tilted her chin, kissing her nose and then her eyelids before taking her mouth in a kiss that immediately made her want more. And then he said, 'So? Spill.'

No accusations. You're asking the question, that's all. 'I saw you on the news,' she blurted out, not at all as she'd meant to start.

'What?' Whatever he'd been expecting, it was clear it wasn't this.

'On the news,' she repeated. 'They were interviewing someone about the cyclone and you were in the background, helping to rescue an old man?' She was looking at him very carefully.

'Well, I'll be blowed.' He grinned at her. 'I'd have sent you a kiss if I'd known.'

She stiffened; she couldn't help it. 'Actually you were already busy in that realm.' She raised her eyebrows questioningly but she had lost him, she could see it in his puzzled face.

'What realm?' he said easily.

'The kissing realm,' she said tightly. What else?

'Rosie, forgive me, but I haven't the faintest idea what you're talking about.'

'You don't remember?' Was that a good sign or a bad sign?

He frowned, his voice holding a thread of impatience.

'We could go on all night like this, so why don't you say what's on your mind and be done with it?'

'You and the canary.' Damn, she hadn't meant that to slip out. Blushing furiously, she qualified, 'You and Alex's sister.'

'Alex's…?' His brow cleared. 'You mean Trixie was in the shot? Is that what you're getting at?'

Trixie? Oh, her name wasn't really Trixie, was it? Her grandmother had had an incontinent poodle called Trixie. 'Not just in the shot,' she said evenly. 'You were kissing.'

He stared at her, his eyes narrowing, and she stared back, not at all sure how he was going to react. She tried to read his expression but she couldn't. She didn't know what he was thinking or feeling. So much for being able to read his face when she challenged him about it, she thought miserably.

'Where does the canary come in?' he asked after a long moment or two, when the only sound was the violent swishing of water from the windscreen wipers and the drumming of rain on the taxi's roof.

Rosalie shifted uncomfortably, and then became aware that the movement emphasised the taut peaks of her nipples through her damp clothes. Kingsley was aware of it too if the look on his face was anything to go by.

He eventually managed to tear his eyes away, saying again, 'The canary? I'm sorry but I don't follow. Why a canary?'

'I… You…weren't supposed to hear that. It slipped out.' Her face felt as though it were going to catch fire.

Dark eyebrows rose. He was demanding an answer.

'I saw her on the pictures of Alex's wedding, when you were the best man and she was the chief bridesmaid. She…she was dressed in yellow.'

He continued to study her hot face for a second more

and then he began to shake with laughter, much to Rosalie's chagrin.

'And she was draped all over you then,' she continued, and sharply now. 'And you looked as though you were enjoying it.'

'Now hold on a minute.' Still grinning, he shook his head. 'Trixie is the baby sister I never had. I indulge her, spoil her, tease her, but the thought of anything along the lines you're suggesting is ridiculous. Damn it, she's a baby.'

'A baby?' Rosalie had promised herself she wouldn't get mad but he was the limit. 'A baby with a thirty-eight, twenty-four, thirty-six shape is no baby, Kingsley, and you might not have noticed but the "baby" has got the hots for you,' she finished somewhat crudely.

'Rosie, she's twenty years old.'

'So? How many men do you know that have girlfriends who are ten, twenty, thirty years younger than them? It isn't exactly unheard of,' she said scathingly.

'You're jealous.' He was clearly delighted and she could have killed him. Is this what she'd suffered the torments of the damned for? She took back all the nice thoughts she'd had.

'Not at all.' She drew herself up and away from him, as regally as the transparent dress would allow. 'I just think it's pretty disgusting to carry on the way she does in public, that's all.'

'You are, aren't you?' It was faintly wondering and actually doused her anger more effectively than anything else could have done. 'You're jealous of a silly little girl who hasn't a grain of sense in her head and is a damn sight more irritating than anything else. The child's a pest, Rosie. She always has been. She drives me mad half the time, if you want to know, but, like I said, she's the kid sister and so I don't mind.'

She stared at him, barely hearing him past the 'silly little girl' bit. He meant it, she thought in amazement. He actually thought that gorgeous young thing was a pest. She still said, 'You were kissing,' in a faintly stubborn voice, unable to give in completely. 'And she definitely doesn't want you for a brother.'

'She kissed me, if I remember, and, as she'd come with the news that the doctors were more hopeful about Alex for the first time since he was injured, I might have held her for a moment. And she's at an age where she's finding her wings—she flirts with any and every man. It doesn't mean a thing.'

She stared at him, all eyes, and his voice changed, becoming softer as he murmured, 'Come here, my love.'

Once she was nestled in his arms he said, 'I can see it's going to take me some time to convince you just how much I love you, but it'll be fun for both of us, I promise. I think I can do it more effectively when I have more time, so how about a long, long honeymoon? I want to learn what you're like in all your moods—sleepy, grumbly, playful, wicked…especially wicked.'

'Kingsley—'

'Say yes, Kingsley.'

'But—'

'Yes, Kingsley.' He kissed her, his mouth demanding her submission, his tongue circling and stroking. He raised his head, aware as well as she was that she was melting against him, her breasts swollen and her nipples hard and puckered against the rasp of his shirt. 'Yes, Kingsley,' he repeated again, the blue eyes holding hers.

'Yes, Kingsley,' she breathed against his mouth. 'Yes, yes, yes.'

'A quick wedding.' He kissed her again. 'Very quick. Yes?'

'Yes.' She was achingly aroused.

'Mmm.' He shifted position slightly, his own arousal rock-hard. 'I've found the perfect method to get my own way.'

The rain was thundering down now, a virtual torrent, causing the taxi to crawl along, but Rosalie didn't care. The storm had broken but she was safe. She would always be safe with Kingsley. He loved her and he understood her, and that was precious. So very precious. He had been worth waiting for.

'Never doubt my love for a moment.' His voice was thick with desire. 'Never. All the doubts, all the fears, we'll deal with them one at a time, together. You're not alone, my love. Whilst I've breath in my body I'm yours.'

She clung to him, wishing they were alone rather than in a taxi in busy London streets. But there was all the future to be alone together; it stretched, bright and wonderful in front of her eyes, dazzling her.

She could give this man all the love she had stored up in her heart because he wouldn't hurt her, they were bound by forces that had brought them together and would keep them together. One beating heart in two bodies.

EPILOGUE

IT WAS a simple wedding, but none the less perfect because of it.

The bride looked radiant in a pale silver dress created from chiffon and lace, and she carried a bouquet of delicate orchids, their fragile petals just touched with pink and threaded through with silver ribbons. Kingsley couldn't take his eyes off her, the love shining out of his face making all the women cry, especially one or two who had harboured vain hopes in their voluptuous bosoms.

The September day was one of brilliant sunshine, and after the reception for family and friends at a lush London hotel there was dancing until late in the night under the stars on the landscaped lawns, the champagne continuing to flow until the last guest retired.

Kingsley had planned a three-month honeymoon in various exotic places, but that night, he'd said, they were going somewhere special. They left the last of their guests still dancing and slipped away together to the limousine Kingsley had waiting, the uniformed driver resplendent and the car seeming to stretch forever as they climbed inside, Rosalie giggling with excitement and champagne.

'Where are we going?' Rosalie felt as though she were in a dream, a dream she never wanted to wake up from.

'Wait and see, Mrs Ward.' Kingsley's eyes were brilliant in the dim light. At some time during the night he had undone his bow-tie, which now hung either side of his unfastened collar, his jacket slung on the seat of the car. He looked hard and dangerous and breathtakingly handsome, and but for the driver she knew she would have ripped his clothes off on the spot.

She lay cradled in his arms in the car as they kissed, their breath intermingling, but when she asked him, plaintively, how long it was going to be before they were alone, he laughed and told her to be patient.

'I can't be.' She turned her face up to him, rubbing her hand over his lower body beneath the concealing folds of her dress. 'I want you.'

She felt his flesh leap and smiled into his eyes as his hand came out and caught hers. 'Temptress,' he muttered huskily. 'Do you want me to take you right now in the back of the car?'

'I wouldn't mind.'

'Well, I would. Our wedding night is going to be long and slow, and I'm going to spend all night showing you how much I love you, and in comfort. I want to touch and taste and explore over and over again.'

The throbbing ache in the core of her that his words had aroused was just penance for her earlier teasing.

When the car stopped Kingsley had been kissing her for a while, voluptuously enjoying her in the warm velvety darkness as he'd used her submissive mouth to slowly build them both to peaks of arousal, and so she glanced up in surprise, flushed and bright-eyed.

'Kingsley, this is…' Her voice trailed away as her eyes widened.

Beth and George had sold up and were due to leave for New Zealand the very next day after the wedding, and Rosalie had been sad at their going, part of her knowing she would miss the sanctuary of their exquisite old house as well as her aunt.

'Yours.' He finished her sentence, before opening the car door and pulling her out. After he'd dismissed the driver they walked to the front door through the perfumed darkness of the garden she had thought was lost to her for ever, and then he was opening the door and pulling her into the hall. 'We wanted a house in England, so why not this one you love so much?' he said softly. 'It's all empty for you to furnish as you like, except for the master bedroom, which I've furnished for us for tonight, but you can change it if you don't like it.'

'Oh, Kingsley...' Words failed her. She wandered out into the sleeping garden at the back of the house before they went upstairs, the velvet sky overhead with myriad twinkling stars and the scents and smells of the wonderful old garden reminding her of the first time Kingsley had come here with her.

And then they went upstairs, and she gasped with delight at the bedroom as he opened the door. The bed was luscious and huge, a magnificent wicked piece of wantonness with soft, billowy covers and pillows galore, one third at the head of it surrounded by carpeted shelving for books or tapes or magazines. The colour scheme was gold and cream, the carpet thick enough to sink in, and the beautiful cream and gold drapes at the window drifted in the slight breeze from the sweet-smelling garden below.

A TV the size of a small cinema—to Rosalie's fascinated eyes—took up one corner, the door to the *en suite* open and showing a wonderful bathroom following the same colour scheme as the bedroom.

'So this is why Beth and George moved into rented accommodation and packed all their furniture off to New Zealand weeks ago?' Rosalie turned round to Kingsley, who was watching her with laughing eyes. 'Oh, darling, what can I say? How can I find words to tell you how much I love you?'

'You don't have to.' He reached out for her, his hands

moving over the perfect loveliness of her as he whispered huskily, 'You've the rest of your life to show me, my darling.'

Her gaze moved to his mouth and she wondered how she could ever have thought it was ruthless. It caressed hers and she closed her eyes, her slight silver frame fitting into the hard, lean darkness of the man she loved with all her heart.

He kissed her heavy eyelids, one after the other, and then her ears, her throat, before returning to her mouth. He undressed her slowly, pouring kisses on every part of her flesh until she was quivering with a need that made her tremble as she undressed him.

He was already hugely aroused, and his impressive maleness caused an involuntary arch of anticipation as he drew her towards the epicurean bed. This was her husband, her love, and in spite of all that had happened in her past she felt as eager and awestruck as a virgin.

He admired and loved her with his eyes, his hands and his mouth, his boldness calling forth an uninhibitedness she wouldn't have thought herself capable of. His tongue, his hands were magic, and as he continued to pleasure her he did things no one else had ever done and she knew she had been waiting for him all her life without knowing it. He was part of her, wound into her bones, her blood and her heart.

Pleasure coursed through her, focused on the places he touched with such loving precision. He seemed to read her mind, to know what she wanted next, what gave her the most pleasure at just the right moment, and she was conscious of thinking she just hadn't known it could *be* like this. This was joy and bliss and erotic fulfilment beyond her wildest imaginings...

'I love you, my darling. We're going to go on and on

and it's going to get better and better. Do you believe that?'

She couldn't believe anything could be better than what she was experiencing right now. She reached her arms to him, drawing him up and over her as she said, 'Please, please…'

He waited no longer, possessing her so completely that their oneness was the only living thing in the universe, every cell and fragment of her body filled with passion and pleasure and him.

This was her life, her future. This was her love.

THE UNEXPECTED
MISTRESS

by

Sara Wood

Childhood in Portsmouth meant grubby knees, flying pigtails and happiness for **Sara Wood**. Poverty drove her from typist and seaside landlady to teacher till writing finally gave her the freedom her Romany blood craved. Happily married, she has two handsome sons: Richard is married, calm, dependable, drives tankers; Simon is a roamer – silversmith, roofer, welder, always with beautiful girls. Sara lives in the Cornish countryside. Her glamorous writing life alternates with her passion for gardening which allows her to be carefree and grubby again!

CHAPTER ONE

CASSIAN lounged contentedly on the roof of the large rented house which he shared in typically cosmopolitan style with two English strippers, a Buddhist from Florida, and a Moroccan herbalist. It was late, the sky a dense black scattered with stars, the air warm and still.

He and his literary agent were watching the snake charmers and acrobats performing in the *Djemaa el Fna*, Marrakesh's extraordinary market square. His agent's mouth had been almost permanently open since they'd emerged onto the roof ten minutes ago and Cassian's dark eyes hadn't stopped twinkling in gentle amusement.

'A tad different from central London,' his agent marvelled with great understatement, goggling at a group of Saharan nomads who were sweeping majestically through the square.

Men in rags, walking like kings, Cassian thought, reflecting on his belief that outer trappings often concealed the real person beneath.

'Same world. Different values and desire. Life stripped to its bare necessities. The need to eat, to find shelter and love,' he observed lazily.

Stirred but not staggered by the scene below, Cassian poured coffee from the silver beaked pot and offered his agent a sweet pastry. After living here for a year, it had all become gloriously familiar to him; the huge lanterns illuminating the storytellers, the contortionists, the clowns and boy dancers, and the crowd of Berbers mingling with an incongruous sprinkling of awestruck tourists.

By now his ears were attuned to the din. Drums, cymbals and western music drowned the hubbub of voices—and also, mercifully, the groans coming from the stall of the dentist who was enthusiastically wielding his pliers.

A willing slave to intense feelings and sensuality, Cassian delightedly inhaled the powerful aroma of humanity mingling with spices and the smell of cooking from the blazing braziers dotted around the square. And he wondered curiously where his passion for living life to the hilt would take him next.

'So,' said his agent in bright cocktail-speak, clearly uncomfortable with the culture shock he was experiencing. 'Now you've finished the book, I suppose you and your son are both going home for a while?'

Cassian sipped his Turkish coffee, appreciating its richness. 'Jai and I have no home,' he said gravely.

And yet... As if to contradict that statement, an image had come unexpectedly into his mind. Instead of the black night and the ochre buildings, the blazing torches and the patchwork of bright colours below, he saw emerald-green hills laced with grey stone walls, ancient woodlands and small stone villages by a cool, rushing river. The Yorkshire Dales. And, specifically, Thrushton.

Astonished, he inhaled deeply as if he could feel the freshness of the champagne air in his lungs. For the first time in his life he felt a pang of longing for a place he'd once known and loved.

That startled him: he who'd spent his adult life passionately embracing a setting, teasing out its darker side to create one of his popular thrillers...and then leaving without regret for new sensations, new horizons.

'Still, you must have a great sense of relief,' his agent persisted. 'You've got your freedom back, for a start. No more sitting hunched over a PC for hour after hour,' he added jovially, attempting to penetrate the mysterious psyche of the man he knew only as Alan Black.

'I never lose my freedom. If I ever felt it was threatened,' Cassian replied quietly, 'I'd stop writing at once.'

'Hell, don't do that! We've got another film producer offering us an option on your next book!' panicked his agent, seeing twelve per cent of a fortune vanishing overnight.

But Cassian had stopped listening. His sharp ears had heard an unusual noise in the narrow alley beside the house. Moving to the low parapet, he could see a man there, curled up in a foetal position and moaning with pain. Someone was running into the darkness of the souk beyond. Without making a fuss, he politely excused himself and went to investigate.

It was a few minutes before he realised that the bruised and battered man he'd hauled into the house was Tony Morris, his old enemy from that very part of England which had sprung to mind so surprisingly at the mention of the word 'home'.

As Tony blubbered and whimpered, and he silently washed the blood from the flabby face, Cassian found his longing for Yorkshire increasing quite alarmingly, the memories coming hot and fast and extraordinarily insistent.

Ruled by his instincts, he acknowledged that perhaps it was time to go back. Time to immerse himself in the landscape which had reached like loving arms into his unhappy soul and given him solace and peace of mind. Time also to face the devils that haunted his dreams.

And then Tony offered him the opportunity on a plate to do just that.

Laura slammed two mugs on the table and doled out the last of the coffee granules with a preoccupied expression. Coffee wasn't the only thing she'd have to eliminate from her shopping list. Poverty was staring her in the face.

'Sue,' she said urgently to her life-long friend, 'I've got to get a new job sharpish.'

Sue looked sympathetic. 'Nothing yet, then?'

'No. *And* I've been searching in Harrogate all this week!'

'Wow!' Sue exclaimed, suitably impressed.

Her friend was the only person who knew what a huge step that had been. It was a month now since she'd lost her job. Night after night, Laura had lain awake worrying about her child's future, his poor health, his fragile state of mind. For Adam's sake she *must* find work! She must! she'd thought with increasing panic.

No work was available in Thrushton where she lived, nor in the small community of Grassington nearby. None, either in nearby Skipton.

Up to now her entire existence had been confined to the rolling dales and picturesque stone villages surrounding the River Wharfe. Of the rest of Yorkshire, she knew nothing— let alone England—and the thought of travelling further to work had made her blanch with apprehension.

It was a stupid reaction, she knew, but not one of her making. If she had ever been born with self-assurance and confidence, then it had been crushed by her restrictive upbringing. If she'd ever had ambition then that too had withered and died, thanks to the critical tongue of her adoptive father's sister, Aunt Enid, and the scorn and cruelty of her father's son Tony.

She knew she was submissive and reticent to a fault. But the needs of her own child meant a radical rethink of her life. It didn't matter to *her* that she wore jumble sale clothes, but she had to earn good money and buy some decent gear for Adam—or he'd continue to be bullied unmercifully.

'I'd do anything,' she said fervently, 'to ensure we can stay here. This house is my…my…'

'Comfort blanket,' supplied Sue with a grin. 'Be honest. It is.'

Laura glared at her horribly perceptive friend and then let her tense mouth soften in recognition.

'You're right. But I need stability and familiarity in my life. Adam too. We'd both go to pieces anywhere else.'

'I know, duck. I think you've got real grit to pluck up the courage to hunt for work in Harrogate.' Raising a plump arm, Sue patted Laura's long and elegant hand in admiration. 'But…it'd be a bit of a nightmare journey without a car, wouldn't it?'

Laura grimaced. 'Two buses and a train and a long walk. What choice do I have, though? Nine-year-old boys can eat for England. Mind you, employers weren't exactly falling over themselves to take me on. I'm fed up! I've exhausted every avenue,' she complained crossly.

'Must be *some*thing out there,' Sue encouraged.

Laura rolled her eyes. 'You bet there is. Lap dancing.'

Tension made her join in with Sue's giggles but it was frustrated resentment that made her jump up and perform a few poses around an imaginary pole. She adopted an 'I am available' face and moved her body with sinuous grace. It seemed an easy way to earn money.

'Crikey. I'd give you five quid!' Sue said admiringly. 'Madly erotic. But then you've got the most fab legs and body. That monumentally baggy shirt would have to go, though,' she advised. 'Wrong colour!'

Hastily smoothing her tousled hair, Laura subsided breathily into the chair and wriggled down her slim skirt— which she'd acquired like most of her clothes from the local jumble sale and which was almost a size too small.

She felt quite shaken by her erotic performance. She was a natural. Perhaps these things could be passed on genetically, she thought gloomily. After all, she was a bastard. That had been rammed into her enough times.

If only she knew what her real mother had been like! Then she wouldn't have to wonder if her mother *had* been a tart, as Aunt Enid had claimed.

'She was a slut!' Enid—her father's sister—had claimed. 'Your mother slept with anyone and everyone. And married to your father, a respectable solicitor! Diana brought the name of Morris into disrepute.'

Laura would never know the truth. Would never know why her mother had been unfaithful. Would never know the identity of her real father. Nobody else knew that she *wasn't* George Morris's child.

As soon as Laura was born, her mother had run away and George had had no choice but to bring Laura up as his daughter. Which he'd resented. That explained his indifference and total lack of affection.

Misty-eyed, she looked around the comfortable, stone-flagged kitchen with its huge Aga and deep inglenook fireplace, wincing as she imagined the uproar when her mother's infidelity had been discovered. And she understood how hard it must have been for her 'father' to accept his wife's bastard.

Together with Aunt Enid, he had created a regime so narrow and unbending in an effort to keep her on the straight and narrow, that she had turned into a timid mouse. Albeit, she thought wryly, with unrivalled domestic skills and a posture a ramrod would be proud of. Pity she didn't have other qualifications. She might be more employable.

'You know, Sue,' she confided, 'sometimes I've felt as though I'm *prostituting* myself at interviews with all that smiling, all that looking eager and charming and willing…oh, I hate it all!'

Close to losing control, she thumped the table, and Sue jumped in surprise at Laura's unusual vehemence.

'Something'll turn up,' her friend soothed, not very convincingly. 'I've got my dental appointment later, in Harrogate. I'll get the local paper for you to look through the Jobs Vacant column.'

'I'll do anything decent and legal. I'm willing to learn, conscientious and hard-working…but the downside is that I'm plain and shy and my clothes are out of the Ark,' Laura muttered. 'I see all the other applicants glowing with confidence in their make-up and attractive outfits and I know they're laughing at me behind their smooth, lily-white hands!' Glaring, she held up her own. 'Look at mine! They're rough enough to snag concrete. I tell you, Sue, I'd be just as good as them, given a lick of lippy, a decent haircut and a ten-gallon drum of hand cream!'

'I've never known you so forceful,' Sue marvelled.

'Well. It's because I'm angry.' Laura's blue eyes flashed with rare inner fire. 'When will the world recognise that appearances aren't everything? That it's what's here—' she banged her chest vigorously '—and here—' her head had the same treatment '—that's important! And what's that removal van doing outside?' she wondered, breaking off with a frown.

'Getting lost,' suggested Sue without interest. 'Nobody round here's moving that I know about.'

Built from local rock in the Middle Ages and enlarged in the Georgian period, Thrushton Hall stood at the far end of the twenty other stone houses that comprised the tiny village, a cheerful cottage garden separating the handsome manor house from the narrow lane outside—which led only to the river.

Laura leaned across the deep window embrasure and peered through the stone mullioned window. Clearly the van driver had missed a turning. And yet the name plaque on the low drystone wall seemed to satisfy the removal men who'd jumped from the cab, because they brought out a flask and sandwiches and proceeded to settle themselves on the wall to eat.

'Well, unknown to us, we've become a designated picnic spot!' Laura declared wryly. A battered four-wheel drive cruised up and drew to a halt behind the small van. 'Here's another picnicker!' she called back to her friend. 'Huh! We'll have a coachload of tourists here in a minute and I'll have to give them sun umbrellas, waste bins and loo facil-ities! Sue, come and…!'

But her words died in her throat. From the Range Rover

emerged a tall, slim figure in black jeans and T-shirt. The breath left her lungs as if they'd been surgically deflated.

'What's the matter?' Sue hurried up, then grabbed Laura's arm with a gasp. 'Blow me! Isn't that…?'

Laura's eyes had grown huge, her lashes dark against the unnatural pallor of her face.

'Yes!' she choked. 'It's Cassian!'

His appearance was so unexpected, so utterly bizarre, that she stood rooted to the ground in numb disbelief while he chatted to the men. And then he began to turn to the house. Like children caught doing something naughty, she and Sue hastily dodged back out of sight.

'What a hunk he's become!' Sue declared. 'He's absolutely scrummy. But…why's he here—of all places?!'

Laura couldn't speak at all. Her mind was whirling, confused by the sight of the dark and sinister figure, whose sudden arrival seventeen years ago—and equally sudden disappearance five years later—had split her family apart.

She'd been ten at the time. Her father had begun to talk of nothing but a female client who'd come to his legal practice. One day he had announced that he was to marry the artist he'd been defending—and that his bride and her twelve-year-old son would be moving in. It was only then that Laura had realised George must have divorced her mother.

Tony, up till then the adored and spoilt only son, had been scarlet with fury at the news. For her, the arrival of Bathsheba and Cassian had been a revelation. Suddenly the house had burst into life with colour and laughter and music and Laura had quickly become familiar with the smell of turpentine mingling with that of the herbs and spices of exotic dishes.

But almost immediately there had been titanic rows over Cassian's behaviour. Laura could see him now; a silent and glowering boy who couldn't behave conventionally and who'd refused to fit into the community.

Vividly she recalled his defiance in the face of Aunt Enid's rigid rules and the way he'd disappeared for days, seemingly existing without food or comfort.

And while she'd envied his independence and stubborn refusal to be anyone other than himself, she'd feared that very freedom he exemplified. He had been untameable, with an adventurous, bohemian past and he came from a greater world than she or her friends could ever know or understand.

And so they were strangers to one another. She had admired and watched him from afar, wishing she had his nerve, envying his daring.

As he had grown into a young man, the depth of his inner assurance had attracted the girls like bees to a honeypot. He was the local Bad Boy, and women longed to be noticed by him. One or two were. The chosen dazed and dazzled girls had huddled in Grassington square, discussing with awe the passion they'd unwittingly unleashed, while she'd listened in horror.

And, she was ashamed to say, with a secret excitement. Not that she'd want to be part of his life at all. He scared her though she didn't know why, and she couldn't fathom what made her heart race whenever she set eyes on him.

It was quickening now, bringing a flush to her cheeks. Squirming with dismay, she took a cautious peek out of the window. Cassian had resumed talking to the removal men, one foot on the low wall, an expressive hand gesticulating as he described something.

A strange exhilaration caught hold of her, something that coiled warm and throbbing in her veins. She stared, mesmerised. Cassian had charisma. He had always been different, magnetic, special.

Laura shot a glance at Sue. Even her sensible, down-to-earth friend was gazing open-mouthed at him, her expression nakedly admiring. And Sue was in a state of tension, her fingers gripping the curtain tightly.

Just as she was, Laura thought in surprise, releasing the creased curtain in embarrassment. She didn't like being disturbed like this and she felt uncomfortable that her nerves were jiggling about all over the place.

Why should he make her pulses leap about so erratically? It didn't make sense. Oh, he was good-looking enough in a foreign kind of way. Handsome, she supposed. But so were many other men who'd walked into the hotel where she'd worked: young, affluent and personable, and she'd been indifferent to them. And they to her, of course!

Bemused, she scrutinised him carefully in an effort to solve the mystery. And felt her fascination go up a notch or two. His hair was still dark—black and gleaming with the richness of a raven's wing—but it was shorter now, the rebellious curls sleekly hugging the beautiful shape of his head.

His face... Well, those high cheekbones and carved jaw would make any woman's heart beat faster coupled with the dark, intense eyes and sexily mobile mouth. She suppressed a small quiver in her breast.

'What's he doing?' hissed Sue.

'Don't know.'

Her voice had been hoarse because his liquid and relaxed gestures had caused the muscles to ripple beneath his black T-shirt in a way that left her breathless.

'He's beautifully toned,' Sue whispered, eyes agog. 'Not over-developed—just perfect. Wow! And he used to be so skinny.'

No, Laura wanted to say. He was always strong and wiry. But she didn't want to betray her ridiculously chaotic hormones by speaking. His shoulders and chest had certainly expanded. Cassian's torso was now a devastatingly attractive triangle of powered muscle and sinew.

She watched him, her eyes wide and puzzled. He was more than just a perfect body. He...

She stiffened, suddenly realising what drew her to him.

Cassian possessed what she—and many others—might search for all their lives. Something that money couldn't buy. Total self-assurance.

She let out her tightly held breath. Cassian was sublimely at home in his own skin, whereas she had lived in the shadow of someone else's rules and had moulded her behaviour to the will of others. She was someone else's creation. He was his own.

And she longed to be like him.

Suddenly he laughed, and she felt a sharpness like a vice in her chest as she was almost bowled over by the sheer force of life which imbued his whole body—his brilliant white teeth flashing wickedly in the darkness of his face, the tilt of his chin, the warmth in those hot, dark eyes.

'Now that's what I call sex appeal!' Sue whispered in awe. 'Isn't he like his mother? What was her name?'

Laura swallowed and found a husky voice emerging. 'Bathsheba.'

'Unusual. Suited her.'

'Exotic,' Laura agreed.

His mother had been the most beautiful and vibrant woman she'd ever known. Bathsheba had dark, wavy hair, eyes that flashed like scimitars when she was happy, and a face with the same classically chiselled bones as Cassian's.

For the five years that Bathsheba had been her stepmother, neither she nor Cassian had taken much notice of her. But then Enid had kept them apart as much as possible.

And tragically, during the time that Bathsheba and her father were together, Laura had witnessed how two people could love one another but be incapable of living with one another. They were torn asunder by their differing views—particularly where the disciplining of Cassian was concerned.

'Bathsheba and Cassian vanished overnight, I remember,' Sue mused.

Laura nodded. 'They *walked* out into the night, taking

nothing with them! I was appalled. I wondered where
they'd live, how they'd cope. George never recovered, you
know.'

Her eyes softened. It seemed incredible that one person
could have such an effect on another. Her stern, unbending
father had died of a broken heart. She shivered, shrinking
from the destructiveness of passion. In her experience, it
had never done anyone any good.

'Well, Cassian's got over his feelings about Thrushton.
He's coming up the path!' Sue marvelled. 'Oh, why does
something riveting like this have to happen, when I'm going on holiday tomorrow?!'

Laura couldn't believe her eyes. 'He's hardly likely to
stay long. He hated this house!' she said, feeling an irrational sense of panic. 'This can't be a social call. He never
noticed me, hardly knew I existed. And he just loathed
Tony—'

She gasped. A key was rattling in the lock. There was a
pause. Cassian must have realised that the kitchen door
wasn't locked at all. The latch was lifted. Laura couldn't
breathe. *Why did he have a key?*

The door creaked open a fraction. And then it was flung
back with considerable force.

In an instant, the room seemed to be filled with him,
with the blistering force of his anger. She cringed back
instinctively by the half-concealing fall of the curtain,
afraid of his potency and bewildered by the physical impact
he had on her.

Cassian simmered with a volcanic rage as he scanned the
kitchen with narrowed and glittering eyes. And all too soon,
the full force of his incandescent fury became focussed directly at her.

CHAPTER TWO

THE smell of freshly baked bread had hit him immediately as he'd opened the door—even before it had swung fully open. Although his senses had enjoyed the aroma, he'd tensed every muscle in his body.

It meant one thing. A sitting tenant. And a legal minefield ahead.

Unsettled, he'd paused to collect himself. He had wanted to be alone here when he first arrived. To chase away the past. That was why he'd left Jai in Marrakesh, exploring the High Atlas mountains with one of their Berber friends.

Instead, it looked as if he'd have to chase a tenant out first! Furious with Tony for not mentioning that he'd rented the place out, he'd thrust at the door with an impatient hand and stepped into the room.

His heart had beat loud and hard as he'd entered the house where he'd cut his teeth on conflict, toughened his character and learnt to deal with Hell. He'd steeled himself.

And then he'd seen Laura.

The shock rocked him. It was a moment before he could collect his wits, a fearsome scowl marring his features and his eyes narrowing in disbelief as he realised the situation.

'*You!*' he growled, his voice deep with disappointment.

Of all people! She ought to have gone years ago, left this house and made a new start in life!

When she flinched, obviously struck dumb by his greeting, he scowled harder still, silently heaping vicious curses on Tony's fat head. Her huge eyes were already wary and reproachful. Instinctively he knew that she'd weep pathetically when he turned her out and he'd feel a heel.

'Hi, Cassian!'

He started, and glanced sideways in response to the cheery greeting from a strawberry blonde.

'Sue,' he recalled shortly and she looked pleased.

In a second or two he had assessed her. A ring. Biting into her finger. Married for a while, then. Weight increase from children or comfortable living—perhaps both. Her clothes were good, her hair professionally tinted.

She didn't interest him. He turned his gaze back to Laura, drawn by her mute dismay and her total stillness. And those incredible black-fringed eyes.

'W-what…are you doing here?' she stumbled breathily.

Cassian's mouth tightened, his brows knitted heavily with impatience. She didn't know! Tony had taken the coward's way out, it seemed, and not told his adopted sister what he'd done with the house he'd inherited on his father's death. Little rat! Selfish to the last!

'I gather Tony didn't warn you I was coming,' he grated.

Her lips parted in dismay and began to tremble. For the first time he realised they weren't thin and tight at all, but full and soft like the bruised petals of a rose.

'No!' She looked at him in consternation. 'I—I haven't heard from him for nearly two years!'

'I see,' he clipped.

The frightened Laura flicked a nervous glance at the removal van. Her brow furrowed in confusion and she bit that plush lower lip with neat white teeth as the truth apparently dawned.

'You're not…oh, no! No!' she whispered in futile denial, her hands restlessly twisting together.

And he wanted to shake her. It annoyed him intensely that she hadn't changed. This was the old Laura, self-effacing, timid, frightened. He did the maths. She'd been fifteen when he'd left. That made her twenty-seven now. Old enough to realise that she was missing out on life.

His scowl deepened and she shrank back as if he'd hit her, then with a muttered exclamation she whirled and fran-

tically grabbed a tea towel, beginning to polish the hell out
of some cutlery that was drying on the drainer. It was a
totally illogical thing to do, but typical.

Cassian felt the anger remorselessly expanding his chest.
His eyes darkened to black coals beneath his heavy brows.

She'd always been desperately cleaning things in an attempt to be Enid's little angel, not realising that she would
never achieve her aim and she might as well cut loose and
fling her dinner at the vicious old woman.

It appalled him that she hadn't come out of her shell.
Well, she'd have to do just that, from this moment on.

'Just stop doing that for a moment.'

Grim-faced, he took a step nearer and she looked up
warily, all moist-eyed and trembling.

'I—I need to!' she blurted out.

'Displacement therapy?' he suggested irritably.

Close up, he was surprised by the sweetness of her face.
It was small and heart-shaped with sharply defined cheekbones and a delicate nose. Her rich brown hair looked nondescript and badly cut—though clean and shiny in the
morning light which streamed through the window. His
sharp senses picked up the scent of lavender emanating
from her.

And signs of fear. Although her body was rigid, there
was a tiny twitch at the corner of her mouth where she was
trying to control a quivering lip. Perhaps she knew his arrival presented some sort of threat to her beloved security,
he mused.

'I—I don't know what you mean!' she protested.

Her whole body had adopted a defensive pose. Arms
across breasts. Shoulders hunched, eyes wary. He sighed.
This wouldn't be easy.

'I realise this is a shock, me barging in, but I didn't
expect to see anyone here,' he said gruffly, softening his
voice a little without intending to.

'Tony gave you a key!' she cried, bewildered.

'That's right.'

'Why?'

He frowned. She'd sussed out the situation, hadn't she? 'To get in,' he said drily.

'But...'

He saw her swallow, the sweet curve of her throat pale against the faded blue of her threadbare shirt. Noticing his gaze, she blushed and put down the tea towel, her hand immediately lifting again to conceal the tatty collar.

His body-reading skills came automatically into use. Obviously she was poor. And she was proud, he noted. Slender hands, roughened from physical work. Pale face... Indoor work, then. She must be on night shifts—or out of a job, since she was home on a weekday.

Not married or engaged, no sign of a ring. But several pictures of a child in the room. Baby shots, a toddler, a school snap of a kid a bit younger than his own son. He felt intrigued. Wanted to learn more.

'I'm confused. That removal van...' She cleared her throat, her voice shaking with nerves. 'It can't...it doesn't mean that...that Tony has let you stay here with me?!' she asked in a horrified croak.

So that was what she'd thought. 'No. It doesn't. But—'

'Oh!' she cried, interrupting him. 'That's a relief!'

He was diverted before he could correct the conclusion she'd drawn. Laura's slender body had relaxed as if she'd let out a tense breath, the action drawing his eyes down to where her breasts might be hiding beneath the shirt which was at least two sizes too big.

Fascinated by her, he kept his investigation going and finished his scrutiny, observing the poor quality of her skirt and scuffed sneakers. Long legs, though. Slightly tanned, slender and shapely.

He felt a kick of interest in his loins and strangled it at birth. Laura wasn't his kind of woman. He adored women

of all kinds, but he preferred them with fire coming out of
their ears.

'Laura,' he began, unusually hesitant.

Sue jumped in. 'Hang on. If you haven't come to stay,
why bring a removal van?' she asked in a suspicious tone.

'I'm about to explain,' he snapped.

He frowned at her because he didn't want her to be there.
This was between him and Laura. Like it or not, Laura
would have to go and he didn't want anyone else compli-
cating matters when he told her the truth.

He'd tell her straight, no messing. Disguising the news
with soft words wouldn't make a scrap of difference to the
situation.

He sought Laura's wondering gaze again, strangely irri-
tated by her quietly desperate passivity. She ought to be
yelling at him, demanding to know what he was doing,
persuading him to go and never return. But she meekly
waited for the world to fall in on her.

He wanted to jerk her into life. To make her lose her
temper and to see some passion fly. At the same time, he
felt an overwhelming urge to protect her as he might protect
a defenceless animal or a tiny baby. She was too vulnerable
for her own good. Too easy to wound. Hell, what was he
going to do?

In two strides he'd breached the distance between them.
With the wall behind her, she had nowhere to go though
he had the impression that she would have vanished
through it if she could.

Grimly he took her arm, felt her quiver when he did so.
Looking deeply into her extraordinary eyes, he saw that she
recognised he was going to tell her something unpleasant.

'Sit down,' he ordered, hating the way she made him
feel. Firmly he pushed her rigid body into the kitchen chair.

And inexplicably he kept a hand on her shoulder, intensely aware of its fragility, of the fineness of the bone
structure of her face as she stared up at him in fear and

apprehension, drowning him, making him flounder with those great big eyes.

'What is it?' she whispered.

Feeling distinctly unsettled by her, he dragged up a chair and sat close to her. Immediately she shrank away from him, covering her knees with her hands primly. His mouth tightened.

He loathed seeing her like this, a slave to her past, to the constant belittling by Enid which had relentlessly ground away her confidence. It had been just like the elements, the wind and the rain out there on the moors, grinding down solid rock over the years. She needed to leave. To find life. Her true self.

Confused by his own passionate views of Laura's future, he plunged in, eager to send her out into the world.

'When I said that I'm not staying here with you, Laura,' he said firmly, 'I meant that *you* won't be living here at all. I've bought Thrushton Hall from Tony. I'm moving in.'

'Moving…in?'

She was blinking, her eyes glazed over as if she didn't understand. He tried again so that there would be no mistake.

'Correct. You, Laura, will have to move out. Pronto.'

Laura let out a strangled gasp. Her stomach went into free fall, making her feel faint.

'No!' she whispered in pure horror. 'This is my home! All I've ever known! Tony wouldn't do that to me!'

'Yes, he would,' Sue muttered. 'He's a loathsome little creep.'

'That's true,' Cassian said in heartfelt agreement.

Laura stared at the implacable Cassian, her brain in a fog. 'This is ridiculous! I live here!'

'Not any more.'

She gave a little cry. 'I've been paying the bills and maintaining the house ever since Tony disappeared! You— you can't turn us out of here!' she said weakly.

'Us.'

Suddenly alert, he turned to scan the photographs around the room, his eyebrows asking an unspoken question.

'My son,' she mumbled, still dazed by Cassian's announcement. 'Adam,' she added blankly as tears of despair welled up in her eyes. 'He's nine.' She saw Cassian's eyes narrow, as he began to make a calculation and she jumped in before he could say anything. 'Yes, if you're wondering, I was eighteen when he was born!' she defied hysterically, bracing herself for some sign of disapproval.

Cassian, however, seemed unfazed. 'You and your son,' he said quietly. 'No one else living with you?'

Suddenly she wanted to startle him as he'd startled her. Panic and fear were making her unstable. A spurt of anger flashed through her and with uncharacteristic impetuosity she answered;

'I'm totally alone. I never *had* a husband—or even a partner!'

Everyone here knew how the travelling salesman from Leeds had flattered her by pretending she was beautiful. He must have seen a gauche, nervous and drab female in ill-fitting clothes and decided it would be easy for his silver tongue to dazzle her. Laura realised now that her transparent innocence, coupled with her teenage desperation to be loved, had been her downfall.

She flinched. There had been one fateful evening of bewilderment and repugnance—on her part—and then the arrival of Adam, nine months later. The shame of what she'd done would live with her for ever. And yet she had Adam, who'd brought joy to her dreary life.

Annoyingly, Cassian took her confession in his stride. 'I see,' he said non-committally.

Laura stiffened. 'No you don't!' she wailed. 'You stroll in here, claiming you've bought Thrushton Hall—'

'Want to see the deeds?' he enquired, foraging in the back pocket of his jeans.

The colour drained from her face when she saw the document he was holding out to her. Snatching it from him, she frantically unfolded it and read the first few lines, her heart contracting more and more as the truth sank in.

This was Cassian's house. She would have to leave. Her legs trembled.

'No! I don't believe it!' she whispered, aghast.

Despite the harshness of her childhood, this house held special memories. It was where her mother had lived. Deprived of any tangible memories of her mother, it comforted her that she walked in her mother's footsteps every day of her life. And Cassian intended to drive her away.

'You have no choice.'

Her head snapped up, sending her hair whirling about her set face. A frightening wildness was possessing her. Hot on its heels came an urge to lash out and pummel Cassian till his composure vanished and he began to notice her as a person instead of an irritating obstacle he needed to kick out of his way.

Her emotions terrified and appalled her. They seemed to fill her body, surging up uncontrollably with an evil, unstoppable violence. She fought them, groping for some kind of discipline over them because she didn't know what would happen if she ever allowed those clamouring passions to surface.

'You don't want this house! You can't possibly want to live here!' she whispered, hoarse with horror.

His calm, oddly warm eyes melted into hers.

'I do. I can.'

She took a deep, shuddering breath but she was losing a battle with her temper. Her child's security was threatened. She wouldn't allow that.

'This is my *home*!' she insisted tightly, clinging for dear life to the last vestiges of restraint. 'Adam's home!'

He shrugged as if homes were unimportant. 'I had the

impression that it was Tony's. Now it's mine. Do you pay rent?'

'N-no—'

'Then you have no legal rights to stay.'

Laura gasped, her hand flying to her mouth in consternation. 'Surely I do! I must have some kind of protection—'

'There could be an expensive legal case,' he conceded. 'But you'd have to go eventually. You'd save time and hassle if you did so straight away.' He smiled in a friendly way, as if that would console her. 'You'll find somewhere else. You might discover that moving from Thrushton turns out to be a good idea in the long run.'

She glared and was incensed when his eyes flickered with satisfaction. It was as if he welcomed her anger!

'What do you know?' she yelled. Dear heaven! she thought. She was losing control, acting like a banshee—and couldn't stop herself! 'It's a stupid idea! For a start, I don't have any money!' she choked, scarlet from the shameful admission. But he had to know her circumstances. 'There's nowhere I can go!' she cried in agitation. 'Nowhere I can afford!'

He continued to gaze at her with a steely eye, his heart clearly unmoved by her plight. And she knew that her hours in her beloved house—*his* house, she thought furiously—were probably numbered.

'It's true. She's dead broke. Lost her job,' confirmed Sue, suddenly butting in. Cassian jerked his head around in surprise as if he, like Laura, had forgotten Sue was there. 'I reckon she can stay put if she chooses—'

'I don't deny that.' Cassian flung an arm across the back of the chair, his eyes relentlessly fixed to Laura's. She flinched as his expression darkened, becoming unnervingly menacing. 'But you ought to know that living with me wouldn't be pleasant,' he drawled.

'Meaning?' Sue demanded.

He shrugged. 'I'd be…difficult.' His eyes seemed to be issuing a direct challenge. 'I'd eat her food, play music late at night, change the locks…' There was a provocative curve to his mouth, something…unnerving in his expression as his gaze swept her up and down. 'Laura, I'm not changing my way of living for anybody, and I have the distinct impression that you'd be shocked by the way I wander about half-naked after my morning shower, with just a small towel covering me and my—'

'Please!' she croaked.

'I'm just warning you,' he murmured with a shrug.

She felt hot. The rawness of his huge energy field reached out to enfold her in its greedy clasp and she instinctively flattened herself against the back of the chair.

She blushed, ashamed to be assailed by the unwanted rivulets of molten liquid which were coursing through her veins. His sexuality was too blatant, too unavoidable. This was something alien to her and she couldn't cope with it. Didn't want it at all. Living with him would be a nightmare.

'It's no use! I can't stay if he's living here!' she declared to Sue shakily. 'Sharing would be impossible!'

'Don't you give up!' Sue snapped. She glared at Cassian. 'Laura's been far too sheltered all her life to manage anywhere else—so you leave her alone, you ruthless, selfish brute. Push off back where you came from!'

Cassian rose, his eyes dark and glittering. 'I'm not going anywhere, whatever insults you choose to hurl at me. I'm moving in, once the removal men have finished their early lunch.'

'Lunch?' With a start, Sue glanced at the kitchen clock and let out a groan. 'Oh, crikey! My dental appointment! Never mind. I'll cancel it,' she offered urgently. 'You need backup, Laura—'

'No,' she said quickly, sick with nerves, hating the wobble in her voice.

This was her battle. Sue was making things worse.

Cassian had visibly tensed when Sue had shouted at him. He'd listen to logic, she was sure, but he wouldn't be bullied.

Proud and erect, she stood up with great dignity, conscious, however, that her five-seven didn't impinge on Cassian's six foot.

And they were now only inches apart, waves of heat thickening the space between them, pouring into her, the heavy, lifeless air clogging up her throat. Laura gulped, feeling that all the power was draining from her legs till they trembled from weakness.

'Well! Are you fighting me, Laura?' he taunted.

Rebellion drained away too when she met his challenging eyes. His confidence was daunting. How could she fight him when he held all the cards?

'I—I...'

'Still the mouse,' he mocked, but with a hint of regret in his dark regard. 'Still meekly huddling in the corner, afraid of being trodden on.'

'You rat!' Sue gasped.

'It's true!' he cried, his voice shaking in an inexplicable passion. 'She can't even stand up for her own flesh and blood!'

'Leave her alone!' Sue raged.

'I can't! She has to go! I have no intention of having a lodger around!' Cassian snapped.

With a whimper, Laura jerked her head away and found herself staring straight at the photo she'd taken of her son on his ninth birthday. Her heart lurched miserably.

Adam looked ecstatic. They'd spent the day at Skipton, where they'd explored the castle, picnicked by the river, and splashed out on a special treat of tea and cakes in a cosy café. Cheap and simple as day trips went, but a joy for both of them.

The recriminations surrounding his conception had been hard to bear. Yet, even in the depths of her shame, Laura had felt a growing joy. This child was hers. And when he was born, her emotions had overwhelmed her, unnerving her with their unexpected intensity.

Love had poured from her and it had felt as if her heart would burst with happiness. She'd never known she had such feelings. Her child had reached into her very core and found a well of passion hidden there.

For hours she had cuddled her baby, his warm, living flesh snuggling up to her. And it had been more than compensation for the hard, unremitting drudgery which Enid had imposed on her as a punishment for her 'lewd behaviour'.

She'd hardly cared because she had had her son to love. Someone to love her back.

Laura squared her shoulders. She would never let him down. Adam was horribly vulnerable and deeply sensitive. Cassian couldn't be allowed to uproot them both. Did he honestly imagine that they'd pack their bags without a murmur, and tramp the streets like vagabonds till someone took them in?

She flung up her head and spoke before she changed her mind. 'You're wrong about me! I *will* fight you for my home! Tooth and nail—'

'To defend your lion cub,' he murmured, his voice low and vibrating.

Her eyes hardened at his mockery. 'For the sake of my son,' she corrected in scathing tones, infuriated by his condescension. 'Sue, get going. I can deal with this better on my own. Besides, I'd rather you didn't witness the blood he sheds,' she muttered through her teeth.

'Sounds promising,' Cassian remarked lazily.

Laura ignored him because she thought she might choke with anger if she said anything. The situation clearly amused him. For her, it was deadly serious.

'Come on, Sue. Off you go and get those molars drilled,' she ordered tightly.

Secretly astonished by her own curt and decisive manner, she pushed her protesting friend towards the door.

Naturally, Sue resisted. 'I can't believe this! The worm turns! This I've gotta see!'

'I'll get the camera out,' Laura muttered. 'Please, please, go!'

'I want close-ups!' Sue hissed. 'A blow by blow account, when I get back!'

'Whatever! Go!'

It took her a minute or two before Sue could be budged but eventually she went, flinging dark and lurid warnings in Cassian's direction and promising Laura a stick of rock from Hong Kong to brain Cassian with if he was still around.

Quivering like a leaf, Laura shut the door, braced herself, and turned to face him. With Sue gone, it felt as if she was very alone. And she would be—till the following afternoon. Adam was going to his best friend's house after school and sleeping over. It was just her and Cassian, then.

Her heart thudded loudly in her chest at the strange pall of silence which seemed to have fallen on the house, intensifying the strained atmosphere.

Cassian was looking at her speculatively, his eyes half-closed in contemplation, a half-smile on his lips.

'It's a problem, isn't it?' he said mildly.

'The camera or the blood?' she flung back with rare sarcasm.

The black eyes twinkled disconcertingly. 'You and me. In this house together.'

The huskiness of his voice took her by surprise. It contrasted oddly with the intensity of his manner. There was a determined set to his jaw and the arch of his sensual mouth had flattened into a firm line.

'You can live anywhere. I can't—' she began.

'You must have friends who'd take you in,' he purred.

'I couldn't impose!'

'You don't have a choice.'

She felt close to tears of anger and frustration.

'You don't understand! I have to stay!' she insisted frantically.

'Why?'

'Because…' She went scarlet.

'Yes?' he prompted.

She stared at him, unwilling to expose her fear. But she saw no other way out.

Her eyes blazed with loathing. 'If you really want to know, I'm scared of going anywhere else!' she cried shakily.

He raised a sardonic eyebrow. 'Then it's time you did.'

She gasped. So much for compassion. But Cassian would never know what it was to be uncertain and shy, or to be uncomfortable in unfamiliar surroundings. Her pulses pounded as her heart rate accelerated.

'There's more,' she said, her lips dry with fear.

'Yes?'

She swallowed. This was deeply personal. Normally, wild horses wouldn't have dragged this out of her, but Cassian had to realise what this house meant to her.

'My…' She felt a fool. He was looking at her with cold hard eyes and she was having to expose her innermost secrets. For Adam, she told herself. And found the strength. Her eyes blazed blue and bright into his. 'My mother lived here,' she began tightly.

'So?'

She drew in a sharp breath of irritation. This wasn't going to get her anywhere. But…he'd adored his own mother. Wouldn't he understand?

'Cassian,' she grated. 'Is your mother still alive?'

He looked puzzled. 'Yes. Why?'

Thank heaven. Maybe she had a chance. 'You still see her, speak to her?'

'She's remarried. She lives in France, but yes, I see her.

And I speak to her each week. What are you getting at?' he asked curiously.

She offered up a small prayer to the Fates. 'Imagine not knowing anything about her. Not even how she looked. Think what it would have been like, not to know that she's beautiful, a gifted artist, and full of life and fire!' Her eyes glowed feverishly with desperate passion.

'I don't see the—'

'Well, that's how it is for me!' she cried shakily. 'No one will speak of my mother and all trace of her was removed the day she left.' Her voice broke and she took a moment to steady herself. 'I wouldn't know anything at all about her if it wasn't for Mr Walker—'

'Who?' he exclaimed sharply.

'He's someone in the village. A lonely old man with a vile temper but he can't walk far so I do his weekly shopping. He gives me a list and money for what he needs. I lug his shopping back, he complains about half of it and we both feel better.'

Her eyes went dreamy for a moment. Out of the blue, Mr Walker had once said that her mother was lovely. In his opinion, he'd said, Diana had been wasted on boring George Morris.

'What did he say about her?' Cassian asked warily.

She was surprised he was interested, but she smiled, remembering. 'That she was passionate about life.'

'Anything else?'

'Yes. He said she was kind and very beautiful.' Laura sighed. 'Since I'm nothing like that, I think he was probably winding me up. When I asked him for more information he refused to say anything else.'

'I see,' he clipped, dark brows meeting hard together.

'The point is that this house means more to me than just bricks and mortar and general sentimentality.' Desperate now, she felt herself leaning forwards, punching out her words. 'Thrushton Hall is all I have of my mother!' she jerked out miserably.

'Surely you must know about your mother—!'

'No! I don't!' Wouldn't he listen to her? Hadn't he heard? 'I don't know what she looked like, how or why she left me, *nothing*!'

She was aware of Cassian's stunned expression and took heart. He would see her plight and take pity on her.

'Cassian, other than the house, I have nothing else to remember her by, not one single item she ever possessed. Everything has vanished. The only actual trace of her is *me*!'

She steadied her voice, aware that it had been shaking so strongly with emotion that she'd been almost incoherent.

'I don't believe this!' he muttered.

'It's true!' she cried desperately. 'I've had to rely on my imagination! I've visualised her in this house, doing everyday things. That is where she must have stood to wash up, to cook,' she cried, pointing with a fierce jab of her finger. 'She must have sat at that very table to eat, to drink cups of tea. She would have stood at that window and gazed at the view of the soaring fells, just as I do. I can imagine her here and think of her going about her daily life. If—if I leave Thrushton,' she stumbled, 'I would have to leave behind those fragile half-memories of my mother. I'd have nothing at all left of her—and the little that I have is infinitely precious to me!' she sobbed.

She saw Cassian's jaw tighten and waited seemingly for an eternity before he answered.

'You must make enquiries about her,' he muttered, his tone flat and toneless.

Laura stared at him helplessly. How could she do that?

'I can't,' she retorted miserably.

'Afraid?' he probed, his eyes unusually watchful.

'Yes, if you must know!' she retorted with a baleful glare.

'Laura, you need to know—'

'I *can't*,' she cried helplessly. 'She's probably started a new life somewhere and I could ruin it by turning up on her doorstep. I couldn't do that to her. If it was all right for us to meet, she would have come to see me. I can't take the initiative, can I?'

He was silent, his face stony. But she knew what he was thinking. That perhaps her mother hadn't wanted to be reminded of her 'mistake'.

Closing her mind to such a horrible idea, she lifted her chin in an attempt to appear tough. Though even a fool would have noticed her stupid, feeble trembling.

'You must learn the truth—' he began huskily.

'No!'

She wrung her hands, frustrated that he couldn't see how scared she was of confronting her mother. Maybe she was flighty. Maybe she'd had a string of lovers. Maybe...

'Cassian,' she croaked, voicing her worst fear, 'I can't pursue this. I—I just couldn't face being rejected by her.'

'I don't think—'

'How the devil do you know!' she yelled. 'She left me, didn't she? Though...I suppose she knew that George would have won custody, whatever she did. She'd run away. He'd been looking after me and was a lawyer, after all. Mother must have known she didn't have a chance. To be honest, I don't even know if there was a court hearing about me. There might have been—and she might have tried to take me with her. I'll never know. Nobody would ever talk about her.' Slowly her head lifted till her troubled eyes met Cassian's. 'Mr Walker said she was full of life. Knowing how *your* mother felt, I understand why anyone with fire and energy would have found it difficult to live here,' she said with dignity.

Cassian looked uncomfortable. 'Laura,' he said in a gravelly voice, 'this is nothing to do with me. Not one of your arguments is sufficient reason for you to stay. Excuse me.'

He strode into the hall. She heard the sound of men moving about, presumably bringing in his possessions. She buried her head in her hands. She'd failed.

Cassian saw her emerging from the kitchen a few moments later, her eyes pink from crying, silver tear-track streaks glistening on her face. He gritted his teeth and continued to organise the stacking of his few belongings in the spacious hall.

Behind his bent back, he could hear the fast rasp of her breathing and sensed she was close to hysteria. And he felt as if he'd whipped a puppy.

'All done, guv,' announced one of the men.

Grateful for the diversion, he gave Len and Charlie his undivided attention. 'Thanks. Great meeting you,' he said warmly, shaking the men's hands in turn.

He slid his wallet from his back pocket and handed over the fee plus a tip, brushing away their astonished refusals of such a large sum of money. What was cash to him? It came easily and went the same way.

Charlie had told him about his new baby and Len was nearing retirement. They could both do with a little extra and he believed passionately in circulating money while he had the earning power.

'I had a windfall. Might as well share it, eh?' he explained. Like an obscene advance from a film company.

'Yeah? You're a gent,' said Len in awe.

'Thanks,' added Charlie, looking stunned.

'Have a pint on me.'

Len grinned. 'Treat the wife to a slap-up meal and a holiday, more like!'

'Buy a baby buggy!' enthused Charlie.

He saw them out, found them shaking his hand again and accepted an invitation to visit Charlie's baby and to have tea and cakes with Len and his wife. After much scribbling of addresses, he returned to the tense and angry Laura.

'What are you trying to do by gossiping out there—drive me to screaming pitch?!' she demanded furiously, her hands on shapely hips.

He stole a moment to admire them. 'Being friendly. Would you prefer I dismissed them with a curt nod and a growl?' he enquired.

She flushed. 'No...oh, you're *impossible*!'

He felt pleased. Her eyes were sparkling, a hot flush brightening her cheeks. If only he could release her emotions...

He bit back an impulse to invite her to stay so he could do just that, and followed up her remark instead.

'I just live by a different code from you. Now...will I push you into suicide mode if I just check I've got all my possessions here?'

She blinked her huge eyes, dark lashes fluttering as she eyed the stack of boxes, his luggage, and three bags of shopping.

'Do you mean...that this is all you own in the whole world?'

'It's all I need. Books, computer stuff and a few mementoes. Plus a few changes of clothes and some food stores.'

'I don't understand you,' she muttered.

'Not many people do. Now, this is what I've decided,' he said brusquely, suddenly needing to get away from the censure of her accusing eyes. 'I'd booked a room in a hotel in Grassington because I didn't know what state the house would be in. I'll go there now and leave you to start looking for temporary accommodation. Someone will take you in for a few days till you can find somewhere permanent. I'll be back in the morning. To take possession.'

He turned on his heel. Flinched at her horrified intake of breath as it rasped through emotion-choked airways.

'Cassian!' she pleaded in desperation.

But he'd opened the door, was striding up the path and

THE UNEXPECTED MISTRESS

ignoring the sound of her weeping. It would be good for her, he kept telling himself, wrenching at the door handle of his car.

She needed to find out the truth about her mother. But first she'd have to stand up for herself, to gain some strength of will—and being forced to move would make her take her life in her hands at last.

He crunched the gears. And accelerated away, angry with her for making him feel such a swine.

CHAPTER THREE

WHEN he turned up the next morning she was beating the hell out of a lump of dough and he couldn't help smiling because her small fists were clearly using it as a substitute for his head.

Her glare would have put off a seasoned terrorist but, knowing how normally reclusive she was, he could only be pleased. This was precisely the reaction he'd hoped for.

'Any progress?' he asked, coming straight to the point.

'No.' She jammed her teeth together and kneaded the bread with a fascinating ferocity. 'If you must know, I didn't try! And if you're looking for coffee,' she said, as he opened and shut cupboards at random, 'you're out of luck. There isn't any.'

He went to find some in the supplies he'd brought, came back and put on the kettle. The bread dough looked so elastic she could have used it for bungy jumping.

'You did discuss leaving with your son, didn't you?' he enquired.

Laura slammed the dough into a bowl and covered it with a cloth. 'You didn't give me a chance to tell you,' she said grimly, pushing the bowl into the warming oven to prove and slamming the heavy iron door with some force. 'Adam's been with a friend. I won't see him till this afternoon after school. Besides...' Her face crumpled and he realised that she looked very tired and pale as if she'd been up most of the night. 'I can't tell him!' she confessed helplessly.

'You can. You're stronger than you think—' he began.

'But *he's* not!'

Quite frantic now, she began to fling fresh ingredients

into a mixing bowl and he began to think that the resulting cake would weigh a ton.

'In what way isn't he strong?' he asked quietly.

'Every way,' she muttered, measuring out flour carelessly. 'Cassian, *you* know what it's like to be uprooted from somewhere familiar. You loved the narrow boat where you lived with your mother before you came here after her marriage, and you loathed Thrushton—'

'Not the house itself, or the countryside,' he corrected, wondering what she'd say if he brushed away the dusting of flour on her nose and cheeks. It made her look cute and appealing and he didn't want that. It was very distracting. 'Just the atmosphere. The stifling rules,' he said, miraculously keeping track of the conversation.

'Well, moving is traumatic, especially when you're a child. Can't you put yourself in Adam's place and see how awful it would be for him to leave the place of his birth?' she implored, pushing away her hair with the back of her hand. 'Making friends is hard for him. He'd find it a nightmare settling into another school.'

'Life's tough. Children need to be challenged,' he said softly. He passed her a coffee.

'Challenged?!' She flung in the flour haphazardly and began to fold it into the cake mixture as if declaring war on it. 'He's sensitive. It would destroy him!' she cried, her face aflame with desperation.

'Here. That'll turn into a rugby ball if you're not careful. Let me.'

He took the bowl from her shaking hands, combined the flour and the abused mixture with a metal spoon then scooped it all into a cake tin. Gently he slid the tin into the baking oven and checked the clock.

She stood in helpless misery, her hands constantly twisting together.

'Thanks,' she mumbled.

'You say your son is sensitive,' he mused. 'Is he happy
where he is at school now?'

She frowned. 'N-no—'

'Well, then!'

'But another one could be worse—!'

'Or better.'

'I doubt it. He'd be such a bag of nerves that he'd turn
up on his first day with "victim" written all over his face,'
she wailed. Her eyes were haunted. 'You can't do this to
my child! I love him! He's everything I have!'

His guts twisted and he had to wait before he could
speak.

'And you? How will you feel, living elsewhere?'

His voice had suddenly softened, caressing her gently.
She drew in a sharp breath and shuddered with horror.

'I can't bear to think of going,' she mumbled pitifully.
'I love every inch of this house. I know it, and the garden,
the village, the hills and the dales, as well as I know the
back of my hand. There's no lovelier place on God's earth.
My heart is here. Tear me away,' she said, her voice shaking with passion, 'and you rip out a part of me!'

'I'm sorry that you will both find it hard,' he said curtly.
'But...there it is. That's life. One door closes, another one
opens.'

Laura gasped at his callousness. It was as she feared. He
was determined on his course of action. She turned away
as tears rushed up, choking her. Her hands gripped the back
of a chair for support as she imagined Adam facing a new
playground, new teachers, new, more intimidating bullies...

'All right, Cassian!' She whirled back in a fury. 'You
open and close all the doors you want—I'm staying put!'

He smiled faintly and his slow and thorough gaze swept
her from head to toe.

'Flour on your face,' he murmured.

Before she knew it, his fingers were lightly travelling
over her skin while she gazed into his lazily smiling eyes,

eyes so dark and liquid that she felt she was melting into a warm Mediterranean sea.

By accident, his caressing fingers touched her mouth. And instantly something seared through her like a heated lance, tightening every nerve she possessed and sending an electric charge into her system.

She struggled to focus, to forget the terrible effect he was having on her. He was throwing her out. Going gooey-eyed wouldn't help her at *all*. Rot him—was he doing this deliberately? Her eyes blazed with anger.

'If you want me to go, you'll have to get the removal men to carry me out!' she flung wildly.

'No need. I'd carry you out myself. I don't think it would be beyond my capabilities,' he mused.

In a split second she saw herself in his arms, helpless, at his mercy…'Touch me and you'll regret it!' she spat, thoroughly uncomfortable with her treacherous feelings.

'Yes,' he agreed slowly, apparently fascinated by her parted lips and her accelerated breathing. 'I think I might.' Equally slowly, a dazzling grin spread across his face. It was at once wicked and beguiling and made Laura's stomach contract. 'But,' he drawled, 'that wouldn't stop me from doing so.'

She blinked in confusion. There were undercurrents here she didn't understand. Somehow she broke the spell that had kept her eyes locked to his and she looked around desperately for a diversion.

'I'd fight you!' she muttered.

'Mmm. Then I'd have to hold you very, very tightly, wouldn't I?' he purred.

Her throat dried. Almost without realising, she began to tidy the dresser, despite the fact she was so agitated that she kept knocking things over.

Cassian came up behind her. Although there had been no sound, she knew he was near because the hairs on the back of her neck stood on end and her spine tingled. Sure enough, his hand reached out, covering hers where it rested on a figurine she'd toppled.

'You'll break something,' he chided, his breath whispering warm and soft over her ear, like a summer breeze in the valley.

'I don't give a toss!' she jerked out stupidly, snatching her hand away.

He caught the flying figure deftly and set it on the dresser. His arm was whipcord strong, his hands big but with surprisingly long, delicate fingers.

'Laura, surrender. You can't fight the inevitable.'

She blinked, her huge eyes fixed on his neatly manicured nails. Her body was in turmoil and she didn't know why. It was her head that ought to be in frantic disarray.

She should be panicking about her eviction. Instead, she was finding herself totally transfixed by his breathing, the cottony smell of his T-shirt, the accompanying warm maleness...

Oh, help me, someone! she groaned inwardly, trying to gather her wits.

'It can't be inevitable! Have pity on us!' she whispered.

'I am. That's why I'm chucking you out. And when I do, would you like a fireman's lift, or something more conventional?' he murmured in amusement, turning her to face him.

Laura's knees weren't functioning properly. She wobbled and he steadied her. He was incredibly close, his smooth, tanned face sympathetic and kind. It didn't make sense. But his gentle smile broke her resistance. For a terrible, shaming instant, she was horribly tempted to reach up and kiss that inviting mouth so that the tingling of her own lips could be assuaged.

Her eyes widened at her temerity. This was madness! Where were her inhibitions when she needed them? She'd never felt like this. Never had such an overwhelming urge to abandon what was decent and proper and to submit to physical temptations!

It was a relief that he couldn't know how she felt. The unguarded, unwanted and definitely unhinged response of her own body shocked her. It felt as if she was glowing. Erotic sensations were centred in places where he shouldn't have reached. It was awful. Like finding she enjoyed sin.

Shame brought high colour to her cheeks. A terrible thought flashed through her mind. Perhaps she was a slut. Perhaps her mother had been... *No!* Her hand flew to her mouth in horror, dismayed where his casual behaviour had taken her.

'Laura,' he murmured, drawing her imperceptibly closer.

'Let me go! I told you!' she moaned, wriggling away from the pressure of his hands and emerging hot and flustered because of the skin-tingling way they had slid down her arms. She moved back warily. 'I don't want you to touch me!' she stormed. 'Let's get this straight! If you do force me out, I'll come straight back in!'

His eyes danced with bright amusement. 'I'd lock the door.'

'I'd break a window!' she retorted heatedly.

'Do you intend your son to use the same point of entry?'

Laura ground her teeth in frustration. Her argument was futile and they both knew it. That didn't help her temper much.

'So you turn out a woman and a child, both of whom were born in this house! How do you think you'll be treated by people in this village?' she flared.

'Like a leper. However, it's not something that would disturb my sleep,' he replied gravely.

No. It wouldn't. Cassian never worried about the opinions of others. In her desperation she tried another tack. A last-ditch attempt to find a scrap of compassion in Cassian's granite heart.

'Adam is asthmatic. Emotional upsets can bring on an

attack. Do you want his health on your conscience?' she demanded.

'That would be unpleasant for all of us,' he admitted. 'What do you suggest we do?'

Her mouth fell open. 'What?'

Quite calmly, Cassian perched on the kitchen table, one long leg swinging freely and his steady gaze pinning Laura to the spot.

'I've bought the house. I want to live in it. So do you. That suggests a conflict of interests. How do you propose we deal with the situation?'

She was astonished. She hadn't expected negotiating tactics.

'Tell Tony you've made a mistake! Get him to buy it back!' she pleaded.

Cassian shook his head. 'No use. He'll have paid off his debtors to save himself from being beaten up again.'

'Again?! What do you mean?' She felt the colour drain from her face. 'Where is he? What's happened to him?' she asked in agitation.

'You're surprisingly concerned, considering Tony's indifference to you,' he observed. 'If I recall, he was the favoured child. He went from public school to university, whereas you were destined to leave school early. It never bothered him that your lives were unequal. You didn't figure in his life at all.'

'There was a crucial difference between Tony and me,' she pointed out sharply.

'Sure,' Cassian scathed. 'He was a selfish jerk. You were a doormat—'

'I—I was…!' OK. She was a doormat. He didn't have to say so! 'I was hardly in a position to demand my rights,' she said stiltedly. 'I had no blood ties with anyone in this house and you know that. It's hardly surprising he had all the advantages. I was lucky—'

'*Lucky?*' he barked, leaping to his feet angrily.

'Yes! They brought me up. I was fed and clothed—'

'You were crushed,' he snapped. His eyes blazed down at her, sapping her strength with their ferocity. 'And you're *grateful* because they offered you the basic human needs! Laura, they systematically browbeat you. They punished you for what your mother did to the oh-so-important George Morris, solicitor of this parish. They turned you into an obedient, colourless, cowering mouse, afraid of opening your mouth in case you said the wrong thing—!'

'Don't you criticise my family!' she cried hotly. 'It's none of your business how we lived! I don't care what you think of me…!'

She gulped. Because she did care. It upset her that he saw her as such a wimp. An obedient, colourless, cowering mouse! That was an awful description. Was she that pathetic?

Muddled, she stood there, her chest heaving, wondering why he was so angry and why she kept losing the composure which had always been such an integral part of her.

That was because he'd flung her into her worst nightmare. He was knocking away all her props. Leaving her with nothing. Perhaps she could plead with Tony herself…

'Tony,' she reminded him, her voice thin with panic. She sat down, shaking. 'Just tell me what's happened to him!'

Cassian felt like shaking her. She still saw justification in the way she'd been treated as a child. And yet cracks were beginning to appear in her armour. Rebellion simmered inside that tense body. She might have been taught to abhor passion but it was there, nevertheless and the thought excited him more than it should.

Inexplicably he'd wanted to press his lips on her pink, pouting mouth and her unavailability had only made the urge stronger. He couldn't understand his reaction. He'd been celibate for a long time and many women had tried to steer him from his chosen path, using all the tricks in the book and then some.

Tricks he could deflect. This was something else. Whether he liked it or not, Laura was reaching something deeper in him without even knowing what she was doing.

Curbing his rampaging instincts, he set about hurrying her departure before her temptations proved his undoing. Women could be dynamite at the best of times. He dare not get tangled up with someone like Laura. That would be dangerous in the extreme for both of them.

Pity, he found himself musing recklessly. It was such a luscious, kissable mouth... And he hungered for it more than was wise.

Grimly Cassian subdued his lurching passions. He could be hard on himself when necessary. And this was essential.

'I met Tony in Marrakesh—' he began at a gallop.

'*Marrakesh!*' she exclaimed, as if it were the planet Mars.

He gave a faint smile. To her, it probably was.

'Stupidly he'd swindled some thugs and they'd beaten him up. I got out the sticking plasters, let him stay for a while—'

'You have a house in Marrakesh?' she asked, wide-eyed.

Cassian perched on the table again. 'No, I rented rooms. Tony hotbedded with Fee, a stripper, who I—'

'*What?*' Her eyes were even wider, her mouth now joining in the amazement. She was wonderfully transparent. 'You...lived with a...stripper?!'

'Two, actually.' Before her jaw dropped any further and she did herself an injury, he added, 'We weren't cohabiting, I hasten to add. Same house, different rooms. Loads of space, no obligations to one another, come and go as you like...a perfect arrangement. No commitment, company when you want it, solitude when you don't.'

'But...strippers?'

Disapproval came from every line of her body. He decided she needed to have her judgement shaken up.

'Don't let the job fool you. Fee's a sweetie, with a very

strict moral code. Comes from Islington. You'd like her. Runs a shelter for sick animals in her spare time.'

'You're kidding me!' she scoffed.

'No, word of honour. It's partly why she let Tony stay. She has a warm heart.'

'I bet. So…what does…''hot-bedded'' mean, then?!' she asked warily.

He couldn't help but smile again, seeing that he was stretching her knowledge of the world a little too fast, a little too far.

'It's not as interesting as it sounds. The strippers worked at night so Tony had the use of Fee's bed in their room. During the day they slept, and he mooched about on the roof. It's flat. A kind of garden,' he explained.

'Warm-hearted or not, I don't see why they'd let a stranger invade their privacy.'

'It was a favour to me.'

'Oh?'

It was a very meaningful and glacial Aunt Enid kind of 'oh', but he wasn't going to explain how he'd got the girls out of trouble with the police, who'd been harassing them in the hope of some 'action'.

'Anyway,' he said, 'I suggested an answer to his cash flow problem. He was relieved to sell up. I got the impression he felt nothing for the Dales.'

'No, he didn't,' Laura admitted.

'Last I heard, he was planning his escape to Gibraltar with what was left of the cash.' He glanced at her sharply. 'How soon can you go?'

She bit her lip. 'You're heartless!' she flung.

He grunted. 'Practical. I'm not good at living cheek-by-jowl with other people.'

'I remember,' she said caustically and he gave a lop-sided grin. 'Cassian…' She paused, then seemed to pluck up courage. 'Let me explain the difficulty of my situation.'

He frowned. 'You've done that already, at extraordinary length.'

'Please! Give me a chance!'

Her huge blue eyes transfixed him. He saw that she was close to tears and felt a pang of sympathy. Even though her plight had shaken him more than he would have liked, he could cope with this. He'd handled any number of awkward situations in his life.

'All right. I'll listen—briefly. But, I warn you, I won't change my mind.'

'Do you blame me for trying?' she asked, her face wan.

'Go on, then. Make your pitch if you think it's worth fighting for. Tooth and nail, I think you said. And Sue will expect to see blood on the floor when she next calls in,' he mocked, deliberately goading her.

Rebellion flared in her eyes and brought a new strength to her trembling mouth.

'She's going to Hong Kong for two weeks. It'll have dried by then,' she said tartly.

Cassian laughed. 'Well give it a go,' he encouraged, eyes crinkling in amusement.

She took a moment to compose herself, knowing that she must be calm. Adam's future depended on what she said and how she said it. This time, she must let Cassian know her son's needs.

'I want to tell you about Adam in a little more detail,' she said gently. 'The kind of person he is. Why I'm so anxious about him.'

Cassian marvelled at the change that came over her. The expression on her face had became suffused with tenderness and he felt his heart soften. She could love, he thought, his pulses quickening.

'Yes?' he snapped.

His curtness had no impact on her at all. She was totally absorbed in thinking of her beloved son. That's pure love, he mused. And marvelled at the luminous quality of her eyes.

'He was born prematurely. I think now,' she said softly, 'that when I was pregnant I did too much physical work around the house for too long.'

'Sounds like Enid. Perhaps she wanted you to lose your baby,' he muttered.

She winced. 'Perhaps. I can't deny that's a possibility. She made it clear that my pregnancy was all the more reason for me to pull my weight. Anyway, he was a sickly baby and cried a lot. I found myself protecting him, watching out for the slightest indication that he might be starting another chest infection. And then, one day, he—oh, Cassian, it was so awful!' she whispered.

'Tell me,' he said softly.

His heart went out to her. She'd been treated very badly. Someone ought to give her a good time, make her happy...

'He had his first asthma attack. I thought he was dying! He was rushed into hospital and put in an oxygen tent. I knew then that he was more important to me than life itself. From that moment on, I've had to watch his health very carefully,' she said, her voice low and so tender that he almost envied the child. 'It's important that he's not stressed. If he's badly upset then he gets an asthma attack. I've had to work around them, of course. It's what mothers do.'

He grunted. 'Work at what?'

'I did a computer course,' she replied. 'I did well, had a natural aptitude, but I had to abandon it. Adam was ill so often that I couldn't take on anything full-time or permanent because I had to look after him.'

'Tough,' he conceded, his eyes narrowed as he studied her.

She showed no signs of resentment that her son's health had imprisoned her in a financial straitjacket. Pure love shone from her eyes. He wondered idly what it would be like to win the heart of a woman with such deep, hidden passions.

Frightening, he decided. She'd expect total togetherness. His idea of hell.

'It's not tough,' she said, her expression tender. 'He's so uncomplaining and I...like being with him,' she added more briskly, as if reluctant to express affection for her son.

'How did you survive? Social Services?' he hazarded.

'No!' She looked shocked. 'I worked for ages as a waitress in a Grassington hotel but the new owner has daughters who can do my job.' She put on a bright smile. 'They're gorgeous blondes with big bosoms,' she explained with a laugh of self-deprecation.

He tried to stop himself, but he found his glance flicking down and the way she was hugging herself revealed more than she knew, the shirt pulling tightly over firm, high breasts, lusher than he could have imagined.

He felt heat suffuse him and frowned with annoyance. He'd seen breasts before. He wasn't a curious teenager any more.

'Pulls in the trade, you must admit,' he said shortly.

'Oh, I can't blame him for employing his family, or anyone who's really attractive,' she said without rancour. 'I have no illusions about myself.'

You should look in the damn mirror! he thought sourly in the pause that followed. How could she miss what he could see? And yet he dared not tell her. For a start, she'd never believe him—and he didn't have time to convince her. Nor would it be in his interests.

'And, as you have already said, you're out of work again,' he said flatly.

'With a sickly child,' she emphasised.

She crossed and neatly arranged her eye-catching legs. Her face lifted to his earnestly. Cassian hardened his heart. The welfare state would provide.

'So?'

'I can't just walk out and rent somewhere. I have no savings. But I am actively searching for a job and when I get it, I'll pay *you* rent. You don't want this house. You can't want it. You bought it out of the goodness of your heart, to get Tony out of a hole—'

'Huh! If he were in a hole, I'd hire an excavator to make it deeper,' he drawled, moved by her situation despite himself. Yet common sense argued that it was still in her best interests to leave. 'I'm not charitable where he's concerned. I'm here because I want to be.'

'But—!'

'No buts. This has gone on long enough. I'll make it easy for you, Laura. A compromise. Pack your stuff. When your son comes home I'll drive you both to a hotel of your choice and I'll pay for you to stay there till you find a job. Can't say fairer than that.'

He leaned back, pleased with his generous solution. Laura looked defeated. For some reason that didn't give him the satisfaction he'd expected.

The muscles in her heart-wrenchingly sweet face tightened as she struggled not to cry and he had a wild moment when he almost moved forwards to take her in his arms and soothe her panic with promises he couldn't keep.

The tears defied her, trickling from the corners of her eyes. Cassian gritted his teeth to stop himself from backtracking.

'I couldn't let you pay our hotel bill!' she croaked shakily.

'I couldn't do otherwise,' he found himself saying.

'I have my pride.'

'So has the entire population of Yorkshire.'

'It's your revenge, isn't it?' she mumbled.

Cassian frowned. 'What for?'

She hung her head. 'For what Enid and my f-father did to you,' she sniffed.

He was appalled. 'No! I—'

'Then *why?*' she wailed.

'That's my business. I want you to go. Don't you see that—'

She wasn't listening. Her head was angled in an attitude of listening. He heard the sound of feet: someone running—stumbling—up the path.

'It's Adam! Something's wrong!' she jerked out, with a mother's inexplicable certainty.

Hastily she rubbed her tear-stained face with her fists then jumped up and flung open the door. Past her rigidly held body, he saw a mud-splattered boy with dishevelled blond hair and a panic-stricken expression come skidding to a halt outside.

'Adam!' she whispered.

Cassian frowned and rose to his feet. The child was obviously in distress, and by the looks of him he'd been in a fight, but neither he nor his mother were making any move towards one another.

They both stood as if frozen to the ground, staring in consternation, some kind of signal going between them that prevented them from physical contact.

A chill went down his spine. Enid's tongue had removed something more crucial than defiance from Laura. It had killed Laura's ability to show love.

'I—I fell over!' Adam claimed, trying to be brave. But his mouth was all over the place.

'Oh, Adam...!' Laura was evidently distressed. Her hands hovered in front of her as if she was desperate to cuddle her son but had been forbidden to do so. 'I—you...! You—you should be at school—'

Cassian could bear no more. He pushed Laura aside and placed a firm arm around the quivering child's shoulders.

'Cup of tea, I think,' he declared cheerfully, easing him through the door. 'Then a scrub down with the yard brush and a bit of TLC for those bruises. Falling over's quite a shock, isn't it?' he chattered, getting the shaken child into a comfortable armchair in the kitchen and crouching down beside him. 'I did it a lot as a child.' He grinned. 'I seemed to get in the way of other boys' feet.'

He tensed when Laura's hand came past his ear and brushed the hair back from her son's forehead to reveal the bruise which Cassian had already spotted. He was an expert on bruises. And bullying. Particularly from adults.

'Poor Adam!' Laura leaned forwards and hesitantly kissed the purple bruise and then briefly touched her son's hot face. 'I'll put the kettle on,' she said huskily, as if overcome.

'Thanks, Mum.'

Adam bent to untie his shoe laces and Cassian knew he was trying to hide his tears. To be strong. To cultivate a stiff upper lip. Anything to stop real emotion from emerging. Emotion was a bad word at Thrushton Hall.

He could hear George Morris's voice now, echoing down the years.

'Stop crying!' Morris would beg the temperamental Bathsheba in horror. Or…'Don't laugh so loud!…' 'Don't dance like that—it's…unseemly, you're a married woman!…' Or maybe 'Calm yourself!…Don't yell…'

Ridiculous. The man had married his mother because he'd adored her exuberance. And then had set about curbing it so that she fitted in with the silent and repressed household over which he'd presided.

It wasn't surprising that the deeply repressed Laura was afraid of expressing her real feelings.

Cassian found the situation interesting. There seemed to be a kind of agreement between Laura and her child. A tacit acceptance, perhaps, that there should be the minimum of affection displayed, one or two small gestures sufficing for deep concern.

Intriguingly, she had put her hand on the arm of the chair where Adam was sitting. Cassian had noticed that Adam had imperceptibly leaned in that direction so that his body was inches from his mother's restless fingers.

He couldn't believe what was happening. This was a kind of distant comfort, practised by two people who didn't dare to let go in case they betrayed their emotions.

The situation struck deep at his heart and he was moved more than he would have liked. Wordlessly, hampered by no inhibitions, he reached out to hug the shaking child and to let him know what human warmth could be like. He rubbed the thin, bony back in sympathy.

'Let's get your muddy shoes and jumper off, shall we?' he suggested gently.

As the child complied with a worrying submissiveness, Cassian reflected that the relationship between Laura and Adam couldn't be more different than the closeness between him and Jai. Laura would be shocked if she ever saw their mutual expressions of love. He and his son had no problems about expressing their emotions.

A surge of longing careered unhindered through him. He wanted his child near him. Missed him like hell. In a reflex action, he clutched Adam more tightly.

'Who...are you?' Adam asked timidly.

He smiled down mistily. 'Cassian.'

The trembling stopped. Tears were knuckled away in a gesture that mimicked Laura's.

'Gosh! I've heard of you!'

He grimaced. 'Don't tell me!' he said, pretending to groan. 'I was surly and rude and ignored your mother while I was here!'

Adam shook his head, his blue Laura-eyes bright with eagerness.

'I dunno about that. But Mum said you knew every plant and insect and bird and you could find your way around the countryside blindfold!'

Cassian glanced at Laura in amusement. 'Your mother is very kind to concentrate on my few good points.'

'Cassian's come to stay,' Laura said, putting a mug of tea by Adam's elbow. Her eyes challenged Cassian to say anything further.

'Oh, gosh, cool!' enthused Adam.

Cassian frowned at Laura. He'd deal with her later. He fixed Adam with a sober but friendly gaze.

'So. Spill the beans,' he said quietly. 'What happened?'

'I—' Adam faltered, clearly unable to look into Cassian's steady eyes and tell a lie. There was a long pause. It was the silence before a confession and Cassian waited patiently for the child to begin. 'Well…at break-time they said my Mum was a stupid feeble wimp, like me, and—and that we're silly drips with marshmallow instead of guts!' he said with a huge, indignant sniff.

There was another pause. Cassian prayed that Laura wouldn't react or speak. The boy needed a silence to fill with words. Any interruption might make the kiddie clam up. To his utter relief, Laura didn't even move and after fiddling with his fingers for a while, Adam began again.

'I t-tried to ignore them, like Mum said, but they pushed me into the nettles then jumped on m-me and pinched my packed lunch!'

Tears rolled down his cheeks again and Cassian felt his heart aching for the distressed child.

'Here,' he said huskily, grasping Adam's hands strongly in his.

'Oh, my darling!' Laura sobbed.

And to Cassian's surprise, she pushed him aside and drew her son into an awkward embrace. She was crying too, utter misery on her face.

Cassian rose, made two more mugs of tea and took the cake out of the oven. It pained him to see Laura rocking her child and trying to control her weeping.

They needed love and support. Someone to give them confidence. Bullying made him feel sick. Even the thought of it disrupted his laid-back approach to life and made him irrational, his emotions churning chaotically as anger, resentment, pity and past terrors filled his head.

He'd been secretly bullied by George Morris. Taunted, spat upon, and beaten by older kids at senior school. The sheer helplessness had made him seethe with rage and frustration.

And he was seething now, hurting for Adam's sake, loathing those who attacked anyone who didn't conform to some imaginary 'norm'.

He couldn't bear it. He wanted to crack heads together, yell, terrify…anything so that Laura and her child would never weep like this again. He wanted to hug them both, tell them he'd deal with the problem, see their tears dry up and their faces turn to him trustingly. To see them smile.

He found himself shaking—whether from passion or fear at where his thoughts were leading, he wasn't sure.

At that moment, he knew that he couldn't turn them out—not yet, anyway. And the cold certainty iced his spine with apprehension.

He was walking into dangerous quicksand. He loathed living with other people. Found their pettiness and knee-jerk rules irritating. Yet the urge to offer a temporary respite for Laura and Adam was so overwhelming that it couldn't be denied. It seemed he cared about them.

He drew in a sharp breath. For a man who needed to be free that was extremely worrying.

CHAPTER FOUR

LAURA crossly banged pans about as she prepared a scrap lunch. How Cassian had persuaded Adam to go up for a bath without protest—and got him giggling as well in the process—she'd never know.

But before she could think straight, Adam had come hurrying back downstairs in a holey old jumper and faded jeans, his face pink and shiny with eagerness as if something exciting awaited.

She supposed it did. Cassian.

Now Adam sat in smiling assent while Cassian gently and expertly smoothed the cuts and bruises with some cream he'd dug from his First Aid kit.

Adam had spurned her usual stuff, beguiled by the promise that Cassian's remedy was herbal and 'brilliant, I use it all the time when I fall off mountains and things'.

Huh! What was she suddenly? Redundant? The mince suffered a fierce pounding with the spoon. Cassian had made her look both callous and, now, hopelessly inadequate.

When she'd seen Adam struggling desperately to be brave, she hadn't known what to do. Should she respect his attempt or give in to her maternal instinct and comfort him?

It had always been an unwritten rule between them that Adam should try to overcome the bullying on his own. He'd made that clear the first time she'd indignantly tried to interfere on his behalf.

But now Cassian had changed the rule. And, even more infuriating, his tactics of firmness, humour and sympathy had worked, defusing Adam's shock and making him feel better about himself.

With vicious strokes, she grated some cheese and put it aside then flung carrots, onions and turnips into the mince to make it go further.

Adam ought to be sitting with his shoulders hunched, chest heaving, clinging for dear life to his asthma inhaler. That's what invariably happened after something like this.

Instead, he was laughing at some improbable tale Cassian was relating about walking in the foothills of the Himalayas—Him*ar*leeas he pretentiously called them—when he'd slid over fifty feet down a slope and ended up in a particularly magnificent heap of yak manure. Huh! As if!

'We ought to let the school know you're here, Adam,' she said shortly, interrupting Cassian's fairy stories.

'Phone them after lunch,' Cassian suggested with a languid stretch.

'We don't have a phone.' Crossly she met his astonished eyes. 'Too expensive. I'll have to go to the school—'

'That's ridiculous!' he protested. 'It's a four-mile round trip. Take off that hair shirt. You can use my mobile or take my car.'

'I'll phone. Thank you,' she muttered.

'Mum can't drive,' explained Adam.

'Perhaps I should teach her,' Cassian growled.

There was a sudden silence. She looked at Cassian, startled and flustered by his remark. Though he looked more than a little startled too. Her heart thudded. Surely this meant she had a reprieve! Long enough for her to learn to drive!

Adam looked impressed. She knew he dearly wanted her to join the human race and acquire a driving licence. But what was the point if she couldn't afford to own a car? Yet that didn't matter. The reprieve did.

'You won't tell them what happened, will you, Mum?' Adam asked anxiously.

'I can't have you being hurt like this—' she began fretfully.

'Please!' he begged, looking petrified. 'You'll make it worse!'

She looked at him helplessly. What did you do? What was right, in the long run? Did she make her son a total outcast by complaining, or was he to be battered on a regular basis?

Extraordinarily, she found herself searching out Cassian, wondering if he had an answer to the problem. She quivered. There was a melting tenderness in his eyes and it confused her.

'*You* were bullied,' she said to him in a low tone, remembering the torn clothes, and the cuts and bruises he'd often be sporting. He'd always told Aunt Enid that he'd been in a fight, but had never asked for help. And suddenly the bullying had stopped. 'What do *you* think?'

'I didn't want adult interference,' he said quietly. 'But that's because I wanted to find my own way of dealing with the bullying. There isn't one solution. Each person has a different need. Some don't have the resources to cope alone. Adam, if you think you can change from being a victim to a winner, then go for it.'

He was wise, she thought, seeing her son straighten as if he was growing in stature. Suddenly she saw that Cassian could help Adam so much. A tremor took her unawares, making her lips part at the thought of Cassian here, taking a part in their daily lives.

'How long are you staying?' Adam asked him.

She winced at the wistful note. Her son was revelling in male company. Suddenly she felt isolated.

'A while. Moving in tonight,' came the easy reply. It was coupled with a dazzling smile.

'Cool!'

She shot a glance at Cassian and found that he was regarding her wryly. The odd sensations crept into her loins again. They were like small spasms, tugging and relaxing.

Quite unnervingly enjoyable. She bit her lip and clenched all her muscles hard.

'...yes, I was twelve when I first came to Thrushton,' Cassian was saying.

'Did you like it here?' Adam asked eagerly.

'Hated Aunt Enid, loved Thrushton,' Cassian replied with blistering honesty.

Adam giggled. 'Why?'

'I regret to say that Enid was a cow. A strict and humourless woman who thought children should be neither seen nor heard. I think she would have preferred them to have sprung from the womb as fully trained adults with a degree in silence and obedience.'

'Cassian!' Laura reproved, while Adam gazed in delighted shock.

'I can hear her voice now,' he said, looking pointedly at her and Laura blushed in bitter recognition because she'd caught herself reproving Adam's small and rare misdemeanours with Enid's sharp little voice. Cassian had the bit between his teeth and was galloping on. 'Her favourite word was "don't",' he said blithely. 'And her tongue had been dipped in snake venom. She had a way of gnashing her teeth that makes me think now that she could have crushed Terminator I, II and III in her jaws.'

Adam laughed, awe-struck by Cassian's frankness. 'But you liked Thrushton,' he said, pleased.

'Oh, yes. Out there...' He paused. Laura gulped, her senses beguiled. His face had become soft, quite beautiful in its dreaminess. 'It's wild and free and open. Magnificent scenery. Takes you at once from your small, inward world and places your life in a greater context. Don't you think?'

Laura was stunned to learn how he'd felt. That was why he'd spent days at a time on the fells. It had been more than an escape from the confines of the house. He'd seen more than beauty in the Dales. Like her, he'd found something special, spiritual, uplifting.

Thoughtfully she listened while Cassian continued to answer the hail of questions coming from Adam, speaking to her son as if he were an adult. It disturbed her that Adam was chattering—*chattering!* when he was usually so monosyllabic!—and it disturbed her that Cassian's lazy, deep voice seemed to be soothing her own agitated mind and slowing her movements till she was wafting languidly about the kitchen and catching herself hanging on every improbable word.

But her son was undeniably happy in Cassian's company. And although she might resent Cassian for being the one who'd taken Adam's mind off the bullying, she was grudgingly grateful.

'Sometimes you must have got soaked to the skin, when you wandered off for days on end!' Adam was saying. 'Wasn't that awful?'

'Not often!' laughed Cassian. 'I checked the chickweed. Failing that, the spiders.'

Adam grinned. 'Chickweed?' he scoffed.

'Sure. It closes up if it's going to rain. And spiders are only active in fine weather. If they remake a web around 6—7 p.m., you can be almost sure it'll stay dry. If it's raining and they're altering their web, it'll clear up. You have to read the signs. For instance, a red sunset tells you that dry air is coming. A yellow one indicates it'll be damp. You can read clouds too. I'll show you sometime.'

Sometime, she thought. Another indication that they wouldn't be leaving soon. Her hopes rose.

'Cool! But…what did you eat?' asked Adam, wide-eyed with admiration.

'Trout, usually. You start downstream, place a light close to the water, and the fish come to look. With care, you can flick one out. I'll show you. There's plenty of food if you know where to look. I can lend you a book about finding food in the wild. But make no mistake,' he warned, 'walking the Dales over a period of days is not something anyone can do—not even an adult. I took no risks, Adam. I learnt the lie of the land first, practised and learnt the art of survival till I could light a fire in a howling gale and tell by sound and smell and feel alone where I was.'

'You mean...' Laura eyed him in amazement. 'You were so determined to escape Aunt Enid that you spent weeks preparing yourself?'

'I think it took two years of concentrated effort before I was sure I knew what I was doing,' he said quietly. Then he smiled. 'I wanted to escape, not die! It was wonderful out there on a starlit night,' he mused softly, his face radiating pleasure. 'The silence was awesome.'

Adam moved a little closer to his new hero. Laura watched, her gratitude towards Cassian a little eclipsed by a wary concern. Adam wasn't tough. She didn't want him trying to emulate Cassian.

'Weren't you horribly afraid?' he asked timidly.

Cassian's eyes liquefied with warmth. 'Sometimes. Especially when the night was black and I hadn't reached the shelter I'd chosen. But I always knew where I was heading, and never left anything to chance. I started with small trips, graduated to longer ones. And each success made me stronger, more confident.'

'And...er...' Adam persisted, 'you weren't popular at school.'

Laura held her breath. He'd slipped the question in as if it were casual. Would Cassian see that her son wanted some reassurance about popularity—and help with the bullying?

'No. Because I was different,' Cassian answered gently, and she felt the air slowly sift from her lungs. He'd be kind to Adam, she felt sure. 'Kids don't like people who stand apart. I was categorised along with the boys with National Health glasses and too much weight. We were bullied as a matter of course. It's a very primitive thing, Adam, a caveman attitude. Part of what they call the biological imperative. That means that it's part of our survival instincts. Oddities are rejected to allow survival of the fittest. The world has moved on since Neolithic times, but unfortunately civilisation hasn't always impacted on some primeval brains!' he finished with a grin.

Adam laughed too. 'What did *you* do when you were bullied? Actually *do*?' he asked with an exaggeratedly nonchalant tone which fooled nobody.

Laura stiffened, turning to face the two of them where they were sitting with cosy familiarity on the old sofa. He'd never talked so openly before. He trusted Cassian, she thought in shock. More than *she'd* ever been trusted. Or were mothers naturally ruled out as confidantes?

'I learnt about pain,' Cassian replied ruefully. He smiled down at Adam, his manner relaxed and inviting.

'Nothing else?' her son asked in disappointment.

'Plenty!'

'What?!'

Eagerly, Adam tucked his legs up on the sofa, his body curled against Cassian's. Laura felt her heart lurch. Her son was looking at Cassian as if he held the Holy Grail in the palm of his hands.

'Well, obviously you know that my solutions won't necessarily be yours,' Cassian flattered, and Adam nodded in sage agreement. 'You'll know that you have to decide how to deal with *your* problem and work out what *you* want—'

'To be tough!' Adam blurted out.

Cassian's arm came about Adam's shoulders and he was nodding as if they both had much in common. To Laura's astonishment, Adam reached up a puny arm and boldly felt Cassian's biceps. She couldn't believe what her reserved and shy son was doing. For the life of her, she couldn't recall him ever touching anyone.

But Cassian was incredibly seductive and…touchable. She went pink, thinking how close she had come to breaking her own rules about personal space.

'My decision exactly.'

'Did you, uh...have the same plan as me?' asked Adam tentatively.

Laura could have wept. Her son desperately needed help and she hadn't seen that. All his stubborn insistence that he was fine had been a cover-up. She couldn't bear it.

'You tell me! I chopped wood,' Cassian confided, perhaps deliberately emphasising the muscle definition of his chest by leaning back, his arms behind his head. Shocked to be distracted, Laura found herself mesmerised by his physique, her throat drying in an instant recognition of his visceral appeal. 'I walked miles too,' he reminisced. 'Climbed hills. At first, I puffed like an old steam train, then I graduated to running up them. I heaved rocks about, making dams on the fells where no one could see me fall or fail or yell in frustration. I suppose that's the kind of thing you've decided to do.'

'Yes!' Adam cried with shining eyes.

Laura felt a shaft of pain that her son had seen a glimmer of hope on the horizon. And she hadn't been the one who'd put it there. She felt a tug of admiration for Cassian's technique.

'Thought so.' Cassian yawned. 'Lucky that everything you need is on the doorstep, isn't it? Logs, hills, rocks. Makes getting fit a piece of cake.' He looked up, saw Laura stupidly holding the saucepan as if she'd been welded to the floor, and smiled. 'No time like the present, Adam,' he said briskly, leaping from the sofa. 'You can start flexing those muscles by mashing the potatoes while I fetch something for pudding.'

'Me?' her son's mouth dropped open and Laura was just about to say that she did all the cooking and housework while Adam studied or rested, when he scrambled up and rushed to her side. 'Right. Er...what do I do, Mum?'

'Bash.''

Tight-lipped, she handed him the masher, wordlessly dropped a knob of marge into the pan and added seasoning.

Out of the corner of her eye, while Adam pounded the potatoes with messianic concentration, she saw Cassian tipping fresh raspberries into a dish which he'd hauled from the cupboard.

'Make yourself at home,' she said tartly.

'I am, aren't I?' he murmured.

She gave him a scathing look and inspected the potatoes. Her brows knitted in a frown at the lumps but before she could say anything to Adam, Cassian squeezed himself between them.

'You're doing great,' he enthused, praising her son where she would have criticised. 'Nearly got all the lumps smashed, I see.'

Adam's eyes rounded in dismay. Hastily he pulled the pan towards him and set about reducing the potato to a creamy consistency.

Laura stood transfixed. Cassian had achieved the required result with consummate skill, craftily ensuring that it was Adam himself who'd decided the mash wasn't up to standard.

'Penny?' Cassian murmured, his palm touching the small of her back.

She felt she'd been set on fire. It had been a mere enquiring touch and yet her body had reacted so violently that it seemed her heart might leap from her breast.

And all the while her mind was teeming with new thoughts, excitement mounting as she examined the idea of praise and suggestion as a replacement for criticism—which up to now had been the only method of shaping a child's behaviour that she'd ever known.

It was as if she'd stumbled on treasure. In a way, she had.

Half-turning, her face now inches from Cassian's, she smiled delightedly into his dark, pooling eyes and instantly became light-headed. Joy was unsettling, she thought warily. Then decided to succumb. What the hell.

'My thoughts are worth more than that,' she said happily. She could have danced. Almost did. Her toes wriggled. She grinned. 'Thank you.'

He raised a heavy eyebrow. 'For what?'

Close up, his mouth looked devastatingly sensual. Again she felt the light pressure of his hand on her spine and she had to struggle to remember what they'd been talking about.

With solemn delight, she met his bone-melting stare. It was the revelation that was making her so delirious. And she wanted to keep her new-found knowledge to herself.

'For showing Adam how to make the perfect mash,' she breathed.

'My pleasure.'

There was a brief pressure on her tingling back and then Cassian had moved away, leaving a cold gap she wanted immediately to fill. With him. To have him close, touching her, gazing into her eyes...

'Inspection!' ordered Adam excitedly, banging the pan in front of her.

She was jerked back to reality. 'Wow!' she marvelled. 'Totally smashed mash! Eat your heart out, celebrity cooks of the world!'

'Bread smells fabulous. Fancy some wine?' Cassian enquired, waving a bottle of red at her.

She beamed, feeling suddenly hedonistic. Wine was a luxury. And a wicked indulgence at lunchtime! 'Yes, please!' she said recklessly, knowing she was being silly, but unable to stop herself. After lifting out the golden brown bread, she picked up a serving spoon—and then on an impulse she handed it to the glowing Adam. 'There you go. Pile the potato on top of the mince, add the cheese, grab the oven gloves and push the dish into the oven. It's ready when the cheese is brown and sizzling. I'm going to put my feet up and luxuriate in the high life.'

Flushed and happy, she sat neatly in the armchair while

Cassian opened the bottle. The sunlight danced on the planes of his face. He looked relaxed and at ease and she felt her entire body responding to his mood, softening and slowing down as if she too were laid back and uninhibited.

Her fortunes had changed. Cassian had now met Adam and seen his needs. Instinctively she knew they'd be staying for a while—and perhaps she could even come up with some means of sharing the house till he grew tired of such a narrow world and drifted off to pastures new.

A little fragment of doubt interrupted her plan, a small voice telling her that Cassian wasn't an ordinary man, that she was already disturbed by his deep sensuality. But she could surely curb her mad thoughts if it meant she and Adam could stay at Thrushton.

Perhaps she could cook and clean and do Cassian's washing in addition to holding down a new job. No man would refuse free housekeeping services!

Dreamily planning, she surveyed him from beneath her lashes. With the enjoyment of a true sensualist, he was passing the opened bottle beneath his nose, his face rapt as he inhaled the aroma. Her senses quickened.

Slowly he filled two glasses and carried one over to her. 'Enjoy,' he murmured.

Their fingers touched as she took the glass. A flash of heat melted in the core of her body and she felt Cassian's sharp exhalation of breath warming her lips before he re-treated to the sofa again. She was afraid he was annoyed by her gaucheness, but he said nothing. Fortunately, he was totally indifferent to her.

Instead, he concentrated on his wine, quietly studying its colour, sniffing it again and then taking an absorbed sip.

'What do you think of it?' he asked, as if her opinion mattered. He shot her a look and his dark eyes suddenly glowed.

She pressed her parted lips together hurriedly and picked up the glass. 'I don't know anything about wine.'

'You have taste buds!' he growled.

She took a cautious sip. And then another.

'Describe what you feel,' Cassian coaxed.

'I feel warm. From cooking,' she said, ducking the issue and omitting to say that he had added to that warmth.

When he remained silent, she concentrated harder, tasting the rich, dark red wine and trying to find words to explain the glorious sensation in her mouth and the wickedly pleasurable feeling as the alcohol pooled seductively in her stomach.

'I love the smell,' she decided, playing safe. 'It makes me feel rich.'

'Let me sniff, Mum!'

Laughing, she held her glass up to Adam who rolled his eyes and declared he was a millionaire.

'Not far off the truth,' Cassian acknowledged. 'Nothing better than good food and wine, to love and to be loved.'

Laura felt a tightening in her chest. He had someone, she thought, quite irrationally disappointed. It had never occurred to her that the wolf that walked alone would have found a soul mate, but there was no mistaking the depth of emotion in his words. He wore no ring, but then Cassian wouldn't allow any woman to curtail his freedom.

'I've got Mum,' Adam said, treading where angels and she feared to tread. 'Who've you got?'

'My son,' Cassian said softly.

Laura almost spilled her wine. She put it down on the table, her mind whirling. 'Your son?' she repeated stupidly.

'Jai. He's ten.'

'I'm nine!' Adam cried in delight.

Cassian grinned. 'I know. Small world.'

Adam began rattling off questions. Quickly she realised that this was why he'd had such a sure and empathetic touch with her son. Cassian had practical experience of his own.

And what, she thought in quite extraordinary agitation,

about his partner? The woman who'd won his heart, who'd slowly, seductively stripped the clothes from that lithe and lean body…

Laura gulped, appalled at herself. Without any reason whatsoever, she was horribly, stupidly, jealous. She wanted to be close to Cassian…perhaps because it would be wonderful to have the power to conquer someone so quietly strong and independent that his very kiss would be an acknowledgement that she was unique among women. She wanted to sit with him, to be enclosed in his arms and to be soothed by his steady calmness…and to be fired by the passions that lay beneath.

Dear heaven, she thought in horror. What was happening to her?

'*Marrakesh?*' Adam's exclamation made Laura jump.

Cassian hastily got up and opened the oven door, taking out the pie then prepared a pan for the frozen peas he'd produced. Now *he* was entering into displacement activities. Anything, he thought, to avoid Laura's captivating face as she dreamed of…what?

All he knew was that his willpower was being sorely tested and every nerve in his body was begging him to go over and relieve his desire to kiss her soft mouth till his senses reeled. Suicidal!

'Yes,' he said, waiting for the water to boil and glad of an excuse to keep his back to her. 'Jai's hiking in the High Atlas mountains with friends. They'll put him on a plane to Heathrow and he'll make his way here in a couple of days or so, I'm not sure when.'

There was a deafening silence. Glancing round, he saw that Laura's eyes were nearly falling out of their sockets.

'A ten-year-old, finding his way on his own?' she said in horror. 'Don't you think that's stretching independence too far? Anything might happen to him! There are bad people out there, Cassian—'.

'Allow me to know how to manage my own son,' he

said irritably. 'Maybe I've arranged for someone to watch over him. Maybe he's thrilled at the thought of planning his own journey. Maybe he has travelled alone before and has developed strategies to stay safe.' His jaw tightened. How dare she assume he hadn't thought of Jai's safety? 'Maybe,' he said sarcastically, 'I don't care if he's robbed or attacked or abducted by—'

'OK, OK, I'm sorry!' she muttered awkwardly.

He grunted and tipped half the frozen peas into the pan, securing the remainder in the bag with a twist tie. He knew he'd overreacted but no one, just no one, interfered between him and Jai, whose life he'd guard with his own.

'Here,' he growled lobbing the bag at Adam. Who fumbled and dropped them. An easy catch. Poor kid had much to catch up on, he mused and softened his expression. 'Freezer?' he suggested, when Adam looked at him with a puzzled frown.

'Oh, yeah.' The lad disappeared into the scullery and the door banged shut behind him.

He remembered that scullery. He'd stood peeling potatoes for hours there, till his hands were raw. And Laura's father had been furious, Cassian thought darkly, because he'd been unable to break Cassian's will.

Of small victories like that, Cassian knew his character had been forged. And consequently he had his own ideas on how to bring up children. Not by making them peel sacks of potatoes, of course! Gradual responsibility. The acquisition of life skills. Knowledge is power.

Hearing Adam fumbling around in the freezer, he took the opportunity to confront Laura. 'It looks as if we're going to be together for a short while. The shorter the better, I think. But while we are under the same roof, you can keep your thoughts to yourself where Jai is concerned. We have our own way of living and we're happy with it. Any problems, bring them to me. You won't nag Jai and tell him to put his coat on because it's cold. You won't tell him to be careful if he decides to cook. He does what he's capable of. Understand?' he snapped.

'So long as Jai's behaviour doesn't affect Adam,' she said, her eyes wide and anxious.

'Maybe that would be an improvement.'

She bristled, as he knew she would. 'How d—?' Adam walked in again and she broke off, biting her lip. 'How long do you think, before you take those peas off?' she amended, filling in the awkward silence. But her eyes told him how angry she was. And he felt a small leap of triumph.

'Now.'

Cassian spun on his heel and took the pan off the heat for straining. But he was thinking all the while that if he strode over and kissed her passionately on that soft, quivering pink mouth then she might unwind a little. And she and her son might begin to live.

She came to his side, fussing with the plates and he let her take over because otherwise he'd grab her arms and pull her against him so he could rain kisses on her long, slender neck and tousle that perfectly tidy hair.

He wanted to muss her up. To murmur wicked, seductive words in her ear, to rouse her beyond her prim and restrictive responses till she cried out his name and begged for him in husky, unrecognisable tones.

Crazy. The lure of the unattainable. Or perhaps he needed the release of sex. If so, he needed a woman who wanted fun and no strings, not the uptight, emotionally repressed Laura who'd probably expect a ring on her finger if he went so far as to hold her hand.

Grimly he sat at the table. Adam chattered and he answered as best he could. The kiddie had a sweet temperament but was as vulnerable as hell. He itched to set him on the right road. Hated to see a child crushed by life, condemned to feeling inferior to others.

Like Laura. He tore off a piece of crusty new bread and

chewed irritably. She'd annoyed him from the first moment he'd set eyes on her, with her mimsy little voice and breathy uncertainty, scuttling to do the evil Enid's bidding. If his mother hadn't told him to leave Laura strictly alone, he'd have dragged the kiddie off on his attempts to toughen himself up. Though everyone would have imagined they'd been up to no good.

Angrily he replenished Laura's glass and his own. He wasn't used to walking on tiptoe around people and the next few days were going to be foul. It was his habit not to pussyfoot around but to be straight with people. If he did that, he and Laura would be in the sack and Adam would be doing press-ups in the garden each morning.

'Is the pie all right?' Laura's anxious voice impinged on his thoughts.

He looked at his plate and realised he hadn't been eating. 'It's great,' he said honestly, tucking in. 'And the bread is wonderful.'

At least she could cook. That suggested *one* sensual delight in her repertoire.

'I'm glad you like it!'

He looked up and was shaken by her pleased smile. His jaw clenched. She was terrifyingly vulnerable too. One wrong word from him and she could be seriously wounded. It was a hell of a burden to carry.

'I'm going out,' he said when he'd finished. 'Excuse me—'

'But...your pudding!' she cried.

Impatiently he sighed. 'It's not compulsory.'

She flushed and he was back into whipping puppies again. 'But...you haven't even unpacked yet,' she pointed out hesitantly as if he might have forgotten.

'I know,' he bit irritably and she had the grace to look contrite. 'But that can wait and I want to walk.'

Before she could come up with some other conventional chain to wrap around his neck, he strode out.

It wouldn't work, he thought darkly, changing into walking boots and slinging a small rucksack on his back. Laura and he would never live in the same world. Somehow he had to force her out. Before he did something he'd regret for the rest of his life.

Or he could sell up. Perhaps coming here had been a mistake after all.

He set off at a blistering pace, walking off his frustrations.

By the time three hours had passed by, the magic of the fells had made his heart sing again. His route had taken him way beyond the ruined buildings of the medieval lead mines above Thrushton, and past the narrow fourteenth-century hump-backed packhorse bridge with its ankle-high parapets, designed so that a train of forty mules could pass with their laden panniers unimpeded.

Taking delight in treading in the footsteps of history, he walked along the corpse way. He could almost feel the weight of the past, hear the mourners as they carried a loved one to the church, along the narrow path and over the treacherous stepping stones from some remote settlement.

From the track he had climbed high above the beautiful valley where the River Wharfe glinted and sparkled far below and as he climbed he felt a soaring joy at being alive.

The air was sharp and clear and filled with swooping swallows creating a ballet in the air. Overcome by powerful emotions which shook him to the core, he sat on the edge of a limestone pavement, watching an adder drawing the last vestiges of warmth from the late afternoon sun.

He closed his eyes, almost pained by the beauty of his surroundings. And he knew then that he had to spend time here. Wanted... His breath knifed in, snapping his eyes open again. Shock ran through his body. For a brief moment it had crossed his mind that this would be a suitable place to settle. To put down roots.

In a dazed blur, he saw himself creating a herb garden and feeding hens. And then, totally unbalanced by such uncharacteristic dreams, he leapt up and headed at a half-run for Grassington, determined to drink or wench away any potential curbs on his personal freedom.

'I can live here,' he muttered to himself like a mantra, his loping stride swiftly devouring the ground. 'But there's no way I'm going into pipe and slippers mode!'

The beer was good. The women less so. He smiled ruefully on his way back to Thrushton Hall. Women had recognised him. Fluttered their lashes in the hope that he'd remember their totally unsatisfactory teenage embraces. He'd raised his glass in acknowledgement and remained aloof. The loner.

And despite the attentions of what he assumed to be the landlord's 'bosomy' daughters, he felt nothing; no desire, no stirring, no interest whatsoever.

Worse, he found himself comparing them with Laura. Her quiet beauty. Solemn eyes of cerulean-blue, the colour of a Mediterranean sky. Untouched lips he wanted to explore. The body of a siren and the innocence of an angel.

A woman alone. Unique. Unaware that she was close to spilling out her long-hidden passions and needing someone who wouldn't hurt her, who wouldn't damage her fragile self-esteem but who would build it up till she realised her full potential.

And he wanted to be that man. Even though he knew he couldn't give her what she would want. Marriage. Security. Two point four children and a mortgage and the ritual of cleaning the car every Saturday morning after doing the weekly shop.

So he had to keep his hands and his eyes to himself. And save them both from disaster.

Trying to settle his thoughts, he walked down to the

river, knowing the narrow path so well that the occasional light from the thin crescent moon was enough when the clouds lifted, and so he did not need to use his torch.

He let the soft rush of water soothe his mind. Listened to the scops owl, the sounds of badgers snuffling up roots somewhere in the mid distance. Simple pleasures which money could never buy.

It wasn't until after midnight that he returned, letting himself into the house silently. He took a deep breath to steel himself. Now he would face the house, at its darkest and most sinister and chase away the memories till only stone and mortar remained.

CHAPTER FIVE

LAURA had been unable to sleep. It bothered her that Cassian hadn't stopped to sort out which bedroom he'd use or even unpacked his night things. Did he think he could come back in the early hours and wake her up, demanding sheets and pillows? she thought crossly.

So here she was, having to stay awake to tell him that she'd made up a bed in the back room. It was typically selfish of him that he did his own thing and never mind anyone else!

Her mouth pruned in. That was him now. Grudgingly she admitted that he had been extraordinarily quiet, but she had been waiting for that slight creak of the door, her ears tuned like interstellar radar to an invading Martian.

Flinging her cosy blue dressing gown over her short cotton nightie, she angrily tied the cord around her waist as if girding herself up for battle.

Her head cocked on one side. Instead of coming up the stairs, he was moving around in the dark downstairs. That was the study door opening. Her eyes narrowed. What was he doing?

She listened but there was no sound from below. Then the boards creaked in the hall and there came the unmistakable sound of the latch being lifted on the dining room door.

Well, she thought grimly, if he was looking for money, he'd be disappointed! Curiosity got the better of her and she tiptoed onto the landing, intending to catch him redhanded at whatever he was doing.

At the top of the stairs she froze as Cassian's dark figure crossed the hall beneath her and glided stealthily into the sitting room. With the utmost care she crept down and by the time she peered into the room her nerves were strung along wires.

He stood with his back to her, his bulk just visible in the pale light which filtered through the thin curtains. He seemed to be listening, his very muscles and sinews straining from powerful emotion as he remained rooted to the spot with that deep inner stillness which was peculiar to him.

Laura frowned. Something about him kept her from calling out. He wasn't searching for anything. More like... making a reaquaintance with the house.

She stiffened, her hand going to her mouth as she realised why he was creeping about like a burglar. Earlier on, he hadn't ventured into the rest of the house but had remained in the kitchen, and briefly, the hall.

Intuitively she knew that he must be reliving bad memories. A chill iced her spine.

'Cassian!' she breathed, aching to see what this was doing to him.

But he ignored her because no sound had emerged from her dry throat.

Unaware that he was being watched from the darkness of the hall, he scanned the sitting room with painstaking slowness. Half-turning, his eyes focused on the inglenook and she felt her heart lurch. In the gloom she could see that his face was bleak, his jaw rigid with tension.

'Cassian!' she pleaded in soft concern.

His body jerked. When he swung around she saw with shock that his eyes were silvered and as hard as bullets.

'This is private!' he said fiercely.

She felt like an intruder in her own house. His house. 'But—'

'Don't crowd me! Leave me alone!' he snapped.

Taking a deep breath, his face set, he strode to the fireplace. Picking up a log from the stack, he weighed it in his hand then sniffed its resiny smell. Slowly he returned it to the neatly-stacked pile. Placing his palm on the massive granite lintel across the fireplace, he stared moodily at the hearth.

Laura swallowed, knowing what must be going through his mind. He'd chopped logs in all weathers and had never complained or run to his blissfully unaware mother. Bathsheba was usually engrossed in painting her wonderful landscapes but, even so, Laura had found it hard to understand why Cassian had suffered in silence.

'I chopped those,' she said, desperate to lighten the oppressive atmosphere. 'My axe technique's improved over the years.'

His head lifted but he didn't look at her. 'I'm not in the mood to chat. Please go. I can lock up,' he said icily, his profile taut and uncompromising.

She bristled. 'I thought I'd better wait up because—'

His eyes blazed at her, black and glittering. 'I'm not a child!'

'But I made up a bed for you!' she protested tremulously. 'You wouldn't have known where to sleep...' She stopped, cut short by his irritable sigh.

'It didn't matter. I would have curled up on the sofa,' he said dismissively.

'But you would have been uncomfortable—'

'Laura! That's my problem, not yours!' He paused, gazing at her in consternation. 'I thought you knew me better,' he reproached.

She was shocked by her reaction to his disappointment. She wanted to understand him, to please him. And she had no idea what she'd done wrong.

'Don't live my life,' he went on, his face tight with restraint. 'Don't fit me into your ordered, conventional routine!'

'I was being thoughtful,' she said unhappily.

He looked at her helplessly. 'I know. You were. Hell.

Where do I begin? We both lived in this house for five years and you have no idea about me, do you?'

'We weren't close,' she sulked.

But, she realised to her astonishment, she'd always longed to be.

'OK. It was a misunderstanding. You were being kind—but I had no idea you'd take it on yourself to look after me. I thought—wrongly—that you knew me better and you'd leave me to my own devices. It never occurred to me that you'd prepare a bed for me—so you can't be annoyed with me for keeping you up.'

'No. Suppose not,' she muttered grudgingly.

He sighed. 'I don't know where to begin. Look, I can see it's hard for you to understand how I live—but please don't think you need to run around after me. I've slept on mud floors and bare mountains. I can take care of myself. To be honest, I'm not comfortable with being fussed over. It's...stifling. It's up to me if I eat pudding or not and it's my fault if I'm hungry as a consequence. I'm an adult. If I choose, I can stay out till morning, sleep downstairs or even outside in a field if I want.'

She was beginning to see his point of view. And she had known how independent he was. Unfortunately habit died hard, and the arrival of guests meant looking after them. She'd forgotten that Cassian wasn't an ordinary man.

'I understand,' she said, subdued.

Did he ever need anyone? Flashing into her mind came the unexpected thought that she wanted to care for him, to make him comfortable, happy. But he'd loathe that! She bit her lip and vowed not to push the lone-wolf Cassian into a domestic straitjacket.

'I know I'm difficult, Laura,' he said ruefully. 'I did warn you. I've inherited from my mother an abhorrence of being organised.'

She smiled and lifted bright eyes to his. 'Oh, yes! I remember her yelling at Father about that! I won't do it again.

You can organise yourself in future. But…if you happen to be passing the back room any time, you'll see I've made up a bed for you there. You won't have to cosy up to a sheep tonight,' she said lightly.

'Thank you. I appreciate your trouble. Goodnight.'

He hadn't smiled back at her attempt at levity. His tone was tight and strained and she knew he wanted to be alone.

'Goodnight,' she said, unwilling to go.

She almost told him what time breakfast would be, but realised he'd expect to sort himself out. He didn't need anyone. Especially her.

Upset at that thought, she left the room, her bare feet silent on the cold stone. Back in the sitting room Cassian gave a harsh exhalation of breath and she hesitated, her pulses racing.

'Hell!' he muttered in the silence. His voice had broken up as if emotion was choking him. 'Give me strength,' he growled shakily.

Laura was appalled. Was he pleading for strength to cope with her? She listened, her ears straining in the stillness of the night.

'You nerd. It's a cupboard,' she heard him mutter.

And her heart seemed to leap to her throat. The cupboard. He'd been banished there more times than she could remember. It had been unlit then, with a freezing stone floor and huge spiders.

Cassian was testing himself. That's the kind of man he was. Before he felt able to stay here, he needed to come to terms with the harshness of his treatment at Thrushton.

Her eyes darkened as her tender heart went out to him. And yet…if he did conquer the past then she would definitely find herself without a home. From her point of view it might be better if Cassian never overcame the bad memories which filled the silent corners of the house.

She could leave him to it. Hope that he discovered he hated the atmosphere still, and that the reminders of her adoptive father and her aunt were too powerful even for him to be comfortable with.

But even as that thought raced through her head, she knew she had to help him. His distress cut into her very heart and nothing would stop her from offering solace, not even his scorn or his anger.

Soundlessly, she tiptoed back to the doorway, initially keeping well hidden in the shadows.

As she'd expected, he stood in front of the cupboard, his fists tightly clenched, his shoulders high. A rush of emotion hurtled through her. This had been his hell. And she couldn't just walk upstairs when her soul was reaching out to him in sympathy.

Quietly she crossed the soft carpet and stood so close to him that their arms touched. For a moment it seemed that he leaned nearer, though she might have been the one to do so. The fact that he hadn't yelled at her was encouraging and she even believed that his tense muscles had relaxed a little.

'Don't do this, not now,' she whispered into the thick, cloying silence.

'I must.'

Stricken by his choked reply, she astonished herself by putting an understanding hand on his increasingly rigid back. Looking up at him, she saw that his jaw was set and his eyes seemed distant as if he remembered every incident, each indignity, the slaps and the punishments which had made up his days.

With a suddenness that took her by surprise, he lurched forwards and wrenched open the cupboard door. The breath became strangled in her throat. His face was white and he was sweating, beads of perspiration standing out on his forehead.

Her fist went to her mouth. 'Oh, Cassian!' she whispered.

He didn't speak. For a long, agonising time he stared into the black recesses of the deep cupboard and she relived her own terror of all those years ago when he'd nonchalantly walked in there, his head held high in defiance as if he were entering a paradise.

The hackles rose on the back of Laura's neck. For the freedom-loving Cassian this must have been a terrible ordeal.

Seconds ticked past and his facial muscles tightened till she couldn't bear it. 'Cassian—'

'Shut me in.'

She jerked in a shocked breath. *'What?'*

'Do it.'

He stepped in and turned, his eyes commanding her.

'No!' she breathed in horror.

He glowered, his jaw clenched. 'Do it!' he commanded.

She gulped. And knew she must. Mesmerised, she clasped the latch in a shaking hand and slowly closed the door. Aghast, she stared at the oak panels with wide, anxious eyes. For several long minutes she waited, cold and shivering, her pulse thundering in her ears as she imagined what must be going through his mind.

There was a light knock on the door. With relief she stumbled forwards to open it again and Cassian emerged: shaking, breathing heavily, but with the light of triumph in his eyes. Laura gave a little cry and ran to him, briefly hugging him before moving back in confusion.

'You're freezing!' he said with a frown. He reached out and rubbed her arms.

'I'm all right,' she croaked, still reeling from the feel of his strong body against hers. 'Are you?'

'Fine.'

His hands were slowing and warmth was flowing into her—though it was nothing to do with any external temperature. She picked off spider threads from his shirt and suddenly felt overcome with the intimacy of such an action.

'I was just worried about you,' she babbled.

'I was OK. I'll put a key on the inside so no one can ever be locked in. It's all in the past, now.'

'I really didn't want to shut that door. It wasn't your favourite place of all time. Was it really awful, being locked in there when you were a kid?' she asked, and could have kicked herself for such stupidity. Of course it had been awful.

'It was a lesson.'

Puzzled, her small face lifted to his. And she saw the strength there, the fierce willpower which she had always admired and envied.

'In what?' she asked in awe.

'Detachment. Mind over matter.'

'But you must have dreaded going in there each time,' she persisted, for some reason wanting him to acknowledge the horror of sitting in a small, dark cupboard on a solid stone floor for hours on end.

'Sometimes, Laura,' he said huskily, 'you have to face your fears to become stronger.'

'But...' Her face grew perplexed. 'Everywhere you look in this house you must see things you'd rather forget.'

'If you can live here,' he said softly, 'so can I.'

'I'm different—'

'You can say that again,' he murmured wryly.

She flushed, wishing they weren't light years away from one another. But persisted with her point. 'We are total opposites. You and your mother were like...like wild birds!' she exclaimed. 'You both craved freedom! I, however, have always been tractable—'

'Laura. Don't be mistaken; we are all passionate about the things we love.' His hot, dark eyes burned into hers till the breath came short and fast in her throat and she could feel the increased pressure of his hands around her arms. 'Even you. You are passionate about your son—'

'Am I?' she breathed in amazement.

'Fiercely. Your love for him overrides everything else.'

His smile dazzled her, sending her nerves into a tailspin. 'As for me, I don't know why I have to be here, only that I felt an irresistible pull the moment Tony mentioned the house. And,' he went on huskily, 'when I saw the sun on the fells, glinting on the drystone walls and Thrushton nestling on the slopes, my heart leapt in my body. I need to be here and I will come to terms with my past. That is just a cupboard and it holds no terrors for me any more. I must live here to make this house ordinary in my mind again. I think it's part of my rites of passage.'

She grasped that, but would never fully understand him, she thought, stunned by how sad that made her feel. She would never know what drove him, pleased him, made him tick. Would never reach the impenetrable depths which made him so fascinating and desirable.

The past and the present collided. Tension had torn at her nerves making them raw. Cassian always unsettled her, turned her life upside down, upset her. She began to cry silently but didn't know why, and turned away blindly so that he didn't suspect.

But he knew. His hands were on her shoulders, strong, firm, comforting. Gently he coaxed her around and then suddenly she seemed to be crushed against him, weeping quietly into his shoulder.

'I—I'm sorry!' she mumbled in dismay, trying to pull back. He resisted her efforts and she was secretly glad. 'I shouldn't—'

His finger lifted her chin and she did her best to stop her stupid sobbing. 'If you need to cry, then cry,' he said softly. 'There's no point in bottling it up.'

There was. Miserably she blinked in a heroic effort to stem the flood, her tongue desperately mopping up any tears which headed near her mouth. Something told her that if she really let go, then all her carefully constructed world would start falling apart.

'I have to stay in control!' she mumbled.

'Why?'

'Of course I must! Everyone should! Where'd we be otherwise?' she said wildly.

'Laura!' he husked.

His hand slid around to cradle her jaw. Through the veil of tears she could see that his eyes were bright, his lips parted in consternation.

There was a tenderness in his expression which made her heart lurch. Suddenly she felt giddy, as if she were being lifted off her feet by a whirling wind and carried into the sky. Her eyes seemed to be closing of their own accord. The sensation persisted, even intensified and she had the impression that there was no solid ground beneath her feet any more.

She could smell him. A wonderful, alien, male smell that tantalised her nostrils and increased the beat of her heart. Beneath her palms his chest was firm, the pressure of his body a delight.

A soft sigh escaped her as she revelled in the contrast between his masculine strength and her own soft yielding.

'Cassian,' she found herself murmuring.

His embrace enfolded her more securely and she felt an extraordinary elation. Although she was intensely aware of her nakedness beneath the robe and thin cotton nightdress it didn't bother her.

Drowsily her eyes opened. A sudden rush of warm breath raced over her face and she tensed expectantly, straining upwards for the wonderful moment when their mouths would meet.

'Would you…?'

Laura smiled invitingly, delighted by his huskiness. 'Mmm?' she prompted gently.

He cleared his throat. 'Would you like my handkerchief or are you all right now?' he shot out.

They both stepped back from one another; Cassian's expression unreadable, hers transparent with disappointment till she managed to haul the shreds of her tattered dignity about her again.

'I'm OK,' she lied jerkily, avoiding his horribly perceptive eyes.

OK? Her whole body was screaming for him, like a child having a tantrum because it has been deprived of a favourite toy.

'I don't know why I cried—' she mumbled.

'You don't need a reason. Or to give me one,' he said softly.

'I'm not a wimp—' she began.

'I know. I think you're brave.'

She met his eyes then, and found herself caught by them. 'Brave?' she squeaked, feeling her body reaching melting point again.

'Strong, too, and determined. It can't have been easy, bringing up Adam on your own with Enid presumably breathing fire and brimstone and calling all kinds of damnation on your head.'

She gave a wry smile. 'It was a bit like that.'

'You could have given him up for adoption,' he suggested.

'Never!' she declared in horror. 'He was my baby! I loved him from the start. I'd have sooner cut out my heart than give him away!'

'I thought so,' he said gently. 'Laura, I want you to listen to me very carefully. This is important.'

He was smiling at her. She responded with one of her own and was thrilled when she saw a glow light up his eyes.

Kiss me, she told him, with every ounce of her being.

'I'm listening,' she said, deceptively demure. And intensely hopeful.

Cassian touched his lips with the tip of his tongue and Laura swallowed, her eyes huge with longing.

'I believe in Kismet. Fate,' he said thickly.

It had brought him here. 'Me too,' she breathed, her face radiant.

Tight-jawed, he folded his arms, a gesture which immediately put a barrier between them. Laura's hopes and dreams began to fade.

'My arrival releases you,' Cassian said, still hoarse, but perhaps with embarrassment and not desire.

Laura stared in dismay, her mouth suddenly unruly and refusing to obey when she tried to stop it quivering.

'From…what?' she mumbled with difficulty.

'Everything that's kept you here. For you,' Cassian continued more curtly, 'the next journey in life is to shake off the shackles of this house and this village and to take your son and yourself somewhere new.'

'No!' she cried in horror.

He frowned down at her, no longer someone she could trust, but a cold and determined stranger.

'You are strong and you are brave, and your devotion to Adam will ensure that you both survive. I know you can do it,' he rasped. 'I'll give you a week to tell Adam and to get used to the idea. After that, you're out on your ear.'

CHAPTER SIX

THE sound of music woke her, seeping through the house with a soft insistence. Glancing in outrage at the bedside clock she saw it was only six-thirty.

Wretched Cassian! She needed that extra half-hour after tossing and turning all night, seething with anger at how badly she'd misread Cassian's intentions! Far from being close to kissing her, he'd been searching for a way to tell her she wasn't welcome in his house.

And now she was horribly, thoroughly awake.

Muttering under her breath, she dived into the bathroom and showered, dressed and made her bed all in record time. And apart from the few moments when she wielded her toothbrush with unusual vigour, her teeth were angrily clamped together for the whole fifteen minutes.

As she passed Adam's room, she saw that the bed was already made. That meant Cassian had woken him too!

Determined to lay down a few ground rules before putting over her housekeeping plan, she stomped down the stairs, astonished to be met by the delicious smell of bacon.

And then she was confronted by the shocking sight of Adam, scarlet in the face—a fever, perhaps—and yet he was checking the six rashers sizzling gently on the grill which he was holding at a very careful arm's length.

She gasped. He was ill. Alone. Cooking without supervision! Of all the reckless, thoughtless...

'Adam!' she exclaimed. 'What the—?'

'Hi, Mum! Shall I do you some?'

She didn't know where to begin her tirade. She identified the source of the music. It came from a small, state of the art personal stereo. The wonderful swelling sound was washing gently through her brain, doing its best to soothe her temper.

But she wouldn't be placated. First she'd deal with Adam's fever. Then she'd find Cassian and flay him alive.

'Sweetheart, your face is terribly flushed,' she said bossily. 'I ought to take your temperature—'

'Morning, Laura. He's fine, it's only a healthy glow. We've been out for a run,' came Cassian's voice from the scullery beyond. 'Found some mushrooms on the way,' he added, coming into the kitchen.

Laura's eyes popped. True to his earlier threat, he was wearing nothing but a bath towel! Acres of tanned, muscular chest speedily impressed themselves on her retinas so indelibly that she wondered if she'd ever find room for any other vision again.

'M-morning!' she gasped.

'Chanterelles, parasols, ceps. Not bad. I've brushed them clean,' he said to Adam, casually adding the mushrooms to the grill and drizzling on a few drops of oil.

She blinked, all the better to clear her fogged eyes and brain and to see the interesting movements of muscle beneath the flawless back, which was so smooth and glowing that she could hardly hold back from reaching out to caress it.

Briefly she let her gaze wander to the narrow hips and the small, tight rear beneath the thin, clinging towel. It was an awful mistake. Terrible things were beginning to happen to her. Delicious sensations. Wicked yearnings.

But sex-god or not, her boring, Aunt-Enid generated conscience told her sternly, this man was ruthless and heartless and she'd better not forget that.

'Now Cassian—!' she began angrily, all set for a showdown.

'Just a sec—' He wasn't paying her any attention, his alert and watchful eyes constantly on Adam. 'Looks great, steady as she goes,' he said in his deep, calming voice, leaning nonchalantly against the Aga rail.

'Will the sausages pop?' Adam asked nervously.

'Not on the simmer plate. You've got a splatter guard, anyway. Just show them you're the boss. The pan will be safe and steady if you hold the handle firmly.'

'Like that?' Adam assumed a more commanding position.

'Perfect,' beamed Cassian. 'It's like everything; success is a matter of application and keeping focussed on the task.'

'The sausies look a bit brown on their bottoms,' Adam said uncertainly.

'You're right.' Cassian handed him the tongs.

Laura sullenly admired his technique. He hadn't said the sausages needed turning, but had waited till Adam had noticed that fact for himself. The edges were rubbed off her anger. She couldn't help but be impressed by Cassian, callous brute though he may be.

She sat down, non-plussed, her gaze sliding surreptitiously back to him as he raised a hand and slicked back his hair which was still wet and shiny from his shower. Absently he rubbed his damp palm on his rear. No noticeable wobble. Taut muscles. Small and neat…

Laura tried to breathe normally. She couldn't cope with so much nakedness, so much male beauty. It was too early. And to make matters worse, she had the distinct feeling that she was being superseded.

A sausage sizzled menacingly as Adam wielded the tongs. And she jumped up again.

'Cassian! The fat—!' she cried in alarm.

'Sound effects, nothing more,' Cassian said airily. 'There's virtually no fat at all, the way we're cooking. He's safe, I promise you.'

She glared. If her son was burned, she'd…

'Great grub, isn't it?!' enthused Adam, failing dismally to turn any of the sausages.

She took a step to help but felt a heavy hand descend on her shoulder pushing her back into the chair. Cassian's carefully draped towel brushed her leg. His hip was an inch from her eyes and she almost craned her neck to follow the delicious aroma of fresh soap that had accompanied his sudden movement.

'Little beggars, sausies, aren't they?' sympathised Cassian, releasing his hold on Laura. 'Oh, well done. They give in eventually. One down, three to go.'

Her mouth opened and closed. The burning imprint of his hand remained on her shoulder.

'What was this about a run?' she queried icily.

She peered hard at Adam for signs of exhaustion. There were none. That should have pleased her but it made her crosser than ever and she felt horribly guilty because of that.

'Cassian asked if I'd like to go with him. We were up before six,' Adam said proudly. 'We walked and jogged and ran then walked and jogged and ran,' he explained. 'It's a good way to start exercise. I could have gone on,' he boasted, 'but Cassian said he was starving so I agreed to come back.'

'Oh, yes?'

Laura's cynical glance made Cassian grin and shrug his shoulders in amusement behind Adam's absorbed back. Cassian was so fit he could have run to London and back without breaking into a sweat. But at least, she thought, Cassian had been careful not to drive her son to the limit of his endurance.

'This is a first. You never eat breakfast,' she pointed out to her son, having tried for years to interest him in more than a meagre slice of toast and a glass of orange.

It annoyed her that Adam didn't answer. He was occupied in looking blankly at the egg which Cassian had handed to him as if he'd never seen one.

'I'll do the first, you do the next,' Cassian murmured,

sotto voce. 'Watch. Small tap with a knife, fingers in carefully, open it up very slowly...break it into this cup and tip it into the poacher.'

He was behaving like a conspirator, Laura thought huffily. For the first time in her life, she was playing second fiddle to someone else in Adam's life. And she couldn't bear it.

To her amazement, Adam managed the tricky operation and grinned up at Cassian in delight, receiving a slap on the back.

'Eggsellent!' Cassian said with a grin.

Laura looked at her giggling son as if he'd betrayed her. 'So now you're a fan of cooked breakfasts,' she said lightly, trying to keep the scouring jealousy out of her tone.

'I didn't have the benefit of fresh air and exercise before,' he said absently.

He pushed back a blond hank of hair with a busy hand and cracked another egg with great success. It was as if he'd scored a goal for Manchester United.

'Hey! How about that?' he cried in delight, taking a bow.

'Brilliant,' conceded Laura, squirming at his pleasure. This wasn't her son. It just wasn't.

Cassian put an arm around Adam's shoulder. They looked very much at home with one another. Her eyes clouded.

'There's plenty for you, Laura,' murmured Cassian, 'if you want some. I bought loads.'

She could be proud and stick to toast and marmalade, or give in to her hysterical taste buds.

'Thanks,' she said stiffly, managing a compromise. 'I'll do myself some in a moment.'

She stalked over to the fridge for the juice and stood in amazement at the sight that met her eyes.

'Is this...yours?' she asked Cassian, overwhelmed by the amount of food crammed into the small space.

'And yours. I just grabbed a few things on my way here.'

'Few?' Steaks. A joint of lamb, chocolate eclairs...
'We...we can't—'

'Oh, Mum!' complained Adam. 'We can! It can be his
rent for staying here, can't it?'

Her teeth ground together. 'You answer that,' she said
sweetly to the amused Cassian.

'The food is for us. My contribution to the well-being of
our stomachs,' he fudged, his eyes mocking.

'Sending us off into the blue, well-fed?' she queried
waspishly, prompting him to come clean about his presence
in the house.

He smiled and didn't rise to her bait. 'With all the exercise Adam's intending to take, he'll need plenty of sus-
tenance,' he said easily.

'It's brilliant having you here, Cassian. And isn't this
music triff, Mum?' Adam declared, going off at a tangent
and totally oblivious to Laura's fury. 'Andean pipes.
S'posed to sound like condors, soaring over mountain
peaks. Condors are big birds of prey, Mum.'

'Are they?' she replied drily.

But she lifted her head and listened to the music, hearing
the sound of wind on feather, the chillingly beautiful echo
of the pipes—as if they were rebounding from one mountain top to another.

She was aware of Cassian watching her intently and lowered her gaze, annoyed to be caught out enjoying the music
and disturbed that her senses had been so deeply stirred.

'I've made Turkish coffee for myself. Want to try some?'
he murmured.

Even now, though she knew his intentions towards her—
eviction—her body trembled at the sound of his low, me-
lodious voice. Even, she thought, wryly, at the crack of
dawn.

If he could have this kind of effect on her, in a kitchen,
with the smell of sausages pervading the air, what could he

achieve over a candlelit dinner for two and a splash of aftershave?

'All right,' she said with a shrug.

Cassian poured some treacly liquid into a small cup from an exotic-looking silver jug with a beaked nose.

'Do you think everything's done now?' he asked Adam innocently.

'Um…yes, I reckon so,' he replied, flushing with pleasure at being given the responsibility to decide.

Laura shrank into herself even further. The two of them dished up and carried their heaped plates to the table. All very cosy, very intimate and chummy. Laura sat sipping the rich, sweet coffee, feeling utterly miserable and gooseberryish.

They chattered, she was quiet. Adam didn't slump as usual, or eat at a snail's pace. And he looked Cassian directly in the eye, instead of that hesitant, sideways glance he normally gave to people.

It was astonishing. In a few hours, her son had changed. A few culinary skills, a jog across the fields, and he'd gained in confidence.

A sharp pain sliced through her and she hastily got up to cook herself some breakfast. She was a failure. Adam had needed a father—or at the very least, a different mother, she thought, racked with guilt. But she'd done everything she could to protect him. Cared for him, sacrificed much. Why then, should she feel deeply inadequate?

Miserably she looked up, hearing Cassian offer her son a lift to school. She almost told Adam to do his teeth but daren't, not with Cassian's dark eyes upon her in warning.

'I'll go and do the gnashers,' Adam declared. 'Um… what do I need today?' She opened her mouth to reply, but closed it again around a piece of sausage, waiting for her son to work that one out for himself. Perhaps because he wasn't used to doing that, there was a long pause. 'I'd better check what lessons I've got and get my stuff together,' he said eventually. 'Then I can do some extra work on my project till it's time to go.'

'Mmm,' she enthused, and gave him a beaming smile of encouragement. 'You do that, darling.'

Adam dashed out and Cassian raised his coffee cup to her in admiring salute. Laura only just managed to stop herself from blushing coyly and joining the Cassian United Fan Club. But she knew how Adam felt, she mused. Heady, happy, pleased.

She glared at the seductive triangle of Cassian's back. He was already clearing dishes and running water for washing up, his feet planted firmly apart on the stone flags as he tested the temperature of the water and squirted in some of the ecologically friendly washing up liquid he'd bought.

Nice feet, she couldn't help but noticing. Well-shaped, with no ugly lumps or bumps. And muscular calves...

Furious with herself for finding him so attractive, she leapt up and stacked plates on the counter, then grabbed a tea towel. All madly domesticated, she thought grimly.

'Now, look,' she snapped. 'We need to talk.'

'Shall we save it till Adam's at school?' he suggested amiably, working away at an eggy plate.

'No! I can't wait! Now!' she hissed.

'You could shout at me more easily if he's not around,' Cassian pointed out, infuriatingly right.

Laura hauled in a huge breath, ready to explode, but she heard Adam thundering down the stairs and shot Cassian a vicious scowl instead.

'All right. Later,' she grated.

'Look forward to it,' Cassian murmured.

'Hey! I just had a thought,' Adam said excitedly, gazing at Cassian with a hopeful expression. 'Do you know anything about Ancient Egypt?'

'Lived in Cairo and Aswan for a couple of years,' Cassian replied and smiled at Laura when she let out a quiet snort. 'What do you need to know?' he asked Adam.

And soon they were both huddled over Adam's project, with fascinating stories being faithfully recorded—stories so well-told and interesting that Laura found herself moving quietly so that she didn't miss a word.

There were tales of Pharaohs, of greed and ambition, murder and achievement—all woven into a tapestry of facts and figures which made them seem all the more believable.

He was amazing. A walking encyclopaedia, she thought, deciding that everything he said was probably true. A devastatingly charismatic man—and already Adam had fallen under his spell.

She couldn't blame him. If she didn't know Cassian's intentions, she'd be sitting goggle-eyed at his feet, too.

Seeing her child's awe-struck face and shining eyes, she knew that he'd be terribly hurt when Cassian revealed that he owned Thrushton Hall. And she couldn't bear to see Cassian leading Adam on. If they did have to leave, then Adam would find it hard to deal with Cassian's two-faced betrayal.

'Time you went, darling,' she said, sounding choked. 'Got everything?'

'Oh, Mum—!'

'Come on,' Cassian said cheerfully. 'Plenty of time tonight to do a bit more after we've had our run.'

'Another?' Adam looked shocked. 'I usually watch TV—'

Cassian shrugged. 'Whatever you prefer—'

'Oh, a run!'

Laura glared. This was hero worship on a grand scale and it had to stop. '*After* your normal homework,' she put in quickly.

'I knew that!' protested Adam.

And Laura felt a shock go right through her. He was annoyed with her, for the first time in his life.

'I suppose I'd better get dressed,' Cassian said loudly. 'I

imagine towels aren't usually worn on the school run. Be down in a moment.'

'Sorry, Adam,' she said quietly, when Cassian had bounded up the stairs two at a time. 'I shouldn't have nagged.'

'It's OK, Mum. I usually need reminding.' They smiled at one another, friends again, both confused by the small crack in their relationship. 'Isn't he fab, Mum?' Adam enthused.

'Fab,' she managed with a smile.

And suddenly the future seemed even more uncertain than ever. If they left, they'd have problems adjusting to a new and hostile world. If they stayed...

She bit her lip. She'd have to watch her own child worshiping the ground Cassian walked on. She wouldn't be needed any more. The truth was, that Cassian had the advantage of maleness. They'd do men's things together.

And Cassian's extraordinary magic would act as a magnet to the impressionable Adam. She had no fascinating experiences, no exotic background or a storyteller's gift.

She just loved her child. And, she thought forlornly, it seemed that wasn't enough any more.

It was a long time before Cassian returned. She kept looking at the clock, wondering when he'd come back and rehearsing what she'd say.

Everything had been dusted twice, all surfaces wiped down, cobwebs whisked away. The house gleamed and smelt deliciously of lavender but it felt empty and silent after the chatter of the early morning.

Prompted by the deathly quiet, she fiddled with Cassian's stereo and managed to make it eject the condor music and accept something called 'Flames of Fire'.

The house throbbed to a deep and intensely sensual music that sent shivers down her spine and made her think unwisely of Cassian's warm eyes and erotic mouth.

Catching herself breathing more heavily than her recent bout of dusting should have produced, she decided to swap the flames of fire for something that didn't make her erogenous zones tingle. Like a party political broadcast. But she never made the switch.

'You there, Laura? I'm home!'

She stiffened at Cassian's voice, coming from the hall. 'Oh, no, you're not!' she muttered under her breath. This was her home. He merely owned it.

'What do you think of the music?' he asked cheerfully, immediately seeming to fill the sitting room with energy.

'I was just going to turn it off,' she grumped.

'Do that. And get smartened up. I'm taking you off to look for a job.'

Her mouth tightened stubbornly. 'I want to talk to you first—'

'Do it on the way.' He waited expectantly.

She tossed her head in defiance. 'Don't boss me around! I don't like being organised any more than you do—'

'But you need a job.'

'I can go on the bus,' she said, cutting off her nose to spite her face. A lift would have been marvellous. But not with *him*.

'Seems silly. I'm going anyway. So if you don't come with me, your heart to heart talk will have to wait till tonight.' He smiled at her sulky face. 'Come on. You might as well use me, mightn't you? And think of the yelling you can do, while I'm driving.'

He was utterly impossible! She glared. 'Put like that...'

With a show of reluctance, she stalked over to the door, expecting him to move aside. He didn't, and clearly wasn't intending to. The stereo whispered out a deeply passionate refrain that made her entire body contract.

Summoning up all her willpower, she slid past Cassian, totally, intensely aware of the feel of his moleskin trousers, the softness of his brushed cotton shirt, the flurry of warm breath that disturbed her hair…and her senses.

Hot and flustered, she scurried up the stairs. Her heart pounded as she scrabbled out of her clothes and dug out her interview suit. Bottle-green, second-hand and badly fitting. Crisp shirt, well-polished court shoes, well-worn. Ditto handbag.

Smooth the mussed-up hair. How had that happened? Cold water on face. Done.

He was waiting outside. Took one look at her—clearly disapproving, from the quick frown—and opened the passenger door without a word.

Composed now, she climbed onto the high step, hampered by her skirt. Cassian gave a brief push on her bottom and she slid into the comfortable seat pink with embarrassment but determined to use her time usefully.

'I have a proposition,' she announced briskly as they pulled away.

'Uh-huh.'

'You know all the reasons I want to stay.'

'Yup.'

Her hands fidgeted nervously in her lap. Cassian reached over to her side and she flattened herself against the back of the seat. With a curious look at her, he turned on the radio and pushed in a cassette.

Laura groaned. Loin-stirring flamenco music.

'Well,' she said stiffly, 'I've thought of a way to solve the problem.'

Cassian didn't look too pleased about that. 'Oh?' he grunted.

'You can live at Thrushton Hall.'

'Thanks. I'm with you so far,' he drawled.

She took a deep breath. The next bit was tricky.

'I get a job, stay at Thrushton too—and pay rent, and I do all the housework and cooking and washing for you!'

She looked at him anxiously. The signs weren't good. Beetled brows, furrowed brow, tight mouth.

'One teeny flaw. I don't need a housekeeper or a cook or someone to do my washing,' he declared.

Her heart sank. She felt stupid for not realising. Cassian would bring over his woman to Thrushton. It was too painful to contemplate.

'I'd forgotten. You've got your wife. Partner. Whatever,' she floundered miserably.

'No wife, partner or whatever. My wife died when Jai was born,' he snapped.

Now she'd hurt him. 'I'm sorry,' she mumbled.

'Laura, please try to tune in to the kind of man I am. I've always looked after myself. I need no woman for that.' His glance seared into her. 'I've never needed a woman for anything other than love.'

Love. He had sounded very sad as if he was remembering the woman he'd adored so much that he'd risked his love of freedom and gone willingly into marriage. And his wife had died tragically. How awful.

There was a long silence. Then timidly she ventured again.

'You and Jai would be alone?'

'It's how we like it.'

'But I could save you from doing domestic things. They're boring. You'd have more freedom,' she enlarged, 'if you didn't have to do chores—'

'You're very persistent.'

'It's very important!' she replied. 'Well?'

'No.'

Her stomach lurched at the finality of his tone. 'Why not? You hate restrictions! Shopping and cooking—'

'I don't shirk responsibility,' he corrected. 'I just don't do things that are unnecessary.'

'Please, think about it—' she begged, horrified that her great plan had been so casually rejected.

'No.'

She pressed her fist to her mouth and tried to stop the tears of disappointment. She'd really failed this time. For a moment she contemplated the abyss that was her future.

It would be terrible. She felt sick. Adam would be devastated. Her head jerked up. Adam!

'In that case…' She choked, swallowed, and tried to find her voice again. 'In that case,' she cried hotly, 'if we're out on our ears at the end of the week, then leave Adam alone! Don't get close to him!' The flamenco rose to a crescendo and she found herself shouting angrily over the fiery beat. 'You'll destroy him, Cassian! You're not blind. You can see he thinks you're Mr Wonderful. You sit there, telling him stories, behaving like—like a *father* to him, the father he's always wanted, and yet in a few days' time you'll be rejecting him! You can't do that!' she stormed, beating her fists on her knees. 'You can't hurt him, I won't let you…' She broke off. He was pulling over, driving onto the verge. 'What are you doing?' she flared.

'Out.' He jerked his head at her.

Her mouth dropped open. 'You don't mean—?'

'No, I'm not abandoning you,' he said wearily. 'But this is important and I can discuss this more easily when I don't have to concentrate on the road.'

'Discuss?' she raged, half-falling out of the car in her eagerness to get out before he helped her. 'There's no point in talking! You won't listen to me. You don't care what happens to Adam and me. You have no heart! It doesn't matter that he'll be distraught because his god has turned out to have feet of clay and that—'

'Laura!' Cassian was shaking her, his grip firm on her arms. 'Laura, *I do care*!'

CHAPTER SEVEN

HE COULDN'T believe he'd admitted that. He felt her freeze, every muscle, every breath in her body halted by his claim.

'What?' she whispered, searching his face.

'I care about Adam,' he said shortly, and released her. 'Come and sit in the sun.'

'I'm all right here!' she yelled.

'As you wish.'

Touched by her wonderful stubbornness, he settled himself on the low stone wall and stared out at the valley, hoping his inflamed senses would simmer down.

Laura had been more passionate than he could have believed possible. Yesterday he'd watched her responding to the music and enjoying the wine, an excitement surging within him as he saw her long overdue awakening to the pleasures in life.

His body had known little rest since. It demanded that he should introduce her to the greatest pleasure of all.

His eyes closed to the warmth of the sun, feeling his very bones melt at the thought of making love to Laura. Despite the terrible green suit.

'Cassian.'

There was a lurch in his loins. She had come to sit near him.

'Mmm?' he grunted.

'If you care—'

'It's because I care, because I see a child longing to be part of the hurly-burly of the world,' he said grimly, determined to deny himself the pleasure he wanted, 'that I'm determined to extract you both from your shell. He must

101

take his life in his own hands. He's desperate to be liked at school. I've never seen a kiddie so anxious to please—'

'What do you mean?' she demanded, suddenly alert. 'Something happened, didn't it? Tell me!' she cried, grabbing his arm with both hands.

He glanced quickly at her fiery eyes and only just managed to drag his gaze away and fix it on a distant peak.

'Oh, some kids making fun—'

'Of Adam?' she cried, aghast.

He sighed, and decided he'd better explain. 'They were actually pointing at—and mocking—what they imagined to be my rucksack. It's orange, you see. Day-Glo. So I got out and told them it was my paraglider and offered to show it to them.'

She frowned. 'You mean those parachutes with a sort of strap seat thing beneath it? You fling yourself off mountains for fun?'

'Something like that.' He was amused by her description of one of the most exhilarating sports in the world. To fly. To soar into the sky, to stay airborne by reading the contours of the ground and assessing the thermals… Breathtaking. 'It's a little more complicated, but that's the general idea,' he acknowledged.

'Then what happened?' she asked curiously.

Bedlam. He grinned and played the whole thing down.

'We got quite a crowd around us. I answered questions about it and then a woman with a letterbox mouth came over and told us all off for not hearing the bell.'

'Miss Handley,' Laura said, her mouth curving into a reluctant smile.

'Yes. The Head. I apologised, said it was all my fault and why and before I knew what was happening, she had me in there giving a talk during her assembly.'

Cassian watched a sparrowhawk spill out the air from its wings, mastering thermals without knowing how.

'I can imagine.' To his relief, Laura sounded drily

amused. Then she frowned. 'I suppose Adam is madly impressed.'

And he sighed. Even now he felt upset by Adam's pitiful delight to be associated with someone 'cool'.

'Adam helped me with my talk,' he said in a low tone. 'Unwrapping my wing. The parachute,' he explained. 'He sat in the seat while I held it.'

He didn't want to say any more. He could see the child's face, bright with joy to be regarded with such envy by the entire school while he talked of flying with black vultures over Spain and with the condors in South America. It hurt him to remember.

Laura was silent. He was glad, needing time to push some steel into his backbone because somewhere a little voice was becoming more insistent, saying that Laura's solution was workable, that he could help them both.

Then common sense reasserted itself. He wasn't God. Shouldn't meddle. She had to find her own way. All he should do was to put her on the road.

Dippers bobbed about on the rocks in the turbulent river below. A heron flapped lazily across the meadow. Far in the distance he could see that a deer had become trapped in a field, enclosed by the high stone walls.

It ran up and down in panic, unsure how it had got there, incapable of finding its way back to safety. He realised that this was what he was doing to Laura and Adam: flinging them into an alien space where there were no recognisable landmarks. Yet, like the deer, they wanted to hide in safety—

'There's a deer trapped!' she cried with concern. And she pointed.

'I know.'

'I forgot. You don't miss a thing, do you?' she said ruefully. 'It's scared, Cassian. Can't we go down the valley and help it somehow?'

'No.'

'Surely we must—'

'Laura, I hate to see it so frightened but we'd scare it even more if we started waving our arms and trying to get it back to the wood. It could hurt itself on the wall—break a leg, perhaps in its panic. Or get caught up in the barbed wire at the top end of the field.'

'It looks so frightened,' she said in a small voice.

He laid his hand on hers. 'It must find its own way,' he said gently.

And, extraordinarily, he wanted to keep Laura safe with him, and not send her out into the wide world. His jaw clenched. He was just missing Jai. Needed company. Someone to hold.

'What is it?' Laura asked softly.

'Jai.' His voice was choked with emotion.

He knew she nodded, though he kept staring straight ahead.

'You're a very caring man. Jai is very lucky to have you as a father.'

He sought her eyes then, almost faltering at the beauty of her misted blue gaze.

'A callous brute like me?' he joked.

She smiled wistfully. 'I know you think you're doing the right thing—that you believe it's "good" for us,' she breathed.

Her face lifted to his, the wind ruffling her hair. And he felt his heart lurch. She was entering his very bones. Shaking the cells in his body. It was purely a yearning for the softness of a woman, nothing to do with her personally.

Do it, a satanic voice urged. Wake her up. Kiss her.

'I think we'd better go job-hunting,' he said in strangled tones, his eyes hopelessly enmeshed with hers.

'OK. But…about us staying on. Reconsider. A trial period. Please.'

Passion suffused her face. She looked radiant. And he could resist no longer. His mouth closed on hers and he

groaned with hunger as she responded eagerly, inex-
pertly...but oh, so sweetly, the taste of her more succulent
than the most exotic fruit, the pressure of her hand on his
arm more welcome than he could ever have imagined.

Her hand slid to his neck. He drew her close, absorbing
her into him, the needs of his mouth becoming more and
more desperate as he sought to kiss life into every part of
her.

To his astonishment, his neck was encircled in crushing
arms, his head forced down till his mouth and thus his
kisses became bruising. Laura had erupted. She was clamouring for him, moaning, crying, urging with a vehemence that startled and thrilled him to the core.

He lifted her onto him, her skirt riding up and her legs
sliding around his waist. They clung in total abandon, not
caring that anyone might drive by—although it was a rarely
used road—oblivious to everything but the sensational release of long-held desires.

Her skin felt like velvet. Her hair tumbled over her forehead, silky and faintly perfumed of rosemary and he explored every inch of her face with impassioned delight.

He was weakening, kiss by kiss. Each wickedly innocent
caress of her work-roughened hands aroused him more than
any artful, silken finger. Laura was without artifice, her passion real and untaught.

That dazzled him, made his head spin with wonder. If
he could have this glorious woman in his bed, he'd...

'Cassian!'

She had tensed. But he hadn't sated himself with her yet.
So he continued to kiss her, to coax her now stubbornly
closed mouth, sliding his tongue over it, enticing it open.

Except that it stayed resolutely closed, despite the sexual
shudders which racked her body.

'Laura,' he murmured pleadingly.

'No!'

Oh, God, he thought, seeing her stricken face. She regrets what she's done. His arms fell away.

She looked down at her skirt, at the long lengths of slender tanned thigh which were making his loins liquid with their promise, and she gasped in horror then scrambled awkwardly away. With his reluctant help.

She turned her back, her face scarlet, eyes huge and glistening. Her skirt found its correct position. Her jacket was buttoned up, her hair hastily pressed smooth. And he saw with a wrench to his heart that her shoulders were shaking.

'Laura,' he ventured gently.

'No! Don't touch me! Don't come near me!' she squeaked.

'We just kissed,' he tried, playing it down.

Just! He'd seen stars. Been in heaven for a while. Dreamed impossible dreams.

Her head lifted and he dearly wanted to kiss the sweet nape of her neck.

'*You* might be used to grabbing women and—and—'

'Kissing them,' he supplied, seeing that she was struggling.

'Well,' she demanded, whirling around, all fire and passion again. 'Are you?'

How he wanted to take her in his arms again! That energy of hers needed an outlet—his, too.

'Not with such spectacular results,' he admitted, thinking how easily she'd aroused him.

She swallowed, as if horrified by his answer. And ran to the car. He didn't help her to get in. He didn't think she wanted to be touched.

He put his hands on the wall to steady himself because his legs seemed like water. His hands were shaking too.

Several deep breaths later, he'd come to the conclusion that he'd made things worse. Laura's hidden depths had come to the surface but he'd been almost drowned in the process. Of course he'd known from the start that Laura wasn't a run-of-the-mill woman. Whatever she felt, she felt fiercely.

So long as he realised that her uninhibited response hadn't been to him, *for* him, but was a reaction to her stifled emotions, he'd be all right. She would never want sex without strings. Whereas that was all he'd allow himself.

He gave her a moment to compose herself. Below, he saw that the deer had gone. It had found sanctuary. Perhaps, he mused, some people thrived better in their own small worlds.

The thought hit him like a sledgehammer. He could be wrong about extending Laura's field of vision, enlarging her horizons.

Yet now he'd kissed her, she could never remain at Thrushton—not if she wanted to stay out of his bed.

He muttered a low curse, went back to the car and settled himself in the driver's seat without comment.

'It never happened!' she whispered hoarsely.

He shot her a cynical look. If she thought he could ever forget that moment, she had another think coming.

The gears ground beneath his jerky grip. 'Let's concentrate on finding you employment, shall we?' he suggested, grinding the words out through his teeth as harshly as he'd ground the gears.

The beautiful scenery was lost on him. He kept blaming himself, trying to understand why he'd acted so precipitously. The desire for pleasure, he supposed. And, for a short time, what pleasure!

Once in Harrogate, he marched her off to a boutique. And, ignoring all her bad-tempered protests, coldly persuaded her that she'd get a job a hell of a lot faster if she wasn't wearing one of Aunt Enid's 'costumes'. If that's what it was.

Sulkily she saw the sense of what he was saying and insisted on paying him back out of her future wages. The assistant whisked Laura off and he lounged in an armchair, being plied with coffee and biscuits by a pretty redhead. Her legs weren't as good as Laura's. Nor her cheekbones.

'What do you think?' trilled the assistant smugly.

He turned his head and gulped like a teenage boy faced with a nude woman for the first time. Only this one was far better than nude. Dressed, she was absolutely breathtaking.

Finding his mouth was open, he closed it and summoned up as near-normal a voice as he could.

'Perfect.'

Laura's eyes had deepened to a startling sky-blue, enhanced by the soft navy dress. It skimmed her body but any connoisseur of women could see that she had a fabulous figure and the unbroken length of the sleeveless dress, grazing her collarbone and falling smoothly to just below the knee, made her look taller and more imposing than before. Helped by the elegant high heels and…surely new, sheer stockings.

As she moved in response to the assistant's instructions, he realised that Laura had incredible poise, her carriage as graceful as a model's.

'And there's a jacket to go with it that matches Modom's eyes,' the assistant crowed, bustling to put it on the increasingly astonished 'Modom'.

'Do you like it, Laura?' he asked dead-pan, entranced by her rapturous face.

She eyed him uncertainly. 'I do. I think it's gorgeous! But I don't think I'd be able to afford it—'

'Your…leaving present, then,' he suggested in clipped tones, finding the words ridiculously hard to say.

Her eyes widened in consternation. 'Leaving! Oh, yes. Leaving.' She gulped. The idea was obviously terrifying to her. He thought of the frightened deer. 'I—I don't know—'

'I do.' Feigning a frown, he stood up and handed over his credit card. 'I'm not hanging around any longer,' he said, with a good attempt at irritation. 'People to see. I've got an office to set up.'

'An office?' she repeated in amazement. *'You?'*

'For a colleague,' he growled. And realised he'd have to be careful if he was to keep his business a secret. 'Come on. That outfit is fine.'

And so with a little judicious bullying and much tutting at his watch, he rail-roaded her into accepting an expensive designer outfit, the shoes too, and a handbag which the assistant hastily found.

By the time they drove back later that day he'd leased a large Georgian building overlooking the green and had ordered the necessary office furniture and computer equipment. Sheila was due any time and he didn't want his charitable foundation to suffer any delays.

He wasn't the only one who'd had a successful day. Laura had four good job offers to consider. Success had wiped away her earlier distress and made her glow with pride. She looked utterly ravishing and he found it hard to keep his mind on the road.

This was a turning point for her, he thought. And wondered if she'd change, and become hard, efficient and slick.

Hopefully not. Since the incident in the restaurant when the waitress had flung banoffi pie over his arm, she'd mellowed towards him. That meant she had a soft heart. May it never harden. Wherever she went.

His stomach sucked in. There it was again. A pain. He didn't want her to go. Suddenly it was difficult to pump breath through his lungs. He felt as if he was panicking and set his mind to conquering his weak and wayward body.

'I'm in a total whirl!' she confessed as they bumped through Grassington's cobbled square. 'Which job do *you* think I ought to accept, Cassian?'

'It's your decision.'

His tone was abrupt enough to make her sink back into her seat and work out the pros and cons of each offer in silence.

Cassian couldn't understand why her success should bug him. What was he afraid of? He wanted her to extend her horizons and to become self-assured. Wanted her to have a better standard of living. Yet her imminent departure filled him with unease. No—be honest—misery. How could that be?

Appalled, his thoughts winged back to Jai again. It must be that he felt lonely. He and his son had never been apart for so long. That was it!

With a screech, he brought the car to a halt overlooking Thrushton village, the relief surging through him in waves.

'Got to ring Jai,' he explained, before leaping out.

Even in her bewildered state and with several job offers to consider, Laura noticed his urgency, the way he fumbled with the mobile attached to his belt and punched numbers with an almost frantic haste. He dearly loves his son, she thought soberly.

And the happiness that lit up his face when he spoke to Jai made her heart somersault. He didn't trouble to disguise how he felt. He looked thrilled, amazed, tender and amused, all in the space of a few moments.

He couldn't keep still, but strode about, gesticulating excitedly with his free arm, occasionally pushing a hand through his hair till it tumbled about in gypsy curls and made him look boyishly appealing.

If only she could be that free, that much at ease with Adam!

'Good news?' she queried, unable to hold back a smile. Cassian looked elated, his eyes sparkling like black diamonds.

'He's heading back!' Cassian leapt energetically into the car, beside himself with delight. 'Arriving later this week, depending on when he can get a flight. Isn't that fantastic?!'

His happiness was infectious and she found herself beaming. 'Wonderful,' she said huskily, wishing she could bring such a light to his eyes. 'We've both got something to celebrate.'

The light died a little. 'Yes. We have,' he said slowly.

And he suddenly jerked around, setting the car in motion again, his profile a confusing mix of pleasure and regret and anger.

Laura was puzzled. In fact he'd been odd ever since they'd met up after going their separate ways and she'd announced with pride how well she'd done in her interviews. His praise had been less generous than she'd expected and it seemed as if he was almost...sorry, yes, sorry, that she would soon be out in the world of commerce.

Had he hoped she'd fail? It didn't seem like Cassian. He was too big-hearted, too adamant that she should stop hiding herself away.

She glanced at him surreptitiously. He was frowning, his mouth grim. The tension in his hands would have been obvious to anyone. Perhaps his day hadn't been to his liking.

'What's wrong?' she asked softly.

His body contracted. He continued to glare at the road. 'Thinking.'

From the harshness of his tone, he didn't want to be disturbed. He shifted in his seat, drawing her attention to the flatness of his stomach, the stretch of soft moleskin over his thigh.

She drew in an involuntary breath before she knew what she was doing. He flicked her a sharp glance and the air seemed to thicken. She could feel her blood racing around her body, scalding her from within and she looked away, quickly.

Already she'd made a fool of herself. Perhaps that was what he was worrying about—wondering if she'd embarrass him in front of his son. She groaned inwardly. He must have been shaken by the way she'd responded to his kiss. Or had she made the first move? It had all been so sudden, so inevitable.

Whatever had happened to her? Had she unwittingly encouraged him? Had he—being acutely perceptive—read the signals she'd tried to hide…and acted on what he knew had been surging within her body?

She cringed, remembering with shame how abandoned she'd been, taking that kiss several stages too far. Cassian must have been appalled.

But… She bit her lip, frowning. Something had snapped inside her and she hadn't been able to stop herself. Her lack of control scared her. She needed to keep a tighter rein on herself.

So what about Cassian? Why had he taken up her unintentional invitation? Racking her brains, she remembered that they'd been talking about Jai. Heaven help her, she thought. She was a love-substitute. Cassian had wanted to be with his son—and he'd kissed her in an expression of his own loneliness.

Idiot! Stupid, arrogant dummy that she was! She stared into the window, seeing her own blurred reflection. A dull mouse; now dressed up in fabulous clothes, but clad in ghastly bottle-green yuk when they'd kissed.

She couldn't believe that she'd imagined he'd been interested in her. Would a man like Cassian ever be attracted to a homebody? Her eyes darkened. No. He'd go for the Bathsheba type: hot, passionate, simmering and unpredictable.

Her fingers touched her lips, every nerve in her body reliving the pressure of his mouth. It seemed that she had become hopelessly addicted to Cassian. Ever since he'd arrived there'd been a current of electricity linking them, setting her on fire.

Adam might hero-worship Cassian, she thought soberly, but so did she, after his behaviour today. His actions had proved him to be the kind of man she'd always admired. Thoughtful to others, courteous, easy company.

Lunch had been such fun. And he'd been so nice to the waitress, when the rather shaky-handed older woman had dropped the pudding onto his sleeve then burst into floods of tears.

To her amazement, he'd jumped up, put an arm around the woman's shoulders and drawn her aside, talking to her for a while and calming her down—totally ignoring the tight-lipped head waiter.

'Her husband's up for shoplifting,' he'd explained, when he finally returned to the table with profuse apologies for his absence. 'She thinks he might have Alzheimer's.'

'That's awful!' Laura had said, her eyes rounding. 'The head waiter was awfully mad—'

'Not any more, he's not.' Cassian accepted a substitute banoffi pie from a smiling waitress.

'Got you a big helping,' the young girl whispered. 'And thanks. That's my Mum you saved from the sack.'

'She'll be OK,' Cassian assured her quietly. 'I've arranged with the management that she can have time off to organise a decent defence—and a medical check for your father.'

For Laura, the rest of the meal had been spent in a haze of admiration. Now watching the houses of Thrushton loom nearer, Laura leaned back in her seat, her head filled with thoughts of Cassian and his kindness to people.

She knew that it hadn't been a show for her benefit. Kindness was ingrained in him. When she'd arrived early at their arranged meeting-point, she'd wandered through a department store and had seen Cassian unfolding a baby buggy while a young woman juggled child and shopping. Carefully he had tucked the toddler in, making it giggle while the mother had stowed away her laden bags. And they'd parted in smiles.

More important to Laura, a few moments later he'd

checked to see if she was in sight—not knowing she was following behind him—and made a point of going around the square to slip money into the hands of the young men who were begging there.

That had really touched her heart and melted any doubts she had about his values. It always upset her to see people reduced to such terrible indignities. Maybe some of them were 'fake'. But plenty were not. How did you ever know?

'Cassian…'

'Uh,' he grunted.

She searched for a diplomatic way to bring up the subject. 'Did you notice the beggars today?'

'Hmm.'

She waited for him to announce his generosity, but gradually realised that he wasn't the kind of person to boast about his good deeds.

'I never know what to do,' she confessed. 'Whether I'm condoning a drink or drug habit by giving them money, or if I'm actually helping them to buy a meal… What do you think?' she asked anxiously.

His mouth softened. She saw his shoulders drop and realised he'd been holding them in tension.

'There's no easy answer, no right or wrong. It's a question of conscience and judgement, isn't it?' he said gently. 'I like to make contact with them. I look into their eyes and talk to them and see if they're still on this planet and then decide. The method works whether you're in Yorkshire or Egypt, Russia or Columbia. However, I do give to the support groups—the hostels and so on. One day I hope that no one will be without a home. It's a basic human right.'

Laura considered this, remembering how he'd stopped to chat to each one, touching them, treating them like human beings instead of parasites or objects of loathing. He is compassionate, she thought shakily. And the knowledge brought her a quiet joy.

'It breaks my heart to think they have nowhere to be warm and safe,' she said in a small voice. 'I can't bear it. So I always give them money even though I don't know how to tell if they're on drugs or not.'

'But you're on the breadline yourself,' he said huskily.

Her eyes were big and dark with distress. 'And I have a home and a child who loves me! They have nothing, nobody! Imagine what that's like, Cassian!'

'I do,' he muttered bleakly. 'Often.'

She felt intensely disturbed by the depth of his caring. He was very special. Even as a child she'd known that. On several occasions she'd come upon him, secretly nursing an injured animal back to health. He had a way with animals; strong, gentle hands and a softly reassuring voice that encouraged trust. Dogs, cats, horses…they all fell under his spell.

Whenever he'd been with animals, there had always been a softening of the surly, angry expression he'd habitually shown to the world. And she remembered thinking how lovely it must be, to be tended with such devotion.

Laura hung her head. What must he think of her? That she was cheap and easy? She shuddered, wishing that she hadn't kissed him with such desperation. More than anything in the world, she wanted him to like and admire her. It baffled her why that should be.

Trying to unravel to mystery, she stole little glances at him, compelled to look, driven to gaze on him so often that he might have been her lover.

She stopped breathing for a moment. Lovers couldn't tear their eyes away from one another. *Love*… Could that explain the huge swelling sensation in her chest? The feeling that her mind had been electrified by a thousand volt charge? That she wanted to bury herself in him, to hold him and never let go?

Her muscles tensed. The extent of her passion was terrifying. Hot and trembling, she slid off her jacket after a complicated manoeuvre with the seat belt. And her senses screamed when Cassian's helping hand brushed her bare arm.

'I can manage!' she croaked.

'I'm sure you can,' he replied in a low and husky voice. 'But it would have been bad manners not to have come to your aid.'

'Sorry,' she muttered, feeling awful for snapping at him.

'It's OK. I imagine you're a bit preoccupied thinking about the jobs you've been offered,' he said generously. 'I'll leave you in peace.'

Peace! If only!

There was a brief touch of his hand on hers. She almost clasped it and gave it a fierce squeeze. Instead, she merely trembled.

Horrified, she realised that she was utterly infatuated with a man she hardly knew. A ridiculous situation.

Except…she felt as if she did know him. Perhaps she'd had these feelings before—when they were younger. She frowned. When he and Bathsheba had left Thrushton, had her sense of loss been so heart-wrenching because she'd believed herself to be in *love* with Cassian? Even at the age of fifteen?

And…had she unwittingly carried a torch for him all these years, perhaps even flinging herself at the salesman from Leeds because he too was dark and travelled about the country and had an air of independence like Cassian's?

Restless with the significance of her half-formed thoughts, she crossed her legs. And noticed his eyes lingering on the curve of her thigh. Her heart beat faster. Then she told herself that all men looked at legs. What she wanted, was a man who was interested in her. And that was highly unlikely where Cassian was concerned.

Anger set her eyes flashing and a fierce shaft of longing tightened her entire body. She wanted him with a ferocity of purpose that she'd never known before. Yet sheer common sense told her that at the best she'd be a woman to kiss and fondle. Nothing more. Nothing deep and lasting.

And in only a few days they would part, perhaps never to see one another again. She felt frantic at the thought, her heart cramping now that they were drawing up to the school to wait for Adam. It was all too late. Cassian would for ever remain a man she adored, his heart untouched.

Overcome with misery, she flung open the door and jumped out, her pulses thumping chaotically. It felt as if her life was disintegrating into tiny pieces. She knew at that moment that she had fallen headlong in love with Cassian.

It was a certain and instant knowledge. She'd always dreamed of being in love. But in her dreams her love had been returned and her lover had proposed marriage. She had imagined a Happy Ever After scenario but life wasn't like that. It was cruel and kicked you down whenever you got to your feet. One step forwards, two steps back.

Cassian had released her emotions; making her angry, afraid and defiant. With the opening of the flood gates, her passion for love had been also released from its prison of restraint, and she had joyfully emptied her heart to him.

But if you stuck your head above the parapet, there was a chance that you might get wounded. And wounded she was.

Choking back the sobs, she stood in forlorn silence, steeling herself to the fact that for the rest of her days she'd never find another man to match Cassian.

She loved him. Wanted him. But knew, with a sense of utter desolation, how hopeless her desires were.

CHAPTER EIGHT

LATER, she changed out of her finery and after a monosyllabic evening she sat pretending to read in the sitting room, while a silent and thoughtful Cassian sat opposite working on his laptop computer.

After school, he'd touched her heart still further by taking Adam for a walk then helping him with his homework and cooking supper. Steak and chips. Treacle sponge. Which Adam helped to make. Then treating Adam to a thrilling bed-time story, all off the top of his head.

Why did he have to be so flaming perfect?! she thought crossly. She was useless. OK, she conceded, maybe she'd landed those jobs and everyone had seemed more than anxious to have her on their staff... That was quite an achievement...

'You've been deep in thought for hours. I suppose you must have decided by now,' Cassian said quietly.

His eyes bored into her and she dropped her startled gaze in case he saw her naked adoration.

'Not yet. Toss up between the legal secretary and admissions clerk in the clinic,' she fudged, having hardly given them a thought at all.

'You must have been a brilliant interviewee.' His gaze held hers and she tried not to sink into a jellied heap but his voice was soft and dark as chocolate and persisted in rippling through her in silky rivers. 'Now do you believe me when I say you can do anything you want, if you want it badly enough?'

She smiled sadly. If only he knew what she really wanted! 'I hope that's true! But my references helped. People said some kind things about me.'

'They told the truth. Anyone can see how genuine you are; that you're honest and sincere and totally trustworthy,' he said quietly. 'It's plain that you'd be a conscientious and dedicated worker, and wouldn't contemplate giving anything less than one hundred per cent to your work.' He laughed at her open-mouthed amazement. 'I'm not kidding! Workers like you are few and far between. You have rare qualities, Laura.'

'Well, they only became apparent when I wore decent clothes,' she pointed out wryly, intoxicated by his words. Rare! She felt delirious from his praise.

'They got you noticed, I go along with that. Unfortunately people pay attention to appearances. But you won those job offers on your own merit so don't put yourself down. It's quite an achievement.'

She felt her breathing rate increase as hope spilled into her dulled brain. What had Cassian said? Something about applying yourself? If she wanted him to notice her, to respect her—and she did, oh, how she did!—then she needed time. Which she didn't have. Unless she very quickly made herself indispensable.

He wouldn't love her, she had to accept that. But could she settle for mutual friendship? Adam would benefit so much from Cassian's strength.

Living with the man she loved—and keeping her adoration a secret—would be agony. But it was better than never seeing him again, and for Adam's sake she must do everything she could to ensure that they remained in the house.

Looking at him from under her brows, seeing his long limbs draped easily over the armchair, she felt every inch of her body becoming fluid with adoration.

Quite subtly, so he wouldn't realise, she'd have to produce such gorgeous meals and make life here so incredibly comfortable, that he wouldn't want her to leave—whatever he'd said about being able to manage for himself.

He'd love being looked after—providing, she warned herself, she didn't ever curtail his freedom.

'You look sad,' she said gently. 'Are you thinking of Jai?'

His eyes flicked to hers and then darted away, his expression bleaker than ever.

'Something else.'

She had to bite her tongue to stop herself from asking 'what'. He'd tell her if he wanted to—and it seemed he didn't. It felt as if he'd slapped her around the face. It was all very fine, being Rare, but that didn't stop her from being excluded from Cassian's inner life.

She wanted to call out *Look at me, I'm here! Talk to me, confide in me!* But she couldn't bear the prospect of rejection. He didn't need her, he'd made that plain.

Her idea wouldn't work, she thought, her fragile confidence wavering. She'd never be able to hold back because she loved him so much. The sensible thing would be to close down. To shut out her feelings and become detached.

Her mouth shaped into a stubborn line. But she didn't want to! She wanted it all—the house, the job, Cassian. *Impossible.* Her eyes filled with tears.

Dimly she heard the trilling of a mobile phone and hid her wet face with her hand in case he noticed that she was being a wimp again.

'Cassian here,' he murmured into the phone and she flinched at his warm, rich tones. 'Hi, Sheila!' he said enthusiastically and she flinched again, this time because she wanted to be greeted with delight like that. 'How's things?'

There was a long pause during which Cassian's brows drew close together and his expression became concerned. Tactfully, Laura rose and slipped into the kitchen, wondering who Sheila might be that she could elicit such affection from him at first, and then reach into his heart to cause that look of deep consternation.

What a cloth-head she was! she thought grumpily, stoically drying her eyes and beginning to set out the breakfast things. Sheila was probably gorgeous. With ninety-four-inch legs, a degree in astro-physics and a background of extensive world travel. Oh, how could she ever have imagined that Cassian would give a damn about her—friend or otherwise?

And supposing he did, what then? They were too different for any relationship to blossom. She'd witnessed a similar disaster between her father and Bathsheba—and they'd been madly in love.

Little Miss Mouse, terrified of her own shadow, living on another planet to Cassian... The tears seeped inexorably upwards, clogging her throat.

'I'm going to bed.'

He'd spoken from the hall, his voice tight with strain. Scowling, she shot a quick look at him, surprised to see how defeated he looked.

Whatever Sheila had said, it had shattered him. Laura swallowed and furiously tried to stem the newly threatening tears. She wanted to affect him like that!

'Night,' she muttered, hoping he'd stay and tell her what troubled him.

He didn't move. It seemed as if all the stuffing had gone out of him. Her body ached with the yearning to run over and enclose him in a hug. But that wasn't her way.

'I'm going into Harrogate tomorrow,' he said flatly. 'Do you want a lift?'

So she wasn't to be his confidante. Bereft, Laura slammed the marmalade on the table.

'No. I'm shopping for Mr Walker.'

'What?'

Conscious that he was barely listening to her, she dealt out cutlery with unusual carelessness. Her life was one long round of fun, she didn't think.

'I told you about him. He's the one I shop for.'' Seeing he was still staring blankly into space, she felt compelled to let off steam. 'He's smelly and bad-tempered and he does nothing but moan and complain. I walk the two miles to Grassington, get everything he wants, walk the two miles back laden with bags, unload his shopping while he pretends I've got the wrong variety and have spent too much, and then I make him a cup of tea, settle him in his chair with a rug around him and we watch TV for an hour together. That's my excitement for the week. That's what I am,' she said with a sob. 'Miss Exciting. I really know how to live life, don't I? No doubt you're *riveted*!'

'Laura!' he cried, his brow furrowed in bewilderment. 'You're upset! Why—?'

'It doesn't matter!' she snapped, turning her back on him.

He pushed her around to face him again but she jerked her head to one side. Unfortunately her tears betrayed her and he gave a sigh then held her in his embrace.

'It does matter.'

'Only to me! And d-don't ask me if it's that time of the month,' she snuffled, 'because I'll scream!'

Cassian merely held her tighter. 'It's been an emotional few days for you,' he murmured in her ear. 'I would be surprised if you *weren't* on a roller-coaster.'

His hand lightly stroked her hair. It was a lovely sensation and she relaxed into him. But, to her dismay, he gently moved back.

'I didn't mean what I said about Mr Walker,' she mumbled. 'I do care. It's an awful life for him being confined to his house.'

'How long have you been doing all this for him?' Cassian asked quietly.

'I don't know. Ever since his wife died. I used to help her do her hair. She had arthritis in her fingers.'

Cassian drew in a long and hard breath. He seemed to be thinking about something and while he did, his finger lazily toyed with her fringe. She froze, afraid that any movement she made might make him stop.

'How badly do you want one of those jobs, Laura?' he asked hesitantly.

Blue eyes met brown. 'Desperately. I need a job to survive, you know that! How else can I afford champagne?' she jerked.

He smiled at her brave joke, took out his handkerchief and handed it to her. 'There's another job you might be interested in.'

'Sounds like an embarrassment of riches,' she commented, handing back the handkerchief.

Cassian pulled out a chair for her and sat nearby. Absently he rearranged the higgledy-piggledy cutlery in front of him and she waited, realising that he was searching for a way to tell her something.

'I...have a friend. A very good friend—'

'Sheila,' she hazarded.

How good, how friendly? her mind was demanding. Very? Bed friendly? Snuggle up together and exchange personal secrets kind of friendly?

He nodded. 'She runs a charitable organisation. Handing out money to deserving causes.'

Cassian's friend *and* with a wonderful job! Lucky Sheila.

'I envy her,' she said with a sigh.

Cassian felt his pulses race. She'd be perfect. Honest, reliable, conscientious and warm-hearted, with a love of humanity and a desire to help people in need. There was no one else he could turn to at such short notice. And yet common sense was telling him this would increase her involvement with him...

'She's had to give it up,' he said, pushing the words out before he got cold feet. The charity had to come first, whatever his doubts. 'She's flying to the States to look after her three nieces. Her sister and brother-in-law were killed in a car crash yesterday.'

'Cassian!' Laura cried in horror. 'That's terrible! The

poor little kiddies. Poor woman! Is someone with her? Do you need to go with her?'

She was holding his hand, giving him comfort. He could feel the firmness of her grip, the roughness of her work-worn fingers and somehow her concern was making his heart tighten as if it were in a vice.

'No. Her partner has gone with her. But...Laura, she's frantic about leaving the charity in a lurch. It's a small operation but it needs someone at its helm, someone who can be trusted not to misappropriate funds. People like that are hard to get—particularly at short notice.'

'I imagine so,' she said in concern.

Amazing, he thought. She had no idea of her qualities. Even now she had no idea that he was alluding to her. He took a deep breath, his passion for the charity overruling any personal wariness.

'Laura, I told her she could go immediately because I knew someone who could do the job.'

She smiled sadly. 'That's great. Sheila must have been relieved—'

'You,' he said. 'I thought of you at once.'

Her eyes widened, the spiky wet lashes blinking furiously. He wanted to kiss her. To take her to bed. He snatched away his hands and she looked upset at his rejection, her lush mouth trembling.

'You can't mean me! You can't be suggesting I take her place!'

He tried to keep his head—even if his body had decided to betray him and go off the rails. He cleared his throat and wondered if he had a cold coming.

'Who better? I've just set up an office for the charity in Harrogate—'

'Well, there you are. That lets me out. How do I get there? It's impossible, Cassian!'

His heartbeat quickened. She'd sounded deeply disappointed. 'You would commute, and get in whatever time

you can. There aren't any rules attached to this job. Or I
could drive you in sometimes. Then *you* will learn to drive.
The charity will supply you with a car.'

Wistfully she said, 'And when Adam's ill?'

'No problem,' he said firmly. 'Much of the time—when
he's ill, or if you have something special you need to do
at home, you can operate from the house—'

'Sure. With no phone, no computer—'

'You're determined to find obstacles,' he said, amused.
'A phone line can be installed. This isn't the Sahara Desert.
In the meantime you can use a mobile. The charity will set
you up with everything you need, including a computer at
home, plus anything else you need.'

'But…the cost—!'

'—would be a drop in the ocean. Particularly if the position goes to someone reliable and honest. There are a lot
of sharks about. Money is a huge temptation and whoever
runs this charity has carte blanche to sign cheques for massive amounts of cash. Appointing the right person is a real
headache.'

'But…wouldn't you like the job?' she asked, puzzled.

'Me?' He hesitated. 'I'm…already employed.'

'Oh. I thought you must be looking for something.
You've only just come from Morocco and you haven't exactly joined the 9—5 brigade,' she explained, looking excited at the prospect of landing the job.

'I…took time off.'

'What do you do?' she asked eagerly.

'Computer work. Laura, never mind me. What do you
think?'

She chewed her lip. 'I don't know. It's a huge responsibility. I'm not sure I could do it—'

'You could! Listen. There's a fund. The income from its
investments can be spent every year. Applications come in
and the fund director—you—'

'Me? A fund director?' she asked, pink and beaming.

He laughed. 'That's what you'd be. And you'd sort through the applications, interview people from the charities applying, and write a cheque to those you think worthy, honest and with sound business plans. Simple. A matter of judgement. The salary would be at least double that of the jobs you've been offered—'

'Good grief! I couldn't take that much!' she protested. 'Not from a charity—'

'For heaven's sake, Laura!' he said impatiently. 'Value yourself! You'd earn it, I can assure you!'

'Well,' she said with a huge smile. 'I can always give the extra away, can't I?'

Typical. The people with least money were the most generous. He desperately wanted her to be financially secure.

'You'll do the job?' he asked, hardly daring to breathe.

'Don't I have to be interviewed? See a board of directors or something?' she asked with a frown.

'I told you. Sheila runs it. The directors are…kind of sleeping. She's left the matter of her replacement in my hands.'

'Why? What's your connection with the charity?'

'I contribute to it on a regular basis,' he said, omitting to tell her he was the only contributor.

She sighed. 'You are so generous. And, judging by the state of your four-wheel drive, you're not rolling in money.'

This wasn't the time to say he wasn't bothered about material goods and if a car moved, then he was happy with it.

'I get by,' he said blithely. 'Forget me. Say you'll do the job. It'll be a load off my mind and I know you'll be cracking at it.'

'I can't believe this! Yes, yes, I'd *love* to. Absolutely adore it!' she replied, her eyes shining brilliantly.

'Fantastic! Thank you!'

In sheer relief he caught her hands and grinned at her, completely bowled over by the delight on her face. Somehow they had moved closer and her lips were recklessly within reach. There was nothing in his lungs, not one breath. The very air seemed suspended as slowly he leaned towards her, a centimetre at a time so that she didn't take fright.

Her eyelids closed, her face lifted and he felt his heart soar as if he were being lifted on a thermal. Gently he placed a hand behind her head and let his lips touch hers. She quivered throughout the length of her body.

'Thanks,' he muttered.

The sweetness of her smile, the tenderness of her gaze, created mayhem in his head. This wasn't happening to him. Mustn't happen.

'I want to kiss you again,' he said with reckless disregard for sanity.

Solemn and painfully beautiful, she seemed to sink more deeply into his arms.

'It would be very unwise,' she said, encouragingly unsteady.

'Why?' he asked, his voice as thick and slow as a treacle.

'Because I'm going at the end of the week.'

His teeth clamped together. He had the impression that she was angling for an alteration to their arrangement. But if she stayed much longer than the next few days, he'd seduce her. And he must not do that. She was too precious, too vulnerable to handle a brief relationship. But a kiss or two would be all right.

'All the more reason to kiss you before you leave,' he murmured, pushing back the knowledge that he was deliberately deceiving himself.

She looked confused. 'Why do you want to kiss me?'

Cassian bit back an exclamation. He'd never been interrogated like this before! Trust Laura. He smiled at her, his finger running down the side of her soft cheek. She gave a little gasp and he knew she longed to let go. It would be

good for her, he rationalised. A release of passion. Hell—
it would be good for him too!

'Your mouth,' he husked recklessly, 'is soft and warm
and far too near for me to ignore it. I like its taste. I like
holding you in my arms…like your scent, the way your
body yields, responds, matches mine for passion…'

She surrendered. With a series of little sighs, she let her
lashes flutter down and allowed her lips to part. Gently he
pulled her close. Felt her heart beating hard against his
chest. The exquisite softness of her high, fast-heaving
breasts and the tight hardness of her nipples, apparent even
beneath the material of her shirt.

His head began to whirl. She wore no bra. It would take
just a movement of his hand and…

He swallowed, checking himself ruthlessly. A kiss. Nothing more.

'You're so beautiful,' he breathed.

Her eyes snapped open, startlingly blue so close to his.
'What?'

The lightest of kisses. 'Beautiful.' Another one, delicate,
whispering, tantalising every inch of his body with the effort of denial. 'Beautiful.'

'Oh!' she sighed in bliss.

He had no reason to be doing this except for sheer sensual pleasure. And pleasure it was. The smell of her, the
feel of her hair beneath his fingers, the way she fitted him…

And he was using her. It wasn't fair. Wasn't right. Somehow he must extract himself from this situation without
hurting her. Hell. Oh, hell, hell, hell.

Just a little more, a voice was telling him. A few kisses,
a little more passion, the pressure of her mouth infinitely
irresistible, the winding of her arms around his neck all that
he could have wished for.

Against his chest her nipples were rock-hard now and

her mouth had become more daring, exploring his with a thoroughness that thrilled and unnerved him.

He had to get out of this, he thought hazily, crushing her closer. Willpower, that's all it took. All! When his entire body throbbed, his blood pounded so loudly in his ears that he couldn't have heard if she'd yelled, when his heart was in danger of going into cardiac arrest and his hunger had never, never been so desperate...

Somehow—who knew how?—he gentled their kisses, moving a fraction of an inch back each time. And wondered how he could do this when she was as hungry as he, willing, dizzy with desire...

'You,' he croaked, like a rusty hinge, 'are gorgeous.'

Her smile was intoxicating, lighting up her whole face. He couldn't leave it like this. She'd imagine this was the beginning of a courtship.

Cassian cursed himself for succumbing. It had been a mistake. Cruel.

He could hardly breathe. Certainly couldn't walk yet. He'd ache for hours.

'I know I shouldn't have done that,' he admitted hoarsely. 'But I can't say I'm sorry. I hope I haven't offended you...' A slight movement told him that she was moving away, both mentally and physically. 'I just had to kiss you,' he confessed with all honesty. 'An impulse. I was grateful—delighted that you'll take on the charity. And...you looked so lovely. Hope you understand. Forgive me?'

His eyes pleaded with her, begging her not to be hurt. Like an angel, she accepted his reasons, saw nothing evil in what he'd done. Perhaps because there had been no evil intended.

Her slow and seraphic smile mesmerised him. 'I understand.' Her eyes lowered, her mouth mischievous. 'It was a thrilling moment and it bowled me over,' she murmured. He tensed, every nerve in his body straining. And then he was stunned by his intense disappointment when she added demurely, 'To be offered such a wonderful, worthwhile job.'

'My gosh! You look terrible!' Laura said in amusement, when he staggered in from his run with Adam the next morning. 'Unshaven, bleary-eyed…what *have* you been doing?!'

'Bad night.'

'Why's that? Bed uncomfortable?' she asked innocently.

He was rescued by Adam. 'Race you to the shower!' Adam crowed, already leaping upstairs in his socks.

But Cassian didn't take up the challenge. He unpicked his laces, put his boots beside Adam's and slumped in a chair.

Now, mused Laura, usefully pouring him a black coffee, is this a man who's sexually frustrated and has spent the whole night trying to stop his hormones holding him to ransom?

She smiled a little smile of triumph. She did hope so! And she hugged her glee to herself that—for a brief time— he had found her mouth quite irresistible.

'I'm doing scrambled eggs. Shall I add some for you?' she asked serenely.

'Uh. Please.'

Grumpy and haggard and bemused. Looking at her legs again, slowly surveying her rear, her breasts… Her eyes gleamed. He was interested. He did like her. Respected her enough to offer her a high value job. That had meant a lot to her. And to top it all, she was both rare *and* gorgeous.

Her mirror that morning had agreed. After a deep, utterly contented sleep, she had woken to find someone else looking back at her—a confident, sparkling-eyed woman who oozed vitality.

She sang happily to herself, adding a few home-grown chives and tiny tomatoes from the garden to a buttered dish and slipping them in the oven to grill. For the first time, she really believed that she could achieve her life-long dream. Her voice strengthened, bursting with joy, the notes clear and true, every inch of her body surrendering to happiness.

Cassian slowly stumbled out of the kitchen, his tread heavy and laboured on the stairs. Her singing grew louder, more ecstatic.

It took Mr Walker only a short time, however, to bring her down to earth again. Morose and uncommunicative, Cassian had acted as chauffeur so that she could do Mr Walker's shopping and then be free to investigate the office in Harrogate.

'I hope you don't mind,' she said hesitantly, when the old man opened the door, 'but I've brought—'

'Cassian!' Mr Walker cried in delight. 'Cassian!' he added with soft affection.

Laura was open-mouthed when Cassian strode forwards and gave Mr Walker a gentle bear hug.

'Tom,' he said fondly. 'You old reprobate! Sitting around like Lord Muck, and letting a tame dolly bird do all your shopping…you ought to be ashamed of yourself!' he teased.

'Man's gotta get what pleasures he can at my age,' chuckled the old man. 'Sight of those legs of Laura's sets me up for the whole day!'

Blushing, the astonished Laura went into the tiny kitchen and began to unpack the groceries, oddly pleased that there was some kind of bond between the two men.

'You know each other, then,' she commented when they both appeared, Cassian with his arm around Mr Walker's frail, shawl-wrapped shoulders.

'Go a long way back.' The old man eased himself painfully into the rocking chair by the iron stove. 'Cassian used to come here when he was a lad. We went fishing together. My Doris lent him books. Great reader, my Doris.

Devoured encyclopaedias, Cassian did… Hang on a minute, lass!' he protested. 'That's not proper ham!'

'It's what you always have,' she said calmly, conscious of Cassian, dark-eyed and silent in the corner.

Mr Walker muttered under his breath, picking over his supplies for the week. 'I've told you I don't like big oranges. And those sprouts look manky. Useless woman,' he goaded, picking up the bill and glaring at it. 'You bring me rubbish and there's twopence more on the bill?' he snapped.

'I know,' she said with a sigh. 'I'm awfully sorry—'

'You're on the wrong track,' Cassian said to Tom Walker, suddenly alert. 'Try attacking something she cares about.'

Mr Walker's watery eyes narrowed. She thought there was the suspicion of a smile on his sour face before he said in contempt,

'Her? She's a waste of space. And her kid's as dopey—'

'Don't you dare talk about my son like that!' she flared, her eyes scorching with anger. 'I can take your bad temper and your ingratitude because I feel sorry for you but Adam's off limits! *Do you understand?*' she yelled, banging the table so hard that the vegetables jumped in shock and rolled to the floor.

To her astonishment, Mr Walker grinned so hard that his toothless gums showed. Cassian was laughing.

'Now *that's* your mother talking!' cackled Mr Walker.

She froze. '*What?*' she ground out furiously.

'I've bin trying for years to get you angry, lass!' he wheezed, tears of laughter running down his face. 'Wanted to see if you'd got your ma's fire in your belly. Almost gave up. All you did was apologise like you was made of milk and water. But you're like her all right,' he said more gently. 'More life in her than most. Lovely woman. Miss her, something chronic, I do.'

She sat down, her legs weak. 'You…you devious, mean

old man!' she said shakily but she couldn't hide her pleasure. 'Am I...am I really like her?'

'Spitting image. Beautiful, she was. Had a temper on her, though.'

'Tell me!' she begged. 'I know nothing about her, nothing! Please! Tell me the circumstances surrounding my birth. Everything.'

'Well, I'm blowed. I thought you knew *that*. Well, let's see. I know George Morris didn't treat her right. Bullied her. Any fool could see how unhappy she was and that she longed to be loved proper, like. Anyroad, she fell headlong in love with the American who took over Killington Manor, down the dale just beyond Little Sturton, where I worked as a groom. Found she was pregnant—and George hadn't touched her for over a year. But, proud devil that he was, he wouldn't agree to a divorce so she tried her level best to settle back into her marriage. Doomed, it was, though.'

'My...father was...American?' she said faintly.

'S'right. Nice chap,' said Mr Walker. 'Jolly sort—'

'More!' she begged. 'I want to know more!'

'More, eh? He was tall, dark, smiling eyes, if you know what I mean. Easy-going hospitable type. Publisher. Crazy about your mother, but then few could resist her lovely nature.'

'All this time I've known you...why...*why* didn't you tell me all this?' she wailed.

'Thought you knew bits and pieces, lass. When I realised you didn't have much of a clue, I thought I'd better keep my trap shut. Not my business to interfere. Wasn't sure you were tough enough to hear the truth.'

'They didn't speak about her mother,' Cassian explained. 'It was a taboo subject.'

'But...*you* knew!' she stormed at him.

'Yes,' he admitted. 'But until you told me a few days ago that Thrushton Hall was the only link you had with your mother, it had never occurred to me that they hadn't

told you the basic facts, or that you had no tangible memories of her—photos, possessions…I still can't believe
they'd do that to you! Poor Laura. This is outrageous…'

Clearly upset, he put his arm around her shoulders.
Gratefully she leaned into him, touched by his anger on her
behalf. She felt nothing but contempt for George and Enid's
refusal to explain her background.

'But why did my…' She checked herself. Never again
would she call George Morris 'father'. 'Why did George
get custody?'

'Because everyone thought you were his child,' Cassian
said gently.

Laura felt a sickening sensation clutch at her stomach.

'Didn't my *real* father claim me? She must have gone
to him, surely? Didn't they run away together? Didn't they
want me?' she asked miserably.

The old man looked uncertainly at Cassian, who brought
her close to him as if protecting her.

'She can deal with it,' he said in low, quiet tones.

Laura's hopes collapsed. 'Oh, no!' she groaned. 'You're
not telling me they're…*dead*?'

Mr Walker's eyes were gentle, his expression loving and
full of regret.

'Both of them, lass. Her and the American. It was filthy
weather. Tractor came out of a field and into the Harrogate
road and killed them outright two weeks after you were
born. He was bringing you and your mother back to
Killington Manor to live with him. George Morris brought
you up as his daughter and only a few of us knew the truth.'

A sob escaped her. She had been so close to having a
truly loving home. And her mother had been denied the
happiness she'd hoped for.

It was unbelievably sad. Laura gave a moan and flung
her arms around Cassian's waist for solace.

'They never said!' she mumbled. 'All these years I privately feared that she'd rejected me, *abandoned* me—led

on by heavy hints from George and Enid. Oh, that was cruel, Cassian, cruel!'

She burst into floods of tears. There were years of weeping inside her but the two men just held her and patted her and waited while she mourned the parents she'd never known.

Dimly she became aware that the men had been talking for a while.

'...say goodbye properly. Got a map, Tom?' she heard Cassian ask quietly.

A map! She felt indignant but kept her head buried in his middle hearing the rustle of paper. Cassian wanted to look at a route to somewhere, when she...

'Just there,' said Tom Walker. 'That little lane...'

'And the gate?' Cassian asked softly.

Her heart turned over. Guilt swept through her as she realised what Cassian was doing. Bless him, she thought. Bless him.

'Take me there!' She pleaded, choking and hoarse, the words disappearing into his soft shirt.

His hand was infinitely gentle on the silk of her hair. 'Come,' he muttered, his voice cracking. 'We'll pick some flowers from the garden. We can make a lovely bunch for your mother from the roses, agastache, helenium, salvia...'

'And if you come round one day, both of you,' said Mr Walker kindly, 'we can have tea and talk about your parents, if you'd like. I'm very fond of you, pet,' he added. 'You're like a dear daughter to me.'

'I'd like,' she said in a small voice. And kissed him. Suddenly she felt overcome with emotion and her arms tightened about the skeletal frame and she held him tight. 'See you soon,' she whispered.

He nodded, his eyes filled with tears. 'Say hello to her from me,' he rasped. 'Good friend. Warm heart. Like you. I promised her, at her funeral, that I'd keep an eye on you. She'd be proud of you, Laura.'

She couldn't speak for emotion. In a blur she saw Cassian clasp Tom Walker's hand, an unspoken message of affection exchanging between them.

'Old times,' Cassian said softly. 'We have a lot of catching up to do, Tom. Till then.'

Gently he ushered Laura out of the door. His arm was around her as they walked along the street to the manor house, guiding her feet, holding her firmly when she stumbled because the tears were obliterating her vision.

But he stood back while she picked the flowers, knowing that this was something she needed to do on her own. These were her gift to her mother.

And even though he waited a yard or so away, his tenderness enfolded her, protecting her like a supporting blanket. Without him she would have broken down. With him, she felt she could cope.

'How did you know that Mr Walker was goading me?' she asked in a pitifully little voice.

'Partly because he's a kind man and I could see from his eyes that his heart wasn't in what he was doing, and partly because I'd been trying to do the same.'

Her eyes widened and accused him. 'Provoke me, you mean?'

'Sort of,' he confessed. 'When you talked about Adam, I could see that underneath you were a woman of deep passions and fierce beliefs. For your sake, Laura,' he said gently, 'I wanted you to find your guts before you were thrust into the world. It's a wonderful and exciting place. I wanted you to enjoy it.'

She heaved a sigh. The end of the week was a long way away at the moment.

'I'm finding my emotions all too easily,' she said jerkily. 'You're stripping away all my barriers and I'm left raw and open and hurt!'

His eyes softened. 'But you're in touch with your heart.'

'It's a painful process,' she muttered.

'There's joy too,' he promised.

'Really?' she mumbled, her face wan.

Because she wasn't sure she believed him. A chill went through her. Passion, she thought, gripped in an icy fear. Was it truly worth the anguish that came with it?

CHAPTER NINE

IT WAS a fifteen minute drive to the accident spot. For the rest of her life she would remember the powerful musky perfume of the roses in the confines of the car, and the comfort of Cassian's reassuring hand on hers when they finally reached the place Mr Walker had described.

'Wait. I'll help you out,' Cassian offered.

So kind and tender. He seemed to know instinctively what to do, what to say, when to be silent.

Her pulses drummed. Her face was almost as white as the mallow flowers in her hands. Shakily she clambered down and lifted her head up high.

Alone, she walked to the farm gate, thinking only of her mother's tragic death and of the American man who had been her mother's lover. Her father. A man she would have loved if she'd known him. What had he been like? She didn't know. She couldn't visualise him.

Her eyes filled with tears again. It was awful, not knowing either of her parents. She bit her lip. For most of her life she'd unwittingly lived a lie created by George and Enid Morris.

Fervently she asked for her mother's forgiveness for doubting her. Laura had been swayed by the endless false-hoods and half-truths. Cheated of her past, deceived, and twisted so that she fitted into a mould of George Morris's choosing.

She could have been lively and passionate and beautiful, given the chance. She might have been the kind of woman who flung her arms around people, like Sue, and breezed through life without hang-ups.

Her heritage had been taken away from her. And now she didn't know what kind of person she was.

And yet despite her sadness, Laura felt the inexorable beauty of her surroundings seeping into her. The lane ran along a valley, eroded long ago by the meltwater from an ice sheet. Close by were the remains of a medieval village, abandoned in the plague. Buttercups made the valley golden in the September sun. In early summer, she mused, the meadows would be a riot of colour, red clover, pignut and cranesbill vying with the buttercups and marguerites.

The high drystone walls were thick with lichen and moss and she reached out to touch the soft green mat covering the massive limestone rocks. Here in this lovely valley she could imagine her mother's spirit. Here she could find solace and comfort.

'I love you, Mum,' she husked, an overwhelmingly powerful emotion deepening her voice and making it shake. She didn't find it odd to be standing in a country lane and talking aloud. It seemed right and natural and it unburdened her heart. She took a deep breath and continued passionately. 'I wish I'd known you and Father! Wish I'd lived with you! Oh, I wanted that so badly. We could have been happy, the three of us.'

Again she thought how different she might have been. More open, less guarded, more ready to laugh and cry. Less afraid to show her love. To be loved.

Her heart aching, a hard, painful lump in her throat, she strewed the flowers about the lane and bowed her head while goldfinches chattered sweetly nearby.

'I'll make you really proud of me,' she promised. 'I won't let myself become like Aunt Enid: mean and caustic, critical and unfulfilled. I will go for happiness…follow my heart. I will hug people if I feel the urge. I won't let my life go to waste, I won't!' she sobbed. 'And I'll help Adam to be strong, now I know how. You'd love him, Mum, Dad…'

She couldn't speak for crying. It felt as if her heart was full of love and sorrow at the same time. It seemed to be expanding from where it had been lying cramped and afraid in her chest. Now it beat with her mother's blood, her father's passion. And she felt whole at last.

She shivered and a moment later she started when she felt a jacket being gently draped about her shoulders.

'You're cold. You've been here a long time,' Cassian said huskily.

Her forlorn, tear-washed face lifted to his, instinctively seeking something from him.

'Hold me,' she pleaded.

With a mutter of concern, he took her in his arms and let her squeeze him as hard as she could. After a moment the violent tensions in her muscles eased and she sagged against him.

'They…sound as if…they were lovely people,' she sniffed jaggedly.

'And you are their child. Remember that. You are like them,' he answered, stroking her back.

'That's a n-nice thing to s-say.'

'Just the truth,' he breathed into her hair. 'Perhaps now you can be yourself. Be free.'

The thought comforted her. She could start again. Despite her anguish, she felt an uplifting feeling. 'Can we walk?' she mumbled.

'Whatever you like, whatever you need. Hold my hand, you're shaking,' he said softly.

With infinite care, he helped her over a ladder stile and into the field beyond. For a long time they strolled quietly with just the plaintive cry of the lapwings eerily breaking the silence.

They found a sheltered spot to sit. They gazed at the view from high above the strip lynchets, the terraced fields which had been hacked out of the hillside centuries ago, even long before the Black Death in the fourteenth century which must have parted so many loved ones.

The wind ruffled her hair and brought sharp colour to her cheeks. This was her beloved Yorkshire. The place where her mother and father had fallen in love and where they had died. And she would do anything to stay here for the rest of her days on earth.

His hand gripped hers tightly. His eyes were like liquid velvet and she felt more cherished than she had in the whole of her life.

And for no reason at all, her tears suddenly cascaded down her face in torrents.

'Laura, Laura!' he whispered, turning her to him.

His lips touched her cheekbone then travelled around her face stopping each tear that fell. She felt a desperate need to be comforted by him, to lose herself in his kisses.

Lifting her mouth, she caught his face between her hands and let her eyes do the asking.

'Kiss me properly,' she moaned.

Cassian stared helplessly. 'Don't mistake what you're feeling,' he rasped. 'You're—'

'I want to be kissed!' she insisted.

'Because you want to be comforted.' He sounded bitter and his teeth were clenched together hard. 'I'll hold you, but I won't do more—'

'Why?' she demanded, shuddering with intense fervour.

'You'd regret it later, when you're not so distraught—'

'I won't!' she whispered, adoring his mouth, the smoothness of his face beneath her fingers.

Desperate to lose herself in his lovemaking, she explored his mouth with a thoroughness that shook her. She laced her fingers through his hair, subtly trapping him, her body pressing hard against his.

It was wonderful when he responded, a groan preceding his impassioned surrender to her wiles. They couldn't get enough of each other, their hands clutching, roaming, invading…

She was caught up in the intensity of her feelings, her mind closed to all but the sensations surging through her frantic body, everything centred on the need to touch Cassian, to be touched…loved, not to miss a moment of life and happiness.

If she loved him, and she did, she wasn't going to waste time being coy. She'd take what she wanted, be what she wanted, obey the call for love that was overriding everything else in her mind and body.

She was crying and gasping, moaning and panting just like him. His hands wove magic spells in her body, every part of her seemingly set alight by his caress.

Each breast quivered, bloomed, tightened unbearably from the gently erotic movement of his questing fingers. The heat of his loins burned into her till she thought she must have reached melting point.

At some time they must have sunk back to the ground. Here, her arms demanded, legs slithered urgently, pelvis arched in throbbing hunger. She was dimly aware that her mouth knew now every inch of his face and throat, the hard satin of his chest, the hollows of his stomach.

Her clothes had largely disappeared, like his, though when he—or she—had removed them she couldn't have said. Her desperation matched his. Her desire to kiss and touch every inch of him was echoed by his unstoppable ravishment.

The surface of her skin felt hot and tingling as if it had been electrified. Each of Cassian's fierce, impetuous kisses stirred her very blood and pushed her to a more intense state of excitement.

'I can't bear it!' she whispered, seeking without success to undo his belt.

She felt him kick away her skirt, and, unhampered, she wound her legs about him so that she could drive her pelvis harder into his body and ease some of the terrible need within her.

His mouth swooped on hers, enclosing, warm and almost frantic in its kisses. The pressure of his hand cupped around the cleft between her legs and even through her small cotton briefs she could feel the heat, the glorious movement of the heel of his hand. And then, with a wriggle, she had ensured he touched her flesh.

'Ohhhhh…'

'Laura!' he croaked.

Her loving hand stroked his face, her eyes anxiously encouraging him.

'Please,' she whispered.

'I—this is not right…I—'

'*I need you, Cassian!*' she rasped. And touched him.

His eyes closed as he did battle with himself. Gently she moved her hand, feeling the leap of power beneath her fingers.

'No, no, no…' he moaned.

'You told me to live!' she whispered, slipping her tongue between his lips. 'I am living. This is what I want. Love me. *Love me!*' she moaned into his mouth.

She mimicked the act of making love, her own body so aroused that she wondered how it could still obey her. But then she was operating on instinct. And love.

Cassian tore his mouth away, his face strained. 'But afterwards—'

'Forget afterwards. This is now,' she said fiercely.

She took his hand, let his fingers meet the throbbing bud between her legs and uttered a long, low moan of pleasure. This was what she'd longed for. Physical release with the man she loved.

The ecstasy in her body was nothing to the joy in her head, her heart and her soul. Cassian would possess her. She would know him and he would know her. If she died tomorrow, she would have been a part of him.

He could feel her mouth bruising his. Heard the little gasps and moans, the outrush of her sweet breath as he rhythmically caressed her. The beauty of her body had stunned him.

The soft mounds of her breasts met his mouth and her nipples rose obediently to his gentle suckling as she bucked and shuddered beneath his arousing fingers.

Too far…he'd gone too far to step back. It terrified him, this sensation of losing total control, of being unable to master his passion. What had she woken in him? he thought, slipping further from reality, mesmerised by the alluring Laura, by her sublime eyes, her hungry mouth and fabulous, irresistible body.

Quite helpless, driven by something he didn't understand, he clawed at his belt and managed by accident rather than luck to undo it. In a moment they were both naked. Flesh to flesh. He trembled, intoxicated by the sensation.

'Are…' He tried again, swallowing back the choking emotion. Pausing only briefly to wonder what was happening to him. 'Are…you…sure?'

There was a beauty about her face, as it swam beneath him, that made his heart turn over. Her dreamy smile dazzled him, leaving him blind.

'Sure,' she breathed. 'More sure than I've ever been.'

A volcano was threatening to burst inside him but he caressed her gently, taking his time till her pleas were so loud and insistent that he knew she was more than ready.

A sense of wonder flooded his mind as he gently eased into her, their bodies sliding so naturally together that they had surely been made for one another.

And then his world exploded. All he knew was that something unbelievable was occurring, a scattering of his senses and a fierce high voltage arousal of every cell in his body.

A storm erupted in his head. Sweet torment surrounded every nerve, tugging and caressing, thrilling and teasing

until he didn't know where he was or what he was doing…only that this was lovemaking at its most awe-
inspiring and this was love with Laura and he never wanted
it to end…

The pounding in his ears blotted out her cries—or were
they his?—and his body erupted in a wild release of joy
and pleasure. Warmth flooded him. And a deep, intense
peace.

Her hands moved lazily over his back. Still in a state of
disbelief, she smiled to herself. This was why people became obsessed with one another, then! Her heart was soaring. As free as that bird she could see high up in the sky…a
lark, surely?

Now she fully understood her mother. When you found
true love and a passion that matched your own, it was hard
to deny. She was so happy. Madly, hugely, ferociously!

'Cassian,' she whispered into his ear.

'Mmm.'

She wound her arms around his neck. He lifted his head
which had been buried in her neck and looked at her as if
he was drunk. Her eyes shone, her adoration plain for him
to see.

'Is it…always like that!' she asked, not sure if she could
physically bear such sweet torment too often.

He kissed her soft mouth. 'Hardly ever,' he said wryly.
'What did you do, Laura? Drug me?'

She laughed and kissed him back. No. She'd only loved
him. Given him everything. 'Good, was I?' she asked
smugly.

His eyes darkened till they were like glittering black
onyx.

'Sensational,' he growled.

She was going under again; the desire flaring up from
the igniting of his body moving over hers. Her eyes closed,
all the better to enjoy the unbearably slow, rhythmical

strokes inside her and the delicious sensations chasing on and in and through each part of her.

'Cassian,' she murmured and slithered sensually against him, provoking him with her body, biting him, enjoying the tension of his muscles under her sensitive hands.

'Sweet Laura,' he said hoarsely, kissing her throat.

The little stabs of energy began to thrust at her and she let them take her over, revelling that she could abandon herself without fear. She trusted Cassian. And so she could dare to behave freely.

''Swunnerful,' she slurred, clinging to him.

He flipped her over, hauled her up, cupped her heavy breasts in awe and flicked his tongue over each engorged nipple. Then his hands pressed on her hips till she felt the deepest, most incredible completion of herself.

And she began to move, watching his face, seeing the infinite pleasure she could give him, aroused beyond belief by the blissful expression on his beloved face.

The climax came hot and fast, rushing up to take her unawares. It shot her up to a pinaccle of sensation and then slowly released her, till she found herself safe and warm in the welcome of Cassian's strong arms.

It was a while before he dressed her. Tired and bemused, she let him do so, offering a leg or an arm like a docile child. She was far to 'high' to do anything for herself.

This was emotion—and she loved it, she mused, as his handsome face contorted with a frown while he tried to manoeuvre her skirt over her hips. With a sigh, she lifted her pelvis. Their eyes locked. Hot passion spilled between them, Cassian kissed her, hard.

'I can't leave you alone!' he muttered.

'Good,' she crowed.

'No, it's not…'

'Why?' She lifted her arms over head, intentionally provocative.

'Please, Laura!' he groaned. 'We have to get back. Harrogate's off, but you'll need to be home for Adam.'

'Is it that late?' she said in stunned surprise.

'We seem to have missed lunch,' he said, amused.

'No, we didn't!' she laughed and he kissed her tenderly.

In a daze they stumbled back to the car. Laura paused for a moment in the lane, trying to visualise her mother as someone alive and vital and very much in love, very loved, chattering happily as her lover drove her and their baby to Killington Manor.

Her mother would have been happy. As happy as she, Laura, was now. A long sigh escaped her parted lips. Today she had found great sorrow and great joy. This, she vowed, would be a relationship that would survive.

'Do you want to be alone?' Cassian asked with typical tact.

They were holding hands and she gave his a quick squeeze of thanks.

'No.' She didn't ever want to be alone again. 'Thank you for bringing me here. Let's go home,' she said, deeply content.

'Tom has told me where your parents' graves are,' Cassian said quietly. 'I'll take you there. And I think Adam should come too.'

She was overcome with gratitude. 'Thank you,' she said again.

They met Adam from school and took him to the small churchyard in a small village beyond Killington Manor, close to the river. Gently Laura told him about his grandparents while Cassian checked the gravestones.

'Here,' he said, holding out his hands to them.

Laura's heart pounded. She swallowed and gripped Adam's small hand in hers. Cassian enfolded them both in his arms, shepherding them towards a small, nondescript stone above an untended grave.

'I can't read it!' she mumbled, her eyes awash.

'It says…''Here lie Jack Eden and Diana Morris'',' Cassian said huskily. 'Then there are the dates…and below it is written; ''tragically taken from this world but together in the next.'' Tom Walker had that stone put up,' he told Laura. 'There was a scandal because George and Enid wouldn't pay for the funeral but those who worked at Killington had a whip-round for it. The house was sold and incorporated into your father's estate. Since your father hadn't changed his will, everything went to some distant cousin in New York. Tom was upset that you had nothing. He has watched over you ever since.'

'People are so kind!' she said shakily. 'I don't mind about the money. I have so much, compared with others.'

'Don't cry, Mum!' begged Adam.

She hugged him hard. 'I'm sad and I'm happy. Do you understand, darling?'

His big blue eyes softened. 'Yes, I do, Mum. I'm sorry they're dead. I'd have liked grandparents. But I'm glad they didn't abandon you.' His skinny arms wrapped tightly around her. 'I love you, Mum,' he said fiercely. 'Everything'll be all right now.'

She smiled and met Cassian's infinitely tender eyes. 'Yes,' she breathed, kissing her son's fair head. 'I think it will.'

That evening, when supper and the run and homework were all dealt with, all three of them sat on the sofa together and talked. And when Adam had gone sleepily up to bed, she curled up in Cassian's arms watching a documentary on TV.

Occasionally he kissed her. But most of the time it was enough that they were close. He was wonderful, she thought happily. And he seemed compelled to touch her. Not sexually, but just small touches; a stroke of her hand, the brush of his fingers down the side of her cheek, the increased pressure of his arm around her waist for no particular reason.

In her book, that meant one thing. Whether he knew it or not, he was rapidly finding he couldn't do without her. She hoped that was true. All her hopes were pinned on that fact.

'I wish I could take you to bed,' he growled in her ear.

'Well, you can't,' she said, secretly delighted with his regret.

'I know. It's torture. I want to fall asleep with you in my arms, to wake and find you beside me.'

'Me, too!' she whispered, overjoyed that he wanted her presence as much as she wanted his.

'I'll take you to the office tomorrow,' he rasped. 'And I will make love to you as you've never known it before.' Abruptly he stood up. 'I must go now, Laura,' he said, desperately running his hands through his hair. 'See you in the morning.'

She couldn't believe it. He needed her very badly. And everything he said suggested that it wasn't just sex but something deeper. Hopefully more lasting.

Walking on air, she floated off to bed and fell into a contented sleep the moment her head touched the pillow.

CHAPTER TEN

'THE blue or the green?' she asked the next morning in the Harrogate office, waving silky scraps of froth, which were masquerading as panties.

'Breen. Glue…Laura!' groaned Cassian, when she gurgled in delight at his confusion. 'My brain doesn't work when you prance around like that.'

'Like what?' She pranced. Tried a little modified lap dancing.

Naked and menacing, Cassian growled alarmingly and came straight for her. She squealed and dashed around the buttonback sofa. But not too fast.

'Temptress,' he muttered, catching her and covering her with kisses.

He bent her backwards, Silent Picture Style, and she fluttered her lashes at him, making Silent Picture Faces at him.

'I think I'm going to like coming here,' she said smugly.

'You won't get sex every time, you know,' Cassian said with a grin.

'Shame! I suppose I'd better get dressed.' Her eyes sparkled, a deep and intense blue. 'Have another glass of celebratory champagne while I shower. Then I'm handing out money to people who deserve it,' she said happily.

'You think you have everything you need?' he enquired.

She paused, her eyes glazing over. He was gorgeous. Standing there absolutely naked, totally masculine and unbelievably thoughtful. His hair was tousled, eyes drugged whenever he looked at her, body…quite breathtakingly beautiful. What more could a woman want?

Yes. She had everything.

'It's all perfect,' she said with a sigh.

Glowing with love, she cast her eyes about her. The offices were gorgeous too. High ceilinged and with the lovely proportions of a typical Georgian mansion, they had been tastefully decorated and fitted out so that the overall effect was that of a comfortable high class home rather than a business empire.

They were in the interview room, having made the best use of the deep cream carpet she could ever have imagined. Their clothes were strewn everywhere. The results of their shopping—wicked and seductive lingerie and two more outfits for her, plus clothes for Adam and small decorative touches to make the office more friendly—were heaped on the comfortable sofas.

When she was ready, she was to employ someone to open mail and to deal with her correspondence. Until then, she could settle in at her own pace. It seemed too good to be true. But it was real enough. She'd seen the letters asking for help and was anxious to get started.

'Thank you for this chance,' she said, beaming with pleasure.

'Thank *you*. You'll be wonderful,' he answered huskily.

Blowing Cassian a shy kiss, she wandered into the huge marble bathroom and turned on the shower. She was to work for a while and Cassian would help her with the mail, then they were going out to lunch.

When they arrived back at Thrushton Hall, Cassian and Adam would go out for their run and then on their return the house would be filled with the sound of laughter and noise and fabulous music, just as it had been last night.

She smiled, thrilled with the change in Adam. He *was* more confident, more feisty. And she'd listened to the sound of Cassian's voice in the house upstairs as he'd read some exciting story to her son, and her heart had seemed fit to burst with happiness.

A fabulous meal was in order tonight, she thought, mentally going through the recipe she'd chosen. With a month's advance salary in the bank, she'd felt able to buy something special to strengthen her plan to be totally indispensable to Cassian.

Fillet of beef rolled in herbs and porcini, wrapped in prosciutto. Her mouth watered as she stepped out and dried herself. Chocolate pots and sharp lemon wedges. Her eyes lit up. He'd adore it, while she'd adore cooking for the men she loved. And tomorrow there'd be succulent chicken in wine sauce followed by bread and butter pudding laced with whisky. Heaven.

'Champagne.' Cassian handed her a glass and switched on the shower for himself.

'To the future. Happiness for all,' she said, lifting the elegant flute, confident now that he'd want her to stay.

He smiled fondly. 'The future. Happiness.'

In a daze of delight she eased on her elegantly fitting Jackie-O dress and then, with great pride she settled at her huge desk with its view across the leafy park.

Her mind was teeming with thoughts of the future— Cassian falling in love with her, the two of them and their sons living happily together, perhaps a child of their own…

The shower door banged in the background and she hastily put her dreams on hold and began to tackle the post.

'So many people needing help!' she marvelled, when Cassian came in.

He grabbed a stack of letters and began slitting them. 'I know. It can be heartbreaking. But we…I mean, the charity can make a difference to some. I suggest you make a rough selection of "Good grief no's" and "so-so's" and "yes, desperate's", and I'll keep them coming.'

Her 'yes, desperate' pile was unnervingly large when they'd finished opening all the letters.

'Supposing I give out all the money in two months and there's none left?' she said anxiously.

'Then you have ten months of twiddling your thumbs,' he said, grinning. 'Relax, Laura. Use your intuition, make some appointments and hear what your favourites have to say.'

Solemn-faced to have such awesome responsibility, she applied herself with a will and began to enjoy the task. Her decision to enter every single applicant on a database had been greeted with approval by Cassian and her fingers flew over the keys as she entered the names and addresses.

'Time for lunch,' he murmured in her ear, seemingly a few minutes later.

She checked her watch. 'It can't be that late!' she exclaimed.

'You've been working non-stop. Take a break.'

'I'd rather continue. Could we have sandwiches?' she asked hopefully.

'I can do better than that.'

Cassian disappeared and returned later with smoked salmon, pasta salad and two wicked cream cakes.

'Pastry on your mouth,' he drawled lazily, when they'd finished. 'No, let me!' The tip of his tongue slid around her lips, making her tremble. 'Tasty.'

'You're supposed to be the office boy today, so go and make me an espresso,' she said haughtily, pretending she wasn't feeling hot throughout her body.

'Mmm. Ever had a fantasy about an innocent young office boy being seduced by his glamorous, high-flying boss?' he murmured, slipping his fingers to her zip at the back of the honey-gold dress. 'Across her executive desk?'

Her eyes gleamed as her body capitulated. She walked over to her desk and without taking her eyes off him, hitched herself onto it, her skirt high on her thighs.

'Come and learn a little office practice, *boy*,' she purred silkily.

She saw him swallow, knew he was hopelessly drawn to her. Elated, she leaned back, unable to believe he found her so enticing.

His mobile rang. He ignored it. And played the game to the full.

'Lunch hours have never been such fun,' she gurgled later, when they were mutually soaping one another in a haze of satisfaction. 'Enough!' she protested, when Cassian came dangerously close to arousing her again. *'Work.'*

Escaping, she pulled on her clothes and shakily returned to her lists. Time passed quickly again and it seemed only an hour or so before they were driving home. Somewhere in the depths of Cassian's pocket, his mobile rang.

'Can you answer that?' he asked.

'Yes, of course.' She dug it out. 'Hello?' she said uncertainly.

'Oh. Where's Dad?'

'It's Jai!' she squealed.

Cassian's eyes lit up like beacons. 'Can't stop here, too dangerous. See what he wants,' he urged.

'He's driving. Can I give him a message?' she suggested excitedly.

'OK. Can you tell him I'm sitting on the wall outside his house?'

Laura's eyes rounded. 'What? You've arrived? This is fantastic. He'll be over the moon—wait, oh, it'll be a good half hour or so before he can get to you—'

'No sweat,' said the composed Jai. 'I can wait.'

'See you soon,' she said happily. There was a casual 'OK' and then Jai rang off. 'He's there!' she told Cassian. 'At the house!'

'That must have been him, ringing earlier. I totally forgot to check if any message had been left. I can't wait for you to meet him. And Adam,' he said enthusiastically. 'We'll pick him up from school first.'

She beamed, thinking of them all together. Just like a family.

'I can't wait,' she replied.

*   *   *

The noise was deafening but she loved it. Jai had brought his father a tape of a local band playing in some market square in Marrakesh. Adam and Jai were excitedly chattering together, heads close, as Jai described the Berber houses in the mountains, where hospitality was so generous that he'd been overwhelmed by the excess of food and love. Cassian sat listening to the tape and occasionally adding to the stream of information coming from his son. His hand gripped Jai's, his eyes resting on his child with naked adoration.

And she was trying to get the meal together, having shooed away all offers of help, while at the same time she was doing her best not to miss a word of Jai's extraordinary tales of mountain passes, verdant valleys and ruined fortresses.

But mainly he spoke of the people. Her mind teemed with images and ideas, astonished that a ten-year-old boy should have experienced so much.

The vividly colourful clothes of the women, who worked in the fields and grazed the cattle and goats. The closeness of the families and the affection between them all. The remarkable fact that wherever they went, even in a remote valley, someone would appear. And that someone either spoke English or knew a villager who did.

She smiled, caught up in the excitement of Jai's arrival, thrilled to see how happy he was to be with his father. He was a handsome child. Dark, rangy, like Cassian, and clearly tough and self-assured. But sunny-natured, laughing a good deal, and never arrogant, never conscious that his life must be so different from most other children's.

Her eyes softened. She would never forget his meeting with his father. Cassian had leapt from the car as if ejected by a rocket. The two had flown together and had remained in a hug for ages; weeping, exclaiming, squeezing.

Without realising, her arm had gone around Adam too.

And she'd felt weepy when her son had cuddled her hard, his small face lifted to hers in love and happiness.

'Isn't life great now, Mum?' he'd said, starry-eyed.

'Great,' she'd agreed. And promised to herself that she'd do everything to keep it that way.

She hadn't stopped smiling since. Lifting the broccoli off the hot plate, she grinned at the laughing men in her life and coughed loudly to attract their attention.

'Supper's ready,' she announced, flushed pink from cooking and deep contentment. 'Jai, it's your choice. Eat here or the dining room?'

'Here, please!' cried Jai. 'It's smashing. Cosy and homely. Can we have candles?'

'I'll get them!' offered Adam, jumping up.

'I'll come too—'

The boys disappeared. Cassian looked up at her and if she hadn't fallen love with him before she would have done so then. There was such pleasure in every cell of his body and such exhilaration in his gleaming dark eyes that her heart somersaulted chaotically.

'He's wonderful,' she said shakily.

'I think so. I'm glad you do,' he replied.

He reached out his hand and she grasped it, both of them grinning idiotically at one another.

'I'd better put the meal on the table,' she breathed, afraid that she'd tell him how much she loved him. And she pulled her hand away.

'Crikey!' gasped Jai rushing in. 'Just look at that beef! Smells stupendous. I can't wait. I'm starving!'

Pleased, she began to carve. 'When did you last eat?' she asked in amusement, watching Jai pile potatoes and vegetables onto his plate.

'Umm… In Skipton, just before my minder put me on the bus.'

Adam giggled. 'I can't imagine what Skipton made of a

Berber in full ceremonial robes standing at a bus stop with
you!'

'Did draw the crowds a bit,' Jai acknowledged. 'But
Karim's got a degree in Psychology so he handled it. I love
England, Laura. People are so friendly and smiley.'

'Are you sure?' she asked, a little astonished.

'I grin at them and they grin back,' Jai said blithely.

'I can imagine,' she said with a smile. He'd charm the
birds off the trees. 'But we don't all have a tame Berber to
help the conversation along.'

Jai laughed and sampled a piece of beef. 'Wowee, this
tastes fab, Laura!' he declared. 'The absolute best!'

'Thanks,' she said warmly, won over by Jai's enthusiasm. 'I wondered what you'd think of the food in this country, after all the exotic stuff you've eaten.'

'But it's exotic here!' Jai claimed.

'Yorkshire?' hooted Adam.

Jai nodded. 'It is, to me. It's foreign. Exciting. I've never
been to England before. Dad's talked about it a lot. In fact,
he hardly ever *stops* talking about the Yorkshire Dales—'

'Exaggeration!' Cassian protested.

'In the last month or so, all I hear,' said Jai with the kind
of affectionate scorn reserved for a wayward parent, 'is how
beautiful it is, how green, the charm of the hills and trees
and little fields and tiny villages. And do you know something, Dad?'

'I'm a bore?' he suggested.

Jai grinned. 'Never in a million years! No, you're right!
This place blew me away. I know why you drooled about
it.' He ducked to avoid an accurately hurled lump of bread.
'Seriously, though…is this going to be our home, now,
Dad?'

'Could you really *live* here?' Adam cried hopefully, before Cassian could answer. But she saw he was frowning
and a slight feeling of unease spread over her. 'We'd have
a great time together,' Adam enthused.

'Yeah! Could you show me the corpse way you told me about?' Jai asked eagerly. 'And…what was it…Li'l Emily's Bridge? And the suspension bridge that wobbles and—'

'All of it!' broke in Adam. 'It's Saturday tomorrow, so I don't have school. We'll go early. And there are the remains of Roman lead mines above the village, and ruins of Victorian mining offices and a forge. It's dead interesting—'

'Dad!' Jai cried, his eyes shining. 'We can stay, can't we? Adam and me'll have a great time—'

He and Adam vied to coax Cassian. Laura suddenly couldn't eat. Her future—Adam's future—had been suddenly pushed to the forefront.

It had been obvious that Jai thought Cassian must be renting the house, as was his custom. She knew that he'd spent two years renting rooms in Morocco, two years in an Egyptian apartment before that, and a holiday home in Madagascar before then…

It puzzled her why Cassian hadn't explained he'd bought Thrushton Hall. Her eyes grew troubled. And she held her breath while he tried to make himself heard over the eager boys.

'I thought we'd stay for a while—' he began.

The boys whooped, waving their forks triumphantly in the air.

'Brill, Dad! Gosh, Laura, you don't mind?' exclaimed Jai.

'I—don't mind.' How could she? She adored him. And loved his father. 'I'd love to have you here,' she said warmly, aware that Cassian was frowning. But it was his own fault. He should have told Jai what he'd done.

Jai leapt from his chair and ran over, giving her a hug which left her breathless.

'It'll be like having a Mum around,' he said, misty-eyed.

'I've always wanted one of those but Dad wouldn't play ball!'

'Jai—' growled Cassian.

'It'll be like living in a real home, with a real Mum,' Jai said, not in the least bit unnerved by his father's ferocious scowl. 'I wish I had one. A Mum, I mean.'

'Is she dead?' asked Adam, with the typical bluntness of a child.

'When I was born. Dad said she was the most beautiful woman he's ever seen. I've got pictures of her, I'll show you. She was terribly clever. A novelist. He's never really got over her—'

'Jai!' muttered Cassian.

'Well, it's true, Dad! You told me you'd never love another woman, remember?'

Laura tensed, her stomach plummeting. This was awful. Could she ever make him forget this perfect wife, who'd tragically died before boredom or familiarity could set in? Who he remembered with rose-coloured spectacles?

'Yes,' Cassian said in a hoarse whisper. His face was unnervingly bleak. 'I remember.'

She felt sick. Cassian looked dreadful. He was carrying a torch for his late wife. Her hopes came crashing about her ears.

'Wish I had a father,' Adam put in, gazing significantly at Cassian, raw hope in his eyes.

She didn't know where to look. Her fingers trembled. The boys were voicing her dreams. Cautiously she stole a quick glance at Cassian. He was frowning at his plate, cutting up a piece of beef into increasingly small pieces.

'What happened to your Dad?' Jai asked gently.

'He didn't stand by Mum,' Adam said, his voice indignant. 'He left her in the lurch. But she's the best Mum in the world. You can share her if you like.'

'Can I?' Jai asked, his face wistful.

Laura's heart jerked painfully. 'Of course, Jai,' she husked. If Cassian would only let her...

'I thought you liked wandering the world, Jai,' Cassian said gruffly, still intent on dissecting the beef out of all existence.

'I do! It's cool!' Jai declared with passion. 'I love new places and getting my education first hand from you and where we are, instead of—'

'Wow! Your Dad teaches you?' Adam asked in awe.

'Yeah. Our life's too nomadic for me to go to school. Dad sets me work—like...doing the shopping in the souk, working out exchange rates, comparing prices and currencies in other countries, that kind of thing. Or...I do a study on the effect of land form and climate on people's lifestyles—that was my last project. Or local art—that's great, I get to talk to some real odd bods. And when Dad's finished writing for the day, we talk over what I've done.'

Cassian had stiffened imperceptibly. He was staring fixedly at the oblivious Jai—who was happily eating—as if he wanted to convey a message. Laura's eyes narrowed.

'Course,' Jai went on, prompting Cassian to tense up even more, 'when Dad's *really* motoring on a book, I have to create my own education. That's quite fun. I brush up on the local language or do a bit of painting. Sometimes I just read and read.'

Laura's mind was racing. Cassian's late wife had been a novelist. And he spent long hours 'motoring on a book'.

'I write thrillers,' Cassian said quietly, plainly reading the expression on her face. 'Under a pseudonym. I tell no one, *no one*, who I am. I don't like my private life invaded. We travel so that I can research a particular setting for a novel.'

'Wow!' Adam's eyes were popping. 'Are you famous?'

'I'll say!' Jai answered, matter-of-fact.

'But anonymous,' Cassian warned, and his son at last took the hint.

'We won't tell anyone. Will we, Adam?' Laura promised.

A writer, she thought. And if Jai hadn't innocently spilled the beans, she wouldn't have known. Even now, Cassian wasn't intending to tell her the name he wrote under. That hurt. He didn't want to share a huge part of his life with her. She felt suddenly flat and depressed. Where did she stand with him?

'You work on a computer?' she asked, remembering how he'd deflected her questions about his job.

His eyes begged her forgiveness for that evasion. 'I do.'

'Anyway,' Jai went on, 'it's a great way to live. I'm not knocking it, Dad. But for a while I'd like to be here. It's a super house, isn't it? And Adam and I are already good mates. Laura's my kind of Mum-substitute. I'd have chosen her out of a million other women—'

'Only a million?' Cassian asked, eyebrow raised.

'Ten,' Jai amended.

'A billion,' Adam said.

She waited for Cassian to make his contribution. An advance on a billion would have been nice. But he didn't.

'Jai, it's OK,' he said instead, quite unusually stilted in his manner. 'We're staying put for at least a couple of years. After then…I'm not sure. You know how it is.'

'Two years!' the boys crowed. Cassian opened his mouth and shut it, his jaw tight.

Laura almost joined in the cheers. She began to feel a little better, knowing that she had two whole years with Cassian. They'd live in close proximity. Judging by the way that they had instantly melded into a happy, friendly unit, they would all get on well. And Cassian would surely not want to break that unit up at the end of that two years.

Maybe she wouldn't ever be as special or as beautiful as his late wife, but she would be an important part of his life. And that was enough for her.

Serene amid the noisy, excited chatter, she smiled indulgently at the boys as their friendship blossomed.

'I'm shattered,' Jai announced with a yawn when they were all sitting in the drawing room around a cheery log fire. 'Mind if I go to bed?'

'Me too,' said Adam.

'I'll make up a bed,' Laura said warmly.

'Will I be in the same room as Adam?' Jai asked, his eyes so appealingly like Cassian's that she laughed, unable to resist his plea.

'If you like!'

She covered her ears when the boys shouted their delight and found herself enveloped in wiry arms, one dark head and one fair buried against her middle.

'I think you're a hit, Laura,' Cassian said in a thoughtful tone.

She heaved a huge sigh of pleasure and put away her niggling doubts about Cassian's love for his late wife.

'Has there ever been a more perfect day?' she marvelled, her eyes desperately hoping that he'd agree.

'It's been eventful,' he replied, with masterly understatement. 'Come on, boys. A quick bath each and bed. I'll tell you about the ghost of the miner's daughter who haunts Bardale Peak if you're tucked up in fifteen minutes.'

'Ten!' cried Adam and led the charge up the stairs.

Cassian followed Laura, his mind in turmoil. He could barely answer her comments as they moved the spare bed into Adam's room and made it up for Jai. He'd get through the next half hour and then he'd have to do some thinking.

She was humming to herself. Her entire face seemed luminous and he couldn't bear the pain that gave him.

'Adam will do so well, with Jai here,' she said softly, her eyes shining with happy tears. 'You...you don't know what this means to me, Cassian,' she continued. 'To see my child transformed, because of you, because he has found a trustworthy friend in Jai, means more to me than if I'd won the lottery.'

He understood. And because he did, because he knew that his own happiness depended largely on Jai's well-being, he felt doubly torn. She and Adam had changed beyond all recognition. Jai wanted them all to live like one big family.

And he...he even wished he could tutor Adam so the two boys learnt together. It was a fatuous idea. Of course it was.

'I'll chivvy those boys up,' he said shortly and knew she was disappointed that he hadn't acknowledged her happiness. She looked at him uncertainly and then went downstairs.

He stood in Adam's empty bedroom and gave a token yell at the boys, his breathing hard and fast. He couldn't allow this situation to develop. Nor did he want to feel this deeply. Didn't want to be possessed, obsessed.

His freedom was seeping away and soon he'd be back in the nightmare of his youth. Trapped. Cornered as surely as if he'd been shut in a cupboard.

The sex was fantastic. But love...that was something else. He didn't want this compulsion to stay close to Laura, to touch her every few moments, to ache with a sense of loss when she wasn't within his sight.

Love struck deep inside you. It took over your muscles, your veins, your lungs and every single brain cell. He would fight it. Stay detached.

'Story!' yelled Jai, hurling himself forwards like a projectile.

Cassian caught him and flung him on the bed, laughing despite his worries. And he did the same to Adam, because the child desperately needed some rough and tumble too.

God. What was he going to do, break three hearts?

CHAPTER ELEVEN

AFTER the story he told Laura that he had work to do, and went into the study, her image—soft, sensuous, loving— imprinted indelibly on his brain.

Of course he couldn't work. He couldn't think, either, and sat in a leather chair morosely nursing a whisky, wishing that life consisted of him and Jai and no one else.

Except…he sighed. Laura filled his mind, intruding on logical thought. Perhaps tomorrow he'd be more able to decide what to do. If the weather was suitable, he'd take a flight and let his instincts dictate his future.

Feeling extraordinarily tired and subdued, he wandered slowly along the darkened hallway to where Laura sat reading recipes in the sitting room.

The firelight cast a glow over her absorbed face. Her dark lashes were thick arcs on her flawless cheeks and her lips were parted as she frowned at the recipe book, perhaps, he mused, working out quantities or deciding which day she'd surprise them with another superlative meal.

But she was a meal in herself. Her lissom body was curled on the sofa, every inch of her desirable from the top of her gleaming scalp to the delicate, beautifully arched feet which he had kissed so fervently that very day.

Something hard and painful cramped in his chest and he bit back an urge to invite her to stay for ever. With a tremendous effort, he forced his voice to sound casual.

'I'm going up. Fantastic supper,' he said, extending his goodnight even though he wanted to hurry away to the isolation of his room. 'See you tomorrow. Night.'

She had risen, her eyes on his. He could turn away with

a curt nod... No. He couldn't. She held him fast, his feet were rooted to the ground.

'Goodnight,' she said softly, coming to put her arms around his neck.

He found himself kissing her, the sweetness of her mouth taking his breath away.

'I'm pleased Jai likes me,' she sighed, snuggling into his embrace more securely.

Unseeing, he stared over her head. Jai's longing for a mother had shaken him—together with the fact that his son had clearly wanted stability, too, a home of some kind.

The wanderer wants a home, he thought wryly. The homebody wants to wander.

'I've never kissed a famous author before,' she murmured into his throat. 'I suppose you're a literary genius and that's why you aren't rich beyond the dreams of Averil.'

He smiled at her joke. And felt safe enough with her, sure of her discretion, to come clean. He didn't want secrets from her. He wanted to share.

'I am rich,' he said gently. 'I just don't keep much of my money. It comes in, I keep what I think I'll need, and the rest—'

'Goes to the charity?' she gasped.

'I trust you not to breathe a word to anyone.'

Her hand lifted to caress his cheek. 'You are the most amazing man I've ever known,' she said shakily.

A wonderful sensation—pride, joy, contentment—meandered silkily through every inch of his body. 'You must get out more,' he chuckled. Kissed her small nose, and beat a hasty retreat.

With a crescent of Day-Glo orange spread out behind him, he checked the wind and cloud formations again. His narrowed eyes scanned the ridge of hills, now lit by the warm morning sun.

Tightening the strap on his helmet, he began the short run to the edge of the hilltop and launched himself into the air.

Freedom.

A huge sigh released itself from his tense chest. It was a long time since he'd flown and he'd missed the sensation of becoming unshackled from the world.

His feelings for Laura were more intense than any he'd ever known, but he had to remember that a permanent relationship came with strings that eventually strangled him.

Yet Jai would love to have her around.

Cassian searched for more lift, found it, and shot up a few hundred feet. Now he could see Thrushton and the manor at the edge of the village. What was it about this place that gave him such a sense of calm and well-being? It was as if he had come home—despite his troubled teenage years there.

Jai and Adam would be exploring Hangman's Wood by now. They'd come back, dirty, dishevelled and talking nineteen to the dozen and Laura and he would listen to their exploits and smile at one another...

He frowned. Laura. Laura, Laura! She never left him alone. Slid into his thoughts and his vision, forcing him to acknowledge how powerfully she had entered his life. Too far, too fast. He had to cool things down. And separation was the only way.

He'd never intended that she should stay. Jai and Adam and Laura had misinterpreted his remark when he'd said they'd be living at Thrushton Hall for at least two years. He'd been referring to Jai and himself. Now he'd have to clarify the situation.

No problem. A straightforward statement of fact. And yet he was shying away from even voicing it to himself.

Slowly he worked his way along the ridge in the direction of Thrushton, as though he couldn't bear to be parted

from it for long. The wind began to buffet him and he had
to stop thinking and focus hard on keeping up in the air.

But he was losing height and the wind was throwing him
around too violently so he made a running landing and
packed up for the day, feeling vaguely unsatisfied.

The flight had been enjoyable but it hadn't thrilled him
as it used to. He found he was hurrying to fold up his
'wing', eager to return…to Laura.

He groaned. Maybe if he steeped himself in her the ob-
session would pall. He'd go back, make love to her… His
body jerked in anticipation and he ruefully stowed the wing
in its sack, recognising that there was only one thing on
his mind. To hold Laura in his arms. To smell her, feel her,
hear her, look at her.

The journey was short, he knew, but even then it took
too long. And when he arrived, shouting to her, struck
dumb by the answering silence, he knew a disappointment
so keen that it unnerved him totally.

He'd wanted to see her smile at him, the cute lift of each
corner of her lips, the whiteness of her even teeth. To listen
to the warmth in her voice with its husky cadences as she
spoke to him. Her scent was in his nostrils now, tantalising
him; the clean smell of the shampoo she used, the subtle
elusiveness of her favourite geranium and orange soap.

But without her presence, there was nothing but empti-
ness in the big house. It was as if it had died.

Quite at a loss as to what to do, he wandered into the
garden behind the manor and passed the time waiting for
Laura by planning a herb garden. It would be dual purpose—culinary and medicinal, and he'd draw on what he'd
learnt from the Morrocan herbalist.

Mint to keep flies at bay. Nettles for pesticide—and to
flavour the soft fruit he'd grow, chives for blackspot and
aphids on the roses… Meadowsweet, heartsease, chamo-
mile…

He couldn't wait to start planting. And what else? Perhaps at the far end of the garden he'd build a chicken run so they could have fresh, new-laid eggs. Extend the vegetable garden of course—

He blinked, and leaned against the sunwarmed wall of the house, suddenly sure—absolutely positive—that he wanted to put down roots here. Not just for two years. For the rest of his life. His mouth curved into a smile, his decision giving him a peace of mind he'd never known before.

'You look happy,' came Laura's soft voice.

It trembled a little, as if emotion bubbled within her and her eyes were luminous. He felt his knees weaken.

'I am.' But he didn't tell her why. And he had to fight his longing to include her in his plans.

'So am I. I've been talking to Tom about my mother. It's so wonderful, getting to know her, Cassian!'

'I'm very pleased for you,' he said, lightly touching her arm.

And suddenly she was nestled up to his chest and the house, the garden, his life, seemed complete again. His lips caressed her forehead while fear and excitement tussled with one another.

Maybe his idea of sating his desire wasn't a good one. It went without saying that Laura gave him the kind of sexual satisfaction he'd dreamed about. But she also made security and a cosy family life seem appealing. When, in fact, it wasn't.

Her fingers laced in his hair. Her laughing eyes were melting into his. Every part of his body was alight, energised, strangely empty. With increasingly drugged eyes, he gazed at her soft lips and let her warmth seep remorselessly into him. He paused, his heart thundering. There was nothing he could do to draw back—his desire was too overwhelming.

'I want you,' he said hoarsely.

Detaching herself, she gave a beguiling smile and walked

to the door, the glance over her shoulder telling him that he was to follow.

And follow he did, hopelessly tied to a woman's smile, soft blue eyes, a lushly mobile body. And hoping that was all. Pure physical lust.

Gently, with near-reverence, he made slow and adoring love to her. The poignancy of her whimpers and sighs caused a bitter-sweetness within him that led him to extend her pleasure until she was almost weeping with frustration.

His climax, and hers, both awed and unnerved him. Nothing could be this good. He was imagining it. No two bodies could move in such harmony, feel so good, offer such mutual rapture, or make him wonder if he'd been bewitched or transported to a heaven.

He didn't want to move, but held her in his arms, lost in a state of unbelievable bliss. And fear. This was getting beyond his control. No one should feel so attached to someone.

It was as if he depended on Laura for his very existence. A lump of terror came up in his throat, his heart beating frantically. And he finally detached himself.

They were both quiet when they wandered hand in hand downstairs later, and he wondered if she too was contemplating their relationship.

His throat dried again. He had to make his position clear. It was only fair.

'Laura,' he croaked, as she began her bread-making ritual. 'I must talk to you. Get things straight—'

'Things?' she asked, her eyes instantly wary.

He took the precaution of staring out of the window. Without her glorious, sexually glowing face in his vision, he'd focus more sharply.

'I think, over the past few days,' he muttered, 'I've known every emotion in the book.'

'Me, too.'

Hearing the smile in her soft voice, he steadied himself,

his hands flat on the work counter. Behind him he could hear the dough being thumped and he hurried on, anxious not to hurt her.

'It's...it's happened so fast, been such a roller-coaster that I hardly know where I am—'

'I know. It's lovely but it's scary, too,' she murmured in agreement.

'We need to slow down a bit.'

He almost smiled at himself. Was this really him talking—advising caution? Was he actually suggesting they lived with their heads for a while, instead of their instincts?

'If you like,' she said casually.

His head lifted in relief. She wasn't going to tie him down, to demand further commitment. A load lifted from his mind and he turned to watch her as she deftly kneaded the dough. Not too violently. Normal. Rational. Serene. And she smiled encouragingly at him, a dazzling smile that made his heart ache.

'I'm glad you feel that way,' he husked.

'I wonder,' she mused, glancing out of the window behind him, 'where Adam and Jai have got to now? They're as thick as thieves, aren't they?' She laughed, her pearly teeth glistening in her rosy mouth. 'I suppose I'll have a heap of washing to do when they come in!'

He knew what she was implying. That their sons were now a unit. But, he thought with a frown, that didn't mean they all had to live together.

'Laura, I don't want to lose what we have, you and me—'

'Nor do I,' she said, her eyes far too tender and mesmerising for him to stay unmoved.

'You know, I hope, that I'm not a man to make commitments,' he warned with quick urgency. 'I don't want to be trapped—'

'What commitments? And who's trapping you?' she asked in amiable surprise. 'You come and go as you like

and I don't ask where you've been or where you're going—'

'It's not just that,' he said gently. 'Let me explain. You
told me once that I wasn't to make Adam too fond of me
because I wasn't going to be part of his life for long—no,
wait, hear me out,' he said, when it seemed she'd interrupt.

The dough was left unheeded on the table. Dusted appealingly with flour as usual, she stared at him wide-eyed,
her arms hanging by her sides.

'I'm listening.' Her voice shook.

'We're in danger here of giving the kids the wrong idea.'

'Are we?' she asked, her eyes piercing blue and startlingly luminous.

He could kiss her. Brush her hair from her forehead,
chide her for coating herself in flour…

He swallowed. This had to be said. 'I'm worried that
we're all getting too cosy. We're moving into Walton territory.'

'Nothing wrong with that, except all those interminable
"goodnights",' she said with a wicked little grin.

No way could he smile. He was too worried. 'And what
if it all goes wrong?' he shot. 'You saw how Jai was about
you,' he croaked, longing to take her in his arms and say
it would be all right, that she wouldn't be hurt. But he
couldn't promise that. 'He wants a mother figure and has
fixated on you. But the last thing I want is for him to be
upset. We don't know what will happen between us, you
and me. We might stay together for a while and part, we
might separate tomorrow. Nothing is certain in this world.
We can't let the boys think we're heading towards something permanent.'

He could feel the pain in her. And it was tearing him in
two. But he had to be honest.

'You can't protect Jai from everything,' she breathed.
'You've taught me that. What happened to seizing the day?
To living life? Learning to cope with disappointments?'

She wouldn't accept what he wanted, he thought with a slicing fear. Laura would want commitment. A husband, children—he'd always known that. She ought to be married to a loving man, not tied to someone who couldn't bear the finality of marriage. His spine chilled. Almost certainly he'd lose her.

And yet honesty and decency made him plough on, even though he knew he was heading towards a separation he'd find hard to bear.

'Jai is impulsive and passionate. He thinks you're wonderful. I'll be nagged to put our relationship on a firmer footing. I can't do that. I'm just suggesting that we can cool things and make this more of a friendly relationship, if we detach ourselves a little.'

'How do you suggest we do that?' she asked, widening her big blue eyes. She looked at him with a suspiciously provocative tilt of her head. 'I do find it hard not to touch you, Cassian. And we look at each other ten times a minute. The boys aren't stupid.'

He frowned. This wasn't going the way he'd planned. 'We'd be less…obsessed with one another if we didn't live together. I never wanted that,' he said with unintentional sharpness. And although he wasn't looking at her—but examining his shoes with intense interest—he knew she had stiffened. 'I said to Jai that we'd be here for two years but I think you all assumed that you and Adam would be part of that set up. Nothing was farther from my mind. You and Adam must live somewhere else. In the village, maybe—there are a couple of houses for sale, or Grassington—I'd buy a house for you both—'

'So I'd be your secret mistress,' she said, suddenly cold.

Alarmed that she was withdrawing from him mentally, he took a step forward. And she took one back. He felt panic welling up inside him.

'We'd have a relationship,' he corrected huskily. 'We'd

spend a good deal of time together, going out with the kids, reading them bedtime stories, that kind of thing—'

'And I'd pop over for sex. Or we'd use the back of your car. Or a convenient field.'

His breath rasped in. 'It's not like that—'

'Yes, it is.' She folded her arms and her eyes were as dark as a threatening storm. 'Just *you* get *this* straight. I won't be used as a substitute mother for your son and to satisfy your sexual demands!'

'Don't misinterpret what I'm saying! We both agree we're going too fast and need to find a way to put the brakes on. This would achieve that. Please don't think I'm using you. I want more than that—' he found himself saying desperately.

'What?' she shouted. 'To fall asleep beside me? To wake up and find me in your arms?' she cried, tormenting him with the passionate words he'd spoken earlier. 'So what do I do? Commute? Leap up at dawn and hurry home? Do I find a baby-sitter to stay in the house so Adam is safe? No, Cassian! I don't want to be at your convenience, at your beck and call. I deserve better. Either I live here with you, or we part. I mean *really* part. You choose. Now.'

He gazed at her in horror, his hand scraping distractedly through his hair. That wasn't what he'd wanted. Just something slower, less threatening to his freedom. He couldn't imagine what it would be like without her...

'I've not made myself clear,' he said, choked.

'Oh, yes, you have!' she raged. 'It's your late wife, isn't it? You think you can't love another woman because she was so perfect. Well I'm not filling her shoes. I have shoes of my own. I am not her. I am me. And if you don't want me as I am, warts and all, then have the grace to say so. But don't use me to assuage your guilt because Jai needs a motherly touch, and don't use me as a sex object for your voracious appetite! It's not fair on me! I want sex too. But I want a hell of a lot more than that from the man I give my body to! So decide whether you want me, flesh and blood and living and breathing—or your late, perfect, beautiful wife who's dead, Cassian, *dead*!'

'You've got it wrong!' he said harshly, grabbing her arms. She put her hands to his chest and pushed, but he resisted, ignoring the flour and dough that now marked his shirt and rushing straight into his explanation. 'My wife wasn't perfect! Not anywhere near!' he hissed, his face ferocious as he remembered, felt the wounds, the misery, again.

'You married her!' she shot.

'And don't I regret it! I fell for her because I was only eighteen and ruled by my hormones and thought sexual pleasure was love. She was four years older with a hell of a lot of lovers in her past and a whore's skill in arousing men. But she didn't have an ounce of tenderness in her entire body! She lured me into a hasty marriage because she was already four months pregnant by another man— *yes*! Pregnant!' he snarled, when Laura jerked in horror.

'Jai?!' she whispered, appalled.

'Exactly,' he muttered bitterly.

'But…he's so like you!' she gasped.

He nodded, sick with misery. 'His mother was darkhaired. Spanish. Hence the similarity. She was beautiful, yes, but only on the outside.' He raised a harrowed face as memories came thick and fast. 'I knew her to be cruel and vicious to animals and her behaviour towards them made me want to retch,' he muttered. 'She had no compassion for the elderly, or those who were less than beautiful, and she made fun of them, ridiculed them unmercifully. Maria was an absolute bitch. I *loathed* her for trapping me into marriage!'

'But she's dead, Cassian—!' Laura said, infinitely caring.

'No. She isn't.'

'*What?*' she gasped.

He felt drained, as if the lie had taken away something

precious to him. His integrity. His belief in honesty at all times.

'She didn't die. I lied to Jai,' he confessed hoarsely. 'I never wanted him to come into contact with her, to learn the kind of woman she was. She'd tried to abort him. Her own baby, Laura!' He thought of the world without his beloved Jai and his eyes pricked with hot tears. 'She didn't care about him. He was a burden, something vile to her, because he'd ruined her figure. When Maria gave birth she dumped the baby on me, then vanished. I never saw or heard of her again and it took years for me to get a divorce and to free myself from her. Jai is not my son but—'

Laura froze. There had been a sound behind her. Ice chilled her entire body. Cassian was staring in horrified disbelief at something…someone…over her shoulder. And she knew before she turned who it must be.

CHAPTER TWELVE

IT WAS Jai. Dirty and dishevelled from his adventures outside. Looking suddenly small and pathetic, his mouth open in an O of despair, his eyes, his deceptively Cassian-like eyes dark and glistening with utter horror.

And then Jai gave a terrible shuddering cry like that of a wounded animal and he'd turned, lurching away in a sobbing frenzy before either she or Cassian could move their paralysed limbs.

'Jai!' he jerked out, in a horrific, broken rasping sound.

Automatically she whirled around, her hands lifting to stop Cassian from following. He cannoned into her, carrying her along a pace or two before he'd grabbed her to prevent them both falling over.

'No,' she said urgently. 'Not you.'

Pain etched deep in his face, his pain hurting her, knifing her through and through as if she was being stabbed over and over again.

'He's my son!'

His eyes squeezed tight as if he recognised the irony of that cry. And she felt the tears welling up in her own eyes and fought them. For his sake, for Jai, she must stay strong.

'He ran *from* you, not *to* you,' she said, as gently as she could. 'Let me go. Give us a while together.'

Without waiting for his reply, she flew into the hall where a bewildered Adam stood, his face as grubby as Jai's.

'Where did he go?' she demanded fiercely.

'Sitting room,' Adam cried. 'But what...?'

She hurtled in there. Nothing.

She bit her lip, wondering if he'd clambered out of the open window. But when she ran to it, she could see no sign of him. Panic made her shake. The child would be so hurt. His world had come crashing down, all the fantasies he'd woven about his mother, the images he'd had of her; lovely, loveable, kind...

And then she heard a stifled, muffled sob. She blanched. It had come from the cupboard.

'Where's he gone?' rasped Cassian from the doorway.

She couldn't answer. But he read her appalled gaze and flinched. Her hand stayed him. Quietly she stepped close to the door and laid her hand on it as if consoling the child within Cassian's long-ago prison.

'Jai,' she said tenderly. 'It's me. Laura.' Her fingers closed on the latch and gently eased it up. But the door was locked. Jai had locked himself in from the inside with the key Cassian had so carefully fitted in the lock. Her eyes closed at the pity of it all. 'Don't cry, sweetheart,' she crooned, love and compassion in every breath she uttered.

The dam burst; from behind the heavy panelled door, she heard a storm of weeping. Anxiously she glanced around. Adam was holding Cassian's hand, his young eyes aghast at the bleakness of Cassian's face.

She had to make things right. She loved Cassian so much that she'd do anything to stop him from hurting so badly. Her hand waved Adam and Cassian back, indicating they should retreat from the room.

'No one's here but me,' she said to Jai. She imagined him, sitting on the cold stone floor, sobbing his heart out. It was hard for her to keep her voice steady because she was so distressed. 'Don't stay in there alone, Jai,' she coaxed. 'Come and cuddle up with me on the sofa. Let me hold you. Just that. Nothing more. And we can talk if you want, or just sit together. Trust me. I know what it's like for you. I heard terrible things about my mother that broke my heart. Come to me. I understand. I've been there too.'

There had been a lessening of the wild crying whilst she spoke and she knew he'd been listening. She held her breath in the long silence that followed her plea. A stray sob lurched out from Jai and then there came the sound of scrabbling, as if he was standing up. Quietly she stepped back. The key rasped and the door opened a fraction.

'Cassian isn't here,' she said softly. 'Just me.'

Around the edge of the door, a wrecked face appeared, the small features screwed up in misery, the dark hair shooting in all directions as if he'd thrust violent fingers through it.

Heartbroken, she opened her arms and with a moan Jai stumbled into them.

'There,' she murmured, guiding him to the sofa. 'Come on. Snuggle up. I'll hold you tight. Cry if you want. I'm waterproof.'

She stroked the weeping child's turbulent curls, her arms securely around him. He clung to her like a limpet and she occasionally kissed his hot forehead, waiting patiently until his tears had subsided. It was a long wait.

'My m-mother was a cow!' Jai wailed. 'She…she didn't *want* me—'

'But Cassian did,' Laura gently reminded him.

'No! He was lumbered with me!' Jai sniffed.

'You know that's not true.' Laura kissed his wet temple and brushed soggy clumps of hair from the furrowed forehead. His tears seemed to have got everywhere, carried on frantic hands. Poor sweetheart. 'Cassian is crazy about you. He really believes you are his son in every way except by blood. He's prouder of you than perhaps he ought to be. The sun definitely originates from your person,' she said with a gentle smile.

'I have a vicious tramp for a mother and an unknown father!' Jai's appalled eyes gazed moistly into her own, seeking comfort.

'That is awful for you,' she acknowledged gravely. 'I thought I was in exactly the same situation as you, once, so I do know how painful it is when your parents turn out to be less than perfect. I was lucky. I discovered that my mother had been maligned and she wasn't horrible at all. My father too. I can't pretend that your mother was really a saint. But maybe she was scared because she was pregnant and unloved. People do terrible things when they're frightened, Jai. They seek self-preservation—think of themselves. That's how the human race is programmed when there's danger about.'

She shifted him more comfortably on her lap, gently wiping his tear-channelled face now that he'd stopped crying.

'Perhaps your father didn't know your mother was pregnant. Perhaps your mother has regretted leaving you, and you are never far from her mind. We can't ever be sure. But there is one thing we do know.'

'What's that?' Jai mumbled, sweetly grumpy.

Her lips touched his soft cheek. 'Cassian loves you,' she said, her voice shaking with passion. 'You are the most important thing in his life. Few people have such love. That makes you very special, very fortunate.'

'He *lied* to me!' Jai railed, screwing up his fists in anger.

'I know,' she agreed, soothing him with her gently stroking hands. 'And that only shows how much he cares. Cassian doesn't lie as a rule. It's a matter of principle to him. He's always honest—sometimes uncomfortably so,' she said, sadly rueful. 'But for you he made an exception. He couldn't tell you the facts about your mother. Perhaps he might have done, when you were older, but you wanted her to be wonderful, didn't you? So he invented a mother you'd adore. And we don't know how much it hurt him to keep up that pretence, how hard it must have been to say that his ex-wife was a paragon of virtue when she had hurt him and deceived him so badly. Do you understand why he felt compelled to lie to you, Jai?' she asked anxiously.

Cassian, listening in silent anguish from behind the door, his hand crushed by Adam's bony grip of sympathy, held his breath. He was nothing without his son. Without Laura.

'Yes,' he heard his son whisper.

Heard Laura murmur something, knew she was hugging Jai, rocking him. He threw back his head and closed his eyes, swamped by relief and gratitude. And admiration. By her tact and loving heart, she had given him the gift of his son. And for that, he could never thank her enough.

She was… He searched for a word to describe her but found nothing that expressed his feelings. More than wonderful. More than compassionate and caring. Selfless, tender, utterly sweet and loveable…

'You OK?' whispered Adam, stretching up on tiptoe to get close to Cassian's ear.

Dimly he saw the blond child's anxious face, saw the same concern and love that Laura displayed so openly. Unable to speak, he nodded, swallowing, and received a friendly squeeze of his mangled hand in response.

'Shall we see if we can call your father in?' he heard Laura say.

'Mmm,' snuffled Jai.

Adam beamed up at him. Laura's smile.

God, he loved her!

'Cassian!' she shouted. 'Are you around?'

He couldn't move. He was rooted to the ground in shock. He loved her so much that his lungs had lost their power and his heart seemed to have stopped beating.

Because he had messed up. He'd been so blind—had feared for his freedom so much—that he'd offered to keep her like some mistress, *like a caged bird*—to appear at his bidding, to make his life complete on his terms.

'Cassian!' she yelled, and Adam tugged at his hand urgently.

Laura wasn't like Maria. She would never trap him. She'd respect his need for space. And suddenly he didn't want that space so badly—he wanted her, to be with her, to be here in the manor and bathing in the warmth of her. Cooking breakfast, doing homework with the boys, exploring the moors, developing the garden…but all with Laura. With her in his heart. With her loving him.

Distraught, he obeyed Adam's desperate tugs and Laura's calls. Like an automaton he walked stiffly to the door, everything a blur because of the tears of despair in his eyes.

'Oh, *Dad*!' Jai wailed.

A body hurled itself at him. His son in all but blood, every inch, every bone as familiar to him as his own. Now Adam, too, was hugging him. And someone…the smell of Laura came to him. Laura. She was drawing them all forwards.

He felt the back of the sofa against his calves and found himself being pushed down. The misery was so intense that he couldn't respond to his son's desperate apologies but eventually he realised how upset Jai was and he managed to put on a show of normality.

'No, I'm fine. Just got a bit emotional,' he said huskily. 'I love you, Jai, Never want to hurt you. I'm sorry—'

'No sweat, Dad. I understand. Laura explained. I'm OK about it. Honest. I've got you, that's the important thing. And now we've got Laura. She's what I dreamed of when I imagined my Mum.'

His son's face swam before his eyes. He couldn't say that Laura was about to leave their lives. It wasn't the time. But his heart felt as heavy as lead despite his cranked-up smile. And he knew he had to be alone to grieve for his lost love.

'Yeah. Great. Now how about you two getting off me so I can breathe and flinging your grotty selves into a bath?' he growled. 'You're a disgusting colour, both of you. Have you been mud-wrestling or something?'

The boys giggled and leapt up. Jai hesitated, then bent down to kiss him.

'Love you, Dad,' he said shakily.

'Love you, Jai,' he croaked.

And then there was the sound of elephants stampeding up the stairs, the sound of yells, water running…

'Cassian.'

Laura's voice, soft and gentle. Her hand stealing into his. What a fool he'd been. Freedom wasn't in being alone, doing your own thing. It depended on many factors.

It was like flying. He could only stay aloft if the wind was right, if the thermals were there, if he manoeuvred his wing properly—and if the wing was undamaged.

To be free he needed a base from which to fly. Somewhere secure and familiar. And he needed to be nurtured by the right person if he was to truly soar up into the heights of joy.

He drew in an agonised breath. He needed to be loved.

'I'm sorry, Laura,' he rasped.

'For what?' she murmured.

'Coming here.'

He couldn't look at her. Not that he'd see her if he did. The tears which he'd not shed through all the bullying, all the terror and desperation, were betraying him now and falling freely down his face. What would she think of him?

He struggled to control himself, to find his iron will. He'd need it. God, he'd need it in the next days, weeks, months.

'How do you mean?' she asked, not moving a muscle beside him.

'If I hadn't come—'

'I would still be a mouse,' she said. 'I wouldn't have a wonderful job. Adam wouldn't know how much I love him.'

'OK. Some good has come out of it,' he granted.

She watched him struggling and longed to help him. But stayed quiet. Patience, she told herself. All would be well.

'I think it would be better for us all if—after a decent interval—I left. You and Adam can stay in the house.'

'Oh.' She thought for a moment. 'Can I take in lodgers?' she asked with apparent gravity.

'Lodge...?' He scowled. 'Suppose so. It'll be your house.'

'And...' Risking all, she said quietly, 'If I fall in love. Would you mind if my lover came here?'

His teeth drove hard into his lower lip. She could feel all his muscles tightening till they were rigid and quivering from tension.

'Your house. Your decision,' he clipped.

His distress, his pain, spurred her on.

'So,' she whispered, snuggling up close. 'When are you moving in?'

For a moment or two she thought he hadn't heard. Not a breath lifted his chest, not a flicker of his eyes betrayed the fact that he was a living man and not a frozen statue.

'What...did you say?' he whispered, desperately trying to focus. He dashed his hand across his eyes and her heart turned over.

'I do love you,' she said, stroking his harrowed face. 'I think you love me. And I want to be with you. I don't care how long that might be. I want you to be free—'

His mouth descended on hers in a hard and impassioned kiss. He was moaning, muttering words of love and delight, saying how deeply he felt and that he wanted to be with her for the rest of his life.

'You mean everything to me,' he said passionately, holding her shoulders and staring intently into her eyes. 'I can't imagine life without you. With you, it's a miracle. An amazing feeling of serenity and exhilaration. Every part of my heart and mind and soul is filled with love for you. I adore you, Laura. Worship you.'

'Whoopee! I've got a Mum!' yelled Jai from behind them.

'I've got a Dad!' crowed Adam.

She and Cassian smiled ruefully at one another. 'And we've got gooseberries,' she giggled.

'I think,' Cassian whispered, 'we'll get the gooseberries fed and up to bed and have a little party of our own down here.'

'Whoooo*oo*!' the boys chorused.

Laura blushed. And turned to the towel-draped boys, her eyes full of love and amusement.

'Go away, you horrible children!' she laughed.

Jai and Adam looked at each other in resignation. 'Huh. Parents,' Jai pretended to grumble. And they scampered upstairs again, screeching with joyous laughter.

Cassian hugged her. 'Rascals,' he said fondly. Then he caressed her cheek. 'I've never been so happy,' he said roughly. 'Not in the whole of my life.'

'I think you might be,' she purred. 'After chocolate torte for supper. And after that…'

The love in his eyes touched her heart. Wonderingly, she reached up and touched his mouth. Then she lifted her face to his and lost herself in his kisses. Now she was truly, deeply happy. And all her dreams were on their way to coming true.

She sighed and sank deeper into Cassian's arms. Perfect love. Perfect lover. She was, without doubt, the luckiest woman in the world.

'Marry me,' Cassian whispered. 'Be my wife. I want that more than anything. I want us to have children. More gooseberries,' he said with a laugh.

Her face was radiant, her eyes sparkling like a bright blue sea beneath a blinding sun. 'I would love to be your wife,' she said shakily. She giggled. 'And to have your gooseberries!'

Cassian gave a shout of laughter and kissed her passionately.

'About time! Thought he'd never ask,' came Jai's stage whisper from the doorway.

INNOCENT
MISTRESS

by

Margaret Way

Margaret Way takes great pleasure in her work and works hard at her pleasure. She enjoys tearing off to the beach with her family at weekends, loves haunting galleries and auctions and is completely given over to French champagne 'for every possible joyous occasion'. She was born and educated in the river city of Brisbane, Australia, and now lives within sight and sound of beautiful Moreton Bay.

Don't miss Margaret Way's exciting new novel, *Cattle Rancher, Secret Son,* **out in February 2008 from Mills & Boon® Romance.**

CHAPTER ONE

AFTER the well-heeled, well-endowed Poppy Gooding left his office in a swirl of silken perfume, Jude carefully wiped any lingering trace of lipstick from his mouth, then straightened his tie.

"Play it cool, Jude," he advised himself.

It didn't help. He knew he'd had about as many of Poppy's come-ons as he could comfortably deal with. He'd never met a girl so oversexed. He suddenly recalled a movie about sexual harassment in the workplace in which the man was the victim. Poppy's behaviour wasn't as dastardly as that woman's had been but her methods of seduction were at the very least questionable. Poppy completely lacked the degree of reserve one saw in properly brought up young ladies—although maybe that thought belonged in the Dark Ages... She most certainly wasn't a virgin, but then virginity wasn't as valuable as it used to be, either. The key point was that Jude had to stop her before she removed her clothes. Or his. He was the guy who'd always considered mixing business and pleasure high risk. In this instance it could see him right out of a high paid job.

After months of trying to fend her off he'd come to the conclusion Poppy had big plans for him. He was even tempted to get it over with and prove a big disappointment. Two of the guys in the firm, fellow associates, had given service beyond the call of duty. Maybe it was a required course of action? At present he was the guy holding out, resulting in a lot of ribbing from his colleagues.

The big problem was that it would be a bad, bad move

5

to offend her. Her father just happened to be his boss,
Leonard Gooding, senior partner in the prestigious firm of
Gooding, Carter and Legge, corporate lawyers. Being invited into this firm usually didn't happen for years, if ever,
but he'd earned a lot of kudos along the way. He'd graduated top of his law class with first class honours. He was a
good athlete, track and field which didn't hurt, either—even
couch potatoes like Leonard Gooding were sports mad. He
could only be thankful Poppy had spent the previous six
months overseas, no doubt spending a goodly portion of her
father's money. It was Poppy, the collector, who'd made the
running almost from the day she laid eyes on him.

Women smiled on Jude. He'd be a fool not to have noticed, though it took them a little time to realize how keen
he was on his bachelor status. He was twenty-eight years
old. There was a lot of exasperating talk about his ''blue,
blue eyes'' among the girls in the office. Blue eyes apparently scored well. The articled clerk, Vanessa, had even told
him she wanted to pass his blue eyes on to her children.
Even so Vanessa didn't put him on the defensive like Poppy.

City life had enforced his entrenched view of women.
Every last one of them was after a husband—preferably a
rich one—they'd been brought up that way. It was intimidating for guys. Some of them thought Jude, as a husband,
would do nicely.

The only thing was, he wasn't in the running. Not yet.
Most guys were happy to start considering marriage when
they got to thirty or so but he wasn't sure he would. Not
that he played unobtainable—he'd had lots of nice girlfriends—but there were huge problems after The Knot had
been tied. Marriage after the marvellous heady flush of the
Big Day was a big letdown. Women seemed to live for the
day alone as if they were no ever-after to occupy their time.
The fabulous wedding dress—it needed to be white, the veil,

the masses and masses of flowers, the picturesque church, the reception, just family and friends that turned into a crowd of four hundred. In his opinion, and on the evidence, they'd been planning it since they changed booties for shoes. The trouble was the excitement didn't last and lots of times neither did the attraction.

Statistics proved too many marriages didn't work out. Some of his clients had been married two and three times and they sure as hell didn't give the appearance of being happy. In fact most of them had a henpecked look. Jude didn't want his marriage—if he ever stopped flinching away from the hazards—to be a dismal failure. He didn't want to see another kid, like himself, suffer. If the saddest thing in the world was a mother losing her child, it was just as sad to be a child losing its mother.

These days he got by playing fancy-free man-about-town. A month ago he'd made it into a list of the Ten Sexiest Men in the city, though he'd never returned the call of the woman journalist who had started the whole nonsense. In any event she turned up a glossy photo of him at a function and used that under the heading Local Heartthrob. There was no point in being outraged. Vanessa had made a bumper sticker of it and somehow managed to fix it to the back of his car. All the beeps and the cheeky little waves finally aroused his suspicions and he had stopped in a loading zone and ripped it off. No one seemed to take it seriously anyway, so he'd shrugged off the ribbing. It was a crazy world. Sometimes it didn't seem worthwhile a quiet, country boy like himself trying to hold the line.

Nevertheless he'd changed a lot since his university days. Now he had to dress in sharp suits, shirts and ties, even his socks had been labelled cool by that journalist. He could kill her. Cool socks? That was a brain wave. His unruly blond hair—always had too much curl in it—was cut just right according to Bobbi his secretary who from the beginning had taken pity on him and told him the in places to shop, even where to have his hair cut. He no longer had short back and sides and as a result it skimmed his collar. He couldn't stop it flicking up all over the place. He'd long ceased trying. The guy at the unisex salon who'd cut it told Jude with a roll of his eyes he was a dead ringer for some famous actor. For an eye-popping minute there Jude had thought the man with the scissors was going to kiss him, but no, he settled for a friendly squeeze on the shoulder.

The fact was he'd taken years to get himself together. He'd always liked to be comfortable, even sloppy. T-shirt, jeans, sneakers. He liked going to the gym, working out, as he was still an athlete at heart—he'd even won a bridge-to-city run. For public display he'd had to change in a hurry; he had to look like what he was, a young lawyer on the fast track, cited to get to the top. At the beginning he hadn't minded Poppy's advances all that much—he was as open to temptation as the next guy—if only she could have kept it low-key.

He'd never expected it would please Leonard Gooding who had the kind of granite face you wouldn't wish on anyone—what if it came out in Poppy's children?—if Jude became involved in a meaningful relationship with his only child. The possibilities for Leonard Gooding's future son-in-law were limitless. Hints were already being thrown around about a full partnership by thirty, access to the top clients. There would be fresh territory to roam, an introduction to the charmed world of the hyperrich. Jude would have to laugh at all their jokes and let them beat him at golf.

Born and bred in the middle of nowhere, a small North Queensland sugar town, Jude sometimes thought he might be able to get used to that kind of life. He hadn't studied as hard as he had to be a loser. His much loved Dad had

been so proud of him. But then he had to confront a formidable truth. He saw no real possibility of ever selling his
soul no matter the rewards.

The only way out for him was if Poppy got interested in
someone else and the sooner the better. He realised however
hard he worked, however smart he was supposed to be, it
wasn't beyond Gooding to turn on him at a moment's notice
and engineer his dismissal from the firm. Leonard Gooding
was a shark.

Jude walked restlessly to the panoramic plate-glass window that overlooked the broad sweep of the River City. At
this time of the afternoon the impressive steel and glass
commercial towers were turned to columns of gold by the
slanting rays of the sun. Any self-respecting shrink could
diagnose his deeply ingrained resistance to matrimony as
the by-product of his childhood. His mother had abandoned
the best and kindest man in the world, his father. She'd
abandoned him, her only child. That single event had influenced his entire mode of thinking.

"My gorgeous boy!"

That was the way she'd used to greet him. What a joke!
It depressed him to even think about it. She'd never meant
it at all. She was only acknowledging that physically he'd
taken after her. He'd been a bright kid going on twelve,
thinking all was right with his world, when she took off for
the beckoning horizons. He only found out years later when
his father finally told him the whole pathetic story, that his
mother had gone away with a rich American tourist who
had been holidaying at the luxury hotel where she was receptionist. His mother in those days was a knock-out. She
was probably still able to turn heads with her golden blond
hair, big melting blue eyes and luscious figure. According
to his all-forgiving father no man could be blamed for falling in love with Jude's mother, Sally. Sally was perfect.

It took Jude years to come to the realisation that when it came to his mother, his father had been one gullible fool. Even as a kid he'd been edgily aware that his mother who the gang he hung around with described as "hot" was a habitual flirt. She gave off allure like a body scent. Probably the rich Texan hadn't been her first affair. At the time his father told him his mother needed a more exciting life. The town was a rural backwater.

"Sally wants a real taste of life. She's so beautiful! She deserves more than I can give her."

Did that excuse being unfaithful? Jude didn't think so. His father had let himself be seen as dull and boring when the fact was he had been a clever, industrious, respected town lawyer. He loved books, revered literature. He loved music, too, classical, jazz, opera and he adored big game fishing. He had such a great sense of humour. Much as Jude's father had grieved, extraordinarily he'd never held a grudge against his wife.

Jude did. Unlike his father he'd never wished his mother all the best. He and his father had been betrayed and Jude had learned the lesson that women weren't to be trusted. They cheated on their husbands. If they didn't get what they wanted, they moved on. If his father continued to love his mother until the day he died, Jude took the opposite stand. He might be thought hard and judgmental, but he hated her for sucking all the life out of his father who died soon after Jude made it into the firm. His father had flown to Brisbane so they could have a celebratory dinner together. He'd been so proud, telling Jude before he left, his dearest wish was that Jude would have a much better life than he had.

"Find the right girl. Marry her. Give me grandchildren. You're the one who always kept me going, Jude. I've lived for you, son. You've done me proud."

Trying to make his father proud was what had given him

the edge, driven him to succeed. Then his father up and died on him. At least he'd been doing what he loved—big game fishing. He and a couple of his life-long pals were out on Calypso when a freak electrical storm hit. The waves, reportedly, had been huge. His father and one of his friends had been washed overboard. Both perished in the Coral Sea. Despite a wide search their bodies had never been found.

How I miss him! Jude thought, grief locked deep inside him. The town had given him all the sympathy in the world when he flew home for the memorial service. He and his dad had always been popular. He was the local boy made good. Now that he had a real chance of making it up to his dad for all his sacrifices his dad wasn't around. Successful as he'd become the loss of his father shadowed Jude's life. There's no end to love in the human heart; no end to grief when love is lost.

Bobbi, Jude's secretary tapped lightly on his door, breaking up his melancholy reflections.

"Manage to get rid of her?" Her hazel eyes were full of wry humour. Bobbi was petite, attractive, power dressed and happily engaged. Since he'd been with the firm she'd proved a real friend and a great legal secretary, loyal, thorough and accurate. He got on well with her sports reporter fiancé, Bryan as well.

"Don't look so damned happy," Jude groaned. "It was really, really hard." He moved back to his desk. "Poppy Gooding has deluded herself into thinking she fancies me."

"And how!" Bobbi choked on a laugh. "I nearly had cardiac arrest when she shoved past me. She mightn't look like Leonard—she must get down on her knees every night and thank the Lord for it—but she's a bulldozer just like him. She only wants you for your body, friend."

"Why the heck me?" he asked in extreme irritation.

He really means it, Bobbi thought. Jude Conroy, every

girl's dream! A drop-dead gorgeous hunk with those dreamy, dreamy blue eyes! He even had a fan club in the building. If she and Bryan weren't destined for each other Bobbi thought she'd have thrown her own cap in the ring.

"Want me to put around the rumour you're gay?" she asked drolly.

He shot her a sharp glance that softened into his white lopsided grin. It made even the faithful Bobbi's heart execute a little dance. If he wanted to, Jude could star in a toothpaste commercial.

"I doubt that would stop Poppy. She'd think she was the one girl who could turn a man around. What I need right now is a vacation."

His cell phone rang when he was walking to his car later that afternoon. It was Bobbi on the line, her voice flustered.

"Listen, I just had a guy on the phone, kind of snarly sort of guy I bet kicks his dog, severely put out you weren't here—name of Ralph Rogan. Says you know him. Wants to speak to you ASAP. Sounded like you were sleeping with his wife. I told him you were due for an important meeting that should break up around four. Number is—your part of the world curiously—got a pen?"

"Give it to me, I'll remember."

She laughed. "Jude, you're a human calculator."

"Right." He had a special thing with numbers. Even as a kid he'd been able to add up stacks of them in his head not that kids used those skills anymore. Bobbi gave it to him and from the area code he immediately identified his area of Far Northern Queensland. He didn't need any introduction to Ralph. Ralph Rogan was the son of the richest man in his home town of Isis and one of the richest men in the tropical north. Jude's dad had been Lester Rogan's solicitor and close confidant. Rogan Senior had trusted no one except Jude's father. Jude and Ralph had gone to school together but they had never been friends. More like adversaries. The hostility was an on-going state of affairs exacerbated by Ralph's "problems" with his domineering father. Rogan Senior had wanted and expected his son to shine, to come out on top. Ralph never had. Even as a boy he'd been to use Bobbi's word, "snarly," a bully who traded on the fact his father practically owned the town and huge tracts of land for development. It had to be something serious for Ralph to get on the phone to Jude. As soon as the meeting was over he'd place a call.

Piercing screams woke him, screams that echoed around the mansion. The minute Ralph Rogan heard his mother's frenzied cries, he knew something was very wrong. It had to be his father. His father had been diagnosed with atherosclerosis, hardening of the arteries. It wasn't surprising after a lifetime of indulgence, eating, drinking, smoking, womanising. Despite the warnings it never occurred to him to give anything up. With any luck he was dead. Ralph had lost every skerrick of affection for that big bull of a man who was his father. He didn't consider he closely resembled his father at the same age.

Ralph shot out of bed, pulling on jeans and a shirt in a great hurry. He didn't bother finding shoes. He rushed into the hallway, covering the not inconsiderable distance to his father's suite in the west wing in record time. His mother and father hadn't shared a bedroom in years. In his arrogance and insensitivity—Lester Rogan thought of his wife and children as property—he'd brought in workman to turn several rooms of the family mansion into a self-contained suite for himself. Ralph's long-suffering mother had no back bone. She was a thin pitiful thing these days and she'd been left out in the cold. His father was like that: a law unto himself. That's what came of too much money and power.

Inside the massive bedroom with its heavy Victorian furniture inappropriate to the climate Ralph found his mother slumped to the floor beside his father's bed. She was sobbing bitterly, her thin body convulsing as though shocked and grieved out of her mind.

"I couldn't sleep. I knew something had happened." She turned her head, choking on her tears. "He's gone, Ralph. He's gone."

"And good riddance." Ralph Rogan let a lifetime of bitterness and resentment rip out. For moments he stood staring at his father's body, his heavy, handsome face dark with brooding, a thick blue vein throbbing in his temple. Eventually he moved to check if his father was indeed dead. A huge man in life, in death Lester Rogan looked surprisingly lighter, shorter, his mouth thrown open and his jaw slack. His eyes were still open, staring sightlessly at the ceiling. Ralph reached down to shut them, but abruptly drew back as if the corpse would rise up and bite him. He didn't want to touch the man who had treated him so badly, who had never shown an ounce of pleasure or pride in him. All he'd received were insults and humiliations, comparisons with that clever bastard, Jude Conroy, the Golden Boy.

"He's dead all right!" Coldly he informed his weeping mother, throwing the sheet over his father's face with something approaching violence. "I'll get Atwell over. He'll have to sign the death certificate." Ralph cast another disgusted look at his mother, before drawing her to her feet. "What the hell are you crying about, Ma?" he demanded in genuine amazement. "He treated you like dirt. He never had a kind word for you. He kicked you out of his bed. He had other women."

"I loved him," his mother said, disengaging herself from

her son's hard grasp and collapsing into one of the huge maroon leather armchairs custom built for her husband. It dwarfed her. "We were happy once."

Ralph's laugh was near wild. "What a load of drivel! It must have been a lifetime ago. There's never been any happiness in this house. You'll have to pull yourself together while I phone Atwell. Where's Jinx?"

"Please don't call your sister that, Ralph," his mother pleaded. "Sometimes you're so cruel."

He rounded on her, tall and burly, deep-set dark eyes, large straight nose, square jaw, already at twenty-eight carrying too much weight. "I didn't give her the nickname, remember? It was Dad. Okay, where's Mel?"

"Here, Ralph." A light soprano voice spoke from the door. "He can't be dead." Melinda Rogan cast one horrified glance at the sheeted figure on the bed, then advanced fearfully into the room.

"He is, darling." Myra Rogan answered, holding out her hand to her dressing gowned daughter. Melinda was two years younger than her brother, a pretty young woman with her mother's small neat features, soft brown hair and grey eyes.

"Well I'll be damned!" Ralph mocked. "He never did a thing the doc told him."

"It's such a shock, Ralph." Melinda swallowed on the hard lump in her throat. Bravely she went to tend to her mother, putting her arms around Myra's thin shoulders. "Don't weep for him, Mum," she said gently, her own eyes bright with unshed tears. Death was death after all. "He never showed you any kindness."

"He did once," Myra insisted, rocking herself back and forth.

"Oh, yeah, when?" Ralph busy pushing buttons on the phone looked towards them to bark.

Myra tried to think when her husband had been kind to her. "Before you were born, a few years after that," she said vaguely. Lester Rogan had taken little notice of his daughter.

"So he never cared for me from day one," Ralph snarled.

"That's not true. He loved you. He had great plans for you." The fact that these plans never worked out was not always Lester's fault.

Abruptly Ralph held up a staying hand, speaking into the phone to his father's doctor.

"Here, Mum," Melinda found a box of tissues. Copious tears were streaming down her mother's face, dampening the front of her nightgown. Once her mother had been pretty, but for years now she had been neglecting herself, horribly aware her husband had no use for her.

"Atwell will be here in twenty minutes," Ralph informed them. "Could you please stop all that hypocritical blubbing, Mum, and get yourself dressed. That man in the bed there—" he jerked a thumb over his shoulder "—has done us a huge favour. At long last we're free of him and his cruel tongue."

"Surely you mean at long last you can get your hands on the money," Melinda challenged, suddenly looking at her brother as though he were the enemy. "You're head of the family now. I tell you what, Ralph, I'll take a bet you'll turn out no better than Dad."

It was hours before Ralph Rogan was able to make his phone call to his old sparring partner, Jude Conroy. Good old Jude, the big success story. The hotshot lawyer. There was no love lost between them. Once when they were kids, around thirteen, Conroy had whipped him good and proper for bullying some new kid, a snivelling little runt, small as a girl, who'd been admitted to their excellent boys' school on scholarship. Ralph had never forgotten lying on the ground, wiping the blood from his nose and his mouth—a loose tooth. It was easy to beat up other kids. It was humiliating to be beaten up yourself. One day he swore he'd get even with Jude Conroy, school hero, champion of the underdog, young lion. Even Ralph's mother had said he'd probably deserved his beating, taking Conroy's side.

His father and Conroy's father had been real close. Matthew Conroy had been his dad's solicitor. Conroy knew all the secrets and he'd taken them down to the deep with him. Now Ralph was going to need a solicitor and loathe as he was to contact Jude, he knew he had to. Matthew Conroy had drawn up his father's will but in the event of his death Lester Rogan had appointed Jude executor.

Lester Rogan's funeral was underway before a young woman slipped into the back pew of the church. She knelt for a moment, then sat back quietly. A navy silk scarf was wound around her hair in such a way not a tendril escaped. She wore a simple navy shift dress. A few people at the back of the church turned to glance at her. Most were caught up in the eulogies, as first Ralph Rogan, then various townspeople walked to the podium to endeavour to say a few words for the late Lester Rogan, whose real estate kingdom included half the town and stretched for miles.

Though everyone tried—some better than others—there was no real feeling, not even from his son who stood with his hand over his heart, face beaded with sweat in the heat, rambling on about what a giant among men his father had been; how his father had taught him everything he knew. This had caused a little sardonic ripple to pass through the congregation that was quickly brought under control. Lester Rogan had not been loved and admired. Over the years he had become as mean as they come. Collective wisdom suggested Ralph was shaping up to be a chip off the old block.

The family sat up the front, son and daughter with their faces blank, Myra Rogan inexplicably weeping uncontrollably as though her husband had been the finest man ever to walk the earth.

Tears of joy, a lot of the congregation thought waspishly. She'd get over it. Probably take a grand tour overseas. There never had been any evidence Lester Rogan had physically abused his wife or children, but he'd kept tight control on them, allowing his wife and daughter little real freedom. At the same time they had benefited from his money. They lived in a sprawling two-storey mansion atop a hill with the most breath-taking view of the ocean. The womenfolk were able to buy anything they wanted—clothes, cars, things to keep them entertained—though Myra Rogan wasn't anywhere near as attractive as she used to be. The expensive black suit she wore with a black and white printed blouse was much too big for her. The stylish, wide-brimmed hat with a fetching spray of dark grey and white feathers, spoiled by her haggard unmade up face.

Jude, who had arrived a scant ten minutes before the service began sat rows back on the family's side of the aisle. How different this was to the memorial service that had been held for his father. Then the old timber church had been packed with mourners spilling four deep into the grounds. Today it was half filled.

People had wept as they spoke about Matthew Conroy's innumerable kindnesses and the generosity which he'd wanted kept private, but the grateful had let their stories out. It was well known and perhaps traded on, in hard times Matthew Conroy never took a fee. He was always on hand with free advice. He listened to people's problems when they came to him, tried to come up with solutions and most often did. Matthew Conroy had spent his life giving service to the community. All agreed he had been a wonderful father to his son. The proof was Jude himself.

No one seems to doubt I'm a winner, Jude thought. They don't know about the scars. The young woman Jude had seen slip into the church late—his hearing was so acute he could near hear a pin drop—was barely visible at the back. It was as though she had deliberately withdrawn into the shadows. Only her skin bloomed. It made him think of the creamy magnolias that grew in the front yard of his dad's house that now belonged to him. Whoever she was, he didn't recognise her. Intrigued, he turned his head slightly to take another look. Immediately she bent forward, her face downcast as if in prayer, or she'd realised her presence had drawn his interest and didn't welcome it.

By the time the service was over, she had disappeared. He even knew the moment she'd left. He thought he knew just about everyone in the town. Obviously she'd arrived fairly recently, or she was from out of town. He really couldn't understand why he was so curious. He certainly wasn't keeping watch on anyone else, not even poor little Mel, who had always wrung his heart.

Jude joined the slow, orderly, motorcade in the hire car Bobbi had organised to be waiting for him at the air terminal, some twenty kilometres from the town. It felt a little strange to be back to the snail's pace of his hometown. No traffic. No nightmare rush hour. No freeways, no one-ways. You could go wherever you wanted with no hassle at all. There was limitless peace and quiet, limitless golden sunlight to soak in, tropical heat and colour, white sand, and the glorious blue of the ocean at your door. The rain forest and the Great Barrier Reef were a jump away. Isis had been a wonderful place to grow up.

The family and the mourners—not everyone who had at-

tended the service came—spread out around the gravesite,
all slightly stunned Lester Rogan was actually dead and being lowered into the ground. He'd always seemed larger
than life, a big, burly, commanding man with a voice like
the rumble of thunder.

The interment took little time. The widow was a pitiable
sight. Who knows what she was thinking. Ralph, sweating
profusely, shovelled the first spadeful of dirt onto his father's ornate, gleaming casket with too much gusto. As Jude
walked over to pay his respects to Myra and the family, he
saw, not entirely to his surprise, the same young woman
who had attracted his attention at the church. She was standing well away from the crowd, taking refuge and he suspected a degree of cover under the giant shade trees dotted
all over the cemetery's well-tended grounds. There had to
be a reason she was there. He could see she was taller than
average, very slender. She wore a simple dark dress that
managed to look amazingly chic, no hat, but a matching
head scarf tied artfully. It completely covered her hair.

Who was she? He wondered if the family knew her. It
didn't appear at all likely she was going to come across the
grass to speak to them, unlike the other mourners who had
formed themselves into a receiving line. They probably
weren't relying on their memories of the late Lester in order
to summon up a few kind words, Jude thought, his eyes still
on the mystery woman.

Myra, to his surprise, reached up to kiss him as he offered
his sympathies which were genuine for her and Mel. Many
the time he'd heard Ralph wish his father dead. Melinda
looked so lost and pathetic he took her into a comforting
hug, allowing her head to nod against him.

"I'm so glad you're here, Jude," she whispered, deriving
strength from her childhood friend's presence. Her own
brother, Ralph, had been incredibly mean to her as a child.

Jude had always been nice to her and she'd never forget that.

"Anything I can do for you and your mother, Mel, I will," he was saying in his attractive voice. Melinda clung to Jude's arm, hanging on his every word.

"This must have been a big shock for you, Mel, even if your dad had health problems," Jude said.

"He didn't try at all," Mel lamented. "In fact you'd swear he was trying to kill himself. I couldn't love him, Jude. He wouldn't let me. You know that."

"He wasn't exactly fatherly material, Mel."

"Whereas your dad was everything a father should be," Mel sighed. "I know how cut up you were about losing your mother, Jude. You were very brave. But you had your dad and he was such a lovely man. My dad was very open about how stupid he thought we were." Melinda dabbed at her eyes with a lace edged handkerchief.

It had an old-fashioned scent like lavender. Heck, it was lavender, the sort old ladies bought. Jude found that a little strange for so young a woman.

Nevertheless he shook his head. "Never stupid, Mel." He comforted her. "You aren't and you know you aren't. It was just your father's way of trying to keep you all down."

"Well he succeeded." Melinda bowed her head like a sacrificial lamb. "Death is always a shock, even when you're half expecting it. He was my father, the most important person in my life. I feel a sense of awe he's gone. You're coming to the house aren't you?" Her soft grey eyes held a plea.

"Of course. I'm executor of your father's will. You do know that?"

"Ralph told us. I'm glad it's you, not a strange lawyer.

We really miss your father around here, Jude. He was very special. Like you.''

Jude gave a rueful smile. ''I'm not so special, Mel. I've got my faults just like the next guy. There'll be a reading whenever your mother feels up to it.''

Ralph, nearby, must have heard. He broke away from a group of mourners to stride up to them. ''Thanks for coming, Jude.'' The hard expression in his eyes didn't match his words. In fact he looked confrontational. Good old Ralph, still mired in his adolescent jealousies and resentments, Jude thought. ''It won't take long at the house before everyone starts moving off. I'd like you to read the will straight after.''

Jude glanced towards Myra doubtfully. ''Is that okay with your mother? She looks very frail.''

''It's okay with me,'' Ralph said tersely, turning on his heel again as though he was the only one who counted.

CHAPTER TWO

JUDE let the procession of mourners' cars get away before
he made a move towards the hire car. As usual Ralph rubbed
him up the wrong way as soon as he opened his mouth.
Now he wanted to get the reading over before he returned
to his family home. He'd taken Bobbi's advice and asked
for his overdue vacation. Leonard Gooding had agreed on
the spot, buoyed up by the fact Jude had managed to pull
off a big, but complicated merger and in the process bring
in new highly profitable business for the firm.

The path through the cemetery to the towering front gates
was wide, but winding, flanked by enormous poincianas in
full bloom. Their hectic blossoming had turned the very air
rosy. The town cemetery was never a gloomy place even
when the flowering was over. He should have had his eyes
firmly on the drive but he happened to glance reflexively at
his watch. When he looked up again, his heart skipped a
beat, and every nerve ending tensed as he hit the brakes.

Right in front of him, a young woman was leaping back
from the driveway to the grassy verge, her frozen expression
betraying her shock at his car's near silent approach.

"Damn!" Within seconds he was out of the vehicle,
watching in dismay as first she staggered then fell to the
grass, thickly scattered with spent blossom. Her heel must
have caught on something, he realized, probably an exposed
root of one of the poincianas.

He had a sensation of falling himself. He was always a
careful driver. There was no excuse. "Are you all right?"

Shoulders tensed, he bent to her, studying her with concern. "I'm so sorry. I didn't realise anyone was still about."

"My fault." Graciously, instead of berating him, she accepted his hand, wincing slightly as he brought her to her feet. "I shouldn't have been walking on the driveway at all. There are plenty of paths."

"Are you sure you're okay? You didn't injure your ankle?" They were a touch away but neither moved back.

"It'll be fine," she said quietly after a minute.

It was balm to his guilt. "That's a blessing." They both glanced down at her legs; classy legs on show in her short skirt. She wasn't wearing stockings in the heat, the skin tanned a pale gold. There was no swelling as far as he could see, but it could develop. "Jude Conroy," he said, holding out his hand.

"Cate Costello." She took his hand briefly, the expression in her beautiful green eyes not soft and lingering like the women's glances he was used to but quietly sizing him up.

"You're new in town?" He found himself staring back, all sorts of emotions crashing down on him like a wild surf. Up close she was even more lovely than his glimpse at the gravesite, like a vision from some tantalising dream. Her eyes had an unusual setting that bestowed an extra distinction on her delicate features. He realized straightaway she possessed an attraction that went beyond the physical though there was no denying that was potent enough.

There was the unblemished creamy skin he'd first noted in the church. Her large eyes, the feature that really stopped him in his tracks were a clear green, with a definite upward curve at the corners. The brows matched. Her face was a perfect oval, the finely chiselled contours off set by a contradictory mouth. The top lip was finely cut, the bottom surprisingly full and cushiony. Looking at her it was difficult not to dredge up the old cliché "English rose" but just as attractive to Jude was the keen intelligence in her regard.

He knew he was taking far too much time studying her, but she seemed quite unselfconscious under his scrutiny. She had to be around twenty two-or -three, but she seemed very self-contained for her age. Her voice, matched her patrician appearance; clear and well modulated. He wondered at the colour of her hair beneath the silk scarf and even found himself wanting to remove it. There was no question she had him in a kind of spell. Maybe it was the witchcraft of the eyes? If he could keep talking to her until midnight maybe she would simply disappear?

As it was, she stood perfectly still, looking up at him, but he had the feeling she was equally well poised to run. "I've been here for six or seven months now," she said calmly in response to his question. "I know who you are."

Women habitually used that line with him. The old cynicism kicked in. "Really? Want to tell me how?"

"Anyone who comes to live in this town gets to know about you and your father," she explained matter-of-factly. "Your father was much loved and respected. You're the local celebrity."

He shrugged that off. "And you are?" Despite himself the words came out with the touch of steel he reserved for his job. Immediately he was aware of little sparks starting to fly between them. Whether they were harmful or not he couldn't yet say.

"I told you. Cate Costello." Her expression became intent as though she was deciding whether she liked or disliked him.

"Are you a friend of the family?"

She stepped back out of the brilliant sunlight into the shade. "Is this an interrogation, Jude Conroy?"

"Why would you see it that way, Ms Costello?" he countered, with a mock inclination of the head. "It's a perfectly normal question."

"If you'd said it in a different tone perhaps. Anyone can see you're a lawyer."

"You have a problem with lawyers?" He didn't bother to hide the challenge.

"I've never had occasion to call on one. But I appreciate they're necessary."

"I do believe so," he drawled. "And you, what do you do?" He made his tone friendly.

He was pouring on the charm, she thought, feeling tiny tremors ripple down her back. "Does it matter? We'll probably never see each other again."

He laughed, suddenly wanting nothing more than to get to know her better. "I can't help be curious."

"Well then," she relented, "I own a small gallery near the beach. It's called the Crystal Cave. I buy and sell crystals from all over the world."

"As in gazing?" Amusement showed in his gaze. He wasn't too far off in his assessment of her. "Obviously you don't have the slanted green eyes of a storybook witch for nothing."

A faint warning glitter came into those eyes. "I have no powers of clairvoyance, otherwise I'd have known you were a metre off running me over. I simply have a loving affinity with crystals."

"Ouch, I don't think I deserved that," he chided. "I braked immediately."

"I'm sorry." Her lovely face registered her sincerity.

"However did you start with your crystals?" An onlooker might have supposed they were good friends or even lovers so intent were they on each other.

"I knew some people who were great fossickers and collectors. They introduced me to the earth's treasures. I shared their love of gemstones and crystals. After all crystals have been used and revered since the beginning of civilisation.'' She looked away from him and those intensely blue searching eyes. The admiration in them was clearly flattering, but there was keen appraisal, too.

"So how can I find the Crystal Cave?" he asked. "I'm on vacation for a month."

"You intend to spend it here?" She looked back in surprise.

"Why not?" He slipped off his jacket, slinging it over his shoulder. "I was born in this town. I'll probably die here. You sound a little like you're wishing me on my way."

"Not at all." Colour rose to the cut-glass cheekbones. "It's I who should be on my way."

"On foot?" He took another look at her neat ankles. "Where's your car?"

"It's just around the corner." She gestured vaguely.

"Okay so I'll give you a lift. You're not going up to the house then?"

"The family don't know me, Mr Conroy."

"I'm fine with Jude," he told her. "I'm sure I'll find your gallery."

She made an attractive little movement with her hand. "That shouldn't be a problem. Everyone knows it. It used to be Tony Mandel's Art Gallery. The living quarters are at the rear. You'd have known Tony?"

"Of course I know Tony," he lightly scoffed. "He was a constant visitor at our house. My dad bought a number of his paintings in the early days before he became famous. I thought he was overseas."

She nodded. "He is. In London. His last showing was a sell-out. We keep in touch."

"So there's a connection?" Accustomed to asking questions, they were springing out.

"A family friend." Her smile conveyed she wasn't about to tell him more. "You really don't have to drive me. I can walk. It's not far."

"I insist. Can't have you hitchhiking." His speculative gaze lingered on her face.

"Why are you looking at me like that?" she questioned, with the tiniest frown.

"Forgive me, but I can't help wondering who you are and why you're at Lester Rogan's funeral when you don't know the family?"

She tilted her chin to look up at him. The knot in her stomach tightened. He had that confident demeanour tall men often have plus the superb body of an athlete. "Does it matter?" she asked, sounding a lot cooler than she felt.

"Damned if I haven't got the feeling it could."

"So you're the clairvoyant now." She smiled sweetly. "What's your astrological sign?" She restricted herself to a brief glance into his eyes. She'd heard he was dazzling, but in his favour he appeared unconcerned with his good looks. What she hadn't expected was the magnetism, the powerful attraction of that white, lopsided smile, the dimple that flicked deeply into his cheek.

"Leo," he was saying, still sounding indulgent, amused. "There's no scientific basis for astrology, Ms Costello."

The sapphire eyes were full of mischief. "I was going to tell you names of crystals you might find useful," she said coolly. "But no matter."

"Gee, thanks. That'd be fun," he lightly mocked. "Can you tell me something now?"

"If I can." She managed to sound at ease, even though the air around them was so sizzling it burned.

"What's the colour of your hair?" He could see he'd

caught her off guard. "I'm intrigued by your covering it up."

"Ever consider a bad hair day?" She cast him a quick glance.

"I'd be amazed if you were having one."

"It's obvious surely? I didn't particularly want to be noticed. But as you seem to be so curious."

Purposefully she raised a hand, lifting the silk scarf from her head. Another movement released the clasp at her nape.

He sucked in his breath sharply.

She shook her hair free, turning her head from side to side to loosen it. The breeze that swept along the driveway sent her hair swirling like a burnished veil. Sunlight reflected off myriad highlights like the prisms of a precious gem; gold, rose, amber, even pinks and orange. He supposed her long glorious mane would be best described as a gleaming copper.

"I can see what you mean about being noticed." Entranced, he nevertheless kept his tone sardonic. "You speak like the scarf was protection?"

She met his eyes again, tucking her hair casually behind her ears. The richness of the colour made her eyes and skin zing. "It doesn't do any harm to protect oneself. I really don't need a lift, you know. Thank you for the offer."

"No sense in walking in the heat. Deal?"

Her quick assessing glance skipped across his face again. "Okay."

They turned back towards the car. "As a copper-head it's a wonder your skin doesn't burn?" he asked conversationally, moving ahead to open the passenger door.

She slid in. "Strangely enough it doesn't, but I do use a good sunblock. The only hats I own were much too festive for a funeral."

"That's too bad. I'd like to have seen you in one." He

had a sudden mental image of her in a wide-brimmed hat weighed down with huge pink roses, something marvellously feminine and romantic. Ironically a hat like his mother used to wear to protect her skin. With a sudden twist of the heart he remembered how he'd fallen early and irrevocably in love with the image of a beautiful women in a picture hat. There were years when his parents had been passionate about their garden, working happily together. They'd even managed a beautiful sheltered rose garden, large, luxuriant shrubs and blooms, despite the humidity and attendant problems of the tropics. To this day he took a lot of pleasure out of sending roses to his dates.

It wasn't until Jude had dropped the mysterious Cate Costello off at her car that he realized she still hadn't revealed what exactly she was doing at Lester Rogan's funeral.

Ten minutes later he arrived at the Rogan mansion, the overt display of the late Lester Rogan's wealth. The house was huge. In his view no architectural gem but impressive for sheer size alone and the tropical splendour of the five acre manicured grounds. The entrance was electronically guarded, the long driveway lined by majestic Royal Cuban palms. A caretaker-gardener's bungalow was off to the left through the screening trees. There was a pool and a guest-house at the back, but surpassing all the obvious signs of wealth, was the glorious blue sea.

There were plenty of cars littering the driveway and the grass. Jude found a spot, his mind still engaged with his meeting with Cate Costello. What could possibly have motivated her to attend Rogan's funeral if she didn't know the family? Or could he take that to mean she just didn't know Myra, Ralph and Melinda, but she had known Lester? In what context? Lester could have bought out Tony Mandel's beachside property that was the most obvious connection. These days with tourism in tropical North Queensland hectically blossoming the land would be very valuable for redevelopment at some future date. If the late Lester had been her landlord, why didn't she say so? What was the big mystery? What was she doing sheltering amid the trees? He hadn't the slightest doubt he'd find out.

An hour later hurried along by a less than subtle Ralph, all the mourners had departed, some of them definitely over the drink driving limit.

"Now's as good a time as any to read the will," Ralph rasped. "You've got it with you?" He threw Jude an impatient glance.

"Of course. I left my briefcase in the hall."

"I'll get it Jude," Melinda offered. She was nearest the wide archway, one of a pair that led from off the entrance hall to the major reception rooms.

"Sure you're up to this, Mrs Rogan?" Jude asked, taking another concerned look at Myra's extreme pallor. "I can very easily come back tomorrow, or the next day."

Ralph's dark eyes shot red sparks of aggression. Here was a young man who was permanently angry. "For cryin' out loud, Jude, how many times do I have to tell you? We're ready to hear it? Right now."

The school bully was still holding up. "I was talking to your mother, Ralph. Not you." Unperturbed Jude looked towards Myra who was giving every appearance of being the next to follow her husband to the grave.

"Mum tell him." Ralph scratched his forehead violently.

"No, Ralphie—no." Myra pleaded, her voice tremulous.

Ralph stared at his mother for a bit, giving a can-you-believe-this roll of his eyes. "Listen," he said very quietly as though addressing someone mentally challenged. "This won't take long then you can take to your bed. For the rest of your life if you like.''

"I think she needs her bed right now," Jude said, trying to keep the disgust out of his voice. "This has been a bad shock."

"Get it over with, Jude," Melinda advised, returning with his briefcase. In her own way she appeared as eager to hear the will as her brother. "I'll look after Mum. She's stronger than she looks. Dad hammered away at her for years."

"Yes, get it over, Jude," Myra's opposition suddenly collapsed, as if she thought both her children were about to ostracize her.

"Okay." Against his better judgment Jude deferred to their wishes. "Mel, you might like to settle your mother in a more comfortable chair." Myra was perched like a budgie on the edge of a small antique chair that looked like it was only good for decoration.

Melinda put her arm around her mother, leading her to an armchair. Myra took her time, her movements those of a woman twenty years her senior. Jude suspected Dr Atwell had given her medication to get her through the service. She was pretty much out of it. Meanwhile, Ralph was shaping up to be as nasty as his late father.

"Sit the hell down, Mum," Ralph confirmed Jude's assessment by crying out in utter exasperation.

"You're awful, Ralph," his sister croaked, as if she couldn't get past the big lump of misery in her throat. "A real pig."

"Like Dad." Ralph looked back at her out of his deep-set dark eyes. "Okay, Mr Hotshot, read the will."

Jude stepped right up to him, two inches taller, a stone or more lighter, but obviously fitter by far. "Jude will do, thanks, Ralph, and a little more respect all around. I'm your late father's lawyer, not your lackey." Jude didn't give a damn about how much money the Rogans had. Never had. It showed in the sapphire glitter of his eyes.

"So take it easy." Swaying slightly from side to side, Ralph backed off. "Surely you can understand I'm anxious to hear how Dad left things between the three of us."

"Of course." Jude took a seat in the armchair nearest the big Oriental style coffee table so he could put the document down to read it. He withdrew the will from his briefcase, the collective eyes of the family trained on him. They wouldn't be seeing shades of his father. Jude bore little physical resemblance to him, apart from his height. He even had his mother's dimple in his left cheek just so he could never forget her.

"Hang on a moment I'll get myself a drink. Anyone else want one?" Ralph lumbered off looking over his shoulder.

"Haven't you had enough, Ralph?" Myra roused herself sufficiently to ask.

Ralph snorted. "Been countin', Ma?" He poured himself a generous shot of whiskey from a spirits laden trolley, tonging a couple of ice cubes into it. "You, Jude?"

"Thank you. No." As instructed, Jude wanted to get on with it, his expression as professional as any lawyer's could get.

Ralph positioned himself on the opposite side of the coffee table, swirling the amber contents of his crystal tumbler, hunkering down his broad shoulders.

Jude showed them Lester Rogan's will with the seal intact. He viewed their faces intently, then he broke open the long, thick envelope, beginning to read with suitable gravitas...

"This is the last will and testament of me, Lester Michael Rogan..."

Instantly he was interrupted by Myra's stricken cry, one of many to be ripped from her throat. Was this for real?

Jude agonised, wanting to shake his head in amazement. She had no reason to love her husband. Mel grabbed her mother's hand and held it. It didn't appear to be a gesture of comfort, more to shut her mother up.

"Would you mind keeping a lid on it, Ma. Is that too much to ask?" Ralph slewed another disgusted look at his mother. "Continue, Jude."

Jude continued, managing from experience to keep his voice perfectly level despite the rippling shock he felt. "This will is to be held in terrorem," he announced, looking up for a reaction.

"What the hell's that? I haven't a clue." Ralph waved his glass, empty now except for a melting ice cube.

It means this will is going to be one big surprise, Jude thought without immediately responding. Any member of the family who contested Lester Rogan's wishes could finish up with nothing. Ralph pre-set to take over his father's real estate empire was visibly disturbed.

"Why don't you let me read on," Jude suggested. "I'll explain all the legal jargon later."

"Fine," Ralph muttered through gritted teeth.

"This relates to disposition of property," Jude advised them. "To my wife, Myra…" Not the usual beloved, that would have been too much to ask. This highly dysfunctional family knew little about love, Jude thought. It took five seconds for Myra to let out another agonized wail this one so sharp Jude winced. Both of her children however ignored her, continuing to stare fixedly at Jude. "To my wife, Myra," Jude started off again, "I bequeath sole possession of the family home, land and all the contents therein plus the adjoining five acres. In addition she is to receive the sum of ten million dollars which should allow her to see out her days comfortably. In the unlikely event she remarry, the house and all land reverts to my son, Ralph. Myra can do what she likes with the contents.''

Ralph made a dramatic grasp at his heart. He had expected his mother was due for heaps more. Lester had to be worth around $85 to $100 million. Everyone knew he'd been shovelling money in! Wasn't Myra legally entitled to a sizeable percentage of the estate? Ralph wasn't sure. What he was sure of was she wouldn't put up a fight. More for him. Like his dad, Ralph couldn't seriously believe another man would lavish love on his mother.

Jude continued. ''To my daughter, Melinda—'' again no expression of affection, this was becoming a habit ''—I bequeath an annual income of seventy-five thousand dollars to be paid from the trust established for this purpose. The payments will continue up until such time as she marries. On her wedding day she will receive as final payment five million dollars.'' No gifts, no mementos, not even a pair of Lester's favourite cuff links. What code had Lester stuck to?

Peanuts, Ralph was thinking, a triumphant laugh escaping him. ''Mean old bastard.'' That only meant one thing. He was the big winner. At long last after all these years of humiliation he was going to score big time. He'd have control of everything. As long as he lived he'd never have to take anything from another living soul. He was powerful. Rich. Ralph's bloodshot eyes began to gleam. He could buy and sell Golden Boy Conroy.

''To my son, Ralph, named after a man he couldn't in any way hold a candle to, I bequeath my collection of sporting trophies and motor cars, my motor yacht, *Sea Eagle*, my portrait by Dargy in the study and the sum of five million dollars in the hope he can do something with himself in the future.'' Jude glanced up. The tension in the room was so thick he could have cut it with a knife.

"Go on, go on." Ralph jumped to his feet as though he'd been attacked with an ice pick. "There's more. There's gotta be more. I'm the heir!"

"Of course there's more, dear," Myra consoled him, albeit fearfully, the pale skin of her face and neck mottled red.

"Of course there's more," Melinda chimed in, characteristically satisfied with her lot. "Please sit down again. Go on, Jude."

Jude felt a certain tightness in his chest. He didn't want to say this. "To Jude Kelsey Conroy, son of the only man I've ever trusted, Matthew John Conroy, a most honourable man, and in recognition of Jude's devotion to his father and his own outstanding merits I bequeath the sum of one hundred thousand dollars knowing he will use it wisely. The residue of my estate, land, houses, rental properties, share portfolio I hereby bequeath to Catherine Elizabeth Costello, spinster, of the…"

Whatever else Jude, more dismayed than pleased with his windfall, was about to say, it was cut off by Ralph's bull roar. It would have been pretty scary to a lot of people.

Jude wasn't one of them. "Do you want to hear the rest of this, Ralph?" he asked crisply. "I should say I knew nothing of my bequest."

"When your dad drew it up?" Ralph snarled with a curl of the lip. "I bloody well *don't* want to hear any more of this." He picked up his crystal tumbler and hurled it across the living room where it smashed to smithereens against a large bronze sculpture of a rodeo rider atop a bucking horse. Rage, shock, contempt was written across his face.

"Did the old fool go mad?" he demanded of them all, though no one came up with an answer. "Catherine Elizabeth Costello. Who is she? Some fancy whore he had on the side? What hold did she have on him? I can't believe this. It's like my worst nightmare. Who is this woman? The woman he wanted to marry? Not Ma?''

Jude was struggling hard to master his own shock. Now he knew for certainty that Cate Costello and trouble went together. He stared at each member of the family in turn. ''Do none of you know her?''

Myra shook her head vigorously. At least she seemed to have snapped out of her catatonic state.

''I know of her,'' Melinda admitted, staring at Jude. She looked the very picture of bewilderment, which seemed to be her general condition. ''She runs a gallery, the Crystal Cave, near the beach.''

''What does that have to do with us?'' Ralph bellowed, reaching down for his father's will with the obvious intention of tearing it to bits.

Jude swiftly removed it from harm's way, while Ralph glared at him. ''You knew about this?'' he demanded.

Jude shook his head ready to give Ralph a good shove if he decided to get nasty. Not that he altogether blamed him. Who was Catherine Elizabeth Costello and what had she been to Lester Rogan? ''You saw me break the seal. I'm as shocked as you are.'' For various reasons he didn't announce to the family he had already met Rogan's heiress. One of them was to protect her, another was to avoid getting into a fistfight with Ralph. Ralph in this mood was as destructive as a boxer with a sore head.

''She's young,'' Melinda frowned hard in concentration, gripping her mother's hand as if it might assist her recollections. ''Younger than I am. She's beautiful. She has the most wonderful hair. The colour's sort of indescribable, red-gold. I've seen her in the town any number of times but we've never actually met.''

''She moved here,'' Ralph growled, banging his muscular arms together. ''I remember now. The chick at Mandel's old place. I've had her description from quite a few of the guys. To think I meant to check her out when I had the time! Dad saw I had as little spare time as possible. I don't get this? What would a good-looking young chick have to do with my big ugly geriatric dad?''

Myra whistled indignation through her nostrils. ''No one could have called your father old or ugly,'' she burst out, in her loyal, long-suffering wife mode. ''He wasn't even sixty. Sixty these days is young I might remind you. Your father was handsome as you're handsome but you'd better lose some weight. And very soon. I'm amazed you can still get into your clothes. For Heaven's sake, Jude,'' She turned her attention away from her near apoplectic son. ''You have to advise us. This has taken us all by shock. You're telling me Lester has left the bulk of his estate to a young woman none of us knows?''

''That's it, Mrs Rogan.'' Jude threw up his hands. ''I don't understand what's happened here. I confidently expected the estate to be divided between the family. I have no idea why your husband did what he did, but as the appointed executor of your late husband's estate, I promise you I'll find out. I have my responsibilities.''

''You bet you do!'' Ralph dredged up a lifetime of jealousy and irritation. He was breathing hard through his large, straight nose, making a surprisingly loud whistling noise. ''I always knew my dad was a mean bastard. I never figured he was a lunatic as well. He's shafted me. He's shafted the whole family. Even when he's dead he's punishing us.'' The destruction of his hopes and dreams was written all over Ralph's face. ''He won't get away with it. The money is rightfully mine.''

''Ours,'' Melinda piped up to keep the record straight. ''Mum's.''

''What the hell would you two know to do with it?''

Ralph glared at his sister, standing up to get himself another drink. "You and Ma know nothing about business. You've spent your life on your backsides. He mightn't have loved you but you had everything else you wanted. You never even had the guts, Mel, to find yourself a job. How many chicks your age haven't actually had a job? Anyone would think you couldn't read or write."

"You can stop that now, Ralph," Myra admonished in an astonishingly severe voice. "I needed Mel at home."

"So both of you could watch the flowers grow?" Ralph threw back his head and laughed. "Ah hell!" He reached out in extreme frustration sending a pile of glossy magazines flying. "You're the big shot lawyer, Conroy, what's your advice?"

"Nice of you to ask me, Ralph. The will would only be invalid if your father had been of unsound mind when he made it," Jude pointed out in a deceptively calm voice. "As far as I know there wouldn't be a soul around who could prove he was. Your mother has rights by law, family home, etc. In that regard, she's been provided for. You and Mel don't actually have rights as such, Ralph. Your father was free to do as he liked with his money. You and Mel have been provided for. In terrorem means in layman's language if any of you contest the will you'll get nothing."

Ralph executed a full turn, swearing violently. He slammed his fist down on the mahogany coffee table, the steam of anger rising off him. "What if the old devil was insane? What if this girl had him wound around her little finger? What if she bamboozled him into making the will in her favour? I wish I knew where she came from."

That makes two of us Jude thought. "You could contest the will on that basis, Ralph," he offered a legal opinion, actually feeling sorry for the guy. "Work the duress angle. But I'm duty-bound to tell you legal proceedings could risk your inheritance. What's more, your mother has first claim on the estate. If you wanted to fight it your mother has to initiate the action. She could lose. That would be a terrible result. What I have to do is meet with this young woman and establish the connection.''

"Even your dad, that honourable man, betrayed us.'' Ralph looked across at Jude with open hostility.

Jude's whole body tensed. "Don't bring my father into this, Ralph. You'd better know right now I won't stand for it. My father carried out your father's wishes.''

"Shame on you, Ralph.'' Melinda's soft voice turned shrill with rebuke. "You know the respect Dad had for Mr Conroy. Dad was always interested in Jude, too. Dad put a lot of store in brains.''

"You were behind the door when they were handed out,'' Ralph taunted his sister. He turned his glance back on Jude. "I bet your dad told you all about it.''

"I've got a couple of things to say, Ralph.'' Jude, who'd had just about enough of Ralph even given the years in-between, looked at him out of steely eyes. "Mel was actually considered a good student, remember? She got good grades.'' He never added "unlike you" but it hung in the air. "My father said nothing whatever to me.'' Jude stood up, quietly returning the time bomb of a will to his briefcase before snapping it shut. "It's called lawyer-client privilege. My father was absolutely clear about his role. I'm very sorry, believe me, your father's will wasn't what you all wanted, and confidently expected. As your father's executor I have to pay Ms Costello a visit.''

"Just be sure you report back to us straight away,'' Ralph threw up his big head belligerently.

"I'm not your lawyer, Ralph,'' Jude pointed out. "I act as executor for your late father's estate.'' He turned to Myra, his hand out, a sympathetic smile in his eyes. "As a family friend, Mrs Rogan, if you do wish to retain me I'll do everything in my power to help you.''

Myra stood up, still holding his hand. ''Thank you so much, Jude. We do need your help. My boy needs help. I can't take all this in. Everything has been such a shock.''

''I can appreciate that, Mrs Rogan.'' And how!

''I'll walk you to the door, Jude,'' Melinda offered catching hold of Jude's arm. ''I'm so glad you're here for us. I guess we'll find out soon enough what this Catherine Costello was to Dad.''

What indeed! Jude felt all kinds of horrors creep along his skin. He and Cate Costello were strangers though they had spoken briefly. Nevertheless he wasn't sure he could deal with the possibility she might have been Lester Rogan's mistress. It wasn't as though such things didn't happen. Rich powerful men, even geriatrics as Ralph had suggested, didn't have much of a problem picking up female trophies. But how could a young woman so beautiful and seemingly so refined as Cate Costello be part of anything so totally ugly? The very idea didn't so much disgust as numb him. Life was so complicated. He doubted he would ever reach a period in life when it wasn't.

CHAPTER THREE

HE DIDN'T mean to deal with the issue today. He wanted time to think about the whole situation at least overnight.

He went home. Jude focused his gaze on the high beach road that was the quickest route to his house at Spirit Cove some three miles from the Rogan mansion. The narrow road, divided by a white line down the middle, clung on one side to the glorious blue ocean; on the other, beyond an open space of lush tropical vegetation were the plantations; sugar cane, banana, mango, pineapple, avocado, new species of tropical fruits some of which he'd never even tasted.

The town had grown, extending much further south along the coast road and up the low indigo hills of the hinterland. The hills, tropical rain forests, were full of beautiful birds, gorgeous parrots, and plants. There were tree dwelling orchids, the dendrobium, the state flower of Queensland, spider orchids, angel orchids, terrestrial orchids, the extraordinary bromeliads with their vividly coloured centre leaves. He knew all those hills. He had explored them as a boy.

The golden disc of the sun was hot and brilliant. There was a bluish haze over the water. Blue water all around, glittering as if a billion metallic sequins had been cast on the rolling surface. Blue sky above. This was the tropics. Ineffable gold and blue.

He'd lowered the passenger window so the sea breeze could waft in. It bore the fragrance of sea water and salt mingled with the tropical fruits that grew nearby and the delicious scent of flowers. The lovely frangipani that grew everywhere in profusion, the common cream-yellow-centred flowers and nowadays almost as many pink and red. There were frangipanis twenty feet high in his home garden and the scent when they were in flower was so exquisitely heady as to be near unbearable. The frangipani were as ubiquitous as the indestructible oleanders of many colours that massed in great numbers around the cove where he was heading.

As he drove he could see draped over every fence and outbuilding a spectacular array of flowering vines; golden trumpets blazing away, the flashy Morning Glory, jasmines in flower all year round, allamandas and black-eyed Susans, the flame vines and the giant solandras. One had to be very careful planting vines in the tropics. They had a habit of running rampant, in no time at all turning into impenetrable jungle.

At least the lush beauty all around him was calming his thoughts. They'd been heading off in all directions, mostly centred on the mystery woman, Cate Costello. She'd fooled him with her clear direct gaze.

He couldn't bear to think of her as Lester Rogan's mistress. For that matter he couldn't bear to think of any man's hands on her which didn't exactly make sense. He didn't even know her. Was it possible there was a biological tie to Rogan? There was no evidence of it in her appearance. She bore no physical resemblance whatsoever to him—no single feature, eyes, mouth, nose, chin let alone the hair colour. Could she possibly be Rogan's long-lost illegitimate daughter? She'd told him she didn't know the family. She'd lied. She definitely knew Lester Rogan. That was a bad start.

He remembered those beautiful eyes, their cool green colour emphasized by her delicate dark brows and thick eyelashes, startling given the copper hair. Maybe that cascade of glowing silk was dyed? Women changed their hair colour all the time. There were lots of things he had yet to learn about Cate Costello. So far he'd learned she was hiding a great deal.

As had the late Lester Rogan, real estate tycoon. Why? His career wouldn't have suffered had he acknowledged paternity of a child other than his son, Ralph and his daughter Melinda. His wife, Myra, was so completely dominated she wouldn't have given him a terrible time had he confided in her or simply produced a surprise offspring as a fait accompli.

Jude groaned aloud. Lester Rogan wasn't her father. He couldn't be. He wouldn't believe it. Wouldn't his own father have known? His dad was one of the few people Lester Rogan had ever been known to confide in.

So what was the story? He let his mind range over a half a dozen scenarios all of which he hated. Surely he hadn't let a complete stranger get under his skin? He wasn't ready for that kind of connection with any woman much less one who gazed into crystal balls. He was depressed, too that she had lied to him. He hated lies.

Minutes later he arrived home. An old fishing mate of his father's, Jimmy Dawson, though not a caretaker as such— Jimmy had his own little bungalow on the edge of the rain forest—kept the grounds under control. At least the jungle hadn't set in. He got out to open the white picket gates, looking up with deep nostalgia at the handsome white house that stood tall against the turquoise sky. This was his much loved home right up until the time he had started his legal career in the state capital. Two storied it was surrounded by wide verandahs with a green painted galvanised roof and glossy emerald-green shutters to protect the pairs of French doors along the verandahs in times of tropical storms. A wide flight of six steps led to the porch.

His mother had always kept two huge ceramic pots planted with masses of white flowers flanking the double doorway with its beautiful stained-glass transom. Towering palms stood in the large, very private grounds, the lawns a carpet of lush green. Obviously Jimmy had seen to the mowing. The wonderfully spectacular poincianas were in full bloom as were the flame trees. On either side of the house the magnolias carried great plate-sized blooms, creamy-white and resplendent over the rich dark green leaves burnished underneath.

The flower beds had not survived although agapanthus, strelitzias, cannas, cassias and gardenias had gown back to the wild. The long fences on either side of the house were totally taken over by a dense screen of King Jasmine. Jude supposed the timber had rotted, teetering beneath the rampant vines which were so strong they were virtually self-supporting. It would be getting too much for Jimmy even with help. Jimmy was much older than Jude's father, around seventy but wonderfully fit and wiry or he had been the last time Jude had seen him about a year ago. A year at Jimmy's time of life was a long time.

He had rung Jimmy to let him know he was coming. The house had been aired. There was milk, butter, cheddar cheese, bacon and eggs, a whole roasted chicken, a bottle of chardonnay, four jars of cumquat marmalade in the frig—cumquat marmalade, brandied cumquats, pickled cumquats, you name it, cumquats were the base of Jimmy's home made specialties—Jimmy like his dad didn't bother growing the miniature fruit in pots like some people. He grew them in long hedges as a windbreak, always teeming with fruit or flower. Jude looked in the bread bin, found a fresh loaf. There was tea and coffee in the pantry, a few more groceries and a bottle of whiskey—he laughed at that.

Jimmy was a great guy, an honourary uncle to him when he was growing up. His throat tightened with affection and gratitude. Jimmy had been organised to go fishing with his

dad that terrible day only another friend of Jimmy's had
stumbled over a snake on his way home from the pub and
got bitten for his trouble. Jimmy, being a drinker, was on
hand to get his friend to the hospital. The rest was history.

"Anyone at home?" he called to the empty house, knowing he would never again get the answer he wanted. "Are
you there, Dad?" Would he ever get over the loss! His heart
gave a little jump as one of the mahogany treads on the
staircase that led off the entrance hall creaked loudly.
Doubtless his father still walked around the house. "Dad,
do you know how I miss you." Jude continued to talk to
himself as he prowled around.

What better place for his father to roam than Spirit Cove.
There was an off-beat story as to why the cove had been so
named. Some sixty years before, a pretty young woman of
the town, known to be head over heels in love with a married man, the owner of one of the district's largest sugar
plantations, had drowned herself there. A lot of people over
the years claimed they saw her at night walking along the
beach. She was always wearing flimsy white draperies that
billowed in the sea breeze. Jimmy who loved telling a good
yarn claimed he'd once got close enough to talk to her before she dematerialised before his very eyes. Oddly Jude's
highly sceptical mother claimed to have seen her once. Jude
remembered her shock had been real.

It only added to the atmosphere. As a boy, alone or with
a friend staying over, he'd stolen onto the star spangled
beach. Much as he wanted the thrill of seeing a ghost he'd
seen nothing and not been surprised.

Jude started to roam through the house with its large
rooms that flowed into each other and led to the huge deck
his parents had used constantly for entertaining when he was
growing up. He loved this area with its beautiful views of
the ocean. One lived outdoors in the tropics.

The rear garden was crowded with fruit trees. Mango, banana, avocado, fig, luminous golden lemons, limes, custard apples, pineapple guavas. No one would go hungry here. There used to be deep vegetable gardens, an endless supply of sweet little cherry tomatoes he would pop into his mouth. But no more. Sometimes in his dreams he saw his parents working happily together in the garden like they used to, his mother's beautiful face protected by one of her big straw sunhats. Those were the days when they'd been a happy family. Or so he'd thought. In reality his mother had probably been planning her getaway.

Why dream of his mother when he'd never had a conversation with her after age twelve. He had no idea what had happened to her. No doubt her second marriage to a rich man had worked out well—always supposing the rich American had married her. He could have half sisters and brothers for all he knew. He would acknowledge any siblings but never his mother. She'd left his father alone to grieve; turned him marriage-shy. To love was to lose. Jude shoved off the clinging threads of desolation.

Settled in or as settled as he could get, he rang Jimmy to thank him, inviting him over next day. Maybe they could go into town he proposed? Have lunch at the excellent little pub? Extraordinarily restless, he pushed through the picket gate to walk down to the beach with its pristine white sand.

The dunes were swathed in succulents with gossamer thin yellow flowers. Swaying coconut palms, some bent at odd angles by the force of the wind, and spiky pandanus threw shadows over the beach. At this time of the afternoon the sea was a rich royal-blue. The ocean had as many facets as gemstones, sometimes sapphire, emerald turquoise, now tanzanite. North of Capricorn was such a beautiful part of the world, the light incandescent. He kicked off his shoes feeling the familiar crunch of sand beneath his feet. He had lots

to think about. Jude found his way down to the hard sand
near the water's edge.

He settled for a plate of chicken sandwiches and a pot of
coffee for supper, eating it out on the rear deck. By seven
o'clock he started to feel he should have called on Cate
Costello that afternoon instead of leaving it until tomorrow.
He was seriously annoyed with himself for getting into a
spin about a girl he didn't even know. He was behaving
right out of character.

Ten minutes later he took to the road, driving into town.
He had every excuse to drop in on her. Perhaps he should
have rung but then she might have taken the opportunity to
slip out. She had recognised him easily enough. She knew
he was Jude Conroy, a lawyer. It would be a simple matter
for a smart young woman like her to put two and two together and realize he was here for the will reading. She said
she didn't know the family but she hadn't been able to stay
away from Lester Rogan's funeral. She had deceived him
and he dealt with totally convincing liars every day of the
week. There seemed little doubt she'd known Lester.
Probably when he was in town one day habitual womaniser
Lester had stepped into the shop and seen her there among
all her pretty glittering crystals, the creamy skin, the long
copper hair, the up tilted green eyes. Jude had heard the old
myths from Ireland about how red-haired women had "the
powers."

Powers or not, she was a man-trap if ever there was one.
As Myra had said, the late Lester Rogan could hardly be
described as old or unattractive. He'd been a big, vigorous
imposing looking man, larger than life, quite out of the ordinary. All through his married life it was an open secret he
took mistresses, but never as young as twenty-two or there-
abouts. They were usually thoroughly respectable widows
and the like. The youngest Jude could recall, a schoolteacher

who had quietly been moved on after an anonymous letter to the Education Department, was around thirty-six. His father had always said mildly, "Les is fond of the women!" Boy, what an understatement! The late Lester Rogan had had no idea what it meant to be faithful, but he could provide his women with the finer things in life. Women were big on such things!

Either Ms Catherine Elizabeth Costello had well and truly come off her pedestal or there was some piece of the puzzle Jude hadn't yet hit on. There was no getting away from it mistress seemed the most likely scenario given Lester's predilections.

When he arrived at the Crystal Cave, the site of Tony Mandel's old art gallery, he saw the place in a pool of semi-darkness. He contemplated it briefly. Little had changed. It wasn't until he got out of the car that he spotted the red sports car nosed right in to the grove of golden canes at the far side of the building. Instantly all the muscles under his skin tightened.

Ralph! It was enough to make the knees buckle. Anger and a kind of panic hit him. When he'd left the Rogan mansion that afternoon Ralph had been drunk. Why hadn't he considered bully-boy Ralph, the hothead, might take it upon himself to come out to where she lived? An awful image flashed into his mind of the girl trying to grapple with a drink inflamed Rogan.

Jude, the athlete, moved with speed, running along the narrow side of the house to the rear garden. His heart was pounding up into his throat, betraying his agitation. Why hadn't he called her? Then he would have known Ralph was there. He prayed that Ralph had only just arrived. Ralph at the best of times had a short fuse, drunk he would be ugly and unpredictable. Eaten away with bitterness and resentment from a lifetime of hoarding up every little snub, every little slight robbed of his inheritance he would be positively dangerous.

The back of the house was well lit. All the exterior lights were on, flooding the deck with its vaulting canopy of flowering poinciana and shining out into the small square of lawn densely planted around the perimeter by a hedge of gardenia bushes. Coconut palms whispered in the cooling breeze, a sensuous sound for once he didn't hear. He caught a great gust of perfume from the richly seductive gardenia, the hundreds and hundreds of white flowers illuminated by the strong security lights.

He was almost at the steps when a night bird darted low over his head startling him but it was nothing like the freezing shock he received when a young urgent cry issued from inside the house.

"Get out! Go away! Please...just go!" It was a cry that imparted fear, intimidation and loathing.

Jude took the flight of steps two at a time, contemplating what he might do to Ralph and to hell with the consequences. Lawyers weren't supposed to get into fistfights, but just let him get his hands on Ralph. His face was rigid with anger and disgust. Ralph Rogan would never change. He wouldn't know how to.

What he saw through the picture windows was a long comfortably furnished room divided into open kitchen and living area. The girl was stumbling back from a menacing Rogan, one of her arm's held up defensively like a shield. Ralph was advancing slowly, but his resolve to manhandle her was sickeningly apparent. The girl's hands plucked at a chair as if she thought to defend herself with it. Her hair spilled copper over a low-neck top that revealed the cleft between her breasts. She wore white shorts, no shoes. She'd been thoroughly at home at her beach house before Ralph arrived. Very soon he'd be on her. She looked as delicate and breakable as a lily on a stalk, absolutely no match for Ralph.

Jude felt the blood rush to his head. He saw Rogan reach for her with his long, powerful arms—he'd never quite realised how big Ralph was until he saw how he dwarfed this girl. He saw Ralph miss her altogether as she retreated on nimble feet, four feet away, this time straining for something to throw. There was the expected fear of a victim in her face—Ralph was a daunting sight—but a courageous defiance, too. Jude recognised she meant to put up a fight. Ralph would recognise it, too, only Ralph would relish it. It would be an opportunity for him to show his power. Her beauty and vulnerability would only serve to increase the lusty sexual appetite Ralph had inherited from his father.

Jude felt a great surge of adrenaline. He threw back the door so violently it had the effect of a gunshot. At the impact both people inside the room were stopped in their tracks. The girl stared at him. She was all eyes—burning emeralds in a milk-white face. Ralph was twisting his big body unsteadily in an effort to confront the invader, his ugly expression abruptly turning furtive.

"Had to be you, Conroy!" he rasped, his voice lifting in volume. "Always rushing to a lady's defence. What do ya—?"

He broke off open-mouthed, as the girl went flying across the room as graceful as a ballerina, her hair a bright turbulence around her. She backed up beside Jude, clearly for protection.

"Thank God you're here!" she gasped. "You saved me."

He wasn't ready to forgive her, in fact he felt unaccountably angry with her. "Perhaps you can tell me why the hell you let him in?" He felt for her hand, hauled her protectively to his side.

Cate recognised the fury in his blazing blue eyes. "I didn't let him in. I was adamant he couldn't come in, but he shoved me back inside. Pulled the door shut. There was no reasoning with him."

"You know him, don't you?" He didn't look at her but there was hard accusation in Jude's tone.

"Know him?" Cate stared across at the coarsely handsome Ralph who now appeared stupefied by the turn of events. "I know of him. He's Ralph Rogan. I've never actually met him until tonight."

"Well, this isn't my idea of coming courting," Jude clipped off, his natural sweetness of manner totally lost. "Caught you, you miserable bastard," he addressed Ralph in a chilling low voice. "Just what were you intending?" Jude took the opportunity to move the girl out of harm's way before starting across the space that divided him from Ralph.

Ralph awkwardly backed up, Jude's anger cutting into him like a blade. "Listen, Jude, I've no argument with you," he blustered, continuing to inch away. "I wanted answers from her. Can you blame me?"

"Harassment isn't the way to go about it." Jude gritted.

Ralph found his breath quickening. He'd learned his lesson years ago, he didn't want to tangle with Conroy in this mood. "She played Dad for a fool," he blurted. "You know that. I wanted her to tell me."

"Don't keep backing up, Ralph," Jude taunted. "I'm itching to take you apart. You never learn do you?"

"What good would that do?" Ralph asked, shifting his body yet again to prevent his muscles seizing. "Aren't you supposed to be our lawyer?"

Cate realized she had to stop this. She moved swiftly, rushing forward to put herself between the two men.

"Don't." Her green eyes pleaded with Jude. "He's not worth it."

"Would you mind getting out of the way?" Jude kept his eyes on the unpredictable Ralph. Ralph could yet try something, but Jude would be ready.

"This is my place," Cate said, not budging an inch. "I don't want to see you get into a fight over me. I want him to leave."

Jude's golden-blond head slowly turned until he met her eyes. "You don't want to ring the police?"

"I want him to leave," Cate repeated, refusing to surrender to tears of relief. "He's mad. He said he was going to set the place on fire. He said he was going to drive me out of town."

"You said that did you, Ralph?" Jude asked in a dead-flat voice. "Ring the police. You can bring charges." He risked another glance at the girl.

"You better not try." Ralph's deep-set eyes glittered malignantly as he made his gruff threat. "Damn you, Conroy. Whose side are you on anyway?" he demanded. "Why didn't you do what you were supposed to do? Why didn't you get the full story out of this little whore?".

Red spots flamed in Cate's cheeks. "I'd be very careful what you say," she said tightly. "For that, I will report you. I'm going to ring right now." She moved with quiet determination. "You can explain yourself to them, you horrible pig." She moved towards the kitchen where she picked up the portable phone on the counter.

"Don't do it," Ralph burst out sharply. "Put it down. Tell her, Jude. I don't want any fuss here."

Jude gave a hard, disbelieving laugh. "On the contrary I'm advising her to ring. I'm a witness. I saw you menacing her and I believe you were about to physically assault her."

Ralph's strong legs abruptly turned to syrup. He crashed

into a chair, wiping his sweating brow with the back of his hand. "Stop her, Jude. I swear I wasn't going to do anything, I was just trying to talk to her. I had no idea she would panic so badly. She went a lot wilder than she's trying to make out."

Hatred was alive and burning inside of Ralph, Jude was sure of it, but so was the bully-boy back-off he remembered from the past.

"I'm sorry. I didn't mean to scare you." Ralph said to Cate, his dark face blotchy with drink and rage. "I apologise."

Cate put the phone down slowly, nibbling hard on her lip. She was a newcomer in town and she had a business to run. She didn't want any scandals if she could help it. "I'm certain you did mean to scare me." She contradicted him flatly. She could have added she feared he wouldn't have stopped at rape. There'd been something feral in his eyes. She'd seen eyes like that before. "There's a small matter of your breaking in," she reminded him. "I was off guard. You flung me away, sent me sprawling. Your purpose was to frighten and intimidate. I shudder to think what might have happened had Jude not arrived."

There was a crazed sparkle in Ralph's eyes. "Jude?" He eyed one then the other. "You two know one another?"

"No, we don't," Jude denied it flatly. "You've been calling me Jude remember?"

Ralph stood up looking decidedly woozy. He held on to the armchair for support. "I don't believe you. You know her. Your old man knew her. Dad, the randy old bastard sure did."

Provoked beyond measure Jude moved in on the other man, for all Ralph's bulk, spinning him around to face him. "I've never laid eyes on Ms Costello until today," he said in a don't-mess-with-me voice. "Nor she on me. My father never ever mentioned her name. I've told you before to leave my father out of it. He was an honourable man.''

''Okay. Okay.'' Ralph tried to break Jude's grip. Gave up. ''This whole thing is bizarre.''

''I agree.'' Jude took his time removing his hand, though his body language didn't change. There was a chance Ralph would swing the moment he turned his back.

''I want you to leave,'' Cate repeated, still looking white and wary. ''I don't want you to ever come back. If you do I will report you to the police. If I have to I'll take out a restraining order. I don't know what you want with me, but I want absolutely nothing of you.''

Ralph struck his forehead as though trying to clear his brain. ''You'd better talk to her, Conroy. I don't know what game she's playin'.'' All the fight seemed to have drained out of him. He looked sick.

Cate's green eyes flicked to Jude. ''Game?''

She was doing a marvellous job of playing the innocent. ''What else could it possibly be?'' Jude found himself saying in a cynical voice.

''Yeah, get it out of her, Jude.'' Ralph took the opportunity to lumber to the door, where he steadied himself with one long arm pressed against the jamb. ''You damned well knew why I came, girl. You're no fool. No sirree! You're one exotic little chick, I've never seen any girl look like you. Dad must have had himself one hell of a good time.''

The girl looked quickly at Jude, her expression stunned. ''What's he raving about? Do you know?''

For a second Jude almost believed her. As an actress she'd get a standing ovation. ''I'm quite sure you know the truth, Ms Costello. You know the reason I'm here in town. You must have a good idea why Ralph decided to visit you, and you can count yourself lucky I arrived when I did.''

''Well, I'll try to!'' she told him sharply, greatly upset

by his demeanour. Everything about him—his eyes, his expression, his body language—told her for whatever reason Jude Conroy had now concluded he didn't like or trust her. What had happened since their last meeting to cause this hostility? "If it comes to that, I don't know why you're here, either?" She showed him an angry, spirited face.

"If you have the time I'll tell you," he shot back.

"That's it, Jude. Call her bluff," Ralph counselled, starting to move onto the timber deck. "She's probably on the game. I'll leave you to it. Just make sure your trip up here hasn't been a waste of time."

Jude watched him lurch away. Spoke up. "You're drunk, Ralph. You shouldn't be driving your car."

Ralph waved a contemptuous hand. "Don't tell me what to do, pal, and don't try to stop me. I've been drivin' for a very long time. The cops don't worry me, either."

"Let's hope they get you." Bolstered by Jude's presence and his palpable air of command, Cate walked to the door and slammed it on Ralph. She was trembling now that it was all over. Or was it? She realised Jude had become antagonistic towards her but for all her problems she found it difficult not to trust him. That was an awfully big step for her had he known it. He'd been furious with Rogan and he couldn't hide that from her. Furious and disgusted, ready to get into a fight. The tension in his naturally graceful body was obvious, small wonder Rogan had backed off.

"Thank goodness he's gone!" She tried to sound calm when she wasn't. She was shaking badly, trembling with outrage.

"You realise he could have harmed you?" Jude was still angry with her, but concerned by what he was seeing. Even given the natural creaminess of her skin she was very pale. Her beautiful eyes were like saucers.

"It did occur to me," she offered shortly. She wasn't

about to tell him the hidden places in her life. "He certainly changed his tune with you."

"Ralph and I go back a long way," he said, his complex feelings swallowed up by a larger concern. "I think I'll make you some tea, if you'll point me in the right direction."

Cate sat down before her legs gave way. "Tea's fine. Milk, one sugar. Sugar in the small yellow canister on the counter, tea in the medium-size one, milk in the frig."

"I ought to check he's gone," Jude said. It seemed possible Ralph might hang about. "Won't be a moment."

He was quick. Cate closed her eyes briefly in an effort to pull herself together. When she reopened them he was back through the door.

"The car's gone. Useless to try to stop him short of knocking him senseless." Despite himself he was touched by her delicacy, the vulnerable quiver in her limbs. Everything about her unsettled him. "He's going to kill himself one day."

"As long as it's no one else." Cate watched him move to the kitchen, deftly going about his self imposed job. The elegance of movement was made more apparent by his height. He found the cups and saucers first go. "So what's the mystery?" she asked. "Why exactly did he come here? Why was he calling me vile names? It wouldn't be difficult to persuade me he's quite mad."

"Maybe he is a touch," Jude said. "You can't think why he came?" He looked across at her, blue eyes probing.

"I think you'd better tell me." She turned her arm to examine a blue bruise.

"Brute!" Jude gritted when he saw it.

"I bruise easily."

"We can talk as soon as you get this tea into you. I've taken the liberty of adding a bit more sugar."

"Oh, dear! I hate it sweet."

"Trust me, you've had a bad fright." It was one she might have foreseen, he thought. The tea brewed, he poured two cups and put one in front of her. "Drink up."

"Later." She was still watching him with a puzzled look.

"No, now. You're very pale. In fact you look to me like you're in shock."

She shrugged. "What woman wouldn't be confronted by that gorilla?" She picked up the cup, embarrassed when her hand shook so badly she spilt a little.

"Did that burn you?" Naturally solicitous Jude moved away to fetch a paper towel. "Give me that." He took the cup from her, setting it down on the coffee table. "Ralph enjoys being mean to women, he's not so crash hot with us guys."

"I'm amazed he hasn't gone to jail." She dipped her head, feeling foolishly nerve ridden.

"Maybe too many women let him off the hook. You could have called the police. Bill Bennett is a good man."

"I realise that."

He felt his old protective streak rising. "A nip of brandy wouldn't go astray. Have you any?"

"No. I'm okay." Cate made a much better attempt at picking up her cup, willing the tremble out of her hand. She sipped at the hot tea, pulled a little involuntary face at the excessive sweetness. "I'm new here. The gallery is important to me. I have to succeed."

His blue gaze that had been kind and concerned, reverted to cynical. "You appear to have succeeded nicely."

"How would you know that?" She contrived to look as innocent as a child. "You haven't seen the gallery?"

"Just let's sit quietly for a moment." She appeared nearly exhausted. It made him frown and rub his chin. One moment she showed fierce defiance the next extreme vulnerability, it must be all part of her reaction to the shock.

Obediently Cate swallowed the rest of the tea in the cup, set it down. "You're being very considerate for a man who's decided he doesn't much like me."

He gave an abrupt laugh. "I haven't made any decision until I sort this thing out."

"What thing? You're in town as the Rogan lawyer?"

Jude raised an eyebrow. "Hey, so you've figured that out?"

"The truth is I'm quite smart, or smart enough. Your father was the town lawyer and I know you work for a top legal firm in Brisbane. It's quite amazing how often you and your father figure in the conversations around here."

"So I imagine you've heard about my mother?" There was the barest suggestion of bitterness in his voice though he tried hard to keep it out.

She hesitated, afraid she might say the wrong thing. She knew all about the walking wounded. "I've heard she was very beautiful and well liked. I heard you and your father were broken-hearted when she left."

"What would you expect?"

"Nothing less. I'm sorry." She spoke haltingly, but sincerely.

The sympathy in her green eyes disconcerted him. "It's all in the past," he said crisply. "Are you able to tell me now why you were at the funeral? You admitted you didn't know the family."

"I didn't realise I had to confide in you," she retorted, the ready sympathy dissolving at his tone. "You're a lawyer. You might have charged me with something for all I know. The fact is I don't know Lester Rogan's family."

"But you knew Lester?" He studied her closely. The colour was coming back into her cheeks. "You had a friend-ship. An intimacy?"

She looked angry and confused. "He was my landlord, you call that being intimate? The closest I ever came to intimacy was passing over the rent."

"Which he collected personally?" Jude asked in a purr-ing voice.

"Can't you sit down?" She stared at him, admiring and not wanting to, the elegant way his lean body lounged back against the bench. "I don't like you towering over me."

"Sorry!" The distinctive dimple flicked in and out. "I thought I was keeping my distance. I'll take a chair." He moved to the two-seater sofa opposite her. "You were say-ing about the rent?"

"Do you want to check if it was too high or too low?"

"Nothing like that. Only if he collected it personally."

"Well, he did." Her answer was brisk. "Every fort-night."

"Fancy that! A busy man like Lester Rogan, a property tycoon no less, took time off every fortnight to call on you for the rent. Didn't you think that a little odd?"

"Actually I did," she admitted, "but who was I to argue? He was the landlord and he seemed to like coming in."

"Why not?" He gave her an enigmatic half smile. "So Tony sold out to him?"

"Don't take it personally."

He looked at her for a while, his expression a mix of amusement and cool speculation. "Did you talk much?"

"Well, yes, we did." She shrugged a shoulder. Her skin was as smooth as satin, the bones light and delicate. "He was a very interesting man. He wanted to know all about the crystals. Rather like you. How it all started. Not sur-prisingly he wanted to know something of my background."

"He managed to get that out of you?" The sarcasm escaped.

Her heart sped up. "You're barking up the wrong tree if you think he was trying to hit on me, Jude Conroy. He most definitely wasn't. He was rather sweet if you want to know. Gentlemanly."

Jude couldn't help it, he groaned in utter disbelief. "Of all the adjectives I could have lavished on the late Lester Rogan, sweet and gentlemanly wouldn't begin to figure. Lester had a wife but he preferred to have fun with other women. Everyone in town knows that."

She could feel the hot anger burgeoning in her. "I could think of a few adjectives for you. One isn't subtle. So what's bothering you exactly? Dare we take it to the hypothetical level? Even if I were mixed up with Lester Rogan— Why are you so angry?"

He met her eyes calmly, though it required an effort. Why indeed? "Maybe because I'm executor of his estate." That seemed reasonable enough.

"What's that got to do with me?" Her eyes opened wide, clear as crystal, windows of the soul.

"Oh, I can't stand another moment of this!" Jude sprang to his feet, pacing the area between kitchen and living room. The back wall was lined with bookcases crammed with books. Ms Costello was a reader it seemed. She also had a flair for interior decoration now that he thought about it. But it was as an actress that she took his breath away.

"Maybe you're allowing your imagination to run away with you?" she challenged. "Instead of pacing around my living room why don't you tell me what this is all about?"

"Try this." Jude resumed his seat opposite her, pinning her eyes. "I do hope you're ready. At least you're sitting down. It's my job to inform you, you figure largely in the late Lester Rogan's will. In fact he has left you the bulk of his estate. The big question looming in the family's mind is why? Would you have any idea? We're all striving to get the clear picture. Who are you, Ms Costello? I'm not trying to insult you, I really need to know.''

She'd been sitting with one slender leg curled beneath her, now she sat up straight lowering her narrow foot to the floor. "Hang on a minute." She held up a hand. "I'm trying to take in what you've just said.''

"You weren't prepared?'' It came out with more cynicism than he intended to show. "Lester didn't drop any little hints?''

It cost her a considerable effort not to throw something at him. She hated the contempt in his eyes, the arrogant tilt of his blond head. "Listen, I've had the most hideous experience with the dreadful Ralph, why do I have to listen to your taunts?''

His mouth compressed. "I'd have thought because I'm the bearer of glad tidings. You've been left a fortune, Ms Costello, many millions in property and shares. You didn't know you were an heiress?''

Cate with the redhead's hot temper, sprang to her feet. "Heiress? Listen, I'm about to freak out. If you're being absolutely serious and you're not drunk like your friend—''

"Friend?'' Jude grimaced. "I resent that. I'm stone cold sober and Ralph Rogan was never my friend. If you've a Bible in the house I'll swear on it. It's just as I said. the late Lester Rogan has bequeathed to you the bulk of his fortune.''

"I don't believe it.'' Shocked and baffled she stared at him, trying to absorb such sensational news.

"I do actually,'' he told her dryly. Green eyes glowing. White skin. Bright copper hair raining down her back. It was all too easy to believe. "I'll read it all out to you. Just say the word. Is there the remote possibility you're his love child?''

"Come on please!" Cate shuddered, turning away in agitation. "You think I'd want to be related to the goon that came here?''

"Strangely enough Ralph can look good at times…he has no difficulty attracting women. He was drunk. Some might find that understandable given the fact he'd sustained a horrendous shock. I know it's unfair, but we can't pick our brothers and sisters.''

"You're having fun aren't you?" she accused him with quiet disgust.

Actually he was having a great deal of trouble taking his eyes off her. He'd never seen a girl look better in a skimpy pair of shorts "I assure you I'm not. This is a very serious matter. I can see the family trying to prove Lester was in the last stages of dementia.''

"He must have been." Cate put a hand against her head. "This is a terrible mistake.''

"The Rogans certainly think so," he offered suavely.

"Obviously you agree." She was confused and disturbed by the changes in him. When they'd met after the funeral he'd been someone else entirely. Smiling into her eyes, charming, sexy. Very, very sexy. Someone who'd attracted her powerfully. Now the atmosphere between them was electric with distrust.

His very next words confirmed it. "I can't think you're being honest with me," he said.

"Oh, I've got that." She shrugged. "Are legal men always so suspicious?''

"I'm afraid so. It goes with the territory. Lester Rogan had to have very good reason to make you his main beneficiary. He had to feel very strongly about you.''

"There's a problem there. He forgot to tell me. In fact

he was nothing more than pleasant every time I saw him. Didn't the family get anything? Surely not?" She stared at him, hurt by his attitude even if she half understood it. It didn't look good for her. "No wonder the son came after me. He was beside himself with rage."

"You risked a fate worst than death opening that door," Jude clipped off, his expression darkening. "You asked a question. I'll answer it. Mrs Rogan, her daughter, Melinda and her son Ralph who took it upon himself to make your acquaintance this evening, all received a considerable bequest. It should keep them happily for the rest of their days if they listen to their advisers."

"Isn't that you?" she abruptly challenged, picking up a lemon from a basket as though she intended to throw it at him. Instead she only held it in her palm, then put it back in the basket. "Did you benefit by the way?" This time she turned the sarcasm on him.

He kept his expression dispassionate. "Why ever would you ask that question?"

"Why ever not?" she countered. "Surely it was part of your studies learning to keep a straight face? You do it well. Everyone knows lawyers benefit handsomely from clients' wills, we read about it all the time in the papers. Sometimes the family get angry about it and take action."

"Which may well happen to you," he pointed out.

"I don't want the money." She shook back her long copper hair.

"You might well say that now." His expression was sardonic.

"I happen to mean it."

"Well, you could give it away," he suggested lightly. "Rehabilitation centres, charities, your friends, young people on the dole, pensioners. There's no shortage of deserving people who need the money."

"Sarcasm is sweet on your tongue. But this is crazy!"

"Of course it is," he agreed, frowning in thought. "So crazy I don't feel like leaving you here on your own."

She stared out at the deck. "You think Godzilla might return?"

She spoke with bravado, but there was something going on behind her green eyes. Jude studied her, trying to figure out what it was. "I have to tell you I have concerns. You need more security around this place if you're going to live here."

"Why would I live here?" She threw up her slender arms looking like a beautiful witch about to launch into an incantation. "Haven't I come into a fortune? I have to face it. I'm an heiress. Isn't that what you just said." She stared back at him, bright flags of colour in her cheeks.

"Ralph never figured on the estate being broken up the way it has been," he answered soberly. "He expected the bulk of it to pass to him by divine right. I have to confess I expected it. You can bet your life the whole town expected it. Of course I can see what the town might think is neither here nor there to you anymore. If you continued to live here, however, everyone would consider they had the right to hear why Lester Rogan did what he did."

"Why don't you look into it?" she challenged, taking a step toward him. "You're the successful lawyer. Precisely how much do you charge an hour?"

"Quite a lot," he said dryly, "but you could afford it now."

She gave a little half laugh with no humour in it. "I'm not afraid to stay here, I'll be quite safe." Inside she was quivering like a plucked string. Ralph Rogan's aggression tapped in to too many old nightmares.

He could see straight through the pretence. "You'll be a lot safer with me. You really should have a good security door fitted. I'm surprised you haven't. And get locks on the windows—this place would be a piece of cake to get into."

As though she didn't know. "No one has bothered me up to now. I'm just a bit strung up at the moment."

A strained pause followed. Jude broke it. "I'm amazed no one has bothered you looking like you do. I would have thought you'd be fighting off callers? Either that, or everyone thought—"

"Thought what?" She lifted her chin, daring him to say it.

"Callers were likely to make Lester angry," he said finally. "If you thought Ralph intimidating Lester took good care not to show you his dark side. Why did you go to the funeral? Why did you cover your hair so you wouldn't stand out? That says a lot. You must have cared about the man. You're holding back plenty and I know it."

She caught the wave of hostility, took a deep breath. "I went to pay my respects. I wasn't alone. There was a crowd."

He nodded. "Yes, small. Lester made a lot of enemies around here. A lot of people thought making enemies was the sort of thing he liked to do. Not you. You knew him as sweet and gentlemanly. Obviously he was heavily camouflaged or you're not being truthful. Whatever you tell me will be treated in confidence."

Anger consumed her. "There's nothing to tell," she said sharply. "My friendship with Mr Rogan can be examined by the whole world for all I care. It was perfectly respectable. He was not my father in case you're thinking of following up that line."

His face tautened. "I need your help, Ms Costello. Would you mind telling me about your parents."

"I do mind actually." She knew she sounded as defensive as she felt. She couldn't control it. "If there had been any connection with Lester Rogan I'd have known about it. I need to think about this. It really is a tremendous shock whatever you may think.''

Tension was showing in her face and her body language, it was mirrored in her beautiful eyes. He stood up, stunned by the way she got to him and his deep dormant emotions. ''We can go over the will any time that suits. I'm having lunch with an old friend of my father's, tomorrow, otherwise I'm free. I'm not happy about leaving you here. I have a house at Spirit Cove, it's the family home, there's plenty of room and you could stay the night. Then I'd know you were safe.''

She felt so jittery she was tempted. ''That's okay. I'll sleep like a baby.''

''I very much doubt that!'' He turned back, his eyes running over her. ''I won't sleep thinking of you here,'' he admitted frankly, aware his own nerves were on edge. What was to stop Ralph from doubling back? ''Why don't you shove a few things in a bag and come with me.''

She swallowed on the hard knot in her throat. Whether he disliked her or not she could see his genuine concern. ''I prefer to stay here.'' She moved away, her movements brittle, a little helpless.

''No, you don't,'' he said firmly. ''I'm involved now. I know how to handle it. You've had a bad fright, I can see it in your eyes. Frankly I consider it a miracle I got here when I did. I don't want to worry you unnecessarily, but Ralph could be anywhere out there waiting for me to go.''

She was very much afraid of that, yet she argued: ''What's to stop him coming back any other night? Day for that matter?''

Jude's eyes raced over her. Her beauty was attacking all his senses. He found those little gestures of her hands strangely moving. She'd be irresistible to any man. He felt desperate to be convinced the late Lester Rogan hadn't been one of them. "I'm going to read Ralph the riot act when he's sober. I think I can put the fear of God into him for a while until we sort this thing out."

CHAPTER FOUR

WHILE she packed a few things, Jude went around the flat checking on windows and doors, not that anyone couldn't have broken in if they wanted to, but Isis was a peaceful, law-abiding town where people still continued to go out and leave their back doors unlocked. He wouldn't advise it, however, for a beautiful young woman living on her own. She needed the proper protection.

She hadn't told him about her connection to Tony Mandel either, or what she was doing in such a back-water, albeit tropical paradise. It baffled him to think she had chosen to live and work in a small coastal town. Most young people headed off to the cities to find work and excitement, returning years later when it was time to opt out of the rat race. His father, a clever man who could have done a lot better for himself career-wise had never wished to live anywhere else. Unlike Jude who couldn't get out quick enough to embark upon his career.

At twenty-eight he was on the fast track, considered pretty damned good, but amazingly he wasn't all that happy. He had Poppy Gooding to worry about for one thing. She threatened to jeopardize his job. He'd never felt more like taking a break, but instead he'd been dished up a dilemma.

"All set?"

"Yes." She came back into the living room, carrying a small overnight bag. She had changed the white shorts for a long sarong type skirt printed in big open-faced hibiscus, pretty blue sandals on her feet. He felt like reaching for her but that would never do.

69

"I'll take that," he said, putting out his hand for her bag.

"Thank you. Do you think I should leave a light or two on?"

He shook his head. "It won't make a difference if you turn them off. I've checked the windows."

"Anyone could get in," she said in a fatalistic kind of voice, starting to switch off lights. "Tony didn't care. He didn't worry about a thing."

"Tony was a man well able to take care of himself. I don't believe in women going short on security measures." He wanted to ask her about Tony but left it until they were in the car speeding away to Spirit Cove. There was no sign of a red sports car anywhere.

"So how did you meet Tony?" he decided to broach the subject. He realised he knew absolutely nothing about her which made his response to her all the more breathtaking. Her profile was as cleanly cut as a cameo, her skin luminous even in the low light reflected off the dashboard.

"It's a long story. I don't think I can tell you tonight."

"Okay. Tony never mentioned anyone like you and I've known him most of my life."

"He's a good friend, a good man," she said softly.

"Yes, he is."

"He painted me."

That piece of information given so simply startled him. "Now why isn't that a surprise?"

He had one of those voices capable of infinite nuances, Cate thought. At the moment, light sarcasm, a touch of self-mockery. She wondered how she'd found it so easy to come with him when she'd been near assaulted, her every sensibility mangled. It was as though Jude Conroy with his beautiful smile had breeched her every defence. It was odd for someone like her who had lived through dark traumas and kept silent about them for years.

"Tony had a special affinity with beautiful things," he was saying, his tone revealing his affection for his father's friend. "Beautiful women, beautiful flowers, beautiful birds, beautiful tropical sunsets. Where's the portrait now?"

"It's at the gallery."

"On show?" He gave her another quick sidelong glance.

"No. It's in my bedroom."

"I'd like to see it."

He said it in no way suggestively, it sounded as though he were just interested. "You can sometime," she promised.

"Big? Small?" he questioned. "Either way it'd be valuable. At home and abroad. Tony is making quite a name for himself."

"It's a big painting actually. A lovely painting. The treatment of light and colour is wonderful."

Jude was thoroughly intrigued. Of course Tony wouldn't have been able to resist her as a model just as he hadn't been able to resist Jude's mother who had also been Tony's model. Cate Costello was not only beautiful she had so much more to her—the obvious intelligence, plus a bewitching quality that was playing havoc with all the defence mechanisms he had in place. "So when did he paint it? Before he went overseas?"

"A long time before that, I was twelve going on thirteen at the time." There was wistfulness, nostalgia in her voice. She'd been a child in a beautiful garden setting shimmering with light—banks of white azaleas behind her—staring out of the glowing canvas with big green eyes. She'd been red-blond then, her skin very white. Later her hair had deepened to its present bright copper.

Jude was battling all the surprises that were coming thick and fast. Her past seemed strewn with secrets. "So you've known Tony for years? What are you now, twenty-two?"

"Twenty-three my next birthday. Do you believe in fate, Jude?"

Even the sound of his name on her lips unsettled him. It sounded so silky—tender. "Yes, I do."

"Tony was a friend of my mother's. He's been a good friend to me."

"And your mother?" He glanced at her quickly. "You used the past tense."

A soft cry broke from her. Pure pain. A full moment of silence, then: "My mother…disappeared," she told him in a near inaudible voice, as though she couldn't endure to let the words pass her lips. "She's never been found."

Jude was utterly stunned. He was upset his question had been so clumsy. Great misery surrounded that heart-wrenching disclosure. "I'm so sorry, Cate. How dreadful for you."

"Beyond dreadful," she said. "A torture."

"I can imagine." The loss of his own mother approached that. "Her name was Costello?" he asked gently, wracking his brains to recall a story on a missing woman called Costello.

"No." She shook her head. "My mother remarried a couple of years after my father was killed in a car smash when I was ten. I loved him very much. He was so full of love and life and energy."

"How have you managed to rise above all this pain?" He wished it was light enough to see her expression. He was struck by the fact, her life like his, had been shattered by conflict and tragedy.

Her head averted she stared out the window. The stars over the ocean were thickly clustered; infinite acres of diamond daisies. "I'm an orphan like you only the chances of your mother still being alive are good. Do you never want to see her, Jude?"

He hesitated as though unsure what he could admit to. Finally he said, too harshly, "I can't let my mother back into my heart or my life again."

"That sounds very final." She winced at the bitter note of rejection even though she knew there was grief and suffering too.

He was quiet for a moment. "It is."

"I'd give anything just to know my mother was alive," Cate said. "To see her one more time." Her voice conveyed a wealth of emotion.

"And she disappeared just like that?" Jude looked directly at her. "There was a search of course?" There had to be…no one just disappeared.

She nodded. "Nationwide. My mother married a man called Carl Lundberg."

The name swam out of his subconscious. "Lundberg. I remember now." The case had attracted a lot of notoriety. Professor Lundberg was an eminent academic, wealthy in his own right, highly respected in the community. It had to be six or seven years back. Mrs Lundberg—she'd been much younger than her husband—had last been seen setting off with the family dog, a collie, on a walk through the national forest reserve adjacent to the Lundberg's large colonial home. Neither she nor the family dog had been seen again.

"It was as though my mother and our dog, Blaze, disappeared off the face of the earth," she said, sounding so lost and mournful he caught at her hand in an effort to comfort.

"I'm so sorry, Cate. Why does so much tragedy come into certain peoples' lives and bypass others? The only route to survival seems to be to accept. I remember it was a very baffling case. The file won't have been closed. The police never give up."

She nodded. ''They were very kind to me but sometimes it's almost impossible to find enough evidence to lay charges. I believe he killed her.''

Jude's heart rocked. He dared not speak for several fraught moments. ''Why would you believe that?'' he asked finally, keeping his tone very calm. ''The investigation would have been very thorough. The husband is always a prime suspect. You must have been around sixteen?''

''He did it,'' she repeated. ''Heaven knows why I'm telling you all this, you're the first person I've spoken to about it in years. He had an alibi of sorts—he claimed to have been at the university all day. He was seen by staff and students on and off and there was never enough to arrest him. Why would anyone suspect such a distinguished man? He had, still has, so many important friends and supporters.

''He acted as though his own life had come to an end. He played the distraught husband to the hilt. I was the jealous, paranoid, difficult daughter that he'd tried so hard to win over but never succeeded. I wouldn't allow him to take my father's place, he said. That was certainly true.'' She gave a brittle laugh. ''As though a man like that, a man in a mask, ever could. At the end of the day the police had nothing against him. I can't blame them for my rush to judgment. I was such a mess.''

''I'm not surprised,'' he said grimly. ''What you're saying is appalling. Obviously with your loss a terrible resentment towards your stepfather held sway, but have you never considered during these intervening years you could have been mistaken?''

''I'm not mistaken,'' Cate said through gritted teeth. ''I hate him. If my mother had never met him she'd still be alive.''

They were approaching the house. Both of them had fallen silent, both struck dumb. Jude was utterly pole-axed

by what he had learned. How could he possibly have foreseen this dramatic turn of events? He'd thought it would be
all routine; finalising Rogan's will, then taking a quiet vacation at home. That day dream had been blasted away.

There was so much he had to find out about the beautiful,
mysterious creature beside him. There was too much he
didn't understand. Why she had moved to this particular
town, so far off the beaten track? What was the mother's
connection to Tony Mandel? At the top of the list, what was
Cate's connection to her benefactor? In view of what she
had told him he now found it impossible to believe she had
deliberately drawn Lester Rogan into her net though the
possibility remained her mother could have bewitched
Lester. Was it possible she was Lester's natural daughter
and Lester found out years later? Jude had learned enough
about life to know just getting through it was a very bumpy
ride.

He'd left lights burning. They moved into the house, he
standing back so she could proceed him. Now that he had
her here he felt fractionally easier. The house was so peaceful, so welcoming with the shade of his father about.

She paused a moment in the entrance hall, with its bright
rug and golden polished floor, looking about her. "This is
a lovely old house," she said gently. "I love tropical ar-
chitecture. I've seen the house from the road many times
and admired it. I like going for drives Sunday afternoon,
looking at the local houses and the pole houses at the beach.
I much prefer this to the Rogan mansion. Glorious views,
but I don't care for the residence."

She moved into the living room where one of Tony
Mandel's magnificent bird paintings hung above the white
painted mantle. The painting, one of a number bought by
his father, was of a group of white jabirus, the tall Australian
storks, with black tails and bills standing out in contrast to

a turquoise-blue lagoon, a deeper blue sky with a trail of white clouds and lush tropical vegetation.

Jude turned on more lights to improve her viewing. That afternoon he'd slashed a dozen flower bracts of the very showy Red Ginger that grew in abundance in the garden, shoving them into a tall glass vase and placing them on the low coffee table as a splash of colour. His mother had always brought lots of flowers into the house. She'd been an expert at arrangements; wonderful imaginative showpieces that utilized a lot of big tropical leaves.

"You must have picked these," Cate said, touching a scarlet sprout. She liked the idea of his wanting to have flowers in the house.

He shrugged, suddenly consumed by inexpressible feelings. "I did my fair share of gardening when I was a kid. There was a time my parents were passionate about their garden."

"It's still a beautiful garden," she said. "Tony's painting looks marvellous up there. He gets a surreal quality into his work."

Jude nodded. "There are others scattered through the house." He didn't know why he added it but he did. "He painted my mother, too. Tony couldn't resist a beautiful woman."

She turned to stare at him, her copper head tilted a little to the side. "Do you still have it or did your mother—"

"Take it with her?" he interrupted more bitterly than he intended. A dead give-away. "She walked out with just the clothes on her back and never returned. The guy she went off with was a rich American. He could afford her."

She looked back at the arrangement of Red Ginger. "How very sad for your father and you. Where's the portrait now?"

"It's on the next floor. Dad did take it down, but evidently he put it back up. Looks like he never could stop loving her. You want to see it?''

"If that doesn't upset you?" For all his controlled demeanour she could see it would be a test.

"Come up. I'll take your overnight bag. The bedrooms are upstairs. It won't take a few minutes to make up the bed in the guest room. An old pal of my Dad's keeps the house aired and the grounds tidy.''

"Jimmy Dawson?" she smiled.

"Do you know Jimmy?" In the act of picking up her bag, he set it down again to stare at her.

"How wouldn't I get to know Jimmy? He's one of the local characters. He often pops in for a "yarn" or to bring me something of interest. He used to be a prospector, travelled all over the Outback. He's got opals, sapphires, garnets, carnelians and topaz. He has quite a collection of agates, too, chrysoprase—Chrysoprase is a translucent apple-green stone he says reminds him of my eyes.''

"A ladies' man is Jimmy," he commented dryly.

"Aren't they all?" she answered brightly enough, then appeared engulfed by unhappy thoughts.

"Come up," he repeated, to distract her, leading the way.

The same mahogany stair tread creaked as they walked up. Her hand clung lovingly to the beautiful carved banister.

The portrait of his mother held pride of place. It dominated the space at the end of the wide corridor. His father's bedroom, the main bedroom his parents had shared, gave directly off it. He'd kept to the bedroom of his boyhood at the other end of the house. There were four double bedrooms with en suite in all. The bedroom he had in mind for her was midway along the corridor.

Jude paused outside it to put down her overnight bag and turn on the light. Cate continued to walk compulsively towards the portrait of Sally Conroy. What she saw was a beautiful sexual woman revealed in her prime. There was no mistaking Jude's resemblance to his mother. The thick curly golden hair, the dazzling blue eyes that drew you in. Sally was smiling, not a big smile more enigmatic, the familiar dimple etched into her cheek. That smile, like her son's, had great power. Cate was lost in admiration thinking Tony must have been a little in love with this woman. The painting seemed brim full of it. Love. Sensuality. Sally was wearing a rose-pink blouse that tumbled off her creamy shoulders and dipped low over lovely full breasts. Quite a woman!

Jude came up quietly behind her. "I'm thinking now Tony must have been in love with her. The whole thing has a voluptuous quality. Or that was my mother."

"You're extraordinarily like her."

"In looks maybe." He answered in a clipped voice. "Let me show you your room. There's a choice if you're not happy with this one, but I think it's the nicer." He stood back while she walked in.

"You're being very chivalrous, Jude." Involuntary tears came to her eyes. She walked across the large room to the French doors giving her the opportunity to blink them away. She knew Jude Conroy's feelings towards her were highly ambiguous, yet he was concerned for her welfare.

"That's me," he said laconically, moving to open the glass doors. Jimmy had already fastened all the green shutters back when he was airing the house. "This has a good view of the beach. I might have to get rid of a couple of pandanus. They've grown huge." He walked out onto the verandah and she followed him, both of them taking in long draught of the fresh salt air.

"It's paradise in the tropics!" she murmured." No wonder Tony spent so many years north of Capricorn painting."

"What's Tony to you?" he found himself asking, leaning

his hands on the white painted balustrade and staring out into the perfumed night.

A broken-hearted sadness swept over her. Would she ever be free of it? "Tony loved my mother. He said he should have married her only my father came along to ruin his chances. It wasn't destined. Tony was destined to become famous. My father was destined to die. My stepfather—" She broke off, abruptly changing the subject. "The air's like silk! Oh, look!" She pointed, voice rising." There's someone on the beach. Where did she come from?"

Jude stared hard into the semidarkness. "I don't see a thing." For a surreal second he imagined he did.

"You must!" Her voice had a little throb of urgency in it. "Out there, look. A woman. Her long skirt is blowing in the breeze."

All right, a game then! "There's no one there, Cate," he said, revealing his scepticism. "You've heard the story, that's all."

"Story?" She turned an inquiring face to him, innocent green eyes, enormous, jewel-like.

"About Spirit Cove's resident ghost." He let his sceptical gaze rest on her. She could have been an angel sent from Heaven only he knew better. She was far more the white-skinned temptress.

"That's no ghost," she protested indignantly. "That's a woman walking on the beach. You don't believe me?"

"'Fraid not." He shook his head.

"Then let's take a look," she challenged. "She couldn't have gone far. Come on. Don't stand there all glinty eyed like I've made her up."

To his astonishment she turned away in a flurry of long hair like apricot silk. She was running down the corridor, down the staircase, making instinctively for the back door.

"Cate!" He caught her up, shaking his head. "I don't believe this!"

"I've got to see her."

He watched her unlock the door, then she was tearing away into the night, so fleet of foot he didn't even have time to grab her hand.

"Cate, Cate, calm down." He had no recourse but to follow her, his eyes adjusting quickly to the gloom. He had to pause to turn on a few more exterior lights in case both of them broke their necks. By the time he reached the picket gate, she was no more than a streak on the sandy path that led to the beach. She could move. He'd say that for her, but the dunes were laced with grasses that hooked into the sand like a trap. Some kind of alarm was in him and he realised, a dangerous excitement that was building every moment he was with her. No way could he allow it to get the better of him. He had to be resolute!

The lights from the deck were almost gone now. She was lost in the starry darkness. He knew a few moments of pure panic. Hell, he was nearly losing his mind over her.

"Cate," he yelled, tough as nails. "Come back here. Come on, Cate. I can't see a damned thing." There was no moon, only a billion stars crowding the black velvet sky.

Which way did she go? Left, or right? She'd been looking towards the right. He knew everyone who lived around here. Most of the residents of the Cove were retirees, getting on in years. They did their walking early morning and late afternoon. He headed off towards the right, the sand pouring into his Nikes. Now he could make out her slender shape.

"Cate, I'd be real pleased if you didn't do things like this," he shouted. It was a wonder she didn't jump into the surf. Why the heck did she have to be so fascinating? It made everything so much more difficult. He daren't let anything happen. Imagine that face on his pillow! That sweet slender body beside him! She was just crying out to be made love to. He had to force himself to remember he was supposed to be the level-headed lawyer with duties to discharge.

She was moving so fast back along the beach she near stumbled right into his arms. "I'm telling you she was there," she gasped, her breath sweet on his cheek. "It's impossible that I imagined her."

He steadied her by holding her shoulders. A big mistake. Her skin was the softest, the silkiest he had ever touched. "Don't worry. It was nothing. I'll take you back."

She stared up at him. Though she actually couldn't see the expression on his face, it was too dark, she felt keenly aware he thought the whole thing might have been a stunt. "Jude, I saw her quite distinctly, that's why I followed her. She was wearing a long white dress."

"Even if you'd run faster you'd never have caught her up," he said wryly. Spirit Cove's ghost had been dead for over sixty years. He found himself putting an arm around her shoulders, excusing it as humouring her. He began to steer her back towards the house. Desire for her was mounting so hot and rapid he truly believed his ingrained caution might be thrown to the winds unless they moved off the beach. This minute. Night alone had special power. People didn't behave quite the same in the dark.

She was still protesting, anxious for him to believe her. "I tell you her long skirt was flapping in the breeze."

"Sure it wasn't a trick of the eye?" He wasn't about to tell her his own mother claimed to have seen a woman dressed in white walking along the beach at night. It wasn't long after that his mother left. He remembered now part of the myth was that the ghost was only seen by those at a crossroads in their lives.

"It was a real woman, Jude." She lifted her head in an

appealing gesture. "She must have gone up the dunes to one of the houses."

"She wouldn't have had time," he considered, shaking his head. "Our house is fairly isolated as you can see. My neighbours are quite a distance either way. It had to be a trick of the eye, Cate, there was no woman. It could have been the sea mist." He wasn't about to get into any discussion on the paranormal.

"Okay." She expelled a long breath. "I can see I won't convince you. I don't want an argument." Nevertheless she promptly broke away, leaving him to run after her yet again. "You're a witch aren't you?" he called, half laughing, half off balance. "All right then, I'll race you to the house. You've got a good start."

She said not a word, but continued to sprint away making good going in the soft sand. She was almost at the white picket gate that closed off the house from the beach when she lost her footing as dune grasses wound themselves tightly around her ankle and held it fast. She went over onto the soft sand, lifting her arms and laughing delightedly.

He thought he'd never heard a sound so exquisitely seductive. "Get me out of this sand trap!" she yelled.

He closed the distance to where she lay. "That's it! No more races for the night. The things you expect of me!" At least they were within range of the lights from the house. They shone on the flowerlike purity of her skin and her long copper hair, the light garments that covered her. He reached down for her and she grasped his hand. He truly only intended to pull her to her feet but somehow he didn't stop until he had her locked in his arms.

It was stunning, but he was kissing her, kissing her. It went on for ages, her soft full lips opened erotically beneath his, the taste ambrosial. His hand somehow was resting high up, alongside her breast. He had only to move his fingers for his palm to cup its exquisite contours. How he wanted to. "Oh God!" he whispered into her mouth. He was losing the battle for control, his blood pounding hot and feverish.

Things were happening so fast he could scarcely follow. He only knew he didn't want to let her go. He couldn't get enough of her. If only he could lower her down onto the sand, pull off that little top, bend his head to her naked breasts. She was doing nothing to curb him. Her body was pressed hard against his, her arousal seemingly as intense as his own.

"Jude, please…" Yet she was holding on to him with both hands. Where was this going to end? In a bed? His tongue played with hers, their bodies thrusting, grinding, one against the other. He had a heart-stopping vision of her naked beside him except for the beautiful silver bracelet she wore around her wrist. The perfume of gardenias clung to her; clung to her clothes, her face, her skin, clung to him. He'd never experienced such a furore over a kiss.

Suddenly the whole sequence changed. She broke away panting, as though she suddenly realized it was very wrong of her to trust him. Both of them were breathing hard, as though they were having difficulty getting enough air into their lungs.

"I'm sorry." For a moment he couldn't think of another thing to say. "I'd no right to do that. The last thing I want to do is frighten you. Put it down to the night." He didn't put voice to his craving though she would have felt his rock hardness against her. He wanted to catch her back, make love to her until she moaned and didn't know whether to faint. He wanted to tell her about his scars, his sense of betrayal and rejection, his childhood baggage, above all. He knew with her own experiences of pain and despair she would understand.

Her answer was no more than a whisper. "It's all right, Jude. We're both off balance."

Off balance yes, but it was perfect. Kisses that made a man tremble. But then he'd wanted to kiss her since he'd first laid eyes on her in the little timber church. Imagine wanting someone so much at first sight! He was more than half in love with her yet he knew so little about her. It was even possible she wasn't as truly beautiful as she appeared to be. Allowing himself to fall further under her spell would be like jumping into a tropical lagoon with no thought of what might be lurking beneath the water.

Neither spoke a word until they were inside the house with the back door locked and the bolt shot.

"I'll go check on the bed linen," he said, giving them both a chance to calm down. "I haven't had much to eat, have you?"

With surprise she realized she was hungry, even ravenous. "I was thinking of preparing something when that appalling Ralph arrived. What have you got?"

"Nothing much." He shrugged, amazed he sounded normal. "We could have an omelette, toast, there's quite a bit of roast chicken left, bacon. Fresh garden herbs in a jar—I like the smell of them in the kitchen. Tea, coffee, a packet of shortbread biscuits. Jimmy left a few supplies but I have to do lots of shopping."

Wisely she didn't offer to help him make up the bed. "I'll whip up the omelettes. I just hope you've got the right pan. That's absolutely vital."

"I'm sure you'll find it," he called back as he mounted the stairs.

When he returned she had set the table in the family room, using the glass-topped wicker table surrounded by four comfortably upholstered chairs. She had found bright yellow place mats, cutlery, condiments, a couple of tulip shaped wineglasses. "I thought we might have a glass of the chardonnay, okay? Help me sleep."

"Sure. Want me to open the bottle?" He was pleased with himself he sounded so cool. She was so beautiful and he had palmed her breast.

"Please. The omelettes are ready." Cate was having difficulty controlling her own excitement. It was like a brilliant dancing light.

"So you found the right pan?" He located the wine opener, deftly uncorked the bottle.

"You have everything one could possibly need."

He just saved himself from saying his mother had been a great cook consequently she'd accumulated every bit of equipment a serious chef would need.

The wine was nicely chilled. He poured each of them a glass, passed hers to her. "Cheers!" He held up his glass in salute.

"Cheers!" she responded. "Take a seat."

He laughed, unaware of the vivid animation in his face. "You walk right into my house and start cooking."

"Hope you like it." She set a plate before him.

"Say this looks very professional!" He stared down at the fluffy concoction on his plate. His didn't turn out like this.

"I'm really good with omelettes." She turned to him with a smile. "Plenty of practice and help from recipe books. I love cookbooks, I love books period."

"So I saw back at the gallery."

"My father always encouraged me to read," she said almost dreamily. "He said very little about his early life but he did tell me once the house where he was born had a wonderful library."

She had his absolute attention. "How interesting! Revealing

as well. A house with a wonderful library probably was quite a house.''

''I suppose.'' From her expression she regretted having said anything at all. ''I didn't have any parmesan so I grated your cheddar,'' she told him, briskly changing the subject. ''I've used your chives as well and I'm afraid six of your eggs.''

''That okay. I'll go shopping tomorrow. This looks good.''

''Eat up before it goes cold.''

''You're going to join me?'' His eyes couldn't seem to let go of her.

''Of course.''

''Hasn't this been an unexpected night?'' He watched her moving around his kitchen as though it were her own. She looked back suddenly and caught him, the colour rising to her cheeks.

''It has indeed.'' She joined him at the table, bringing with her hot toast and curls of butter in a white bowl.

She'd worked fast. He was amazed how hungry he was. Amazed about everything. She was almost a total stranger yet he felt as though she'd always been in his life. That wasn't easy to understand. He allowed himself to toy with thoughts of a soul mate. Two wandering souls destined to be joined. Maybe there was something in it after all.

The omelette was so good. ''Have you someone in your life, a boyfriend?'' he asked after a while. Hell, he hadn't planned on saying that. Why did he? Answer: because he desperately wanted to know.

She shook her head, put down her fork.

''I have no idea why I asked you that,'' he said.

''Particularly when you've half convinced yourself Lester Rogan was my sugar daddy.''

It was his turn to shake his head. "I can't believe you'd go in for that sort of thing."

"You don't want to believe?"

They exchanged a long glance. "I surely don't. Besides, you've got too much character and depth. And you're wounded. You've got a wounded heart."

"Takes one to know one, Jude," she said quietly.

They shared the bottle of wine and afterwards he made the coffee, the two of them moving of one accord onto the spacious deck. "I think I saw a ghost tonight," she confided, having arrived at her conclusion. "What's more I'm prepared to stick by it."

His low laugh made her tingle. "What are you trying to do? Frighten me to death?"

"I'm not afraid of ghosts," she said.

"I don't believe in them. I can't."

She studied him with those jewel-like eyes, the pupils extended tenderly. "That's not true, Jude. I'm sure you feel your father moving about the house? You feel him as a gentle presence. You smile to yourself when the tread creaks on the staircase."

He couldn't deny it. "How do you know that?"

"Maybe I have extrasensory perception. Maybe losing my mother so suddenly, so violently, is part of it."

"You're sure violence was done, Cate?" There were so many secrets to be drawn out of her.

"Yes, it seemed like a futureless future without my mother. I only pray it was fast." She focused on the floodlit garden with its abundant fruit trees.

"Listen to me, Cate." He reached for her hand. "It'll be all right."

She shook her head. "It'll never be all right."

"Was your stepfather a violent man?" That was not rare

even in a man of culture. He could have been the classic street angel, home devil Jude thought.

"That's what makes it so unreal." She couldn't keep calm with his thumb warm on her pulse. She made a pretence of wanting her coffee and he let her go. "He never laid a finger on her. There was no physical abuse but she came to fear him."

A strange feeling passed over Jude, like a surge of dread. "It sounds like you feared him, too. He must have been very controlling?"

In front of his eyes her whole body went rigid. "He was. Mum almost had to have his permission to go out the door." Her eyes glittered with tears she blinked fiercely away.

It was all he could do not to take her protectively into his arms. "I understand why you couldn't bear to live in the same house as him."

She lowered her head, biting her lip. "I never ever want to lay eyes on him again, but I know I will."

"Cate, one way or another it will come right." His words came like a solemn promise.

"Not in a thousand years!"

"I understand how you feel, but survival is dependant on acceptance, we both know that. Ultimately we have to move on. Are you absolutely sure your mother wasn't planning a new life somewhere? My father trusted my mother. So did I. Look what she did to us."

Cate nodded. "She failed you. I'm so sorry. But my mother would never have left without me." She cleared her long hair from the side of her face. "I was sixteen years old, I wasn't even finished high school. We loved one another. She has never touched her bank accounts nor used her credit card. In March of next year she'll be declared legally dead."

He could see she was broken-hearted. "You hated the man who replaced your father?" That happened, too.

"He never replaced him." Her expression changed to one of swift contempt. "He was charming to begin with—they always are—he entertained a lot. Everyone liked my mother. She was a wonderful hostess and so pretty."

"She would be if you resemble her."

"I don't," she murmured. "I'm my father's side of the family. I have the Costello colouring. Or so my father told me."

"You don't know your father's family?" he asked in surprise. "You've never had any contact?" That, too, was extraordinary but it happened.

She shook her head. "No. I think there must have been some trouble, some family rift. Besides, they're a long way away. Ireland. West of Ireland, I think. One day I'll find out, but so much has happened. My father came to Australia on his own, I know that. He was fresh out of university, an architect. He joined a firm in Sydney, although apparently he never saw eye to eye with them about anything. He went into private practice, but eventually he became a university lecturer. That's where my parents met Lundberg. It had to be the worst day of their lives."

"So what happened after your mother disappeared?" He stared at her intently. "Feeling as you did how did you continue to live with your stepfather?"

"I didn't." She shuddered. "Not even vacations. My mother had a close friend, Deborah, and she took control. She suggested to my stepfather it would be best if I boarded until I finished school. He was very much against it, but she managed to persuade him. I think she exerted some sort of pressure. She never liked him, either. After I finished school, I hit the road."

"Hit the road? Pardon me? What does that mean exactly?"

She looked back at him, a strange little smile hovering on her lips. "You surely don't think I was going to stay around even with Deborah to protect me."

"You're obviously afraid of him?" His face darkened.

"Jude, I'm waiting for him to turn up one day," she confessed.

He reached out and took her hand. "If you're afraid of him why don't you do something about it?"

"Like what? Take out a restraining order? They don't work. Much better to hide."

"Is that why you're here?" He shook her fingers as though he wanted to shake it out of her. "You're hiding out?"

"Tony and I worked it out between us. He knew what had happened to my mother. He was devastated but I never told him what was happening to me. I didn't even understand what was happening—I told you I was a real mess. It seemed it was impossible to get through to anyone outside Deborah. Everyone admired him you see, he was—is—Professor Lundberg, and he gave lots of money to the university."

He could well see how it was. "So where were you before you came here? The years in-between?"

"I've been a gypsy," She laughed. Not a happy sound. "I've never been in any one place for any length of time except for two years as a governess on an Outback station. I was safe there. I'm safe here. Or so I thought before Ralph Rogan arrived, and then you turned up with your mind-blowing news."

"Which we haven't really touched on."

"Not tonight." It sounded like a plea. "I just can't handle it tonight."

"Okay. And this business with the crystals?"

"My Outback friends and my own wanderings. Eventually I started to make good overseas contacts. People have been so kind and helpful to me. People who love crystals generally love people. Perhaps the crystals influence their lives. I've learned such a lot."

"Why did you leave?" he asked, wanting to find out every last thing about her.

She shrugged evasively. "The children, a boy and a girl, twins, went away to boarding school. I had to move on or stay and marry someone. There's a shortage of women in the bush, but marriage isn't on my agenda."

"Why not?"

There was a profound sadness in her face. "I'm a bit like you, Jude. I don't think I could ever trust anyone enough to marry them."

"There's a statement, Cate."

"I can't change how I feel. Trust is something that has been stolen from me. But somehow you've reached me. Maybe it's because you know all about heartbreak." She lifted her face to the sparkling stars. "I think I'll go to bed, if that's okay with you? I feel really odd, all keyed up yet exhausted. I don't seem to be able to take in all that's happening. In fact I have no idea what the heck is going on."

"Me, either," he declared.

The light caught in his blond hair. In the balmy salt air it was a mass of tousled waves and curls. She had actually felt those waves and curls beneath her hands. It was a source of wonder. She thought she might be coming seriously adrift.

"Tomorrow when you're feeling better we'll have to discuss the will."

"I don't want his money, Jude," Cate said, beginning to gather up the coffee cups and saucers. "I don't even want to discuss it. To tell you the truth, I don't actually believe it. Lester Rogan was nothing to me, I swear. The only reason he came into my life was as my landlord.''

''For all that he's left you what most people including me would consider a fortune.''

She didn't even ask how much. It didn't belong to her anyway. ''I'll take getting my mother back, Jude,'' she said sadly and turned away.

There were rough times ahead.

CHAPTER FIVE

THE HOUSE was silent when he woke up. He turned his head to check on the bedside clock. The digital display told him it was almost half eight. God, he'd slept in. Why wouldn't he? With Cate half way down the corridor he hadn't drifted off like a baby. He'd tossed and turned for hours, his body in a high state of arousal. Not remarkable after those passionate kisses. She shouldn't have laughed like that, she shouldn't have parted her mouth for him.

"Come on, Jude buddy, get up!" He issued himself the instruction.

There was movement in the grounds, the murmur of voices. He pulled on a pair of shorts, ran a hand over his unruly hair and walked to the balcony.

"Jimmy, that you down there?"

A moment later Jimmy appeared from beneath the balcony, a nuggety little man with a shiny brown nut of a pate. "Howya goin' there, me boy?" He gave Jude a huge conspiratorial wink.

"You're early!"

"You've been in the city too long, son. I've been up since five. I've got Catey with me."

"Have you now?"

Cate appeared, dressed in the same sarong-type skirt with a different top, sleeveless, low-neck, yellow to match the yellow hibiscus on her multicoloured skirt.

"Good morning!" She turned a smiling face up to him. "Jimmy's been keeping me company."

"Enjoying meself," said Jimmy with relish. "Ya betta come down, son. Catey's starvin', aren't ya love?"

"I am now. The admiral Jimmy has brought fresh croissants and little Danish pastries from the bake shop," she told Jude, reaching out to pick an avocado off a tree, cradling it in her hand. "I love avocados."

"Then you'll have to try me guacamole, Catey, with home made tortilla," Jimmy suggested helpfully. "I use pita bread at a pinch. I reckon no one makes it better," he added modestly. "I've had it tons of times in the West Indies when I go over for the cricket. 'Struth, seems to me those West Indians eat avocados at ever meal. Bigger ones than that, love. They breed 'em huge! You oughta try me guacamole with poached chicken and a cumin flavoured sauce."

"Only if you cook it, Jimmy," she teased.

"You're on. Are ya comin' down, son?" Jimmy peered up at Jude again.

"Sure. Give me five minutes."

He made it in less, face splashed with cold water, hair brushed, a white T-shirt to team with his shorts.

Jimmy was reclining in a sea grass chair in the family room adjoining the kitchen, while Cate was busy making the coffee. "Catey has been tellin' me about last night," Jimmy said with an expression of great disgust.

Jude shot her a quick glance. "Okay, Cate, what did you tell?"

"Nuthin' about you two, you galah," Jimmy reassured him with rough affection. "That brute of a Ralph! A real bastard like his dad. Now there was a guy who hated his fellow man."

Cate set the coffee to perk. "I've got a big surprise for you, Jimmy," she offered wryly. "Lester Rogan left me a lot of money which gave Ralph a very good reason to come calling."

Jimmy sat up, looking dumbfounded. He tore his eyes away from Cate to stare at Jude. "What is that all about? Ya not going to tell me Les finally turned religious?"

"Come on, Jimmy, we both know Lester wasn't a practising Christian," Jude scoffed. "The fact is Cate claims to have no idea why Lester left her the bulk of his fortune."

The astounding news set up a facial tick beneath Jimmy's right eye. He leapt to his feet curling his fingers strongly around Jude's arm. "Jude, me old mate, the worst word in that sentence is "claims." If Catey says she doesn't know why Les left her the whole caboodle she doesn't."

It was Jimmy in champion mode. All he needed was a crusader's cape, Jude thought. "Legal word, Jimmy," he said, only half humorously. Jimmy's wry fingers had the grip of a sand crab.

"Isn't that just typical Les!" Jimmy exclaimed, letting go of Jude's arm. "I swear he hated Ralph more'an Ralph hated him. You're not gunna tell me Les left poor old Myra out in the cold? A lost soul if every there was one. What a life of wedded bliss she's had with Les! What about Melly? I ask ya, is she ever gunna grow up? And Ralph, always snarling. He is the man's only son however. Les surely didn't forget about them?"

Jude's gaze moved in Cate's direction. She was giving all her attention to setting the table. Or so it seemed. In the centre was a copper bowl filled with vibrant orange hibiscus. He loved little touches like that even if they did remind him of his mother. She had one tucked into her hair. "They've all been extremely well provided for if you don't count the fact they're the man's family. It never occurred to any of them, including me they wouldn't get the lot."

"Ya dad knew," Jimmy scratched his bald pate. "I wonder what he made of it."

"You bet your life he didn't think Lester had gone senile."

"And Matty told no one?"

"It would have been unethical for him to do so, Jimmy. You know that."

"This is amazing. I'm gobsmacked."

"We all are, Jimmy," Cate said dryly. "In fact I feel threatened. That's why I'm here with Jude."

"A real gentleman is Jude," Jimmy smiled a big smile. "I hope he stays that way," he cackled.

Jude laughed. Jimmy looked as though he knew what Jude's night had been like.

"European style breakfast this morning," Cate informed them. "Come along now. It's ready."

"Have you made me tea, love?" Jimmy asked. "Coffee brings on cardiac arrest."

"I already knew to make tea for you, Jimmy." Cate reassured him, bringing the teapot to the table. "Coffee for the two of us, Jude. Okay?"

"Fine." He held her chair while she slid into it.

"Gee, these look good. Melt in the mouth," Jimmy said, helping himself to a croissant. "I suppose they're life-threatening as well. Everything you read tells you to stop eatin' this, stop eatin' that. Which, I'm pleased to say I mostly ignore. So…" He buttered his buttery croissant lavishly, then added a big scoop of his own cumquat marmalade. "Nuthin' occurs to you, love, about Les?"

Cate shook her head. "No. I have no idea why he named me in his will. I look on it more as a disaster than a miracle, Jimmy. You've come into the gallery—"

"Barged in more like it," Jimmy interjected.

"When Mr Rogan was there," Cate finished off.

"Wasn't gunna leave you alone with that old lecher," Jimmy explained, his voice dripping disgust.

Cate looked straight into Jude's narrowed, watchful eyes. "I promise you I never saw that side of Lester Rogan. I never saw him as an ageing Casanova."

Jimmy scoffed. "Les could have given Casanova lessons."

"Please, Jimmy, you've never really listened to me," Cate pleaded. "It wasn't like that at all."

"No, it wasn't me, darlin'." Jimmy fired up. "Lester was smart enough to register I was right on to him. Me and Gwennie."

Jude's eyebrows shot up. "You can't mean Miss Forsyth?"

"The very same person," Jimmy said with satisfaction. "Gwennie and me have been keepin' our eye on Cate since she arrived in town."

"You've no idea how kind they've been," Cate looked toward Jude, the sweetest expression on her face. He wouldn't have been human if that smile didn't make some of his anxieties melt.

"Watchin' over her like a couple of guardian angels," Jimmy said, looking happy. "Oh my, won't Gwennie be shocked! We thought we were protectin' Cate from Les now he's gone and left her a bloody fortune. Gwennie will want to start up an investigation. Ya know what's she's like."

Jude was forced to smother another laugh. Gwennie was Miss Gwendoline Forsyth—town character who claimed to have regular out of body experiences—former teacher of English, History (Modern and Ancient) Speech and Drama, at Saint Agatha's private school for girls in Cairns, until her retirement. That had to be over a decade ago, putting "Gwennie" square in her seventies. "I think the two of you better leave that to me," Jude suggested. "How is Miss Forsyth these days? Still doing her astral travelling?"

Jimmy laughed. "With clouds for her magic carpets. She

was in Tibet the other day, she and the Dalai Lama were burning incense together. She's fine. She still goes runnin' on the beach and she's seventy-five.''

"She's a running-walking advertisement for exercise," Cate laughed. "I just hope I look and feel as good if I ever get to Miss Forsyth's age."

"And she's got perfect teeth," Jimmy said, sounding proud. "Look at me I've got fillings." He opened his mouth and tapped his back teeth. "None of which helps Cate here. What are we gunna do about Ralph?" Jimmy addressed Jude while Cate refilled Jimmy's empty cup. "We can't have him botherin' Cate."

"No, we can't," Jude clipped off. "Cate needs protecting. I'll sort it out, Jimmy. It'd be a huge help if we could establish the connection between Lester and Cate. There has to be one. So, Cate—" he looked across the table at her "—I need to go over a few things with you, including letting you read the will. You were too upset last night."

"I'll go if you want to talk privately," Jimmy offered helpfully, regarding one then the other.

Cate shook her head. "No, Jimmy. Please stay. Jude may be stopping just short of saying it, but I know he's sceptical."

"He is a lawyer, darlin'," Jimmy snorted.

"I've got nothing to tell." Cate spread her hands.

"Why did you come up here, Catey?" Jimmy asked earnestly. "Ya never did tell us. Gwennie reckons you must be on the run from somebody. A beautiful girl like you burying herself in a little sugar town."

"This is magnificent country, Jimmy," Cate protested, meeting his eyes. "Where the rain forest meets the reef, isn't that it? I enjoy the peace and the beauty, I love my gallery. I sell quite a bit when the tourists come into town."

"Ah, darlin', you could be a movie star," Jimmy chortled, an admiring look on his face, tanned to the texture of soft leather. "I'm an old man seventy and more and I can't take me eyes off ya. She's beautiful, isn't she?" Jimmy appealed to the silent Jude.

"And mysterious." Jude shot Cate a sapphire glance.

"Look, I think I should go." Jimmy rose to his feet. "That tea was lovely, Catey. You make it just right. It's an art, you know. You two need to talk. What about if I ask Gwennie to join us at lunch, Jude? Cate must come of course."

"That's nice of you, Jimmy, but I really should open the gallery," Cate responded, sounding not all that determined.

"Struth, love, you're rich!" Jimmy burst out laughing. "You can afford to come to lunch. Gwennie knows more about the Rogans than anyone. She taught poor little Mel and I know Myra used to confide in her. Gwennie has to be the best listener in the world. She might be able to see some connection?"

Jude's expression was doubtful. "When did Lester Rogan settle in the district exactly? He was around all my life, Ralph and I are the same age."

Jimmy scratched his polished pate. "It had to be a year or two before he married Myra. We were all placing bets on which local girl he was gunna choose. Not that Myra wasn't pretty in those days but it helped a lot her dad was makin' quite a bit of money buyin' and sellin' land. He was one of our first developers as a matter of fact. He was the one who got Les into the business, though Les didn't come up here penniless like most young fellas. He had money behind him even then. From where I don't know. Never talked about a family. Not as far as I know. Gwennie might remember something. She was invited to the weddin'. I wasn't. I wasn't far enough up the social scale. Ya mum and dad went."

Jude's expression momentarily darkened, imagining his father thinking he was going to be happily married forever. "Ask Miss Forsyth by all means," he said eventually. "I'd love to see her again. She might be able to clear up a few things as well. Okay with you, Cate?"

"We need all the help we can get, don't we?" Cate answered, nodding her head.

Let's hope it's something you can live with, Jude prayed.

On his way to the front door Jimmy turned back to Jude with a question. "A table for four at Elio's? Inside, or out?"

"Out," Jude nodded. "I like it in the courtyard. Make it for 1:00 p.m."

"Ya won't know me, Catey, when you see me wearin' some nice duds!" Jimmy promised.

"I'll look forward to it," Cate was still smiling when she began stacking the cups, saucers and plates. "We ate every last crumb of Jimmy's welcome offering," she said lightly, aware of the seriousness of Jude's expression. "I'll need to go back home." She moved towards the kitchen. "I can't hide out here forever."

"I suppose not." Not if he had to continue to hold her at arm's length. Cate Costello was the most powerfully intriguing woman he had ever met. "This whole business is very odd." He turned his head so he could continue to look at her. "People don't leave a fortune to total strangers, or near enough."

"They just leave it to dog's homes, cat's homes and the like," she offered half flippantly.

"People who do that generally have no one else in the world. Lester Rogan had a family."

"Yet he bequeathed the bulk of his fortune to me." She swept her hair back over her shoulder, a sure sign of agitation. "Do you think I can see the will please?"

"Of course. I'll go get it." Jude heard the edginess in her

voice. He was feeling more than a little on edge himself. For someone who had laboured to maintain a fail-safe self assured facade Cate with very little effort was putting him into a spin.

When he returned with the document he placed it in her hand. "Go to Page Two."

"Thank you." She wandered back into the living room, taking a chair at the glass-topped table. Every now and again she looked up at him, her expression grave. "This will was made over two years ago. Before I even came here. It revokes all other wills."

"Yes," Jude confirmed briefly. Ralph had previously been the main beneficiary.

"It says here I own land, houses, buildings. Even the gallery is mine—"

"Money, everything."

She shook her head helplessly. "He gave no indication he would ever do such a thing."

"Tell me again what you talked about?"

He sounded calm and courteous but Cate wasn't happy with the glitter in his eyes. "Jude, what good would that do?"

"Let me decide. He asked you about your childhood; your mother, your father, your stepfather, your entire life before you fled up here?"

She stared into his handsome, charming face, seeing another side to him. The professional. "Why do you give me the strong impression you're not believing a word I say?"

"That's not true!" He angled his dark golden head at her. "But I need answers, Cate. You need to come up with them."

She shook her head almost angrily. "I've told you I don't have any answers."

Jude took a seat opposite her, holding up a palm. "You're

not telling me everything, Cate. I'm sure there are some things you prefer left in the dark.''

"Like what?'' she asked, a warning brightness in her eyes. "Next you're going to say I was sleeping with Lester Rogan.''

"Were you?'' he asked bluntly.

She made to jump up, but he reached out and held her fine narrow wrist, not applying any pressure, but locking it all the same. "Cate?'' he asked quietly.

"You're working on that assumption and I bitterly resent it,'' she said, waiting for him to remove his hand. Such a disturbing sensation. Warm, tingling, never bruising. "Lester Rogan may have been a lustful man but he didn't act that way around me.''

"So there was nothing sexual?''

"How many times do I have to tell you,'' she asked in despair.

"Forgive me, but I have to come up with something to put the brakes on the Rogan family. You saw Ralph in action. He's in a very dangerous mood.''

She looked away. "He chilled my blood, and on the subject of 'sexual' if you hadn't arrived I doubt if he would have backed off. He's a pig.''

"Sure. You don't have to convince me. Running through our options, next on the agenda is a blood tie. You don't see that as a possibility?''

Her green eyes filled with something like horror. "Until I came up here I'd never seen Lester Rogan before in my life.''

"Tell me about your parents,'' he invited quietly. "Start with your mother. I know it's a terribly painful subject but can you try? Would your mother have known Lester Rogan at some stage of her life?''

"No, she wouldn't,'' Cate moaned in frustration.

"How would you know? For all his faults and failings Lester Rogan as a young man would have been a pretty impressive looking guy. Plenty of girls hang around Ralph for that matter."

"That's a mystery to me," Cate said acidly. "I think he's horrible. I can't think my mother would ever have been involved with someone like Lester Rogan. She was only twenty when she married my father. Tony on his own admission loved her and wanted to marry her but she gave her heart to Dad."

"What was your mother's maiden name?" Jude asked

Cate rose from the table quickly. "I'm sorry, Jude, but I can't talk about my mother. It's all too raw and alive."

"Please."

"Courtney."

He stared up at her. "Please try to bear with me for just a moment. She was born in Australia?"

"Yes. My father wasn't. I told you last night, he was born in Ireland. He was a clever, cultured man, a gentleman. I was so proud of him."

"I wonder if it's possible he knew Lester Rogan?" Jude mused.

"They weren't in prison together if that's what you mean?" Cate countered sharply, visibly becoming more upset by the moment. "You're a lawyer, Jude, not a policeman."

"I'm sorry. I don't want to upset you but lawyers and policeman have something in common. They both have to carry out investigations. We're trying to establish the link between you or some member of your family to Lester Rogan. Surely Rogan's an Irish name? Rogan, Regan, Reagan?"

"So what?" She sat down again, staring at him. "Irish immigrants poured into Australia. There are more Irish outside Ireland than in. Nearly everyone here, apart from Asian migrants, have antecedents from England, Ireland or Scotland. Lester Rogan had a broad Australian accent. He may have been very rich but he didn't speak like an educated man. I suppose you would have to call him a rough diamond. My father had a lovely speaking voice. I can't see any connection whatever to Rogan. I'd like to go home, Jude.''

The room seemed very still. Just the two of them trying to absorb what was happening to them, neither able to put aside that inflammatory incident on the beach. ''I'll take you.''

''I'm sorry if I sound ungrateful.''

Abruptly Jude pushed his chair back and stood up. Just looking at her he experienced an upsurge of primitive desire that shocked him. He had to move to curb it. Losing control could turn out to be disastrous. This beautiful creature had suffered enough. ''We do have to talk, Cate.'' He reverted to his professional voice. ''I have to say as well, I'm not at all happy about your staying at the gallery at night.''

''I don't have any option.'' She willed her voice not to tremble. Ralph Rogan had frightened her and she didn't frighten easily. Her mind seized on an image of him lumbering towards her, the scraping sound of his shoes, that peculiar look in his eyes.

''I repeat, you can stay here.'' Maybe he was too chivalrous for his own good? What did he really know about Cate Costello beyond the fact she was so beautiful and so poignant she made his heart melt. Then there was her traumatic background, the mystery of her mother's disappearance, the questions hanging over the stepfather. Had the stepfather been instrumental in the mother's disappearance or were Cate's suspicions fuelled by distrust and dislike?

There were dangerous and disturbing depths to the whole story.

"You'll be quite safe," he tacked on when she didn't speak.

"Will I?" She gave a brittle little laugh. "You're not looking for an affair, are you, Jude? Something to tide you over the holidays?"

"That would mess things up good and proper wouldn't it?" he said harshly. "I'm attracted to you, Cate. I can't hide that. Not after last night, but I have a job to do. I don't want you back at the gallery for a very good reason. Even if he was warned off by me and the police, I don't think Ralph would have the brains to stay away. To make it worse, he drinks. He's been getting drunk since he was fourteen years old."

"So you think he'd harm me?"

"Cate, you think so, too."

"Maybe I could stay with Miss Forsyth?" She bit her lip, considering." I know she'd take me in at the drop of a hat. She and Jimmy have been very kind and supportive."

"So you're scared of me?" he asked with a half smile.

She looked into his sizzling blue eyes trying to fathom her exact emotions towards him. "What do you expect me to say, I'd rather be with you?"

"Well…I come with the house. There's plenty of room here. As I recall Miss Forsyth's place is pretty much on the small side. I'm sure she's filled it with her amazing cats. She's a teeny weeny bit crazy, you know."

Cate's tense expression eased into a smile. "Eccentric," she corrected. "Aren't you worried Rogan might come here? Knowing you were sheltering me would make him very angry."

"Angrier than he is already?" Jude raised a mocking brow. "Don't worry, I'm sure the last time Ralph and I came to blows is still fresh in his memory. We don't have to discuss it right now. Let's get you home."

CHAPTER SIX

FIFTEEN minutes later Jude turned off the beach road and into the cul-de-sac where Cate had her gallery. She no longer had to rent it, he thought. It was hers thanks to Lester Rogan. To any reasonable mind that bespoke a connection Cate up to date had vehemently denied. There was nothing unusual about that, he'd often had to wade through client's lies and omissions, but to this day Cate Costello was the most mysterious of them all. She no longer needed to work…it had fallen to him to confirm overnight she had become a multimillionairess. That should solve all her financial problems for a lifetime. But she had other huge problems. Top of the list, the previously cited main beneficiary, Ralph Rogan, Lester's only son.

The instant they pulled into the parking bay Cate turned to him. She was all eyes and delicate high cheekbones, her soft luscious mouth free of lipstick. For some reason he found that incredibly erotic. The now familiar throb of desire started up in his loins. Was it possible a woman could reach out and touch not only a man's body but his heart and soul? The worst possible scenario was she could be playing him like a flute.

"I don't want to go in." The expression on her face held more than a trace of alarm.

He smiled, endeavouring to humour her. "I can understand that, Cate, but we have to. You want to check on things…change for lunch."

"He's been here." A little frisson rippled visibly through her body.

"You mean again?" He caught her mood, tried to steady her with a hand on her shoulder. "If you don't want to go in, stay here. Let me check it out."

"No, we'll go together." She hesitated only a moment. She unbuckled her seat belt and sprang out of the car with near kinetic energy making not towards the gallery entrance but the rear of the house.

Jude sprinted after her thinking it was becoming a habit. He closed in on her, making sure he was first to pound onto the deck.

"Is everything okay?" She waited at the bottom of the steps, staring up at him, a little breathless, holding her side. Her whole body was tense as piano wire.

He looked through the picture windows, cold anger sweeping over him. Even knowing Ralph and what he was capable of he could scarcely believe his eyes. "Stay here," he said sharply.

The back door had been jemmied open. It gave with the slightest push. Inside was pandemonium. The place had been ransacked. There was not a piece of furniture that hadn't been disturbed or thrown over. The large book case at the far end of the room was built in otherwise Jude was sure it would have been sent crashing to the polished floor. As it was, the books were scattered, some obviously flung, all over the room. It was immediately clear Ralph had taken his revenge.

By the time Jude walked into the bedroom, involuntarily sucking in his breath in anticipation of what he might find, Cate was at his side. She stared in horror at the upheaval. Her clothes had been dragged out of the walk-in wardrobes and flung to the floor. Drawers had been pulled out of chests the contents spilled. Ornaments were smashed. Inexplicably the portrait of her as a girl had escaped any sort of violation.

No accounting for that, Jude thought, when so much other damage had been done.

The bathroom was heavy with scents from the contents of a variety of broken bottles that littered the tiles; perfume, bath salts, mouthwash, fragments of blue and white porcelain from bathroom accessories. One quick look then Cate turned around with a strangled cry making for the gallery. There was a very strong lock on the door. She had the key.

As she opened it Jude felt the knot in his stomach tighten. There were only two ways into the gallery. Through the front door which she'd had the sense to fit with a wrought-iron security door, and this rear door opening into the living quarters. With any luck at all Ralph or his hireling—that had to be considered—hadn't been able to get so far.

Cate snapped on the lights, transforming the gallery into a fireworks of coloured light. "Thank God!" she moaned, in relief.

Jude stared around him, initially with answering relief then fascination that temporarily overrode his shocked anger. He remembered the gallery from Tony Mandel's day, but Cate had transformed the white walled art gallery into a glittering crystal cave. The interior had become a kaleidoscope of colours as the recessed lighting fell upon myriad shapes and designs; chunks of aquamarine, amethyst, rose quartz, obsidian, the extraordinary glitter of fool's gold, other shades of purple, orange, yellow, green, deep violet shot with a lovely blue colour. The crystals were ranged all around the room, adorning the long shelves fixed to the walls, and artistically positioned on free-standing pyramids and circular towers made out of chrome with white marble shelving. It was another world. A world filled with treasures from the earth.

"This is extraordinary," he said. "Beautiful!"

"Thank you." She was drawn to stare into his handsome

face as though it were a magnet; as though there was no one else in the world to cling to. She could still taste his mouth, this near stranger. See his face when she closed her eyes.

"We have to be grateful he couldn't get in," Jude's blue eyes were still glued to the crystal collection. "Or maybe he was disturbed. It's Ralph's work of course, Ralph or someone he hired to do his dirty work for him. It wouldn't be the first time. Then again Ralph might have derived maximum satisfaction from doing the job himself. We'll have to call in the police, Cate. He can't be allowed to get away with this."

Her stunned anger was quickly passing into a desperate need for caution. "Or we could simply ignore it. Keep quiet," she suggested.

Jude shook his head emphatically. "I'd feel a whole lot better if we let the police take a look at this."

"What if it wasn't Ralph?" A shadow fell across her face.

He made a little jeering sound. "Who else, Cate? After what's happened."

"He wants us to call the police. He wants the whole story to come out. He wants the town to feel sorry for him and angry with me. He won't be caught anyway, he'll have a water-tight alibi for where he was last night. Off the top of my head he'd say he spent the night with some girl. She'll swear to it."

He flashed her a sardonic glance. "I know all about Ralph and his friends. I've known for years. His DNA would be all over the house. Of course he could account for that from his previous visit." He added with regret.

"Exactly. I don't want to call in the police, Jude. I want to keep this quiet."

She seemed genuinely panicked. He wanted to draw her

into his arms, wipe that urgent look of appeal off her face. "You've got an enemy, Cate. There's a big flaw in your decision. Next time he'll target the gallery. Think of all the damage he could do, that's some collection!"

She, too, looked around the gallery; at the beautiful crystals she had arranged so artistically. "I'm glad you like it. Surely I can have a security system fitted today? Or as soon as possible. I should have done it at the beginning when I first came here."

"That would have been a good idea."

"Everyone seemed so friendly, so open and honest. He couldn't afford to smash the front windows. The Harveys aren't that far away, they would have heard it. Surely he didn't come back in that flashy red sports car?"

Jude shrugged. "It's the closest he's got to a getaway car. Maybe he wore some kind of disguise," he suggested acidly. "A baseball cap pulled down over his eyes, sunglasses, a goatee beard. Ralph's none too bright. Then again he could have had one of his social misfit friends do the job for him. Sounds reasonable given your portrait wasn't touched. Maybe the guy who broke in didn't recognise you as the subject? It's very beautiful, by the way."

Cate nodded. "Tony is a gifted artist. I would have been terribly upset if the painting had been damaged. It has great sentimental value for me."

"And monetary value," he pointed out dryly.

"It's Tony's work," she said, turning away from his keen eyes knowing he was struggling to make sense of her and her story. "I'll feel better once I clear up."

Jude glanced at his watch. "I'd better cancel lunch."

"You go." She turned her face back to him.

"Don't be ridiculous." He didn't intend it but his voice was close to brusque. "I still think you should call the police, Cate. You must establish there's been a break-in."

She tucked a long swing of copper hair behind her ear. "Please, Jude, I don't want to." She was so acutely aware of him it made her nerves jump.

"Why do I have this constant feeling you're holding something back?" he demanded.

She shut her eyes tight, small white teeth gritted. "I'm not. Believe me. I better get started."

He reached into his pocket for his cell phone. "Give me a minute to ring Jimmy, then I'll help you. Keep out of the bathroom with all that broken glass. I'll take care of that job."

"What kind of a bastard would do this?" Jimmy asked, looking around him at the senseless mess.

"I'll give you a clue, Jimmy," Jude said, his expression grim. "It starts with an R. You're looking at the result of a half an hour's clean-up work by the two of us. You should have seen it when we came in. We've just finished putting the books back."

"And he's gone and broken ya lovely lamp, Catey!" Jimmy mourned. "I can't understand why you don't want to talk to the police, love. Bennett's a good bloke. They're there to protect you."

"Jude has done a good job so far." She smiled in Jude's direction but he didn't smile back.

He held up his hands. "I wanted her to report it as well."

"Now the gallery would have been the real prize," Jimmy mused.

Jude shrugged. "Too much of a risk putting a brick through the front window. Thankfully Cate went to the trouble of putting an excellent lock on the door leading into the gallery. Or I guess Ralph could have thought enough is enough, leave the gallery for next time. This could be the start of a campaign."

"Yeah, well…" Jimmy scratched his bald head. "We can throw a spoke in that."

"You bet we can!" Jude rasped. "I've called in Hazletts to fix up a few surprises including a surveillance camera." Jude righted a couple of bar stools. "Cate can afford it now," he added dryly. "He should be here shortly."

"So what can I do?" Jimmy asked. "He's a miserable son of a bitch, that Ralph. A coward, too. He's got a couple of no-hopers among his mates. Could have been that guy, Kramer. Drop-out. Leads a useless existence. Could have done it for a price. Kramer doesn't fit in with most folks but Ralph keeps him in his entourage."

"I'll be sure to ask Ralph when I see him later in the day," Jude said in a voice full of intent. "You can help me here, Jimmy, if you like, while Cate gets busy in the bedroom."

"Fine." Jimmy lost no time getting to work.

Miss Forsyth was uncharacteristically speechless when she surveyed the chaos in the bedroom.

"I respect the fact you want to keep this quiet, m'dear, but I have to tell you I side with Jude and Jimmy on this. I think you should have called in the police. Someone has to teach Ralph Rogan a lesson."

Cate looked back at the tall, spare, elderly lady who had befriended her. Miss Forsyth was impeccably dressed in what Cate thought of as her "daytime uniform." Today it was one of her pristine long-sleeved pin-tucked white cotton shirts with a Nehru collar worn loose over baggy beige linen slacks, tan leather sandals on her feet. Her woolly snow-white hair that had in her youth been a riot of tight chestnut curls was drawn up and back into a knot. Her facial bones were very prominent, balancing the distinguished beak of a nose. Cate felt a surge of affection for her. "He has been taught a lesson, Miss Forsyth," she said. "By his father. I know Jimmy can't hold anything back from you, so you'll be aware I'm Lester Rogan's main beneficiary."

Miss Forsyth gave a genteel sniff. "It's the kind of surprise that could cause one to drop dead of a heart attack." She reached down to pick up a few dresses still on their hangers. "There's something I need to ask you, m'dear. Did you already know Lester and were forced to keep quiet?"

Cate returned Miss Forsyth's shrewd gaze. "I never heard of Lester Rogan before I came to this town. I've been over and over this with Jude. He's been very kind even when I feel he hardly believes a word I say."

"A true gentleman is Jude," Miss Forsyth nodded approvingly. "As for not believing you, you must consider it is an odd story. But odd stories are the best of all. There has to be a connection, you're just missing it."

"Try as I might I can't think of it, Miss Forsyth," Cate assured her, walking back and forth from the bed to the wardrobe.

Miss Forsyth crouched down to pick up some scattered T-shirts. "In one of these drawers, dear?"

"The top one, Miss Forsyth. You don't have to do anything. Please, sit down."

"I'm not in my element doing nothing." Miss Forsyth began folding the tops neatly and placing them in the top drawer of the teak chest. "Let's face it. The will has made Ralph very, very angry. That is to be expected. It's not something any family would want to hear. He was such a cruel man, Lester. He gave his family such a bad time. That's when they saw him. He was away from home such a lot, supposedly working on his deals but I suspect he was getting up to a whole lot of things more exotic."

Cate paused in what she was doing to look back at Miss Forsyth with perplexity. "Like what?"

Miss Forsyth shrugged a shoulder. "Lester started up relationships at the drop of a hat. Myra had a very difficult job trying to track him down. In time she learned not to bother. I shouldn't be surprised if Lester Rogan had offspring all over the place."

"Well don't look at me," Cate said, feeling like she was actually in limbo. "My mother loved my father. He was the only man in her life."

"I'm sure, m'dear. Don't get upset. We're talking hypotheticals."

"Besides, I already told Jude I resemble my father's side of the family. I have his colouring. That's settles it as far as I'm concerned, if it even needed settling. The connection doesn't lie there. Why he was so nice to me, I don't know. Why he left me the bulk of his fortune I don't know, either. I'm not happy about it. I don't want his money. I know you and Jimmy were worried every time he came into the gallery but he just wanted to talk."

Miss Forsyth spoke in a calm, soothing voice. "What were you talking about? Go ahead, my dear. Tell me," she urged. "I'm listening. I only want to help you."

Cate shrugged helplessly. "I know that. But it's as I've told you before, Miss Forsyth. It was mostly general conversation. We spoke about the crystals, their properties. He was very interested in them and he bought a number of pieces. He liked to hear about my time in the Outback as a governess."

"Did he manage to coax out of you your history?" Miss Forsyth asked, staring at Cate thoughtfully.

Cate flushed. "I told him a little about my childhood. My mother and father. Not much. We spoke about Tony, of course. Tony sold him the gallery, which it appears is now mine."

Miss Forsyth lay down a garment she was folding and

refolding without much thought. She looked at Cate across the bed. "Why is it you don't speak about your past life, m'dear? We respect your privacy of course, but you know you're among friends. Surely you can trust us? There must be a connection somewhere for Lester to have written you into his will. One could almost conclude you are family in some way. That could be a vital key to the mystery."

"No way, Miss Forsyth." Cate took a deep steadying breath. "Honestly. No way either was I Lester Rogan's toy girl."

Miss Forsyth gave a disgusted click of her tongue. "That's not a point we need cleared up, m'dear. I would never have thought that in a million years."

"I think it's crossed Jude's mind," Cate said unhappily.

"That upsets you obviously." Miss Forsyth flashed another of her razor-sharp grey glances.

"Definitely."

"I must tuck that to the back of my mind. Jude's a lawyer, m'dear, executor of the estate, he's obliged to think of everything. I'm sure it only took him another ten seconds to realise that theory is out of the question. I have a feeling it could have something to do with your parents. Whatever his failings Lester was perfectly rational, not demented. This puzzle has a logic to it, a verifiable explanation. Who is it who can help you?"

Cate sat down on the side of the bed, hugging her slender body with her arms. "My parents can't tell me anything, Miss Forsyth. I'm an orphan just as I told you."

Miss Forsyth shook her head, clearly seeing herself in the role of detective. "You're an orphan now, Cate—I am so sorry such a thing had to happen to you—but you and your parents had a life together. Somehow Lester Rogan was tucked away in the past. He might have known your parents before you were old enough to remember him. The connection must have been very strong to survive all these years. Lester was not a doer of good deeds. He was no philanthropist, he was a mean man, he enjoyed being mean. He enjoyed cracking the whip over his family. Maybe this inheritance is in the nature of retribution. Lester knew for a couple of years he was a prime candidate for a heart attack or stroke. Finally he may have wanted to put his life in order.''

Cate sighed. ''What a pity he couldn't have taken into account all the upset his will would cause. He would have known his family's reaction, how shocked they would be, outraged might be a better word. And what about me? Didn't he consider he might be exposing me to actual danger? He knew his own son. I've heard Ralph Rogan has a job controlling his temper at the best of times.''

Miss Forsyth too sat down, collapsing lightly into an armchair, a flush perhaps of intuition crossing her papery cheeks. ''Maybe Lester badly wanted to make amends without letting any skeletons out of the closet, m'dear?''

Cate couldn't answer for a moment. She felt like a few skeletons were watching her right now. ''What he has done,'' she said finally, ''is put me at risk.''

The security man took some time installing the new system. The rest of them, Jude and Cate, Miss Forsyth and Jimmy worked together to restore order, Miss Forsyth powering along like a woman in her thirties. She even made the suggestion with the air of confident assertion that was so much a part of her that she would make sandwiches for lunch.

No one refused and in no time at all, a very interesting selection appeared, arranged in a gingham lined basket. She had consulted no one regarding the fillings choosing them all herself from what Cate had in the frig and the pantry. Both areas mercifully hadn't figured in the attack which

turned out to be a real bonus. There were chicken and avocado triple deckers with a pat of mayonnaise and a sprinkle
of chopped walnuts, crab meat and cream cheese, paper thin
turkey breast with ginger and mango chutney and a few
sprigs of rocket, all washed down with very good iced tea.
They were all hungry. Afterwards Jimmy draped an arm
around Miss Forsyth, bending to peck her noisily on the
cheek.

"I wouldn't be a bit surprised if one of these days we
end up married, Gwennie?"

She laughed. "Wishful thinking, Jimmy. I'm too set in
my ways not that you're at all serious. You know I'm never
likely to say yes—much better to be friends."

"Spoken by a woman who climbed out of a bathroom
window on her wedding day," Jimmy chortled.

Cate couldn't tell if Jimmy was joking or not. "Did you
really, Miss Forsyth?"

"No. Absolutely not." Miss Forsyth prodded Jimmy hard
in the chest. "How dare you try to soil my reputation,
Jimmy. I climbed out the bathroom window to escape my
dear fiancé, the dullest man I have ever known. I'd spent a
good hour listening to him rehearsing a sermon—he was a
clergyman you see—but I was simply driven to leave. I
didn't actually choose him you know. My mother did. Of
course he was mortally offended but I made up my mind
there and then he'd never get me to the altar so I broke off
the engagement. Broke my mother's heart, so she said. I
don't think I'd have made a good vicar's wife in any case,
I actually like to speak my mind. The high point in my life
was travelling the world before I finally settled in these won-
drous, alluring tropics. I crave the heat and the colour."

"You're English Miss Forsyth," Jude said. Miss Forsyth
still retained what Jimmy called her "hoity-toity" accent.

"Anglo-Irish family," she corrected. "I always thought

Lester Rogan had more than a hint of an Irish accent hidden away there,'' she mused with a frown. ''He was at pains to get rid of it for some reason. In my opinion he exaggerated his Australian drawl.''

''That's true,'' Cate considered, on reflection. ''He had two voices actually. I'd forgotten about that.''

''He had two personalities more like it,'' Jimmy crowed.

''Is it possible Ireland was his homeland?'' Jude put the question to Miss Forsyth.

''He claimed he'd lived in Australia all his life, that he was born here,'' she answered giving it frowning consideration.

''But you doubted that?''

''As I said, there was something about his accent if one listened carefully. It was a hybrid. In later years he favoured what is known as ocker but he didn't speak like that in the early days.''

''Cate's father was Irish.'' Jude shot a glance at Miss Forsyth, studying Cate's face along the way.

''Yes, I know.''

''Could it be Cate's father and Lester Rogan were somehow connected? Related perhaps?''

Cate flared. ''Even if that were true, which it isn't, why would Lester Rogan leave me a fortune simply on the strength of a distant relationship?''

''Who said distant, Cate? This is an important avenue that has to be checked out.''

''He didn't leave a letter, Jude, to explain his actions?'' Miss Forsyth asked. ''One might have thought so. Dear Matthew would surely have persuaded him?''

''No letter.'' Jude shook his head, his eyes still on Cate's troubled expression. ''I've been right through Dad's files, but I can double-check.''

''Matty would have known of the connection surely?''

Jimmy said. "Les would have confided in him, he told ya dad things he told no on else. Course no one was to know ya dad would die so early."

"Indeed, yes," said Miss Forsyth. "A tragedy! Really Lester put everyone in a terrible position," she shook her snowy head ruefully. "Look at poor Cate, I dread to think what might have happened to her had you not arrived last night, Jude."

Jude's eyes were a blue blaze. "I couldn't force Cate to make a complaint but I can talk to Ralph. And his mother."

"Poor Myra has no control over Ralph," Miss Forsyth said with authority. "Parents can be as big a disappointment to their children as children are to their parents. Myra has absolutely no force of character and, as a result, Lester walked all over her. Never did love her, you know, poor little thing. She was just another piece of property he snaffled up. Married her because he thought it would be the smart thing to do. His father-in-law taught him everything about the real estate business, property development. Lester's rise was meteoric."

"Sure was!" Jimmy exclaimed. "He started to make it big only a couple of years after he married Myra. Not that he didn't have a fair bit of his own money. Where did he get that, I wonder? Basically he was a bit of a larrikin I always thought. Not a gentleman like ya dad, Jude. If only you had your dad to talk to, he could tell you all we need to know."

CHAPTER SEVEN

JUDE found Ralph sitting behind his father's desk in the study of the Rogan mansion. He hadn't rung ahead to say he was coming. That would have given Ralph the opportunity to takeoff. Melinda had let him into the house, her small pretty face alight with pleasure. Now she stood at the door of the study, obviously wanting to be part of whatever discussion was about to take place only her brother barked at her.

"All right, Mel. No need to hang around. You can go. Jude wants to talk to me, not you."

Jude looked at Melinda with a sympathetic smile. "I'll see you before I leave, Mel. What I have to say is for Ralph's ears. How's your mother?"

"Doing what she always does," Ralph exploded. "Lying down. You'd think she was the only woman in the world who'd lost a husband. Not a loving husband who was damned good to her, either. A real bastard."

"How can you talk like that, Ralph?" his sister protested, her fair skin turning beet-red. "You must have hated Dad."

"Fact is you did, too, Mel. Why don't you grow up? Get yourself a job. There must be something you wanna do?"

"Have you got to be so offensive, Ralph?" Jude protested, mouth tightening. "Or are you going to spend the rest of your life injuring your mother's and your sister's psyches. Haven't they had enough of that? Haven't you?"

"Maybe I'm more like my rotten father than I thought," Ralph sighed, suddenly sounding sad.

"You don't have to follow the very same course. You

can change, Ralph. You can commit to shrugging off the past and looking towards the future. As for Mel! She could travel,'' Jude suggested. ''There's a big wide world for you to see, Mel.'' He turned his face to her. ''I'm sure you would benefit greatly from the experience.''

''She'd be too bloody nervous to try,'' Ralph scoffed, not about to change overnight. ''She'd rather stay home and lead the same old miserable life.''

''And it must be as miserable as it gets, with you for a brother,'' Jude said. ''If I were you, Ralph, I'd have a care how I spoke to my mother and sister. This isn't your house. This isn't your study and that isn't your chair. The house belongs to your mother.''

''That's right, Ralph,'' Melinda piped up, looking as though she hadn't realised that fact until it was confirmed by Jude. ''Mum could throw you out.''

''Don't make me laugh.'' There was a malicious glint in Ralph's eyes. ''Mum doesn't understand a thing about anything, even running this house.''

''She can find out,'' Jude retorted. ''She can hire a house manager, start with a housekeeper. All these things are easily attended to. I'll find her someone to help her manage her financial affairs, Mel, too, if that's what she wants. I'm here to help.''

''Of course you are.'' Ralph rocked back in his late father's custom made leather chair. ''You're the man. The knight in shining armour.''

''Trust me,'' Jude's blue eyes blazed. ''I'm here to look after your mother's and sister's interests, that goes for Cate Costello as well. Would you like to tell Mel what you got up to last night before I tell the whole town?''

Ralph's mouth fell slightly ajar. ''You wouldn't dare.''

''Don't be ridiculous,'' Jude looked at him with contempt.

"What did he do?" Melinda ventured timidly into the room, pulling at the fingers of her right hand.

"Can you understand plain English?" her brother shouted in frustration. "This has got nothing to do with you, Mel."

"It might be best if you go, Mel," Jude advised. "You've enough grief in your life."

Melinda stood motionless for a moment, staring at her brother. "One day you're going to do something really horrible, Ralph."

"If you're not careful I'll do it right now." Her brother stumbled to his feet.

"Sit down, Ralph and don't move," Jude said in such a way Ralph found himself doing it. "You're in enough trouble as it is."

"Could I get you something, Jude?" Melinda asked. "Tea, coffee a cold drink?" She cocked her head, rather like a bird.

Jude felt his heart ache for her. What a hell of an upbringing both Mel and Ralph had had. "I'm fine for the moment thanks, Mel. We might have a cup of coffee together before I go."

"Lovely!" Burning spots of colour went straight to Melinda's cheeks.

"She fancies herself in love with you, silly little twit," Ralph told Jude after his sister had left the room, closing the door behind her.

"Nonsense!" Jude brushed that off. "Exactly how often does Mel see me?"

Ralph ignored that. "Yeah, well, if you don't want to listen. Poor old Mel has had the hots for you since we were kids. Even I know that's not your fault, part of Mel's problem is she's only good for daydreams. Plus you're the sort of guy who takes a woman's breath away. Isn't that right? Even up here we get the papers."

Jude shrugged. "That was probably the dumbest article ever published, but I haven't come here to chat about me. I really want to talk about you and your recent activities."

"Uh-huh," said Ralph, rocking back, his hands behind his head. "I know I didn't handle myself well last night but I did apologise. I was drunk. Up to my ears in booze. I—"

"And you came back." Jude cut him off. "You ransacked her flat?"

"No way!" Ralph looked the very picture of innocence. "You're off your trolley."

"I don't think so. Your DNA is all over the place."

"So what?" Ralph curled his lip. "I've admitted to calling in on the conniving little bitch."

"I won't listen to your calling her names, Ralph," Jude warned, pulling up an armchair to the desk.

"Oh dear, got you in as well has she?" Ralph hunched his broad shoulders. "I guess she's beautiful if you like the type. I don't. After I left you I drove over to Amy Gibson's place where I crawled into her bed. Ring Amy if you like, she'll vouch for my whereabouts," Ralph added in triumph.

"So what do you have to buy her?" Jude asked. "Only a fool would believe you. You had opportunity and motive, also you get people to do things on your behalf. The police will be asking you more questions, Ralph." Given Cate's refusal that simply wasn't true, but Jude allowed it to pass in the hope it might catch Ralph out.

"Yeah, well, they won't put me at the scene," Ralph countered aggressively. "Someone else had to tear the place to pieces. Not me. A lot of guys in town are mighty interested in her. Maybe she sucked a guy in then told him to get lost. She sure turned her attention on Dad and look where it got her. The old goat was her lover."

Ghastly thought. "I know different, Ralph," Jude said, thinking such a discovery would affect him drastically. "Go near her again, threaten her or her property in any way and you do it at your peril. I mean that. I'll fix you and I'll fix it you wind up in court. Courts take a very dim view of stalking and harassment. You always were a bully.''

Ralph was looking wary now. ''For hell's sake, aren't we suppose to be working together? That girl, that redheaded bitch, has stolen my inheritance. I'm the rightful heir. The only son. Who the hell is she? If she wasn't his mistress, what else? Just because she looks so angelic doesn't mean she didn't work frantically to ingratiate herself with my fool of an old man.''

''Except no one in the world would agree with that description of your father.'' Jude pointed out very dryly.

''He did come to fancy classy little chicks. Little chicks with big green eyes and long silky hair.''

Jude shook his head with emphasis. ''I might have agreed with you for about five minutes, Ralph, but not now. There's a story behind all this.''

''Of course there's a story!'' Ralph exploded. ''There has to be. Is it possible she's his byblow? He had countless affairs in his life. Half the time Mum never knew where he was.''

Jude knew that to be completely true. ''I promise you I'll carry out an investigation and report back to you. In the meantime, Ralph, I'm here to deliver a warning. Keep off the grog and keep away from Cate Costello.''

Ralph still looked like he was slightly drunk. He hadn't shaved, a couple of days dark growth on his cheeks and chin. ''You two are getting pretty close, aren't you?'' he asked in a snide voice. ''Anyway what does it all matter?'' Abruptly he lost all aggression, sounding depressed.'' How are you going to fix it? I can't possibly sit still and let a total stranger get away with family money. I know you wouldn't. You'd fight like hell, don't tell me you wouldn't. The whole thing's crazy.''

Jude nodded. "I agree. So does Cate Costello I'd have you know. She swears she had absolutely no idea why your father would do such a thing.''

Ralph swore violently and waved his arms in the air. "Who would trust a woman? Would you, Jude? Didn't your mum do a real wicked thing without warning. She ran off with some Yank. Left you and your dad to fend for yourselves. That's women for you,'' Ralph swore again.

"It's not sex they're after. It's money. Lots of it. It's always been the same. They sell their bodies on the street. They sell them in swank hotels. Prostitutes. Society women. It's money they're after the same way men go after power. What's she doing up here anyway? Hell, she could have followed Dad up here. Ever thought of that? Maybe she was Mandel's little girlfriend at one time. Attractive bloke, Tony, even if he was old enough to be her father. Maybe Mandel leaked news of a filthy rich property developer up in Isis with an eye for the ladies. Who knows?'' Ralph's dark eyes looked tragic.

"There's another angle, Ralph,'' Jude said. "Did your father ever speak of his childhood, where he was born? Did he have family?''

Ralph stared back, rubbing his hand over the dark stubble on his face. "Struth I'll have to have a shave! I tell you I feel stripped of my inheritance, by a total stranger. I was the heir apparent. Now look what it's come to. As for Dad! We'd all have gone into shock if he'd ever confided in us about anything. He was the kinda guy who left everyone wondering. He told Mum once before they married he lost his whole family when he was young. I'm not sure now he didn't kill 'em, or maybe he just wished them all dead. I can't tell you anything about my father's background. He's one of those people who just appears out of nowhere."

"There are ways to get information. Miss Forsyth detected the hint of an Irish accent or inflection tucked away there?"

Ralph gave an acrid laugh. "How the hell would she know?"

"She came from an Anglo-Irish family."

"She's a Pom. I thought she was smart but she must be a bit stupid after all. Dad's accent was pure Ocker. What has Irish got to do with it anyway?"

"Cate Costello's father was born in Ireland. He died some years back so we can't speak to him."

"About what?" There was genuine confusion in Ralph's handsome beefy face.

"About some possible link, Ralph. We need some answers. I don't blame you or your family for feeling betrayed, I do blame you however for your attack on Cate Costello. I'm convinced she's the innocent victim in all this."

"Victim?" Ralph hooted. "She's rich! Big-time rich!"

"There are circumstances here we don't know about. I'm asking you to give me a little time."

Ralph shifted back and forth in the huge armchair. "Aren't you going back to your city job?"

Jude shook his head. "I'm not going anywhere for a while, I'm on vacation. That should be time enough."

Ralph looked like he was hurting badly. "I'm not going to let her get away with this, Jude," he warned. "I can't live with what Dad's done. He owed me."

Jude gave him a long straight look. "Legally he didn't owe you anything, Ralph. As it is you inherited a tidy sum. Most people don't see that kind of money in a lifetime. I know it's nowhere near what you expected."

'I'm not going to be defeated," Ralph said. "She's not

the pure little thing she's pretending. She could be treacherous. Men lose themselves in a woman's face, we're like little boys when we want them but it takes time to find out about their hearts. You should know that, Jude.

"Find out about her." Ralph went on earnestly. "We've never been friends. I can never learn to like you. Not after the way my dad held you up to me as a role model. I was never smart or special enough, but you were, and your father loved you, you needed each other. Dad didn't need us. Strangely enough I'm clear on one thing, I trust you as a man. I trust you as a lawyer, executor of my father's estate. Find out about her, Jude. Find out what she's been up to. If we learn the real truth about her, we might be able to cut a deal."

Jude stood up. "Don't forget I've got a deal for you as well. Who knows what you planned when you called on Cate early in the evening. She thought you meant to attack her. Maybe you didn't ransack her place yourself but we both know you could find someone to do it. Probably Kramer—I bet you told him to wear gloves. There better not be any more attempts to frighten her much less harm her. I could just as easily bash your head in today as I did years ago. I wouldn't want to do that. I dislike violence and I'm a lawyer. Tell your friend, Kramer, I'm pointing a finger at him as well."

"There'll be no trouble," Ralph growled. "Tell that to your little girlfriend. All she's had so far is a protest. You promise me you'll look into it?"

"I have to look into it, Ralph. The key is somewhere in past lives. I'm sure of it."

By the time Jude arrived back at the gallery, the living quarters had been completely restored to order. Late afternoon sunshine spilled through the large picture windows falling on a beautiful arrangement of the sacred blue lotus which grew in abundance in the North. One perfect large open flower was at the lowest level of the tall arrangement, sitting on an open leaf. He could see two buds, two pods, tightly furled leaves and open leaves all displayed in a lotus shaped bronze vase. Cate was bending over it making slight adjustments to the tallest, soaring leaf. He felt the urgency to go to her startling. He'd heard about a coup de foudre. He appeared to have caught it full blast.

She broke off what she was doing the moment she saw him. "How did you go? I've been so worried."

"No need." He walked through the open door, seeking to reassure her. "Ralph was at the house and we had a talk. He as good as admitted he had someone trash the place. It was in the nature of a protest he said, I rather think it won't happen again. I'm pretty sure Ralph didn't do it himself. Like you said he has a girlfriend to vouch for his whereabouts, but he gave the order. That's a beautiful arrangement." He wanted so much to touch her it hurt. "Where did you get the flowers?"

"Jimmy brought them back for me. He knows I like the Japanese Rikka style of flower arrangements. I studied it for a while though to become a master would take a lifetime."

"Well, you've done a pretty good job. That's beautiful."

"Thank you." Her hand caressed a furled bud. "The buds are the hope for the future. You have such exquisite water lilies here in the tropics. The large leaves are so decorative, don't you think? Miss Forsyth actually gave me this pot. It's very old. I love it."

He didn't reply and she sought his eyes. "You're doing rather a lot for me, Jude. Going to see Ralph Rogan. I've seen how dangerous he can be."

He heard the faint tremor in her voice. "Ralph has been warned off. Did you ask Miss Forsyth if you could stay with her for a night or two? I take it Hazlett has finished up here?''

"Only just. It took hours. The alarm emits quite a din. If anyone should try to break in the whole neighbourhood is going to know about it.''

"Good,'' he said with satisfaction.

"I didn't say anything to Miss Forsyth,'' she confessed. "Actually she asked me if I'd like to spend the night with her. I thanked her and told her I'd be perfectly all right here.''

"Will you?'' He stared into her eyes.'' I was hoping you'd come back and stay with me at least until your nerves settle. Mine, too, for that matter.''

She averted her bright head. "I can't, Jude.''

"Why not? It's not as though I'm proposing an orgy. Nothing is going to get out of hand. I just want you under my nose until things cool down. We could buy a bottle of wine and some seafood for dinner. We can pick up everything we need for a salad at one of the farms along the way. It's the perfect time for you to tell me all about yourself. I need to know.''

"I don't want to leave the gallery,'' she said, though it cost her an effort.

His blue eyes trapped her. "We activate the security system. That's what it's all about.''

Cate slowly let the breath in and out of her lungs. Why was she making it so easy for him to sweep her off her feet. Where were the strong defences she'd built to avoid all kinds of grieves?

"Cate,'' he said gently. "I know you have something to tell me.''

"Hasn't everyone something to tell?''

He shrugged. "Probably, but your story is more shattering than most. I won't let anything threaten you. No one is going to bother you, that includes me. You've had two bad experiences. Give yourself a little time to get over them.''

''I've had worse experiences,'' she said.

''Maybe it would help to tell someone about them,'' he said very seriously. ''Look at me, Cate.''

For a moment she didn't respond. ''Was it really only yesterday we set eyes on each other?''

''I've no idea,'' He gave her a self-deprecating smile. ''You're a witch. You've cast a spell on me.''

''What kind, though?''

''The mysterious kind,'' he said.

She stared up at him with unreadable intensity. ''Then take every precaution.''

He let his eyes linger on her lovely face. ''Thank you for the warning, Cate. I intend to.''

Jude hand-picked the wine—a multiaward winning sparkling as an aperitif, and a beautiful riesling that would go well with the seafood. The seafood in the Great Barrier Reef waters was plentiful and superb. They bought oysters, prawns, crab and crayfish; fresh rolls and a chocolate and almond strudel that had just come out of the oven at the bakery. Cate said she could make a avocado and papaya salad from what was growing in Jude's backyard. Along the beach road they stopped at a farm to buy lots of freshly picked herbs and salad greens, Jude getting into animated conversation with the owners, a married couple of Italian descent he had known all his life. Cate was introduced, smiled upon warmly, both sent off with much more than they actually paid for.

''Is this a celebration?'' Cate enquired, when they were back on the road again.

''Why not?'' He threw her a lazy grin.

''Please don't say it's because I've come into a fortune.''

"Did I say that?" he retorted.

"No. I know you came here as executor of Lester Rogan's will, Jude, but I'm hoping you're going to be my friend."

"What do you think I've been doing?" he chided her.

"Questioning me whilst being very kind. Observing me while I'm not looking. All the time thinking, is it possible she could have been…?"

"Rogan's mistress? It's a thought that would enter anyone's mind, Cate. Rich men of any age can attract beautiful young women. We all know that. We see it and read about it all the time. It didn't take me long to reach the conclusion there was no relationship."

"Sexual relationship."

"Don't brood about it," he advised. "Minutes ago you were laughing with the Pagliaros."

"They accepted me because I was with you. I wonder if they'd have looked at me differently if they'd known Lester Rogan had left me so much money?"

"Money alone has a certain cachet," he said dryly. "They took to you because you're a beautiful young woman with a poised, friendly manner. I took to you the instant I laid eyes on you. That was in the church when you were trying unsuccessfully to melt into the shadows. I took to you even more when we began talking."

"And now?" She glanced at his handsome profile.

"I told you. You've laid a spell on me." He was silent a moment then added rather sombrely, "Women have such power."

"What are you thinking about right now?" she asked. "Please tell me. What made you look so grim all of a sudden. Is it something about me?"

"Of course not." He sought to reassure her. She sounded slightly unnerved.

"Then what? Are you thinking about the mother you loved?" she asked with great seriousness.

"The truth, Cate?" His eyes were a blue blaze. "I think of her frequently. You'd think with all the years that have passed I'd think of her less and less but it's not working out that way. Neither of my parents have disappeared, they're locked into my mind. They come to me in dreams. Strangely enough they're happy dreams when my mother loved my father and me."

"You've never tried to find her, Jude?" Cate shook her head thinking she couldn't let such a thing happen. For all Jude's natural charm of manner, the blond hair, the blue eyes and that "heartbreaker" smile, she had come to realise he wasn't a man to be trifled with. Not him or his emotions.

"She doesn't want to be found, Cate," he told her tersely. "Otherwise she would have contacted us. She simply walked out of the house and out of our lives."

"Yet she looks so beautiful in her portrait. She looks a loving woman."

"The loving didn't last." His voice held betrayal. "At least not for us."

"That is so, so sad. I know what's it's like to be desperately lonely for a mother's love. That terrible morning, our last morning together, I kissed my mother goodbye. A hurried peck I so regret. I was late for my lift you see. I told her I'd be home late. There was a rehearsal for the school play, Romeo and Juliet. I was Juliet. I was excited about it, I loved acting. When my friend's mother dropped me off late that afternoon she was gone. I rang around everywhere. All her friends. One of our neighbours told me she saw my mother heading off with our dog for a walk in the forest. That was hours before. I got on my bike and rode until it was dark but there was no sign of her or Blaze. When my stepfather came home he rang the police. I never saw her

again. It's truly dreadful when someone just disappears.
There's no coming to grips with it. There is no conclusion.
My stepfather is a monster. I hate him.''

Jude understood from the vehemence in her voice there
was more to tell. Whether he would reach the status of
trusted confidante he didn't yet know.

What am I doing here, Cate thought, unpacking her overnight bag in the welcoming white and yellow guest bedroom
with its touches of blue. This wasn't the sort of thing she
would normally do, yet here she was spending another night
at Jude's home. The sea breeze was blowing the filmy white
draperies at the open French doors so she went to tie them
back with their yellow silk cords. That done, she paused for
long moments to look out at the beautiful ocean front setting
with its profusion of palms and pandanus. In the afternoon
sunlight a golden glitter was coming off the brilliantly blue
water, bordered as it was by mile after mile of pristine-white
sands.

She loved Jude's house. It seemed to her so romantic.
She loved the way all the doors in the house opened out
onto that glorious view. She had lived in far more formal
houses, in a cooler climate but she loved the rather glamorous informality and the streaming floods of sunlight.
Many the Sunday afternoon she had driven out to Spirit
Cove just to park near Jude's house and admire it. Jimmy
had told her so much about his friends the Conroys. Father
and son. She had recognised Jude the moment she laid eyes
on him just from Jimmy's description. Jude was certainly
very handsome with an easy effortless charm that could,
however, turn into moments of sombre brooding.

She wasn't scared of him in any way. One only had to
look at Jude to know he wasn't a man who would ever harm
a woman. The truth was she was scared of herself. It was

getting to the stage where he had only to beckon and she would follow. That in itself was extraordinary. Always with admirers and she'd had them, she was the one to back off. She could have found herself a husband a dozen and more times during her time in the Outback.

Out there women were outnumbered by heaps of bush bachelors desperately looking for a wife. Nice guys, too. Manly and caring. One could almost say courtly. Women were a precious commodity and treated as such. Unfortunately, psychologically speaking she was damaged, still caught in a trap of helpless anger and grief. At twenty-two nearly twenty-three she was still unable to cast it off.

Or was that the past? Jude Conroy was handling her very easily. She couldn't bear to think of it as manipulation? In fact the strange bond between them was going ahead in great leaps and bounds. Apart from the strong physical attraction neither of them was able to deny, was it because bad things had happened to them when they were children? Both of them were orphans. Both had suffered the disastrous consequences of having their mothers simply disappear from their lives. Great losses like that changed one's inner landscape.

Successful as Jude had become as a lawyer she knew from the way he spoke a great deal of bitterness, anger and grief continued to hold sway. She wondered if he was involved with someone. He had to be. Women didn't let men like Jude get away. She decided she would ask him. That kiss he had given her on the beach had been so passionate, so shattering, she found it hard to believe he could kiss her like that and be seriously involved with someone else. Or had it been simply associated with the moment? She had been in an overexcited and agitated state. She truly believed she had seen a woman in a long white dress walking on the beach. She still believed it. She would go on believing it even if the whole world put it down to imagination. She had eyes. It was painfully obvious she had a vulnerable heart.

A tap on the door had her spinning her head. "Oh, hi, Jude," she said, trying to smile when she had the sensation her blood was sparkling, rushing, instead of moving calmly through her veins.

"I thought I'd come collect you." He moved across the spacious room to join her, the sun catching the bright honey-blond gloss of his hair.

"I'd fallen into a daydream," she tried to explain. "This cove is an especially beautiful part of the coast. I love your house. I'd love to live here. I'd love to swim morning and evening, go for long walks, work in your beautiful garden. I'd restore the flower beds, tropical flowering is so brilliant it would be an easy task. I love the lemon tropical netting on my tester bed there, the polished floors, the oriental rugs, the furniture, the wicker and rattan and bamboo, all the Thai pieces and the Chinese garden stools. I adore the huge deck. It's a wonderful place for entertaining."

"It's where we're going to have dinner." He smiled, looking into her expressive face.

"Perfect," she sighed.

"So what else would you do with the house?" he asked sounding both pleased and amused.

"It's possible you wouldn't let me do anything. May I ask you a question, Jude?"

"Sure. Fire away." He looked down into her lustrous green eyes.

"Do you have a girlfriend?"

He gave her a slight and dangerous smile. "At the risk of sounding immodest I'm phenomenally popular at the moment."

"Really? And where is the lucky woman? Or is it women?"

"Woman," he said. "She's the senior partner's daughter."

She shied away from that. It made her unsettled and unhappy. "Does she work with you?"

"No, thank goodness!" He reverted to sardonic tones.

The constriction in her chest miraculously lifted. "You mean she's a huntress?"

"Aren't you all?"

"Shame on you, Jude. I'm not hunting you."

"Poppy is." He gave her his heart-catching lopsided smile.

"What does she do?"

"She likes to ambush me in my office," he said dryly.

"But you're a big boy. I would have thought you'd know how to handle yourself."

"It's not as easy as all that, Cate." He shook his head. "I think her father actually approves of me as a son-in-law."

"You don't have your heart set on promotion, a spot of social climbing?" she asked as casually as she could.

"Seriously, Cate, I don't want to lose my job. I've worked very hard to get where I am. I have the feeling Poppy has the potential to turn nasty. She's a girl who only knows about getting what she wants."

"Is she beautiful?" She almost hoped he would tell her this Poppy was plain, but of course she wouldn't be.

"She's a blond bombshell," Jude confirmed her worst fears.

"How very fortunate for you." She brushed a lock of hair out of her eyes.

"And she's irrelevant," he said. "Actually I'm hoping she'll find someone else while I'm away."

"Kissing strange women on the beach?" she countered, bittersweet.

"Well, well, Cate Costello," he said softly, "you sound jealous?" He lifted his hand to tuck flying strands of copper hair behind her ears. "If you must know, ours was a kiss unparalleled until, I guess, the next time."

Sexual desire was exciting. It could also be full of woe. "What do you want from me, Jude?" she asked. There was so much going on between them.

"To spend time with you," he replied." To get to know you, to help you if I can. It sounds like there's been an absence of love in your life."

"I could say the same of you," she said quietly. "You've laid a few of your grieves bare. Are you telling me the truth about Poppy? Have you made love to her?"

"I'd like to hear about your love life," he parried. "I've dated a lot of girls, Cate, but I've never been bewitched until now."

He lifted his hand slowly to place his palm against her cheek, a gesture so tender, so seductive, Cate felt herself dissolve.

"What is it, Cate?" he asked with intensity.

"Surely everything I'm feeling is on my face," she met his eyes.

"I'm aching to kiss you." The tautness of his handsome features gave his longing away. "I've been aching to kiss you all day. Kiss your perfect lips." In a strong movement that revealed the depth of his hunger, he put his arms around her, one hand pressing into her back so he could gather her closer into his body.

It was so overwhelming one part of Cate urged her to pull away before she was lost. She needed to keep control of herself but control was spinning away. She wanted to be wild and free. Her breasts were in urgent contact with his chest. He smelled wonderful. Masculine, fresh, clean, salt, sandalwood, a note of vanilla.

"I'll let you move away if you want to," he muttered. "Only I want you to know I'll take the greatest care of you."

Care? She couldn't keep the sadness at bay. Didn't he know how easy it would be for him to break her heart? Yet her head fell back, flagrantly inviting him to kiss her throat. Her breath was lost as he did so, his lips moving passionately over the creamy arch, up her chin to the corner of her mouth.

Everything was a glorious, hot, sun-filled silence. The sound of the waves breaking on the shore was totally hushed; the loud swish of the palms. They might have been enclosed in a capsule, she flushed and burning, wanting the ecstasy of his holding her, stroking the side of her mouth with his thumb, gently pressing into the flesh.

What need she had! She wanted more than anything to be close to him. He was physically perfect to her. It was as primitive as mate finding mate. Everything was so easy with him. So acceptable to her. She let him caress her, welcoming his touch.

"Let me look at you. You're so beautiful."

She thought she moaned. She must have because his gentleness turned into a kind of delirium, so passionate, so splendid, she was opening up her mouth to accommodate his tongue. Her arms came up to lock tightly around his neck. She was trembling so violently she had to hold on to something. Hold on to him. She had no armour. No protection now. She needed this level of intensity to ease her own desperate aches.

Jude, too, was trying desperately to come up for air. "Oh, Cate!" he breathed into her mouth. He was losing his sense of everything outside of her. Before his driving male need engulfed him he jerked his head back. What must she think of him? He fancied he could feel her body flinching. Or was it simply a fast trembling? "Cate, I'm sorry. Things get so easily out of hand with you. I don't have any excuse. I brought you back here. But I want you to trust me." He caught her chin, turning up her face so he could read her eyes.

"I do trust you!" Her voice was barely audible.

"It's just so unbelievable what's happening!" Still holding her closely Jude stared out over her head, to the blue sea. "Normally I'm so cautious, but you've got through all my defences." The truth was he was perturbed at his own excesses.

"You shouldn't be afraid to care, Jude," she whispered, her green eyes glistening.

"Don't tremble please." He was trying to soothe her, except he had to let her go. "Look what I've done to you," he murmured with regret.

Cate lifted her head. "Jude, I'm not hurt. I wanted you to kiss me. I'm just a little shaky that's all. I haven't been kissed in a long while. And never like that!"

"Why not? You're so beautiful. You could have any man you wanted."

"Oh, yes," she said wearily, "but I don't want one. I don't like men."

He frowned as dark thoughts he'd refused to consider started to gather in his head. "Could that have anything to do with your feelings for your stepfather?"

"Don't let's talk about him," she said emotionally, fighting an impulse to burst into tears. Even the swiftness and hyperarousal of her feelings for Jude was terrifying in its way. "Look, why don't we go for a walk on the beach?" she suggested, trying hard to steady the tremble in her voice. It might help. No talking, no crying, no kissing, no listening to her heart instead of her head. "Tropical sunsets are glorious."

"As you wish." Why the hell, when he was normally so in control, was he allowing his emotions to soar to extremes? It had everything to do with her. At that moment he honestly believed he didn't have enough strength to withstand her. And he was the one who had promised to keep her safe.

This wasn't a good situation. He'd always thought of himself as a self-sufficient person. Cate Costello with her alluring green eyes had stopped that notion dead in its tracks. Or maybe she had brought him back to the real world?

CHAPTER EIGHT

THE DAYS flew for Jude though his intensive enquiries in relation to Lester Rogan's past weren't bearing any fruit. It was as though the man hadn't existed before he arrived in North Queensland. Finally Jude had to consider calling in a good private investigator to help out. He knew the right man, ex-army intelligence.

He'd tried to elicit information from Myra about her late husband, but Myra appeared to have accepted him at face value. If she'd asked questions in the early days of their courtship Lester Rogan had got by telling her absolutely nothing beyond the fact he no longer had family. From Myra's admittedly hazy recollections he had never mentioned Ireland in any context except once to become extremely angry and upset over the death of some famous race horse over there. Myra couldn't remember anything else. A state of affairs not unparalleled in other relationships where husbands managed to lead double lives and have other children tucked away, Jude had found.

Dermot Costello was a lot easier to get a trace on. Jude was able to establish his arrival in Australia, his career as an architect, followed by his stint as an academic, a career which came to an abrupt tragic end in a car crash in which he was a passenger. The Lundberg case proved the easiest of all to research from the newspapers, though what had happened to Mrs Lundberg, Cate's mother, was by far the hardest mystery to crack. It was difficult indeed to see any connection between Cate's parents and Rogan. Harder yet to see any connection to the Lundbergs or Cate's stepfather,

a wealthy, influential man who had resumed his distinguished academic career. Cate had never mentioned there
had been a first Mrs Lundberg who had died of a rare heart
condition a few years into the marriage.

So Lundberg had lost two wives? Tragedies no man
should have to endure. Or something more sinister? Highly
respected members of the community were still capable of
destroying lives. Power and cruelty often went hand in hand.
Jude had come to believe Lundberg at some stage must have
betrayed an infatuation with Cate. Her aversion to him appeared to have strong sexual overtones.

Cate had spent that second night at his house and then
insisted on returning home. He saw her for a short time each
day as he saw the Rogan family. There were no more dis-
turbances at the gallery. Ralph had made no further attempt
to approach Cate, but Jude knew Ralph was just barely biding his time. He'd even heard from Jimmy Ralph was going
around town trying to find evidence of a sharp decline in
his father's mental condition; rambling conversations, bad
business deals and the like. According to Jimmy who had
his ear to the ground, Ralph hadn't yet humiliated himself
by telling the town of the disposition of his father's will.

"What he's tryin' to do is find proof his old man was
going ga-ga," Jimmy chortled. "He'll have a job on his
hands."

That indeed was the question. Was Lester Rogan before
his death in full possession of his faculties? Even that question was irrelevant. Lester had had Jude's father draw up a
new will naming Cate as his main beneficiary two years
previously. Though Jude had searched through every scrap
of paper his father had kept on Lester Rogan and his affairs,
there remained the possibility his father had stashed a file
elsewhere, for safe keeping.

For the time they were apart, Jude pictured Cate back in

his house. He had an excuse to get her there by asking her to help him conduct a search for a possible missing file. If he tried very hard he could keep his mind on the job.

She arrived midmorning of the following Saturday with the glorious weather of the week giving way to an ominous build-up of incandescent storm clouds. Such a display building up over the sea presaged the start of the late afternoon thunderstorms that were so much a feature of the tropics on the verge of the Wet. They were spectacular but short lived.

"Thanks for coming." He allowed himself the luxury of kissing her cheek and caught a drift of her special fragrance. The last thing he wanted to do was frighten her away. He realized there were lots of things Cate was trying to block out. But she leaned towards him, seeming to give a little sigh. Did she know what hope that offered him?"

They walked up the short flight of steps together to the porch. "I think we're in for a storm," she remarked.

"For sure." He surveyed the sky, brilliantly blue over the house, threatening over the ocean.

"Find out anything more?"

"Not much I'm afraid. Lester Rogan might have descended from another planet."

"Maybe Rogan's not his name?" Cate suggested, "Maybe he reinvented himself."

"Very possibly," Jude murmured, ushering her inside. "The big question is why? Like a cold drink? I've actually got some home made lemonade. I had to use up some of the lemons. There's a glut of them."

"Lovely. Where are we going to start?" She looked up at him her glowing copper head tilted to the side.

"Where would you think? Where would my father be likely to hide a document he didn't particularly want anybody to find?"

"The bookcases in the study spring immediately to

mind," Cate said, having glimpsed the room the first night. "My father was always pushing newspaper clippings or scraps of information he wanted to keep in among the books. I saw him do it often."

Jude considered for a moment. "My dad didn't do that as far as I can recall, he was strictly methodical. But we can try."

It was a fairly daunting task. There were legal tomes, countless reference books, books on international law, economics, science, many fields of knowledge other than the law. His father had been interested in so much. History, music, mathematics biographies of famous people mostly nineteenth and twentieth century.

"This is a major undertaking," Jude said, leaning back against his father's desk. "And that doesn't include the innumerable files relating to Dad's clients. I've read everything I can find on Lester Rogan."

Cate let her eyes roam around the large airy fan cooled room. All the windows and shutters were open, affording a beautiful view of the side garden. "Your father must have been a very well-read man," she commented.

Jude glanced at his father's high-backed leather chair. He fancied he could see his father sitting in it, head bent, poring over some papers. "He was indeed. Far better read than I'll ever be and far more learned. In many ways he wasted his life here. There was talk of making the shift to Brisbane when I was about ten or eleven. He had connections with various law firms and he was concerned about me and my tertiary education. There was no more talk after my mother took off. He lost all heart. Or what heart he had was for me."

"You loved him very much?" she asked, wishing she could ease some of the pain away.

"I did. I do. He was the sort of man who did everything

to help people.'' Jude stared back into her eyes, nearly groaning at their look of tenderness. For him? ''All of which convinces me Dad wouldn't have left you with a huge problem.''

Cate looked away. ''He probably didn't expect to die so early, Jude. Any more than my father. He and a colleague were on their way to a meeting, only they met up with death instead. Surely your father would have asked Lester Rogan about me? Who I was? From all accounts he could handle Lester Rogan.''

''Rogan trusted him.'' Jude nodded. ''They weren't exactly friends, but he did go big game fishing with Dad from time to time.''

''On the face of it, the will isn't fair. I shouldn't inherit over his wife and children.'' Cate insisted.

''Hold on. We haven't solved this yet. Dad must have put the truth of the matter down somewhere. We could have an investigation conducted by a professional but it could take much longer than you think. The big problem is we don't have much time. Ralph has a short fuse.''

''At least he hasn't come near me.'' Cate couldn't control a shiver. ''We'd better make a start.''

His mouth curved into that lopsided smile. A smile that bombarded her senses. ''Which means I might keep you here forever,'' he warned.

She reached out and gently touched his cheek. Sharp, sweet sensations. ''I could make it through dinner.''

''Catherine. Cate. That sounds very provocative?''

''I've missed you,'' she merely said and turned away.

Cate chose one end of the floor to ceiling bookcase which occupied an entire wall of what was a large room. Jude started at the other, running his hand across the spines of the law books that filled the shelves.

By midafternoon despite an exhaustive search they'd found nothing. "I'll make coffee," Jude offered.

"Fine." Cate only nodded. This whole business of her inheritance was beyond her. There had to be some documentation to explain why Lester Rogan had done what he'd done. Her back ached a little but her resolve was firm. She pulled out a leather-bound volume on the voyages of Matthew Flinders, checking there was nothing between the pages.

On the opposite side of the room a dozen or so clients' files fell to the floor with such a clatter it gave her a start. Probably they'd been dislodged by Jude earlier. Her natural reaction was to pick them up and return them to the shelf. It was only when she was shoving them back she realised a wad of what looked like newspaper clippings had stuck to the back wall.

Cate reached for the roll as though it had a special message for her.

"Sick of it?" Jude turned his head to ask as Cate walked into the kitchen. "Cate?" His smile disappeared at the expression on her face. "What is it? You've found something?"

She shook her head from side to side as though she couldn't make sense of anything. Then she passed him what she had in her hand.

"Newspapers clippings!" Jude frowned. There was utter silence while he read them. "What does this mean?" He looked up at her, his blue eyes disturbed.

"It means your father knew all about my mother's disappearance. He kept the clippings, didn't destroy them." She brought her hand to her trembling lips.

"But what does that prove, Cate? My father was interested in all sorts of things. Your mother's disappearance was national news.''

She moved closer, upset darkening her eyes to emerald. ''Do you think he could have known her?''

Jude lifted his wide shoulders, swallowed on the hard knot in his throat. ''I can't see how.''

''Why did he bother to cut all this out?'' She stared at him with those huge, helpless eyes.

''At the moment, Cate, I don't have any idea about anything.'' He kept his voice calm. ''My father wouldn't have hurt a fly.''

''Maybe, but he was helping a man just about everyone hated. Lester Rogan. Could Rogan have known my mother?''

Jude was seriously jolted. ''Or could Rogan have known Lundberg? Though what motive he'd have for getting involved with your stepfather I can't imagine.''

''Let's look some more,'' she urged tautly, already turning back to the study.

Jude followed her, coffee forgotten. ''Where did you find them?''

''Over there.'' She pointed. ''Your father did stuff things into bookcases after all. The files almost jumped off the shelf.'' She indicated which ones.

''And the clippings were behind them?''

''Rolled into a tight wad.''

''Okay, so we shift them all,'' Jude decided, his expression grim.

Jimmy found them some thirty minutes later. ''What's goin' on here?'' he asked in some wonderment.

Neither responded immediately. Finally Jude said, ''You can help, Jimmy. We're trying to find some documentation, some written evidence of the connection between Rogan and

Cate.'' He didn't mention the newspaper clippings. He knew now Cate hadn't told anyone apart from him her mother's tragic story.

"Right. What are we looking for? Something shoved into or behind a book. Is that it? 'Struth, we'll be here for a month of Sundays. Matty had a book on everything. Where do you want me to start? It's like looking for a needle in a haystack. I bought you a little present by the way, Jude. Thought you could put it up on the wall.''

Jude tried to listen to his friend, but felt too stressed. "Thanks, Jimmy,'' he said absently.

"Aren't you gonna ask me what it is? Hang on a minute, I'll get it. Left it in the hall. Thought you should have it.''

He returned in a few moments carrying what looked like a small painting wrapped in bubble paper. "I don't know how long I've had this, but I reckon it's rightly yours.''

"Thanks Jimmy,'' Jude repeated.

"Well open it, son. The big search can wait a minute.''

"I'm sorry, Jimmy,'' Jude stretched his long arms above his head. "This is infuriating. We've established Dad knew who Cate was.''

"So who am I?'' Cate asked emotionally.

Jimmy went to her, patting her shoulder. "Settle down, love. What's the matter? You can tell Jimmy.''

"I don't think I can face what this is all about,'' Cate said.

"We'll all face it together,'' Jimmy said. "What do you think, son?'' He shot Jude, who was studying his gift, a glance full of affection.

Jude was slow to answer. "I really appreciate this, Jimmy.''

"Then that makes me happy,'' Jimmy said quietly. "Reckon we can find a place for it. Maybe over there?''

He pointed to a section on one wall where a small collection of framed photographs hung.

"Let's do it," said Jude. "Go on helping Cate while I find the hammer and a hook."

"May I see it?" Cate asked after Jude had left the room.

"Of course, love." Jimmy gave her his big affable grin. "It's just a photograph of Matty and his mates on board *Calypso*. Matty was a great big game fisherman. Yours truly is in it too. Good old Lester, another bloke, his friend, and a visiting American film star who was crazy about fishing our Reef waters. We took him out whenever he blew into town." Jimmy picked up the framed photograph, an enlarged glossy from a Cairns newspaper and passed it to her. "Those were the days!"

"You go back a long way, Jimmy," Cate smiled.

She looked down at the photograph. It was then she lost her breath. "Ah, Jimmy!" she moaned, putting the photograph down quickly as though the ebony frame burned her. Bone white she moved into an armchair, lowering her head over her knees.

Jimmy stared at her, shocked. "Catey, what is it? Are you feeling faint, love?"

No response from Cate. She just kept her head down.

Jude coming back into the room reacted swiftly. He went to Cate dropping to his haunches and throwing Jimmy an order over his shoulder. "Get her a drink of water."

"Right, son." Jimmy took off.

"We've been too long at it, Cate. I'm sorry." Compulsively his hand found her nape, soothing, steadying. "This has all been too much for you."

Jimmy returned with a glass of water, putting it into Jude's outstretched hand. "Drink some of this, Cate." Jude raised the glass to her lips.

"I don't think I can swallow."

"Try." He held the glass while she drank from it. "Why don't you lie down on the sofa for a while."

"Yes, love," Jimmy chimed in. "You look awfully white."

Cate let her head fall back against the leather armchair. The tip of her tongue drew beads of water from her lips into her mouth. "The man in the photograph, the man standing next to Lester Rogan is my father." She shut her eyes briefly as if for strength.

Jude stared at her, his heart doing a tumble. "So that's our connection!" He expelled a long breath.

"You're certain, love?" Jimmy turned back to the desktop to reexamine the photograph.

"As certain as I am of my own face."

Jimmy whistled through his nose. "Ya dad, what was he called, love? What was his name? I've never met anyone outside you, called Costello. What was his Christian name? We probably only got around to Christian names."

"Dermot," Cate said, sounding ineffably sad.

Jimmy shook his head. "Never heard that, either. What about Derry?" Jimmy's voice had a questioning inflection. "Now Derry I've heard. I seem to remember Lester acted as though he'd know this Derry all his life. Only Derry was posh. Spoke very correct like Gwennie whereas Lester was anything but. Yet they were friends. Only time I ever saw him, though. Never again."

Jude who had been sitting on the floor at Cate's feet, lifted himself upright. "Feel a little better, Cate?" he eyed her with concern. This rush of information was startling to him let alone her. There was little colour in her lovely skin. "The shocks are coming a bit too thick and fast, aren't they? But we do have a lead. We know of a connection between Lester and your father. I think the answer lies back in

Ireland. Back in their past, Cate. Your father's family could prove to be our best link.''

Cate struggled to clear her head in a terror of confusion. "I don't know my father's family, Jude. It would be difficult to try to speak to them if my father couldn't. He left home. He travelled as a young man to the other side of the world. Doesn't that say something to you? It was because he could no longer live in his own world. If Jimmy gained the impression Lester Rogan had known my father all his life that means they both lived in the same town or the same district.''

"One was a gentleman. One surely wasn't," Jimmy said slowly, measuring every word. "It's a start. I remember your dad being very good-looking in the Pommy way—I know now he was Irish but I thought then he was English, the skin, you know. Kinda languid if you know what I mean. Maybe graceful is a better word. Not tough like Lester. You can see it right here, the difference in the two men." Jimmy tapped a finger at the glass covering the photograph. "Lester came up real hard, I'd say. Ya dad didn't. But somehow they were bonded." Jimmy turned his full attention on Cate. "Don't you find it amazin' I should bring this photograph over today? I've had it hangin' on my wall for thirty years."

"I wonder if Myra could remember back that far?" Jude asked thoughtfully.

Jimmy shook his head. "Poor Myra has trouble rememberin' what went on yesterday. They weren't livin' together at the time. I mean they weren't married. She could remember somethin' I suppose. Ya dad couldn't have been at the weddin', Cate. Gwennie went and she'd remember the name, Costello. Trust me, Gwennie forgets nuthin'.''

Cate's eyes sought Jude's across the room. "I think this will get worse, not better," she said.

CHAPTER NINE

THE STORM held off until around five-thirty. Jimmy had left an hour earlier to escape it, as great silver laced cumulus clouds raced over the sea like a tidal wave. Soon after Jude had shifted Cate's car into the double garage in case hail attended it.

"I think we'd better close the shutters," he advised with an experienced glance at the now livid sky. Menacing streaks of green and purple rent the billowing grape masses while great gusts of wind gathering force whipped up the white caps on the rolling waves and sent them crashing onto the shore. In the garden and on the strand the fronds of the towering palms were tossed around like silk ribbons. The birds, the brilliantly enamelled parrots, the rose-pink galahs and the beautiful little emerald lorikeets crowned with red, blue, yellow and purple screeched loudly as they winged for shelter in the monumental mango trees that grew in the back garden.

A peculiar fragrance like burning incense hung on the air.

"Not nervous, are you?" Jude asked. Cate was staring fixedly at the lurid sky.

"No, but I haven't seen a sky like that before."

He laughed. "You haven't been here long enough. Tropical storms are volcanic but brief. It's the cyclones you have to watch out for. Better go in, Cate. It's going to come down in a moment."

With the shutters closed one inside of the house was surprisingly dark. She went around turning on a few lights but when Jude came in from the front verandah where he'd been

153

stacking chairs away, he started turning them off. "It won't be for long, Cate," he assured her. "It's an electrical storm, best if they're off. You know not to touch the telephone or the T.V. turn off your computer. Don't stand too near windows and doors." Even as he spoke the remaining light dramatically dimmed.

"It's coming in from the sea, but we can pull the curtain back. It will lighten the room. The awning over the deck is excellent protection but we'll have to keep the doors shut. It'll get hot, but no help for it!"

"It looks dangerous out there," she said, a hand to her throat. "I wouldn't want to be out on a boat." The minute she said it she felt a lurch of dismay. She turned to him her face showing her distress. "I'm so sorry, Jude, I forgot." Too late she remembered Jude's father had been lost at sea.

"Dad died doing what he loved," he said simply. "He wasn't frightened of storms, but he had a proper respect for the sea. I used to love to go out on the boat with him. Took Calypso out myself often enough. Jimmy might have been lost too had he gone with Dad that day."

"The element of chance," Cate said. "Who would have thought Jimmy would choose today to present you with that photograph? If he hadn't, we might never have known my father had been in this part of the world, let alone met your father. It's all incredible to me. I feel it's not real, but a dream."

"It's real enough," Jude said. "We're getting to the truth. The key to Rogan's will lies in the past."

"But that isn't going to satisfy Ralph and his family?"

"No, it won't. I know you find it disturbing but I suppose it's possible Rogan and your father were related? I think the mystery surrounding your mother's disappearance confused us. I don't think there's any connection there. That's an altogether different issue."

"One that desperately needs closure," Cate said. "I pray one day the truth will come out."

"I hope so too, Cate," Jude replied gravely. For the first time it came into his mind he should do something about finding his own mother. She could reject him again, reopen old wounds, but Cate's tragic story made him suddenly think it was worth a try.

"Maybe my father and Rogan were both outcasts?" Cate was saying, her arms folded around her body as she stared out at the storm. "Each in their own way condemned to leave their families behind. The world can be a pitiless place."

"Natures get distorted in the absence of love," Jude said, knowing it to be true.

He walked to where she stood, wanting to rock her like a baby in his arms. It was much too late to banish Cate Costello from his life. The decision was made when he first laid eyes on her. "We can watch the storm together," he said in a quiet voice.

"Put your arms around me," she asked, without looking at him. Waves of excitement were mounting in her, shooting off like so many Roman candles.

"Cate you know where this could lead to," he said into her hair. "You're far too beautiful for me to resist."

"I want to forget everything for a little while."

"Is that the only reason?" He turned her to look at him.

"Sex can be very liberating." There was more than a hint of bravado in her tone.

"I asked if that was the only reason?"

Her expression changed. "You know it isn't." She leaned forward, letting her head rest against his chest. "I trust you, Jude. Something about you speaks to me directly. I'm going to tell you something I've never spoken to anyone about. I felt somehow I'd be exposing my mother and I lived to protect her. For about a year before my mother went missing I had to endure the most excruciating sexual attention from my stepfather.''

Though he had begun to suspect something of the kind he had to brace himself against the shock. ''He surely didn't—?'' He couldn't seem to get his tongue around the word. Not Cate. He put his hand beneath her chin, made her met his eyes.

Cate sighed deeply. ''No. I'd be locked up in a prison if he'd tried that. Only once did he actually grab me, kissing me, fondling my breasts. I nearly fainted from the shock. It was horrible. Demeaning. A frightening experience. My mother wasn't home, she was at a committee meeting. I reacted like a wild thing kicking out. I let him know I'd tell all his colleagues at the university. I'd tell Deborah. I'd tell everyone. Never once did I say I'd tell my mother.''

Jude took her shaking hand, kissed it. ''Because you didn't want to hurt her.''

She inhaled deeply, fighting for control. ''I found it astounding right from the beginning that she was attracted to him. But she must have loved him. Why else would she have married him?''

''Maybe she was the sort of woman who needed a man to take care of her. She had a daughter to rear.''

''It was my fault,'' Cate tightened her arms around her body. ''He told me he married my mother because of me. Can you imagine how that made me feel? It was my fault my mother married him. My fault!''

There was moaning heartbreak in her voice. Outside the deck lit up in a lightning flash. ''You surely can't believe that, Cate. You are not to blame in any way. Your stepfather was sick.''

She laughed bitterly, bending her head forward so her hair screened her face. ''No one we knew would ever have accepted that. I think Deborah became suspicious of him in time.''

''What about your mother? Her maternal instincts? Are you sure she had no inkling of the true nature of his feelings for you? What a terrible problem it presented?''

''She would have had to leave. She did leave.''

''She couldn't have done it deliberately if she loved you.'' Deeply concerned for her, Jude argued strenuously.

Cate looked at him with great brooding eyes. ''No, she didn't.''

''Did you tell the police any of this?''

She shook her head. ''It was a dilemma. I was too ashamed. I raved on about what a Jekyll and Hyde he was but I never said anything about his…touching me. I loved my mother so much I didn't want to tarnish her name. Oh, Jude, can't you understand? I was all mixed up. A school-girl.''

''Of course I understand. Could you tell the police now?'' He stared at her gravely.

She reached up to touch his cheek. ''If you were right beside me. You make me feel so much better. Back then I knew I had to keep extremely quiet about what he did. I feared him. He has a marvellous talent for making people believe whatever he says. He was so convincing and he's very rich—people respect money as though that makes you a good person. He thought with my mother out of the way he could turn me into anything he wanted. I was his step-daughter. He acted as though I belonged to him.''

''So it was one long nightmare?'' Jude asked grimly.

''Hell was more like it.''

''But you had the courage to get away.''

She looked as though she had no courage left. ''Now I'm in another unbearable position. I don't want Lester Rogan's money, Jude.'' There was a slash of colour in her cheeks.

"His family can have it back. As a lawyer you know what to do. I can deed it back to them or whatever. I don't even want to know what link there was between my father and Lester Rogan. If the truth was acceptable it would have surfaced by now. I always sensed Lester Rogan's interest in me wasn't normal."

He picked up on that sharply. "You've never said that before, Cate."

"It wasn't sexual," she was aware of the censure in his voice. "I'm certain of that."

"Even so, you should have said something."

"Maybe you should consider I don't know how to answer questions." She moved closer to the French doors. "Since I lost my father I've led a scary life. Lundberg wisked my mother off. It was like she was the object of a campaign only the campaign was me. My mother and I were enslaved by her marriage to him. She deferred to him on everything like he was some god. He was Professor Lundberg you know. So clever! I was suffocated by his interest in me. What you see, Jude, is the result, I'm sorry if you're disappointed. I'm tired of it all. In coming up here I thought I'd left the past behind, only it has followed me. I'm condemned to relive it."

Her words, so low and rapid, were almost lost to him as the wind screamed across the deck.

He went to her determinedly, drawing her away from the glass doors. Forked lightning sizzled through the dark clouds, creating a beautiful deadly pattern, before it lit up sea and sky in its blinding radiance. Thunder followed, rolling then cracking like a massive military bombardment. Cate literally jumped and he put his arm around her seeing them both reflected in the smoky glass. She looked a white skinned fragile creature beside him.

The wind tore at every door and window, seemingly hell-bent on getting in. Jude felt his own nerves very finely balanced. It had little to do with the storm. He had lived through countless storms and a few spectacular cyclones but the powerful stirrings in his flesh were all caused by a girl who'd had her adolescence stolen from her.

The rain came down. At first a few giant spatters that resounded like artillery on the corrugated iron roof, then a deluge. Silver sheets of water that put the guttering under tremendous pressure.

"This is barbaric!" she whispered in awed fascination, turning her face momentarily against his shoulder as a great jagged fork of lightning slashed down the sky. It illuminated the beach where the vision of a woman in a long white dress was said to appear and disappear in a luminous mist.

He could feel the trembling right through Cate's body. He put his arms around her holding her close to him while the storm screamed around the house seeking entry. A massive clap of thunder that banged the shutters made her gasp. She lifted her face to him, a touch of hysteria in her green eyes.

"That was close."

"Storms frighten you."

"That clap of thunder was like the end of the world." She stared up at him marvelling that he, on the other hand, looked extraordinarily vital. His hair in the rain was a mass of golden ringlets, clinging to his handsome skull.

Her gaze communicated a strange desolation to Jude as if she were renouncing something. Him? He couldn't let that happen. He couldn't let her get away.

With one hand he grasped her long silky hair, the ache so bad, he lowered his head to kiss her. Softly, softly, her lovely mouth parting under the weight of his desire. The intimacy between them had developed at such velocity he thought he'd been waiting for her all his life. For all the

convulsive excitements he felt he had to remain mindful of
the traumas she'd suffered. His inner voice listened intently
to the signals coming off her.

He continued to hold her, a groan coming up from the
back of his throat as he pressed kisses all over the face, her
throat, her small delicate lobes, murmuring to her all the
while, keeping his tone soothing, his touch fluid, drifting
lightly over her shoulders to the upper curves of her breasts
revealed by the jade camisole she was wearing. Though his
own needs were driving he sought to keep them under control. He wanted only what she wanted. To use the slightest
force would be to betray her. That would break him to
pieces. She had suffered enough.

But she was moaning under his kisses, the slow movement of his hands, the urgent little cries muted by his mouth.
Around them was the voice of thunder; the tumultuous
sound of the rain drumming on the roof, causing the guttering to overflow, pouring water onto the deck.

The open-mouthed kisses continued, his hand pressing
into the back of her head, she was so beautiful! He pulled
her in tighter.

After a while, how long?, she seemed to sink against him
as if her legs could no longer support her. It was then he
lifted her, the whole fragile weight of her, carrying her to
the long sofa, still with his mouth at her creamy throat. He
sank to his knees while she lay there, one arm flung above
her head, he trying to beat back overwhelming desire. It
must have shown in his face because she put trembling fingers to the buttons of his shirt, slipping them one by one,
allowing her hand to move across his chest. That small cool
hand burned.

He could hear the heavy thud of his heart as his mouth
dipped to hers. This time he crushed it because he couldn't

keep the extreme gentleness up. His passion was too fierce. It overflowed.

"I have to see you, look at you." His voice sounded slurred. He was drunk on her beauty. Her green eyes clung to his as he pushed the narrow straps of her camisole top off her shoulders. She was wearing a strapless bra with lace cups beneath. In an ecstasy of longing he bowed his head to suckle each erect nipple that showed duskily through the delicate material, now damp from his mouth.

Finally, because he was driven to, he lifted her upper body slightly so he could release the hook. Then he took her naked breasts into his hands holding like they were the sweetest of fruit.

I've fallen in love, Cate thought. Me who has hidden from love for a long time. She had never known such tenderness, such exquisite delicacy from a man's strong hands. He was peeling the clothes from her as he might peel a peach, slowly, gently, giving her time to stay him if she wanted, but she had entered a zone of physical rapture.

An extraordinary thing was happening to her. With her eyes tightly closed she felt his hands begin to explore her body, the silken, supple, yielding flesh. She could feel the faint tremble in his warm fingers as though he found her utterly beautiful.

So this was what falling in love was like? Only a lover could demolish the strong defences she'd taken refuge behind.

"Cate?"

She had to clutch at him, every nerve rippling, electric.

"I hear you." Slowly she opened her eyes on his taut handsome face, feeling the heat rise from her skin.

"I want to take you to bed." He watched her intently with those blazing blue eyes. "I want to make love to you properly. I have protection."

"You can't protect me from you." She lifted an arm to encircle his neck, her fingers spearing in to those crisp golden curls. "I knew what would happen when I said I'd stay." She smiled at him, a smile of deep significance for Jude.

It held trust and something equally as powerful. Pure desire. He put his arms beneath her, gathering her up as though she was the most precious of creatures. "You're sure?"

"I am."

Exultantly he carried her through the house and up the stairs to his bedroom...

Outside the storm continued to rage unabated, but neither Jude nor Cate noticed. Their limbs coiled, hands clasped, their mouths passionately locked, they were sealed off in another landscape. One so extravagantly beautiful and full of sensation they never wanted to leave.

Sunlight lay on the polished floor and on the rug, highlighting the vibrant colours in the design. The sea breeze played with the unlined cream curtains at the French doors. He lifted himself onto an elbow staring down at her. He thought he had never seen anything lovelier in his life. Long dark russet eyelashes lay against her cheeks. Her lips were faintly parted, her breath quiet. The sheet had fallen back to reveal one creamy rounded breast. Very slowly he traced the dusky pink aureole around a nipple with one finger, moving ever closer to the sensitive bud.

Sex with Cate was the kind of sex that had never happened to him. He'd thought he'd had good sex, even great sex at times, but what had happened last night he didn't know he could find a word for. Rapture? Ecstasy, agony? Complete loss of self? He still had the delirium of passion in his blood.

Her beautiful body stirred beneath his hand. Her nipple

thickened and hardened. He bent his head over her, kissed it then her mouth. Deeply.

"Good morning," he murmured, when he finally raised his head. "Are you all right?"

She looked up at him, green eyes wide. "All right?" she asked in a kind of wonderment. "Yes, yes, yes! I've never felt better in my life." She pulled his face down to her. "I think I might stay here forever."

"That's good," he said very softly, "because I don't think I can bear to let you go. You're amazing."

"So are you." She moved to accommodate her body to his. "Make love to me, Jude. You're so good at it."

"But then you make it so easy." He stripped the top sheet off them, dropped it to the floor...

Afterwards they showered together, soaping each other all over. It took time. Kissing, caressing...Jude lifted her off her feet to take her again.

"I must go to the gallery," she said much later. "I have work to do even though I can't think of anything else but you."

"I have a meeting, too," he said, thrusting his arm into a blue cotton shirt. "I have to report to dear old Ralph. Keep him happy."

"Oh, Ralph," she groaned. Cate was fully dressed now, brushing out her long copper hair. "I meant what I said, Jude. I don't want anything to do with Lester Rogan's money."

He looked back at her, his eyes moving over her lovingly. "I can understand your feelings, Cate, but don't come to any decision before you know the full story. We're searching through Dad's things when maybe we should be searching through Lester's? He may have a bank box stashed away. I'm sure Ralph has already checked his father's safe.''

"I don't think I could bring myself to see Ralph Rogan again, Jude," Cate said. "I don't know how he's controlling himself when he's completely unpredictable."

"Leave him to me," Jude told her calmly. "What time do you close the gallery?" He picked up a brush, ran it over his thick, curly hair.

"Five." He looked so blazingly handsome, so wonderfully masculine, Cate thought she should really be wearing sunglasses. After such intimacies, such glorious lovemaking she felt warm and happy inside but she knew only too well life was cruel. In the golden heat she couldn't suppress a shiver. Experience had taught her happiness could be spirited away overnight.

Jude was smiling at her, the dimple flicking in his cheek. "I'll pick you up." He quickened his pace of dressing so he could get her car out for her. He had an intense desire to make life easier for Cate in any way he could.

CHAPTER TEN

WHILE Cate at her gallery was tending to a party of Japanese tourists in search of high quality crystals, Jude was closeted with Ralph in his late father's office.

Jude had shown Ralph the framed photograph of his father and friends on board Calypso some thirty years before. Now Ralph was staring down at it, resting his head in his hands. "This is her father?" he asked for perhaps the fourth time.

"I've already told you, Ralph. It is."

Ralph's dark gaze was sober and direct. "And Jimmy swears this man and Dad acted like friends?"

"More than that, Ralph. Jimmy gained the clear impression they were life-long friends. At the very least they'd known one another for years. Cate's father was Dermot Costello, he migrated from Ireland in the early seventies, I checked it out. I checked out his career as an architect and academic as well. He was killed in a car crash when Cate was ten. Her mother remarried. I didn't find a thing on your father before he arrived in North Queensland."

Ralph shifted his attention from Jude back to the framed photograph. "Dad was a mystery man. You'd swear he didn't have another life before he came here. He didn't talk about himself, his family—even he must have had one—he certainly never said anything about being born in Ireland. This Costello guy looks like some guy in the movies."

"Too damned soft!" Ralph hissed through his strong white teeth. "They couldn't have been related. Look at Dad! Hell, I could be looking at myself."

Jude nodded. "I've been searching through all my father's files and papers," Jude said. "It's a big job, I haven't finished yet, but what about your father's papers? I assume you checked out the contents of his wall safe and that desk?"

Ralph snorted. "I would have checked the safe had I known the combination."

"You don't know it?" Jude asked in amazement.

"You don't really think Dad told me. He was obsessively secretive."

"But he'd have to tell someone? He knew he was dying. Your mother doesn't know?"

"Don't you think I'd have gotten it out of her?" Ralph groaned. "I'm fully prepared to call in a guy who knows how to crack safes."

"You've checked all the drawers of that desk?" Jude asked. "He must have kept the combination close."

"Couldn't have been closer," Ralph said. "In his head."

"Why don't we try something?" Jude raised himself out of his chair staring at a painting on the wall behind which he knew there was a safe.

"You don't really think we could come up with the combination?" Ralph gave a scornful smile.

"It's not unusual for people to use numbers that have some significance. Birth dates, lucky numbers."

"Man, you could search forever," Ralph said.

The search in fact took less than ten minutes. After a number of tries with numbers, Jude turned back to Lester Rogan's massive mahogany desk. He found the combination to the safe, pasted carefully to the underside of a bottom drawer.

"Hell!" Ralph said. "Why didn't I think of that?"

Jude shrugged. "Didn't take much imagination."

Jude unlocked the safe. Ralph reached in.

*   *   *

Late morning as Cate was answering another tourist's questions about crystals associated with spiritual development, a stunning blonde wearing a chocolate-brown leopard print camisole with a cream lace trim and tight-legged cream pants entered the gallery.

Cate smiled at her. "Won't be a moment. Feel free to browse."

"I will." The blonde proceeded to move around the gallery on four-inch heels humming tunelessly.

A few minutes more and Cate had boxed and gift wrapped a particularly beautiful aquamarine sphere, more green than blue, that emitted a gentle energy when held in the palm. The Asian tourist on a day trip to the mainland from her luxury resort on a Great Barrier Reef island thanked her with a charming bow and left.

Cate approached the young woman with the spectacular figure. She was holding a rainbow obsidian to the light. "Are you looking for anything in particular?" Cate asked pleasantly. "That crystal is supposed to bring gratification and enjoyment to one's life."

The blonde turned her voluptuous body full on to face Cate. "You surely don't believe all that twaddle?"

Cate ignore the rudeness. "Crystals have been revered since the dawn of time," she said in a normal friendly tone. "They've been found in the ancient tombs of Egypt, Babylonia and China. The Mayan, Aztec, Celtic, American Indian and African civilisations used crystals, the treasures of the earth in their ceremonies. Many people believe crystals act as catalysts to assist in all kinds of healing processes. The Asian lady who just left the gallery uses crystals for meditation, others for protection. It's a big area of study."

"Spare me." The blonde put the lustrous chunk of volcanic glass back onto the shelf. "You're Cate Costello, aren't you?" She looked Cate up and down.

"I am." Cate knew immediately her visitor wasn't somebody who would brighten her day.

"Poppy Gooding," the blonde announced, her eyes continuing her close inspection. "Jude's girlfriend," she added by way of explanation. "A little bird tells me you've been spending some time with him?"

Though she was shaken, somehow Cate retained her poise. "What little bird would that be?" she asked, knowing she wasn't going to like this one little bit.

"You sure you want to know?" Poppy raised a pencilled brow. "I hope Jude hasn't been sleeping with you, dear, because his loyalty is very important to me. We're going to be married."

"Of course you are," Cate said in the ironic voice of one who knew all about bitter blows. "You're going to be happy forever and ever."

Her visitor looked shocked by her answer. "What's the big joke?" she demanded, with considerable indignation. "I'm deadly serious. I'm up here in this godforsaken place to tell you to lay off my man."

Cate looked past Poppy Gooding's smooth tanned shoulder to the courtyard. "Why don't you deliver that message to Jude," she suggested. "As a matter of fact you can do it right now. He's just pulled up."

"Wonderful! I've got to see him!" Poppy went rushing to the door, in the process losing one of her backless sandals. "Jude!" she screeched out the door, a sound that assaulted more than charmed the ears.

How's that for a greeting, Cate thought. She swiftly positioned herself behind the counter. She might as well look out. Poppy was surging towards Jude like a crocodile surging through a tropical lagoon. It was a wonder she wasn't shedding her clothes while she was at it, Cate thought bitterly. What do I really know about him? Cate, so new to happiness, was starting the familiar slide into bleakness. Had she forgotten men were born liars?

Poppy didn't bother to control her desire even though there were lots of people about. She flung her arms around Jude, kissing him so passionately Cate thought it would take time for Jude's lips to heal. Afterwards Poppy threw back her blond head in an excess of joy at their reunion.

"What a fool I am!" Cate moaned quietly to herself. She had come to understand resignation. But surely a man couldn't commit to a woman the way Jude had committed to her that very morning and have plans to marry the boss's daughter? A woman who looked so damned happy to see him.

Why not? Men couldn't control their sexual urges.

Go away, the both of you! She had to escape again. Go someplace else. She thought of New Zealand. That wasn't far enough. Fiji? She dredged up Jude's remark about Poppy Gooding being irrelevant. She was tempted to go out and tell him what she thought of him, but she had too much pride.

Jude! she mourned. Only this morning he'd been the answer to her prayers. The man she'd been born for. As for the fortune Lester Rogan had left her? They could give it to a retirement home for cats.

Cate left her post at the window, hurriedly picking up the Closed sign and hanging it on the glass door. She couldn't leave because she would have to go past them to get to her car, but she could lock herself in her bedroom and shut the blind. When they'd gone she could come out again and open up shop.

Why? At that point she really didn't know what she was

going to do. She thought she'd been through enough, but it seemed the pain of loss was her dismal lot.

Outside in the courtyard Jude had seen the Closed sign go up on the door. He caught sight of Cate's face. The freeze hit him like a blast. Of course he would change that as soon as he could but first he had to deal with Poppy. He'd always known one day Poppy would present a problem.

"What did you say to Cate?" he asked, not at all nicely.

But Poppy laughed gaily. "I told her I was the girl you were going to marry. You are going to marry me, aren't you, Jude, darling?"

"Don't be so ridiculous," Jude said. "Isn't it time you realised you can't get everything you want, Poppy? Like my head on a plate? Marriage is a very serious business, not a hunt."

"So?" Poppy opened her dark eyes wide. "Don't you think I'm taking you seriously enough, darling? I've travelled all the way up here—actually I'm staying on Hayman I want you to come over—just to be with you."

"Who told you I was here?" Jude asked tersely.

"Jude, darling, it's easy to find out anything if you really want to. I even found out about your redhead. I forgive you. I suppose you were bored."

"I'm madly, deeply, irrevocably in love with her," Jude said. His blue eyes were so fierce they looked like they were capable of starting a fire.

"Love her," Poppy shrieked, throwing her full lung power behind it. "She's ugly. She's got no bust. I hate her hair. I bet it comes out of a bottle."

"I wouldn't care if it did. Yours looks great. But no, Cate's colour is natural. She's beautiful, Poppy. Perfect. You've deluded yourself into thinking you're in love with me. You're not. You don't even know me."

"Of course I do," Poppy fumed, moving her body right up close to Jude's. "You've led me on, Jude. You know you have. You let me know what you had in store for me and dad approved of you. Do you know what that could mean? What do you suppose he'll say when I tell him you've thrown me over?"

"Why don't you tell him the truth, Poppy? You decided it was only infatuation. You're over it."

Poppy lifted her head with the greatest disdain. "You're not going to get off the hook as easily as that, Jude. No—one—dumps—me." She reached out to smack a hand into his chest with every word.

"I know a couple of guys who did. Do your worst, Poppy," Jude invited, turning away from her. "I'm thinking of leaving the firm anyway."

"Without references," Poppy yelled after him, the expression on her face too vindictive to ignore.

Jude paused. "That might lead to complications for you, Poppy. You have quite a reputation. Let's face it I could bring charges for sexual harassment in the workplace."

In front of his very eyes, Poppy ground her jaw just like her father. "What did you say?" She stood feet apart, hands on her hips.

"You heard me. Think about it. Go for help. Frankly I think your best chance is to say you dumped me."

Jude knocked at the rear door of the gallery. "You must let me in, Cate," he called, urgency in his voice.

She didn't answer.

He rang her on his mobile, got the answering service. "Love is supposed to be trust, Cate," he said after the beep.

She was having none of that. He rang again with another message. "Poppy Gooding is not and never has been part of my love life. She's nothing more than a spoilt brat who's going to get me the sack.''

He prayed she'd respond to that. She didn't. She was going to ignore him when he had vital news to impart. He rang again with another message. "I'd push an important document I have with me regarding your father under the door only I'm worried I'll set off the alarm. Please, Cate, don't go into remission.''

It only took her a minute to rush from the bedroom where she'd been sprawled on the bed with the back of her hand over her eyes. She came to the door, unlocking it and throwing it back. "How dare you say that!" Her green eyes held flames. "The only sick person around here is you. She came into the gallery looking like a rock star. Did you see how tight her clothes were and those heels! She told me you were going to marry her.''

"And you fell for it?" Jude groaned. "Didn't I tell you about this, Cate?''

"You told me she was irrelevant," she snapped.

"She is. The man who marries Poppy Gooding for all the luscious body is going to die of boredom.''

She stared back at him with contempt. "Luscious body? So how long into the relationship did it take for you to find out let alone get bored?''

"Cut it out, Cate," he said sternly. He shifted her bodily out of the way, striding into the living area. "I know you've had a hell of a life but if we're going to stay together you have to trust me.''

"As if any woman would be crazy enough to trust you," Cate said in disgust.

"Okay." His blue eyes slashed her. "You don't have to put up with me a minute longer than necessary. You've got big problems, Cate and I don't know whether you're capable of solving them. How do I know sex to you isn't a bit of a game? Why should I trust you with my heart? Bad things have happened to me, too, you know, I still know how to reach out. You apparently don't or won't. This document—'' he threw it down on the coffee table ''—was found in Lester Rogan's safe. In it he confesses to having stolen a very valuable diamond necklace belonging to your father's grandmother, Lady Elizabeth Costello more than thirty years ago. Your father was blamed for it. He was a younger son and in some financial trouble at the time. Nothing too serious, the sort of debts a university student with a rich father runs up.''

As Jude spoke, obviously angry and disillusioned with her, Cate sank into a chair, almost beyond hearing.

Jude continued. ''Rogan is related to you I'm afraid. He's your father's half brother. Illegitimate as they used to say. Your grandfather must have had an eye for a good-looking woman. Rogan's mother lived and worked on a small farm, one of a number, owned by the Costello family who must have been local land owners. Rogan told no one of course. He kept the theft to himself, no doubt he thought your family owed him, to my mind they did. When your father migrated to Australia to all intents and purposes disgraced, Rogan followed. He told no one about the necklace and had it broken up so he could dispose of the stones. Apparently the necklace was a known piece.'' Jude looked up at Cate but her face showed no emotion so he went on, ''He kept in touch with your father up until your father's death. He knew about you and all about your mother's disappearance. He determined towards the end of his life he was going to make it up to you for the terrible injustice he'd done to your father. It's all there, Cate. He goes into a lot more detail than I'm saying. He must have genuinely cared about your father who never looked down on him or denied the rela-

tionship like the rest of your family. Your father treated him
as a brother.

"I'll go now. Read through it carefully. Come to a decision. Personally I think you're entitled to a good deal, you
and your father's memory. Rogan prospered greatly from
the sale of the diamonds in that necklace. He wants the full
story to be known."

Cate sat for some time after Jude left. A sense of unreality
had overtaken her. Every one in her life had treated her like
a fool. Every one of them had secrets. If her father had
privately acknowledged Lester Rogan as his half brother
why hadn't he presented him to his family, her mother and
her? Or in turning into a pillar of society had her father
rejected the relationship? She would never know. Couldn't
Lester Rogan at some point have told her he was related to
her? Obviously not. She was the one who had to be kept in
the dark. Had Rogan been instrumental in some way in getting her up here? Tony replying to one of her letters had
encouraged her to make the move, telling her about the gallery. Had Lester Rogan influenced Tony's offer? Then, on
top of everything, she had Poppy Gooding burst in on her
claiming she and Jude had enjoyed a relationship close
enough to discuss marriage.

Hadn't her trust in the world been shattered when she lost
her father? Utterly destroyed with the disappearance of her
mother? As she'd thought so many times chaos was everywhere.

Sunk in her sad reflections Cate was slow to hear footsteps coming across the deck. Startled she looked up to see
Miss Forsyth holding her hand up to the window, peering
in. Miss Forsyth spotted her, waved.

Cate rose from her chair and went to the door.

"I say, m'dear, you don't look happy?" Miss Forsyth

greeted her, grey eyes keen. "Aren't you well? Is that why you closed the gallery?"

"It's a long story, Miss Forsyth," Cate said. "Please come in."

"I'm not disturbing you, Cate?" Miss Forsyth looked her concern. "You seem to be speaking with an effort?"

"I had a falling out with Jude," Cate explained.

"I see," Miss Forsyth nodded sagely, as though she knew exactly what that might mean. "May I ask about what?"

Cate gave an odd little laugh. "You mightn't believe this but his girlfriend pursued him up here."

"You don't mean that silly Poppy person?" Miss Forsyth asked, sounding amazed.

"How do you know about her?" Cate was equally surprised. She waved Miss Forsyth into a chair.

"Jude must have told Jimmy a little bit about her." Miss Forsyth made herself comfortable, rearranging cushions. "Jimmy tells me everything as you know. I think Jude looked on her more as a work hazard than a girlfriend, m'dear. Isn't she his boss's daughter? I'm sure Jimmy told me that. And she chased him up here? Mind you Jude is the sort of young man the girls chase. That smile and the blue eyes! So you were jealous?"

'It's really weird what happens to me." Wearily Cate shook her head. "Do you believe in love at first sight, Miss Forsyth?"

Miss Forsyth smiled. "I'm not going to argue with a man of Will Shakespeare's intelligence and knowledge of human nature. Are you telling me you're in love with Jude?"

Cate nodded. "I was on Cloud Ten this morning, until she arrived."

"And Jude is angry you don't trust him?"

"That's actually not true, I do trust him. The fault lies in me. I'm one of those people in the world who have lost their capacity to trust. I can't believe in happiness, or rather I can't believe in happiness for me. Up to date I feel I was born to lose out.''

"Because you have a sad story to tell. Wounds to heal. I've felt it all along. I've said to Jimmy many a time, there's a girl who has suffered. Why don't you tell me all about it, m'dear,'' Miss Forsyth urged, her expression wonderfully kind. "It does no good to keep so much in. I believe we're put on this earth to help each other and I desperately want to help you.''

"You're such a kind woman, Miss Forsyth. You and Jimmy have been very supportive right from the beginning. You deserve to know." Cate met the older woman's eyes. "I only wish what I have to say weren't so terrible but I have the feeling you'll take it all in your stride. You're a strong woman, a good friend."

Cate leaned forward, picking up the document Jude had left her. She remembered the sternness of his expression. She'd thought before today one didn't trifle with a man like Jude Conroy.

"I have a letter from Lester Rogan right here, Miss Forsyth. Written in his own hand. It's a confession to a crime of theft he committed over thirty years ago, but first I want to tell you about my life before I came here. I'm sorry I haven't done so before, but it was so traumatic. I'm still trying to cope. Anyway, you deserve to know."

CHAPTER ELEVEN

"So we've got a situation here," Ralph Rogan summed up an hour-long family discussion at the dinner table. He regarded his mother and sister with brooding dark eyes. "We've got to sort it out.

"She's our kin." Melinda shook her head from side to side, still in a state of shock. "How could Dad have kept that from us? He's known about her existence for over twenty years. Her father was Dad's half brother. I don't believe it. That makes her our what?"

"Your cousin, dear," Myra said, shuffling her knife and fork. "Your father was a very strange man, but I believe what he did haunted him for the rest of his days. It was bad."

"He must have been desperate," Ralph said. "Those people, the Costellos must have had everything. Dad had nothing. He must have watched them up at the big house while he and his mother probably lived in poverty or near enough, the lot of them looking down their fine patrician noses."

"That doesn't excuse what he did, Ralph," Melinda reasoned, her eyes and eyelids, pink from crying.

"Especially when he left someone else take the blame," Ralph added harshly. "I wonder if her father ever suspected Dad was the one?"

"Who knows!" Myra shrugged. "He must have had his suspicions. Must have. Lester always had a dark side to him. Even then. He never loved me, he married me because he considered it a smart business move. It was a takeover. His bankroll was no more than ill-gotten gains."

"He stole so he could have a future," Ralph frowned at his mother darkly. "He was just trying to survive."

"Don't condone it, Ralph," Melinda pleaded. "What must she think of us?"

"Who cares what she thinks of us," Ralph growled. "No matter what Dad did then, he made his own fortune since. That fortune should have been left to us not her. She's not going to have it."

"Perhaps she's entitled to it," Myra said. "Or a lot of it. It's horrible her mother disappearing like that. People simply don't vanish off the face of the earth."

"Some do," Ralph grunted, obviously not interested. "She might have wanted to get away. She might have committed suicide. Who knows? It doesn't matter to us."

"She's our cousin, Ralph," Melinda pointed out, a catch in her voice.

"You want a cousin?" Ralph glared at her, venting his turbulent frustrations. "This is bloody hard to take. All right—" he threw up a hand "—maybe she's entitled to something, but not what Dad left her. I swear, we're going to hang on to that. The way Dad treated us! Then the old hypocrite up and leaves her a fortune. He must have felt he was buying his way into heaven."

"So what time does Jude want us all to meet?" Myra asked fatalistically.

"Ten in the morning." An odd smile played around his mouth. "You know he's sweet on her," he said, staring at his sister.

"How can he be?" Melinda blinked. "He barely knows her."

"Sorry to disappoint you, sis." Ralph lifted his beer glass and drained off the contents. "It was obvious. You've seen her and you've seen yourself in the mirror. Why would he look at you?"

Myra drew a long breath. "You know, Ralph, you're genuinely cruel. You take after your father I'm afraid. I've had so much unhappiness in my life and I simply bowed under it instead of putting up a fight. I let your father get away with all his crimes and misdemeanours. I've allowed you to treat me and your sister with contempt, when neither of us deserve it. That's over. You must leave this house."

"You're turning on me, too?" Passion blazed in Ralph's face.

"To tell you the truth, Ralph, I no longer care about you," Myra replied quietly. "You've killed all my love. You'll be better away from us anyway. Your father didn't leave any of us penniless. You've got plenty."

Ralph stood up yanking his chair back from the table. "Don't think I'm going to let things stand," he said in a hard, jarring voice. "So she's family, of sorts. I'll hire the best lawyers in the country to make her hand most of it back."

"Go to litigation and you could lose everything," Melinda reminded him, then added in a clear mocking tone. "Why don't you marry that old sexpot Amy Gibson? Make an honest woman out of her. You've been using her for years."

"Whereas you're missing out on sex wholesale," Ralph gave a humourless laugh. "No one going to marry you, Mel. You're a born old maid."

"Don't be so sure," Melinda called as her brother left the room. "Mum and I have lots of plans for after you're gone."

Jude arrived at the gallery around nine-thirty for the ten o'clock appointment at the Rogan mansion. That allowed him a few moments to speak to Cate privately before they made the drive. He'd spoken to Cate briefly by phone the previous evening regarding the meeting he'd set up with the family. He half expected her to decline, she sounded played out. For that matter he was far from on top of the world. Her lack of trust in him had hit him where it hurt. There was also the stunning fact somewhere around midnight as he sought to get Cate out of his mind by prowling the house, he'd uncovered another secret he dearly wished had been left untold. He'd found hidden in an old trunk in the attic, one he thought had only contained his favourite childhood books, a bundle of letters his mother had written him from her new home in Connecticut.

Would he ever get over the shock? Would he ever clear his father's duplicity from his mind? He'd read one at random, couldn't bear to read more. Not then. Maybe not ever. The letters began some months after she went away; stopped after several years. His father had never told him.

Why? Why had his father kept his mother's letters from him? Had his father feared he might have wanted to join his mother in America? Had his father feared being left totally alone? Like Cate, Jude was reeling under the impact of so many disclosures.

She greeted him quietly. She was dressed more formally than he had yet seen her in a beautiful lime silk dress with a purple silk border. She had pretty lime coloured high heeled sandals on her feet. Her beautiful hair was pulled back from her face and arranged in an elegant knot at her nape. She wore earrings. He had never seen earrings on her before.

She looked exquisite. Boundlessly beyond him.

"I take it you've given careful consideration to everything Lester Rogan had to say in his letter?" he asked her, sounding far more a lawyer than a lover.

"Of course." She inclined her head. "I showed it to Miss

Forsyth. She arrived yesterday after you'd gone. We discussed it for quite some time."

"As have the Rogan family. I spoke to Mrs Rogan briefly this morning. She and Myra want very much to meet you. They're nice people, Cate. For all Rogan's money they haven't had an easy life. You need have no worries there."

"The Rogan family is the least of my worries, thank you Jude. I can't think Ralph is looking forward to seeing me again?"

He let that pass. "Mrs Rogan has asked him to leave the family home, something she's never had the courage to ask of him before. The women will be much happier without him."

She turned to meet his eyes. "I meant what I said about not wanting the money, Jude."

He shrugged. "It won't help to give it all back to Ralph. If you really don't want it, there are plenty of very worthy charities. But Lester Rogan wanted absolution, Cate. He wanted forgiveness."

"He should have looked for it at home. I suppose there is the question of compensation for my father's family. The necklace was probably very valuable. I can't imagine it's worth today."

Jude stared at her lovely withdrawn face. "Let's get this meeting over first and see what they all have to say. I advise against any immediate decisions. You're in a highly emotional state. You've had to withstand shock after shock."

She bit her lip. "I'm sorry about yesterday."

"So am I," he said briefly. "Shall we go?"

Myra looking better than she had in a long while greeted them at the door. Her gentle eyes took only a few seconds to weigh up the lovely young woman who stood so composedly beside Jude. A wave of emotion passed across Myra's face. She reached for Cate's hand.

"Welcome, my dear," she said warmly. That broke the ice. Spontaneously, both women leaned forward to brush cheeks. "Good morning, Jude." Myra's emotion filled eyes moved on to him. "Please come in, both of you. We're in the living room."

Melinda sprang up from her armchair immediately they walked in, a smile that echoed her mother's on her small, pretty face. After a moment Ralph dragged himself up.

Jude prayed for a miracle. Most of all he prayed he could find a way to make Cate really love him. She might have dinted his pride but pride couldn't be allowed to stand in the way of love.

There was a long silence as they drove home in the car. Both of them felt they had talked themselves out. Cate made no objection when Jude suggested briefly they could go back to his place rather than the gallery.

Good, he thought. You trust me.

They were barely inside the door when he drew her to him, holding her lightly not wanting to make her the least bit nervous. "You did wonderfully back there, Cate," he said. "I can't imagine anyone doing it better and in such a difficult situation. You've made quite a number of concessions but I guess they're yours to make. The family seems happy. Even Ralph."

"I'm not interested in the real estate business anyway," Cate said, moving gently out of his arms. "You were right about Myra and Melinda. They're sweet. I never expected they would accept me so readily."

"Why not?" Jude shrugged, following her into the living room. "They're prepared to care about you, Cate. You took the wind out of Ralph's sails in a matter of minutes. He thought he was going to have a big fight on his hands.''

"I just wanted to be fair, Jude.''

"I know.'' Jude felt the tension build up in his chest. It was all or nothing now. Love or heartbreak.

"When I feel calmer about all this I'll clear my father's name,'' Cate was saying, her head bent in a pose of contemplation. "I'll also compensate his family for their loss of the necklace.''

"Your family, Cate,'' he pointed out quietly.

"Maybe.'' There was a sad curve to her lips. "But they let my father go out of their lives. I can't forgive them for that. They didn't care if he had a family here in Australia. They wouldn't care about me.''

"What do any of us know?'' Jude asked, broodingly. "I was so sure my mother totally abandoned me, but I was wrong. I had a momentous find last night. I've been waiting for the right moment to tell you.''

She turned about, smiled at him. Not a full smile. More like she was pained or holding something back. "What is it?''

It took all his willpower not to go to her and pull her into his arms. Kiss her over and over. Her mouth, her neck, her eyes, her cheeks. But nothing against her wishes. "A bundle of letters,'' he said, his voice vibrating with emotion. "I don't think I would have found then only I couldn't settle after our senseless argument. It left me quite shattered. Poppy Gooding means absolutely nothing to me, Cate,'' he insisted, his blue gaze searing. "I thought you should have known that. I thought you'd realize I couldn't possibly make love to a woman like I've made love to you and be involved with someone else.''

Colour burned in her cheeks. She moved closer with no

hesitation. "I'm sorry, Jude. I have trouble believing in happiness."

"You doubt I'm madly in love you?" His voice held a
tormented note.

"It's all the baggage I carry, Jude. Forgive me." Her
beautiful green eyes focused on him with intensity. "Tell
me about the letters. Who were they from?"

He made a bewildered gesture with his head. "They were
from my mother to me."

There was such a haunted look in his eyes Cate felt her
own eyes sting. "How extraordinary!" she said, a faint
tremor running through her body. "And your father didn't
ever show them to you?"

"No." Jude's voice revealed his sense of betrayal. "I
lived with him all my life. I loved him, trusted him, yet he
kept my mother's letters from me. I could only read one
last night—I was so shocked, mostly with Dad—but I intend
to read the lot today. I have to make some tough decisions
now. My mother wanted me to come to her."

"I'm sure she did," Cate answered softly, "but you can
understand your father's reason for not showing the letters
to you? He was terrified he might lose you. He would have
been devastated twice over." Cate moved the few remaining
steps towards him, her eyes reflecting her depth of feeling.

"I wouldn't have left him," Jude maintained. "I know
what happened to him when Mum left, the grief he suffered.
But I would have contacted my mother. I would have written. I could have seen her some time. Oh, Cate, I loved her.
You don't know how much. She hurt us both dreadfully,
but I wish I'd known about the letters."

"Of course you do." Cate studied his handsome, an-
guished face. The vulnerability of his expression tore at her
heart. "But you can still do something, Jude. Most likely
your mother lives in the same place and even if she doesn't

you could trace her, explain why you never got her letters. Your mother didn't go missing like mine.''

Jude looked up, saw Cate's pain. ''I'm so sorry, Cate. One day something will come to light, you'll see. The police never really close the books on these cases. They'd have their suspicions regarding your stepfather, but obviously they weren't able to charge him with anything. You never did tell them your stepfather's interest in you had disturbing sexual overtones. You should. I'll go with you. Your stepfather if he was involved in your mother's disappearance will make a fatal error one day,'' Jude predicted. As he said it, he believed in his heart that would happen.

''She's not alive.'' Cate dipped her head. ''I have to accept that. But your mother is. You can find her, Jude. You have to make peace with your mother before you can move on.''

He gave a twisted smile. ''We could really build a case for some heavenly intervention here, so many strange things happening to shed light on what really went on in the past.''

This time her smile didn't flicker and disappear. It blossomed. So beautiful it made him think of springtime, flowers, a time of renewal.

''Have you thought it may be the spirit of our parents sending us these messages, Jude?'' she asked, a shining light in her eyes.

He put out a tender hand to stroke her cheek. ''It seems to me, Cate, that's not impossible. You have to admit it's all very strange. Oh, come here to me!'' he groaned, hauling her to him as though he couldn't remain another moment away from the exquisite comfort of her body.

A soft cry issued from Cate's lips. It sounded like pure bliss.

''I've come to realise I'll have nothing if I don't have you,'' Jude muttered, burying his face against her creamy throat, catching the scent off her skin. "I love you in that dress. I hope it's easy to get off." He moved to kiss her with yearning, as if it were his salvation.

"I'm sure you'll find a way," Cate whispered. "If you can't, I'll help."

His laugh was exultant. "No need. I've figured it out already." He gazed into her beautiful eyes, his expression turning serious. "Being with you I feel whole again, Cate. I haven't felt that in a very long time. I don't want us to fight about anything. It's a terrible thing to fight, especially about things that aren't important."

"Then let's start again," she suggested sweetly, her expression very tender and soft.

Love for her burned in him. He smoothed her hair, revelling in the length and its silken feel. "Why start again, when I loved you at first sight? I can't let you go, Cate. I want us to be everything to each other. I never thought I could say this, but I've come to believe we have one true soul mate in life. I'm overwhelmed that I've found her. Now that I have, I want her to marry me. Will you, Cate?"

She felt as though a dazzling light was all around her. A miraculous sensation not easy to dismiss. "You know I will," she said.

"My love!" He bent to kiss her deeply, powerfully, as though he meant to reach her soul. "I want us to face life together," he told her after he lifted his head. "Wherever we decide that might be. I'll be saying goodbye to Gooding, Carter & Legge but there are other firms. I might even start up my own. There's plenty going on in the North these days and I don't ever want to part with this house."

"Oh, no, I love it!" Cate said with fervour. She had loved it from the beginning, its flowing warmth, its serenity, the streaming golden light.

"So do I. And it's welcomed you." He held her beloved

body fast.'' You've even seen our resident ghost. It's supposed to appear to people at a crossroad in their life, you know, so the legend goes. I want us to be full partners, Cate. I want us to take on all the joys, all the risks. Anything, as long as we face it together.''

She leaned back in his arms, green eyes luminous, her expression divinely happy. ''Marry me must be among the loveliest words in the language.''

''You've made me believe that, too.'' It was true. The love he thought stolen from him was like a power within him. ''Life would be pretty empty without a soul mate. Fate drew us together, Cate. It wasn't chance.''

''No.'' Cate had to whisper her agreement her heart was so full. ''We need one another, Jude, to be complete.''

It was a message Jude welcomed with all his heart. ''Do you want me to carry you upstairs?'' His blue eyes as he looked down on her were ablaze with desire.

''I'd like nothing better,'' Cate sweetly said, her silky arms sliding up to tenderly encircle his neck.

A new life was opening up before her and it filled her with wonder.

THE ROYAL HOUSE OF NIROLI

...International affairs, seduction and passion guaranteed

Volume 5 – November 2007
Expecting His Royal Baby by Susan Stephens

Volume 6 – December 2007
The Prince's Forbidden Virgin by Robyn Donald

Volume 7 – January 2008
Bride by Royal Appointment by Raye Morgan

Volume 8 – February 2008
A Royal Bride at the Sheikh's Command by Penny Jordan

8 volumes in all to collect!

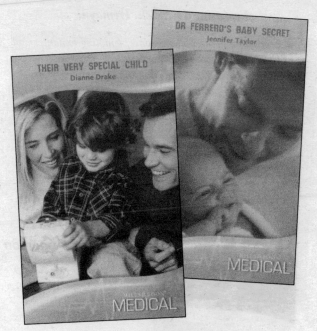

MILLS & BOON®
MEDICAL™
Proudly presents

Brides of Penhally Bay

Featuring Dr Nick Tremayne

A pulse-raising collection of emotional, tempting romances and heart-warming stories — devoted doctors, single fathers, Mediterranean heroes, a Sheikh and his guarded heart, royal scandals and miracle babies…

Book One

CHRISTMAS EVE BABY
by Caroline Anderson

Starting 7th December 2007

A COLLECTION TO TREASURE FOREVER!
One book available every month

MILLS & BOON®
MEDICAL™

Proudly presents

Brides of Penhally Bay

A pulse-raising collection of emotional, tempting romances and heart-warming stories by bestselling Mills & Boon Medical™ authors.

January 2008
The Italian's New-Year Marriage Wish
by Sarah Morgan

Enjoy some much-needed winter warmth with gorgeous Italian doctor Marcus Avanti.

February 2008
The Doctor's Bride By Sunrise
by Josie Metcalfe

Then join Adam and Maggie on a 24-hour rescue mission where romance begins to blossom as the sun starts to set.

March 2008
The Surgeon's Fatherhood Surprise
by Jennifer Taylor

Single dad Jack Tremayne finds a mother for his little boy – and a bride for himself.

Let us whisk you away to an idyllic Cornish town – a place where hearts are made whole

COLLECT ALL 12 BOOKS!

Available at WHSmith, Tesco, ASDA, and all good bookshops
www.millsandboon.co.uk